# Leave it to PET!

### The Misadventures of a recycled Super Robot

4

Give me order!

**Story and Art by**

3 1901 04888 3302

Leave It to PET Vol. 4

STORY & ART BY Kenji Sonishi

Translation/Alexander O. Smith
Touch-up Art & Lettering/John Hunt
Cover & Book Design/Frances O. Liddell
Editor/Traci N. Todd

VP, Production/Alvin Lu
VP, Sales & Product Marketing/Gonzalo Ferreyra
VP, Creative/ Linda Espinosa
Publisher/Hyoe Narita

MAKASETE PET KUN Vol. 4
© Kenji Sonishi 2006
All rights reserved. Original Japanese edition published by POPLAR
Publishing Co., Ltd., Tokyo. English translation rights directly arranged
with POPLAR Publishing Co., Ltd., Tokyo.

The stories, characters and incidents mentioned in this publication are
entirely fictional.

Printed in the U.S.A.

Published by VIZ Media, LLC
P.O. Box 77010
San Francisco, CA 94107

10 9 8 7 6 5 4 3 2 1
First printing, January 2010

www.vizkids.com          www.viz.com

# Contents:

# Leave it to PET!

The Misadventures of a recycled Super Robot

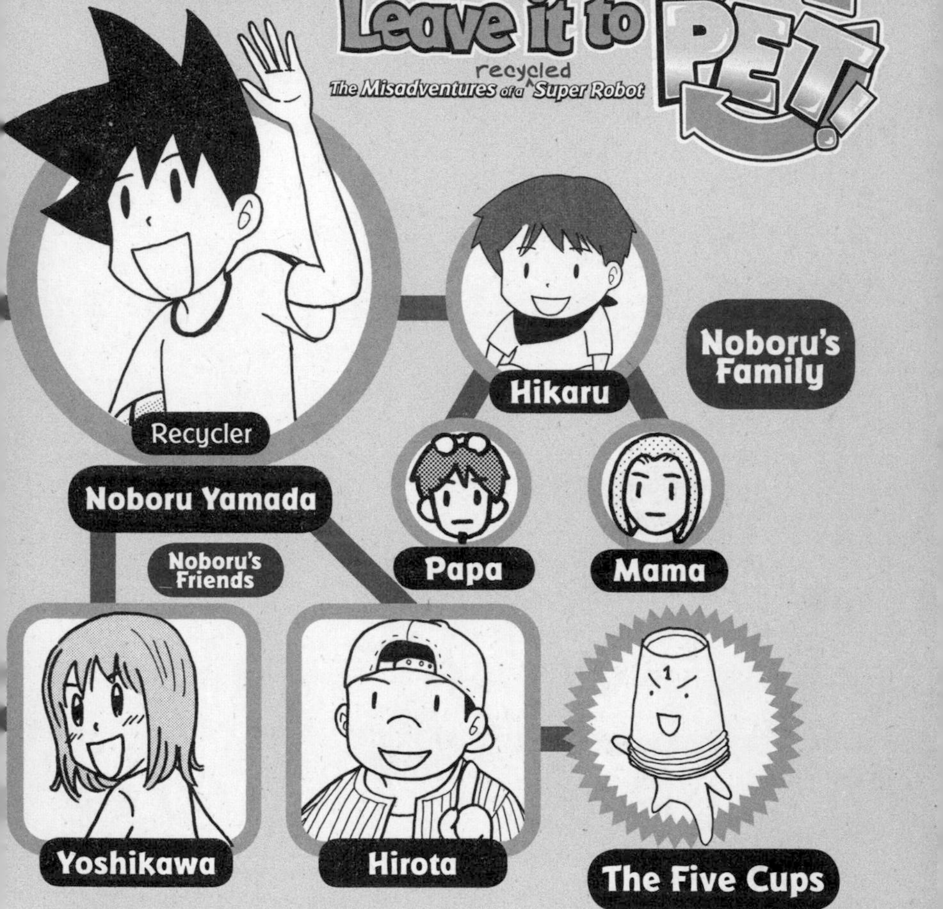
Recycler
Noboru Yamada
Hikaru
Noboru's Family
Papa
Mama
Noboru's Friends
Yoshikawa
Hirota
The Five Cups

## The Story

**A plastic bottle gets recycled and comes back as a helpful robot!**

Meet Noboru, your average Japanese elementary school student. One day he finds a plastic bottle in the park and recycles it. Then the bottle comes back as the robot "**PET**"! **PET** can transform, combine with other robots, and use special **PET** gadgets! Together with his sister, **Alu**, and friend, **Plaz**, **PET** saves Noboru from all kinds of trouble... At least that's the idea.

# Who's Who

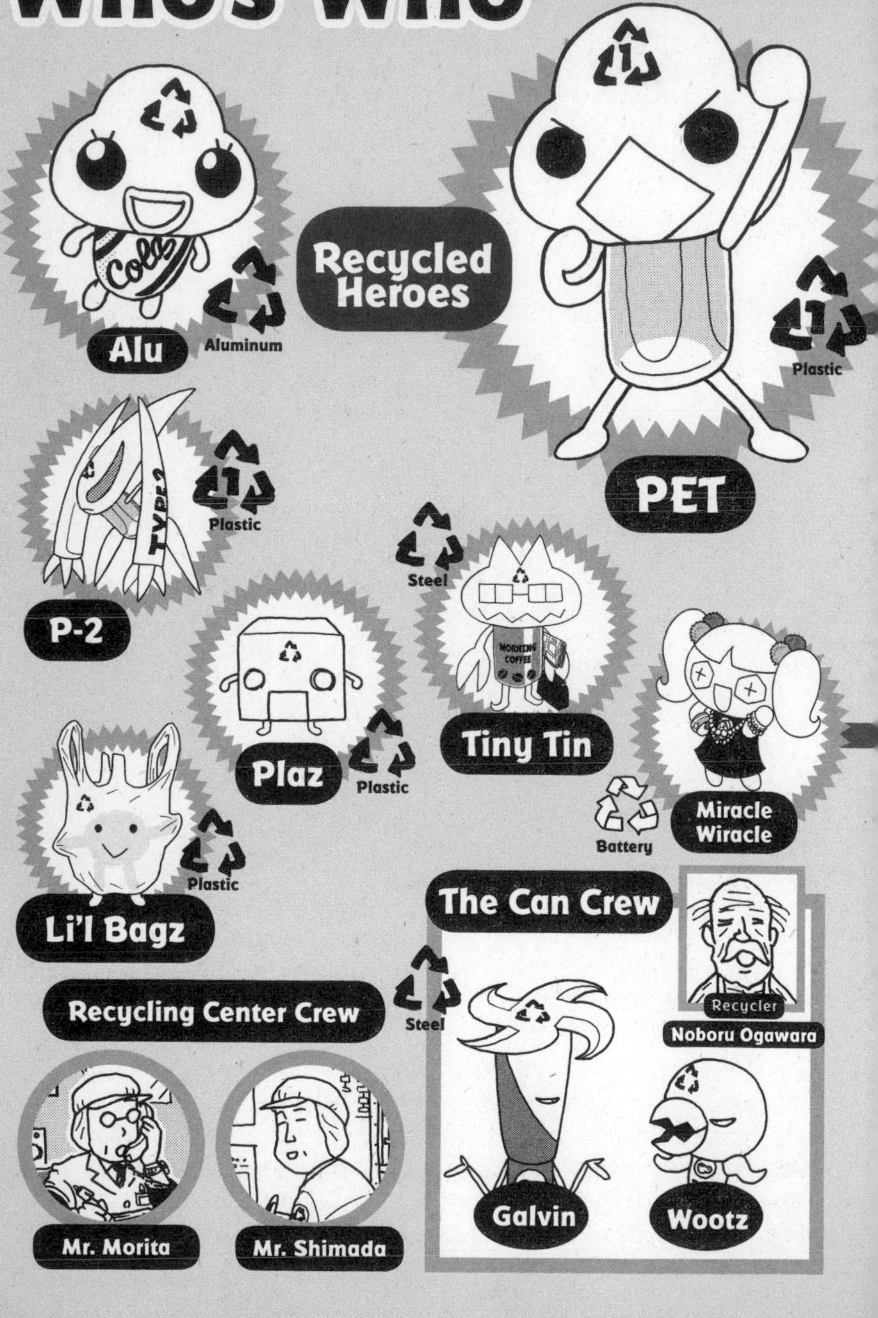

Recycled Heroes
Alu
Aluminum
PET
Plastic
P-2
TYPE2
Plastic
Plaz
Plastic
Tiny Tin
Steel
MORNING COFFEE
Miracle Wiracle
Battery
Li'l Bagz
Plastic
Recycling Center Crew
Mr. Morita
Mr. Shimada
The Can Crew
Steel
Galvin
Wootz
Recycler
Noboru Ogawara

# PET's Haiku*

TINY TIN DOES NOT
LIKE WASABI. IT'S TOO HOT
FOR THE MAN OF STEEL.

*A haiku is a type of Japanese poem
that is three lines long. The first line
has five syllables, the second has
seven, and the third has five again.

**CHAPTER 1**

# PET's Honey Hunt

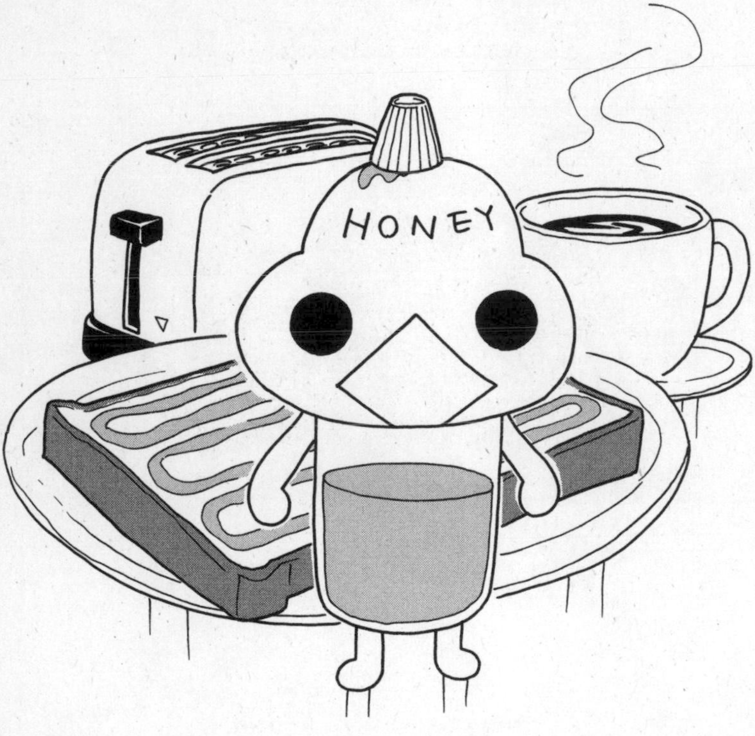
HONEY

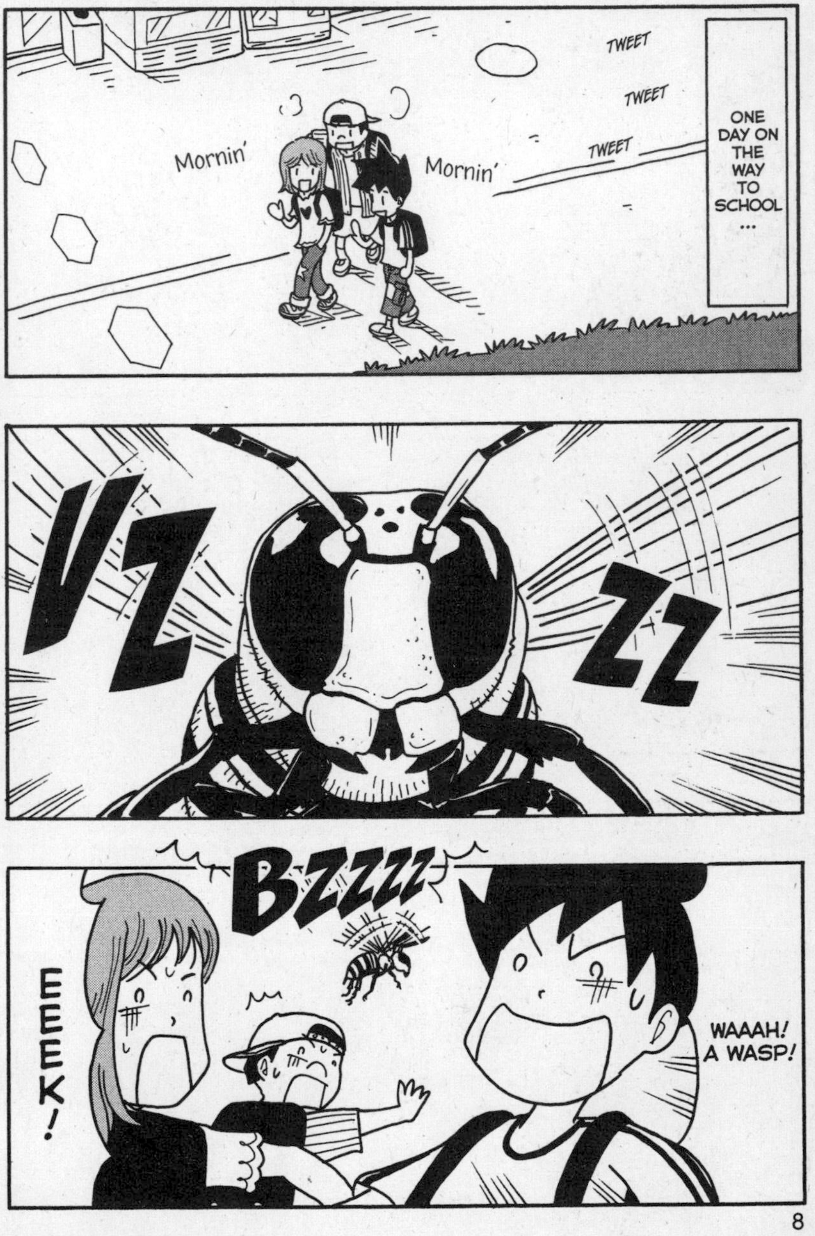
ONE DAY ON THE WAY TO SCHOOL...
TWEET
TWEET
TWEET
Mornin'
Mornin'
VZ
ZZ
WAAAH! A WASP!
BZZZZ
EEEEK!

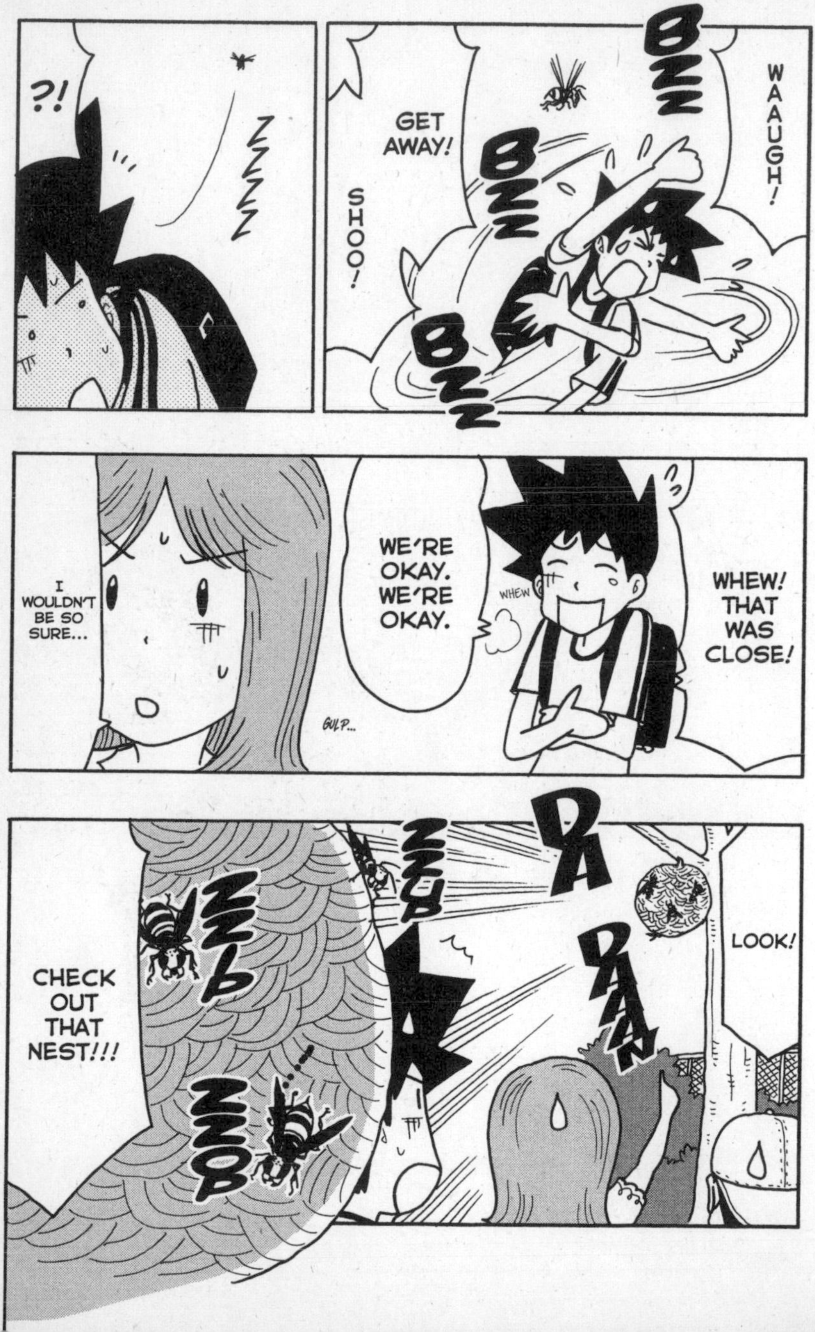
WAAUGH!
BZZ
BZZ
GET AWAY!
SHOO!
BZZ
?!
ZZZZZ
WHEW! THAT WAS CLOSE!
WHEW
WE'RE OKAY. WE'RE OKAY.
GULP...
I WOULDN'T BE SO SURE...
LOOK!
DA
DAN
CHECK OUT THAT NEST!!!

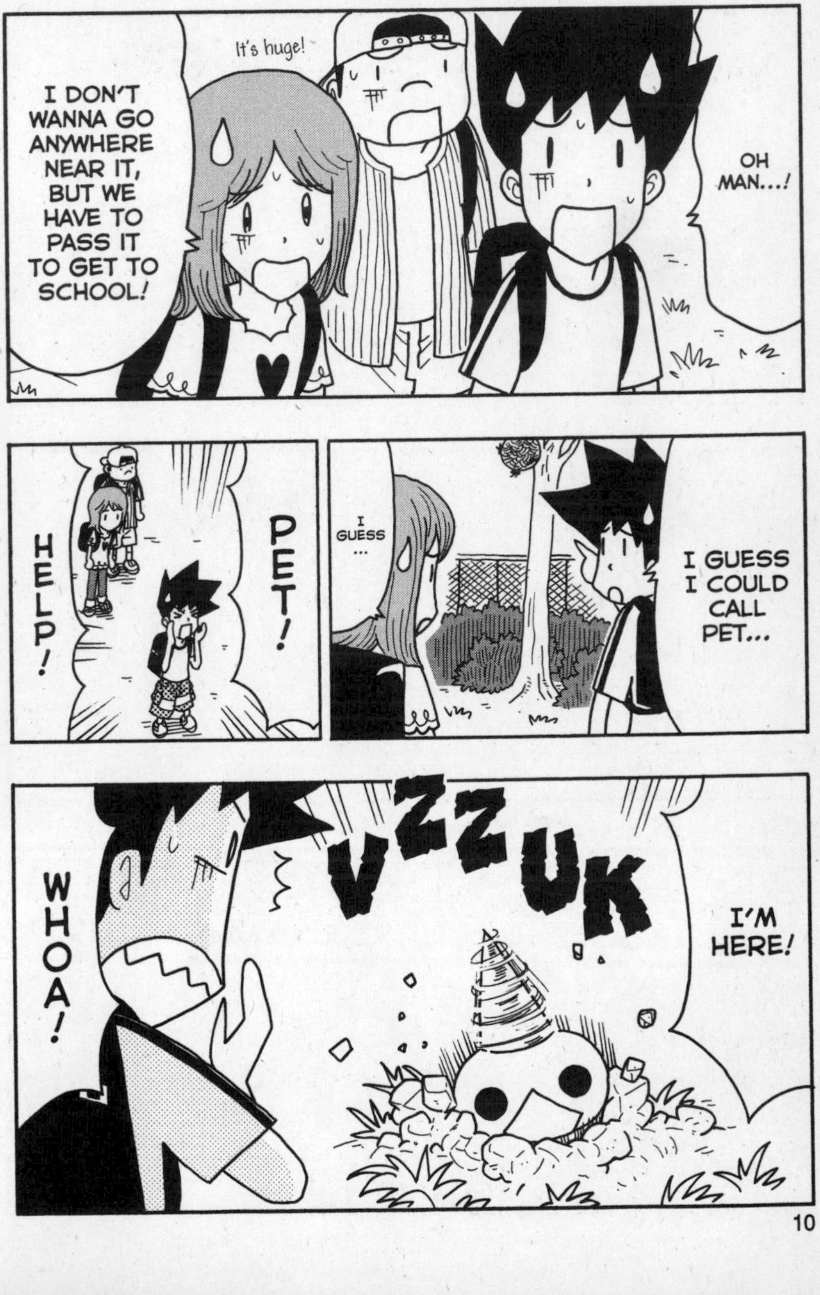
OH MAN...!
It's huge!
I DON'T WANNA GO ANYWHERE NEAR IT, BUT WE HAVE TO PASS IT TO GET TO SCHOOL!
I GUESS I COULD CALL PET...
I GUESS...
PET!
HELP!
I'M HERE!
VZZUK
WHOA!

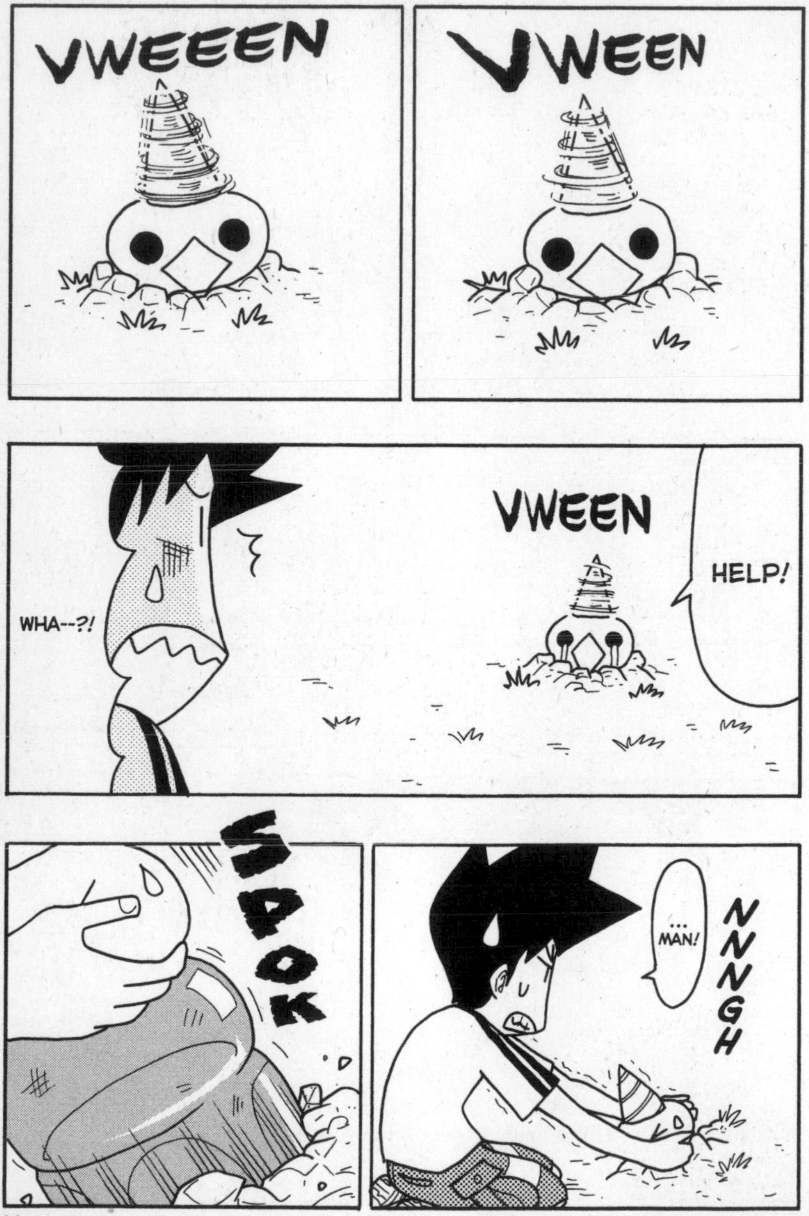
VWEEN
VWEEEN
HELP!
VWEEN
WHA--?!
NNNGH
...MAN!
SPOK

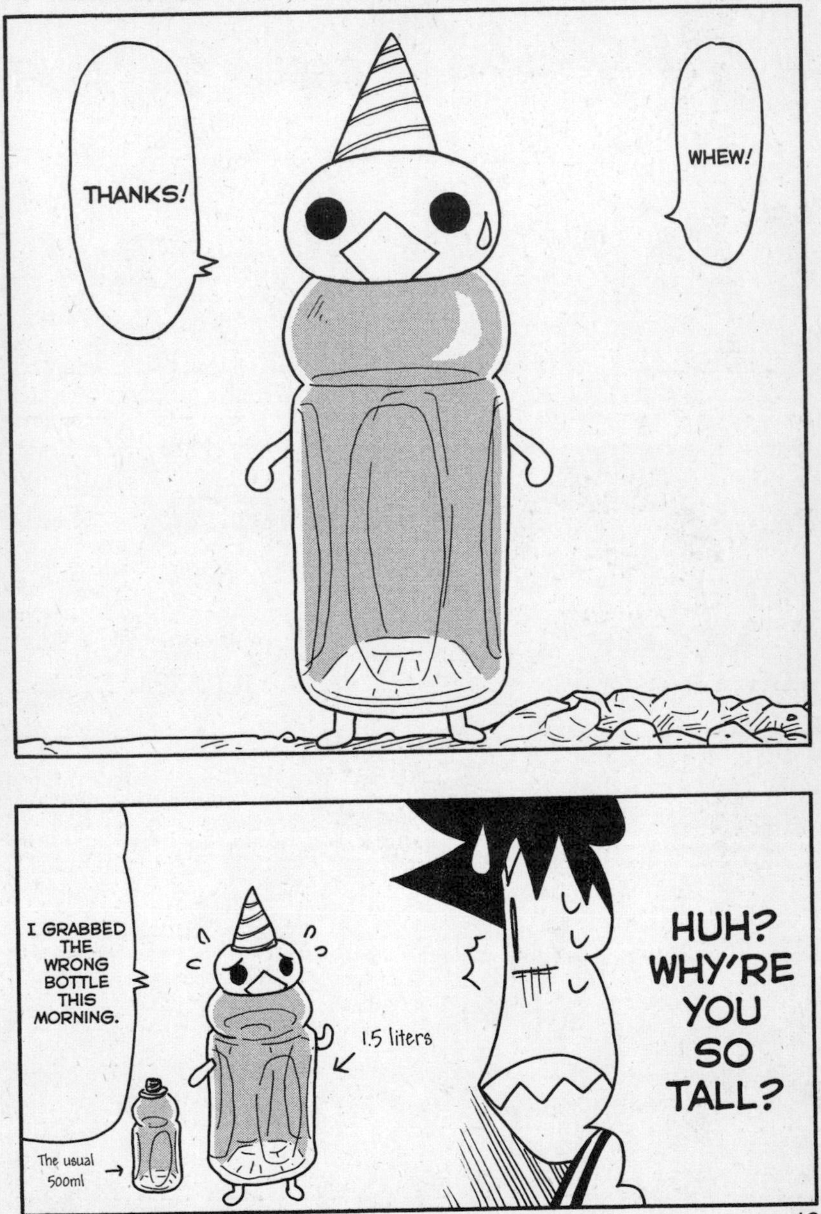
WHEW!
THANKS!
HUH? WHY'RE YOU SO TALL?
I GRABBED THE WRONG BOTTLE THIS MORNING.
1.5 liters
The usual 500ml

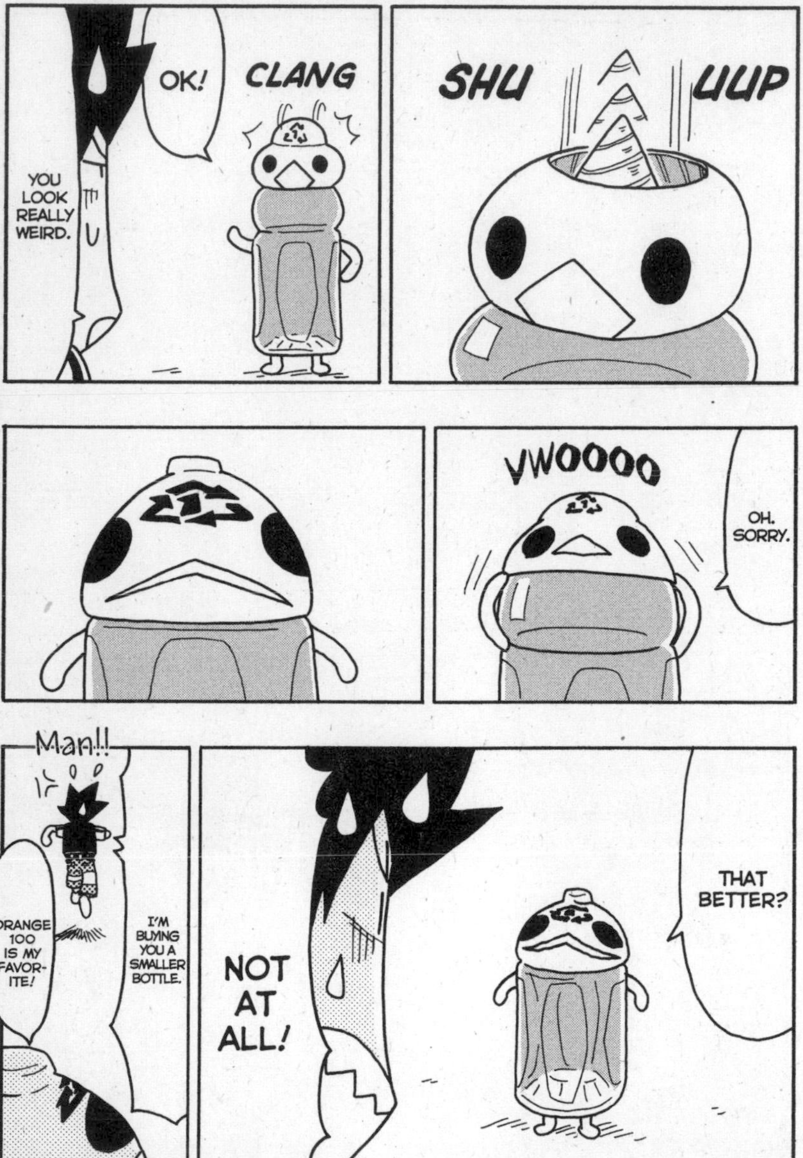
SHU
UUP
CLANG
OK!
YOU LOOK REALLY WEIRD.
VWOOOO
OH. SORRY.
THAT BETTER?
NOT AT ALL!
Man!!
I'M BUYING YOU A SMALLER BOTTLE.
ORANGE 100 IS MY FAVOR-ITE!

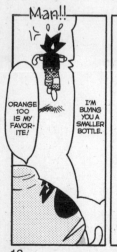

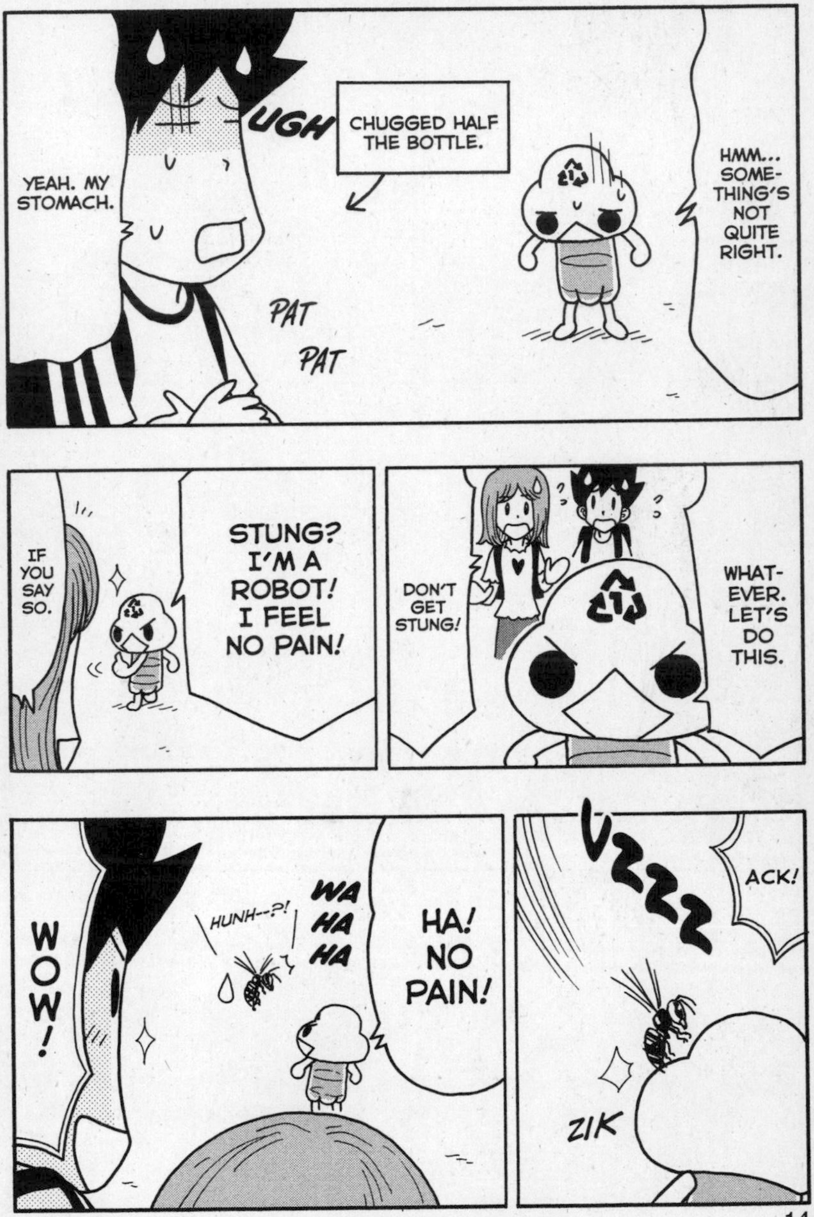
HMM... SOME-THING'S NOT QUITE RIGHT.
CHUGGED HALF THE BOTTLE.
UGH
YEAH. MY STOMACH.
PAT PAT
WHAT-EVER. LET'S DO THIS.
DON'T GET STUNG!
STUNG? I'M A ROBOT! I FEEL NO PAIN!
IF YOU SAY SO.
VZZZ
ACK!
ZIK
HA! NO PAIN!
WA HA HA
HUNH--?!
WOW!

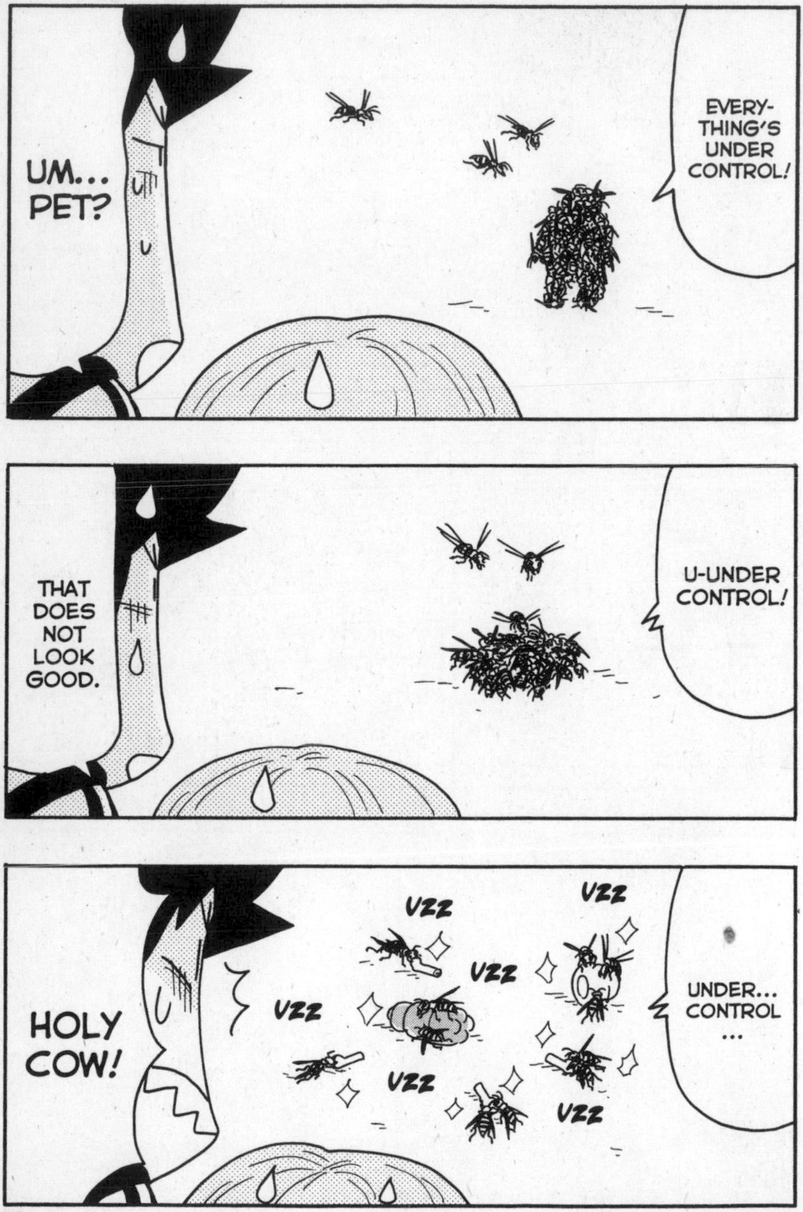
EVERY-THING'S UNDER CONTROL!
UM... PET?
U-UNDER CONTROL!
THAT DOES NOT LOOK GOOD.
VZZ
UNDER... CONTROL ...
VZZ
VZZ
VZZ
VZZ
VZZ
HOLY COW!

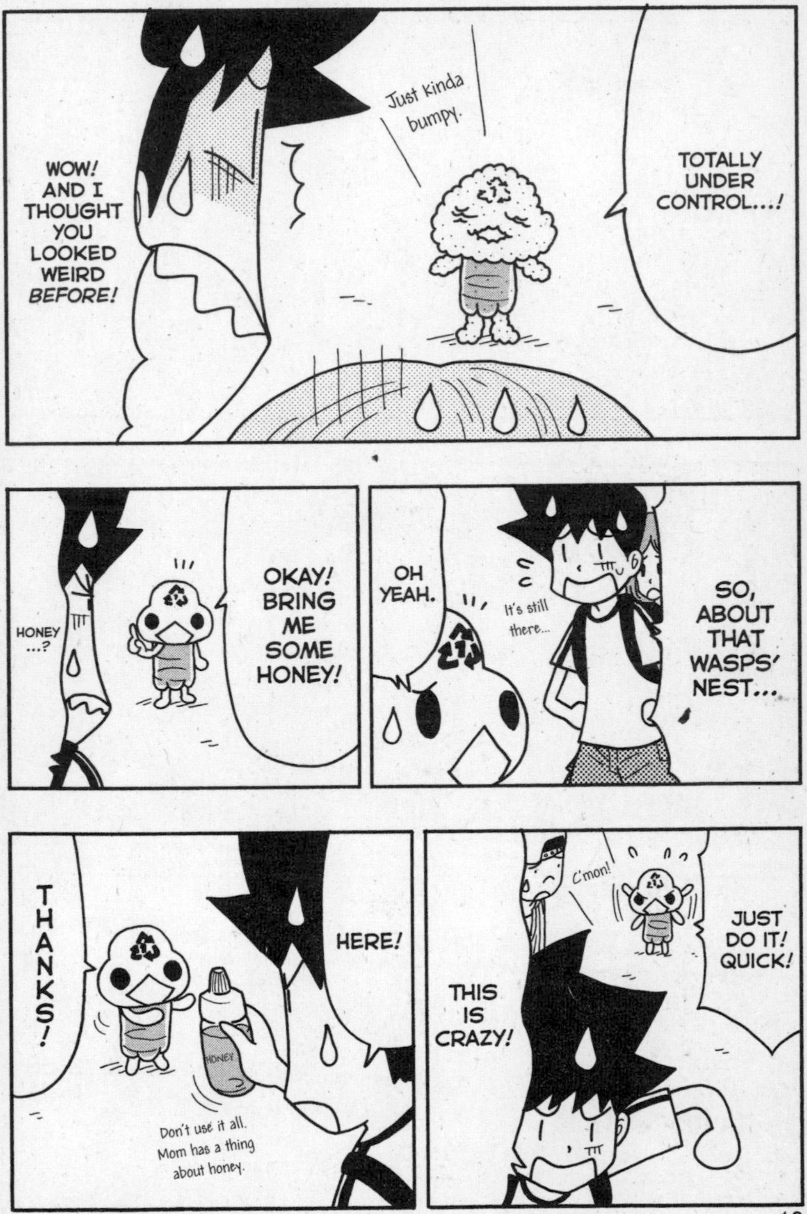
TOTALLY UNDER CONTROL...!
Just kinda bumpy.
WOW! AND I THOUGHT YOU LOOKED WEIRD BEFORE!
SO, ABOUT THAT WASPS' NEST...
OH YEAH.
It's still there...
OKAY! BRING ME SOME HONEY!
HONEY...?
JUST DO IT! QUICK!
C'mon!
THIS IS CRAZY!
HERE!
THANKS!
HONEY
Don't use it all. Mom has a thing about honey.

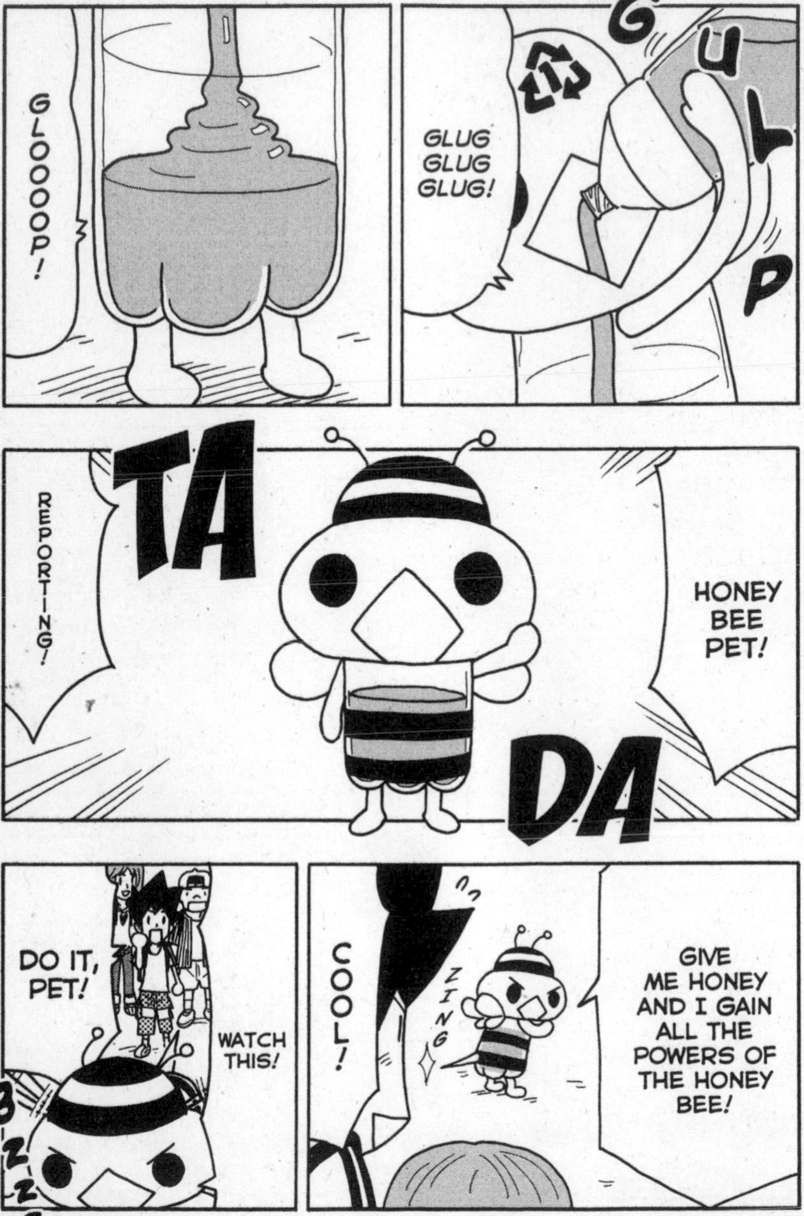
GULP
GLUG GLUG GLUG!
GLOOOOOP!
TA DA
HONEY BEE PET!
REPORTING!
GIVE ME HONEY AND I GAIN ALL THE POWERS OF THE HONEY BEE!
ZING
COOL!
WATCH THIS!
DO IT, PET!
BZZZZ

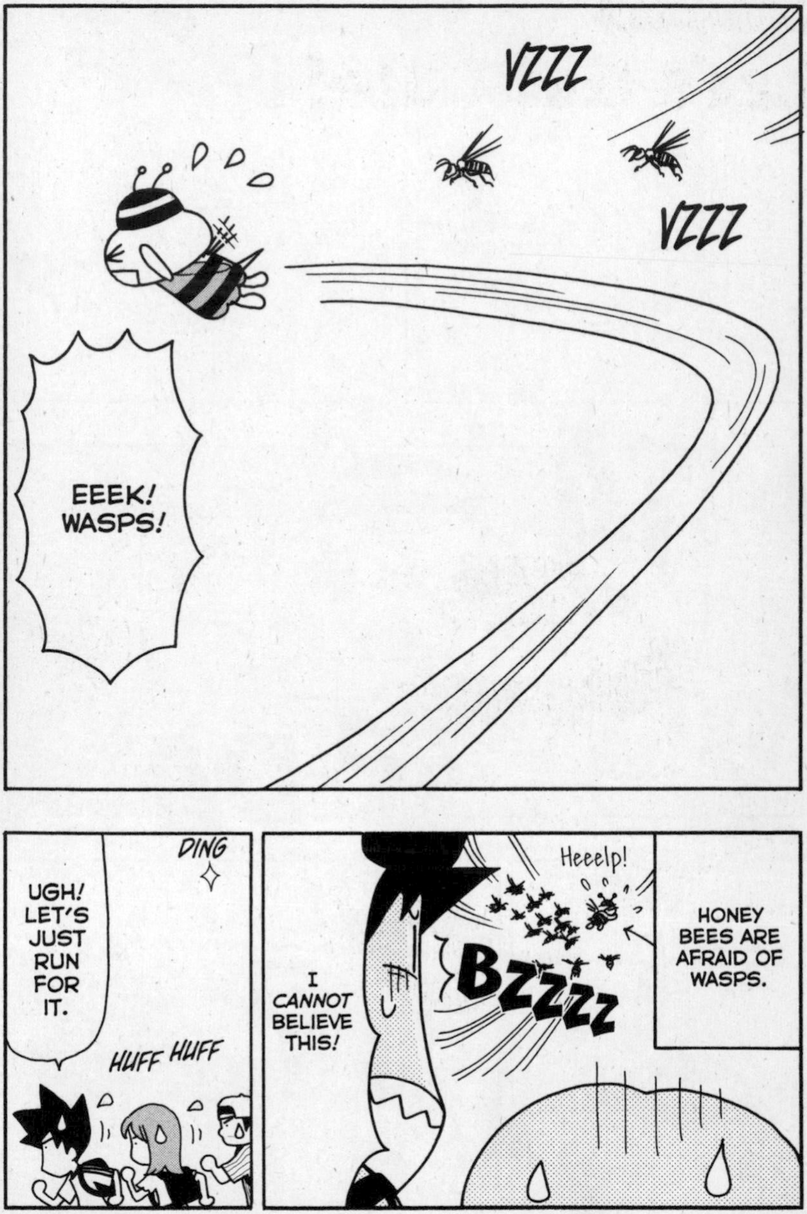
VZZZ
VZZZ
EEEK! WASPS!
HONEY BEES ARE AFRAID OF WASPS.
Heeelp!
BZZZZZ
I CANNOT BELIEVE THIS!
DING
UGH! LET'S JUST RUN FOR IT.
HUFF HUFF

CHAPTER 2

# Let's Get Cute!

Under control!
Under control!

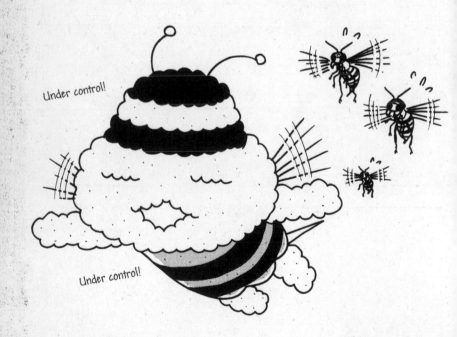

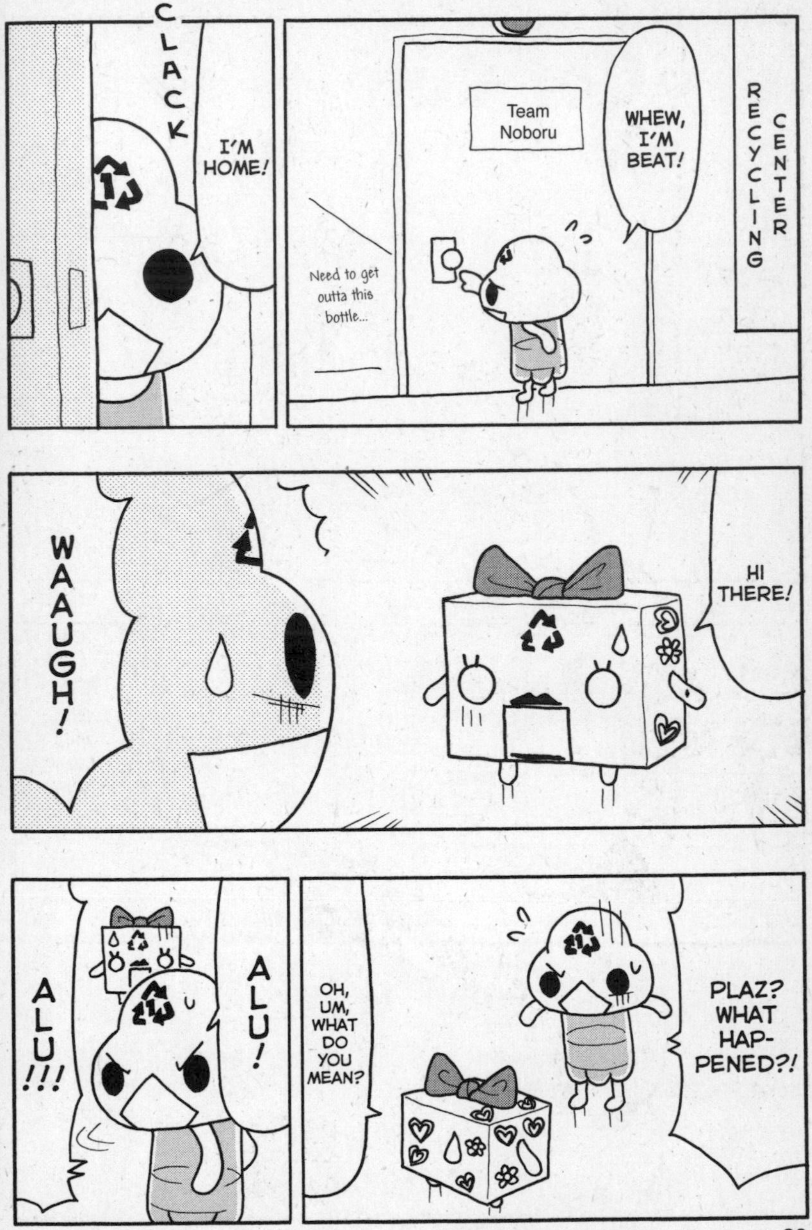
RECYCLING CENTER
WHEW, I'M BEAT!
Team Noboru
Need to get outta this bottle...
CLACK
I'M HOME!
HI THERE!
WAAAUGH!
PLAZ? WHAT HAP-PENED?!
OH, UM, WHAT DO YOU MEAN?
ALU!
ALU!!!

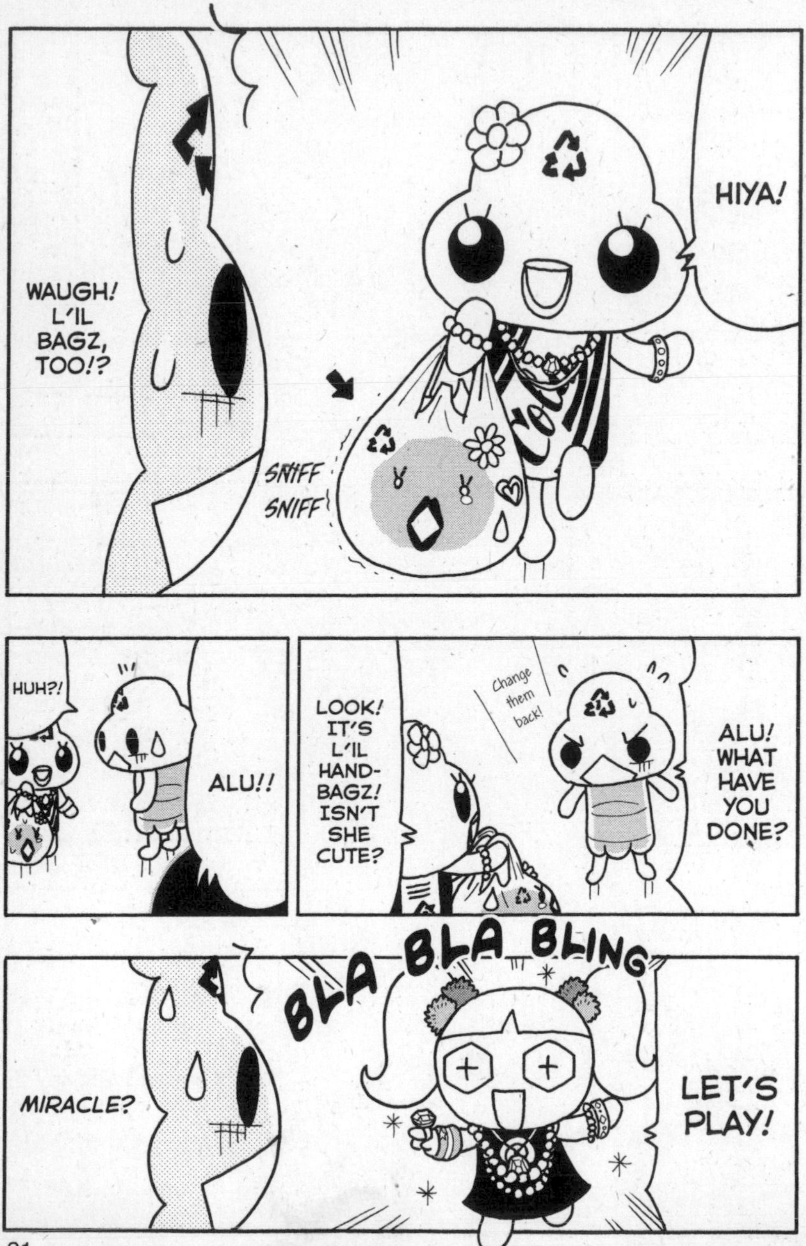
HIYA!
WAUGH! L'IL BAGZ, TOO!?
SNIFF SNIFF
ALU! WHAT HAVE YOU DONE?
Change them back!
LOOK! IT'S L'IL HAND-BAGZ! ISN'T SHE CUTE?
ALU!!
HUH?!
BLA BLA BLING
LET'S PLAY!
MIRACLE?

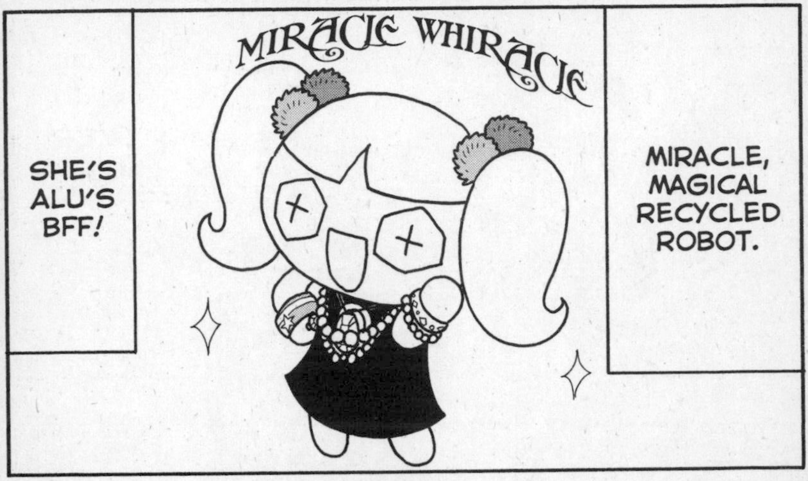
MIRACLE, MAGICAL RECYCLED ROBOT.
MIRACLE WHIRACLE
SHE'S ALU'S BFF!

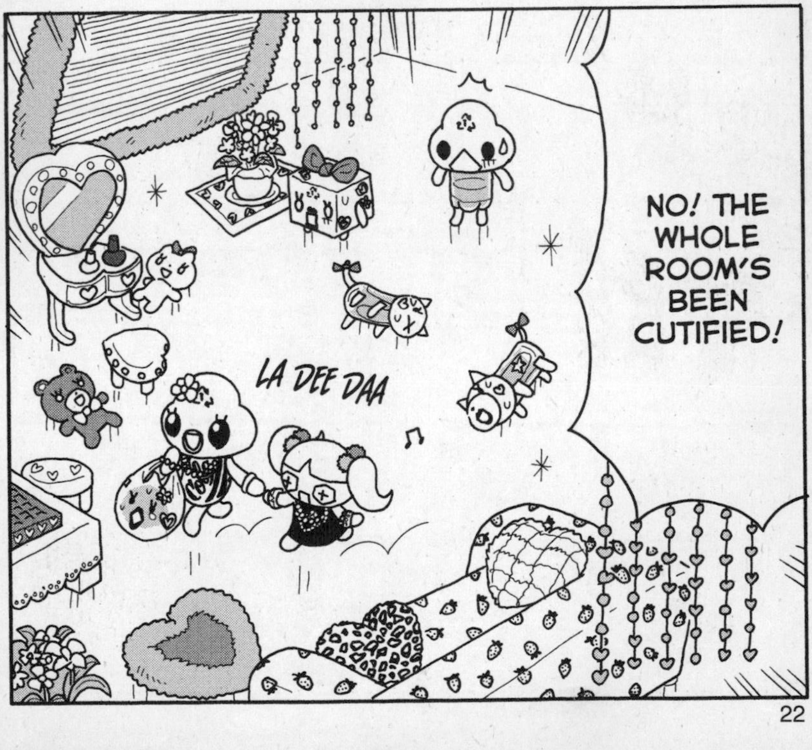
NO! THE WHOLE ROOM'S BEEN CUTIFIED!
LA DEE DAA

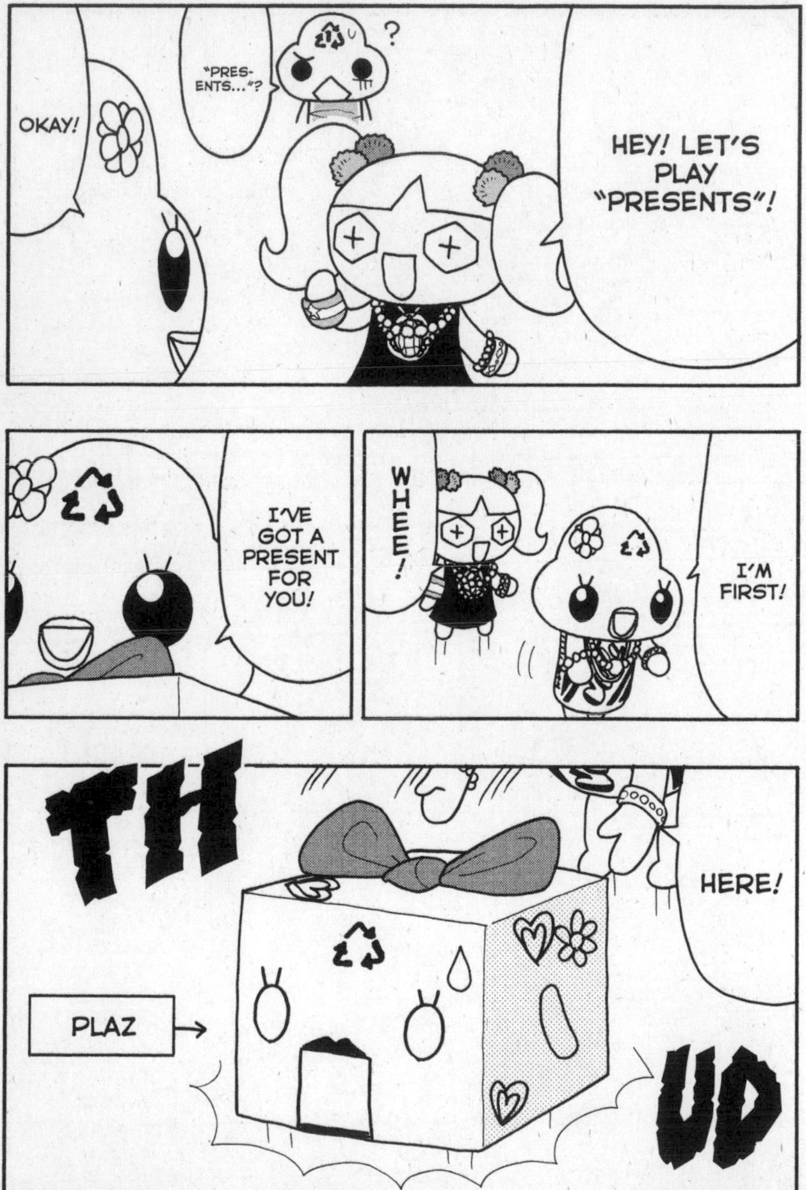
HEY! LET'S PLAY "PRESENTS"!
"PRES-ENTS..."?
OKAY!
I'M FIRST!
WHEE!
I'VE GOT A PRESENT FOR YOU!
HERE!
TH
UD
PLAZ

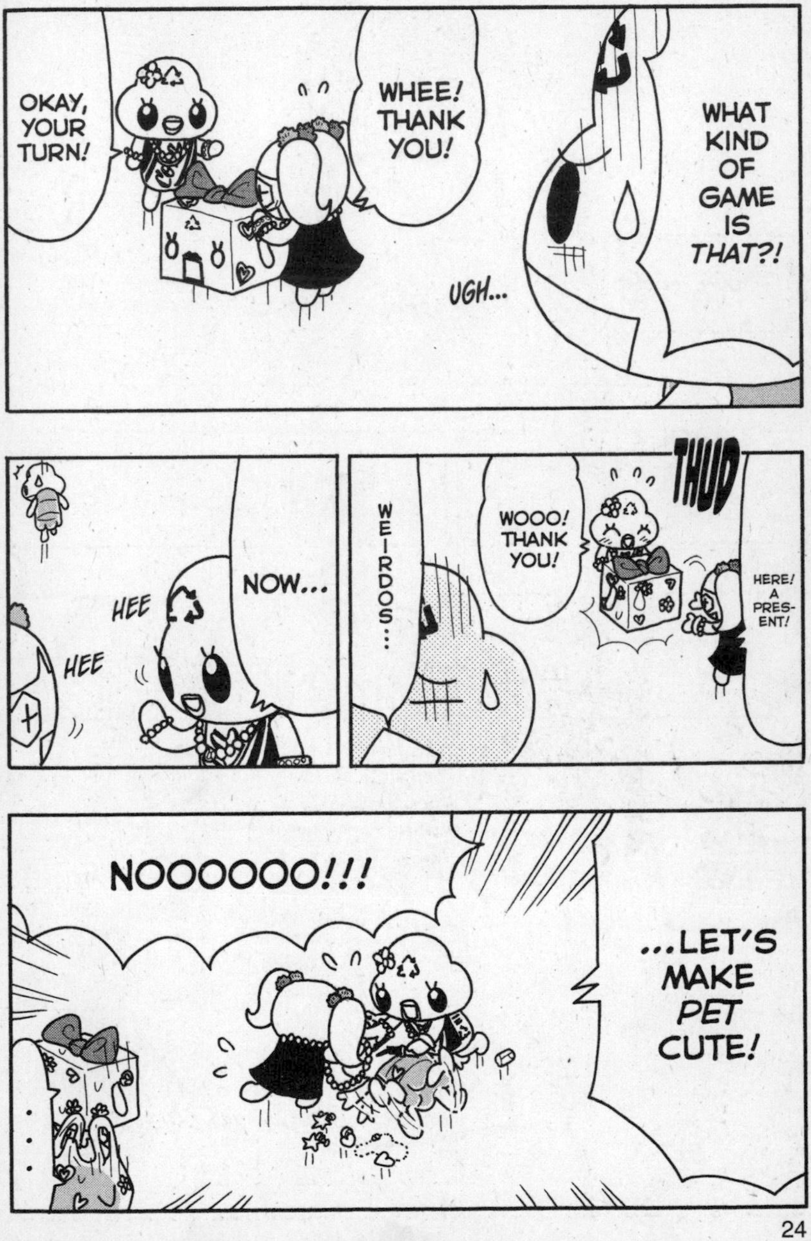
WHAT KIND OF GAME IS *THAT?!*
WHEE! THANK YOU!
UGH...
OKAY, YOUR TURN!
HERE! A PRES-ENT!
THUD
WOOO! THANK YOU!
WEIRDOS...
NOW...
HEE
HEE
...LET'S MAKE *PET* CUTE!
NOOOOOO!!!

## CHAPTER 3 None Like It Hot!

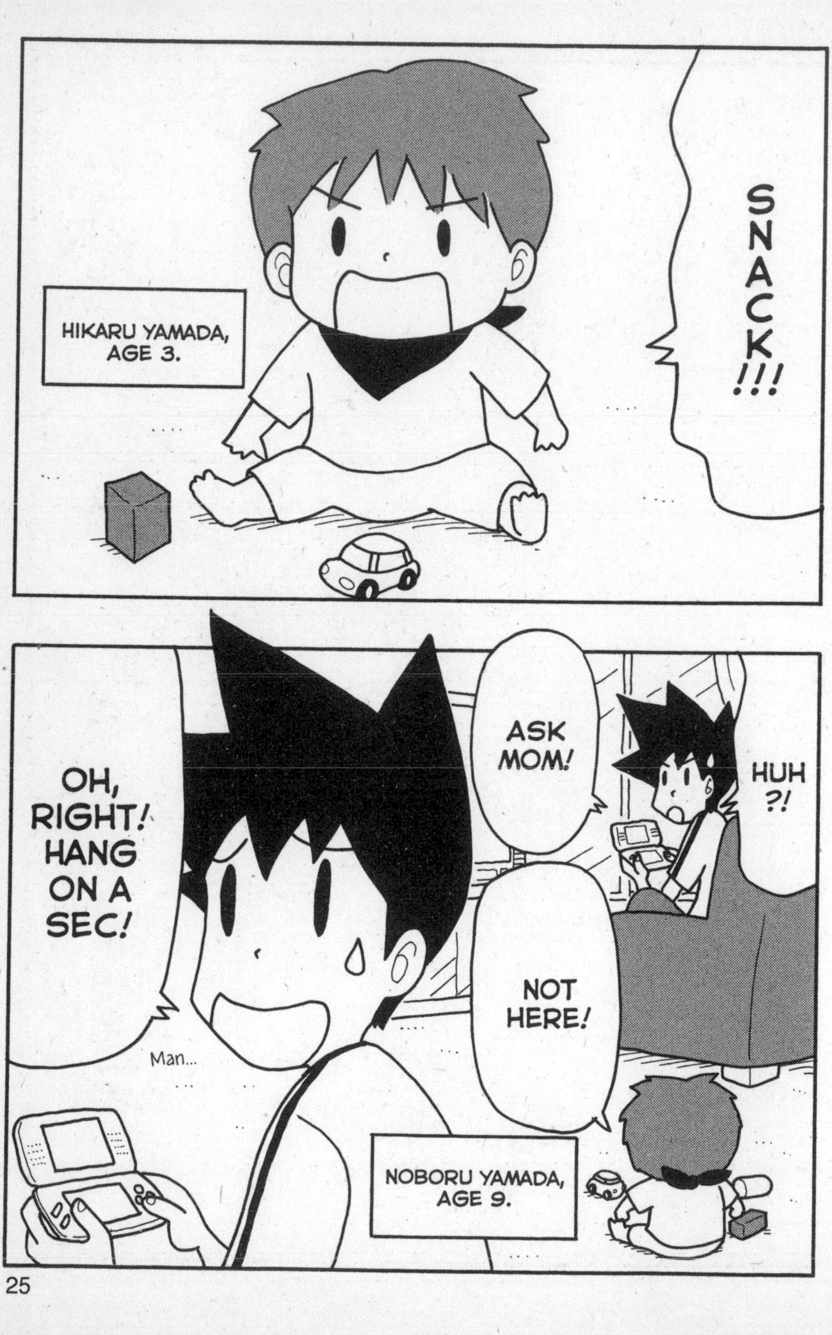
SNACK!!!
HIKARU YAMADA, AGE 3.
HUH?!
ASK MOM!
NOT HERE!
NOBORU YAMADA, AGE 9.
OH, RIGHT! HANG ON A SEC!
Man...

## CHAPTER 3

# None Like It Hot!

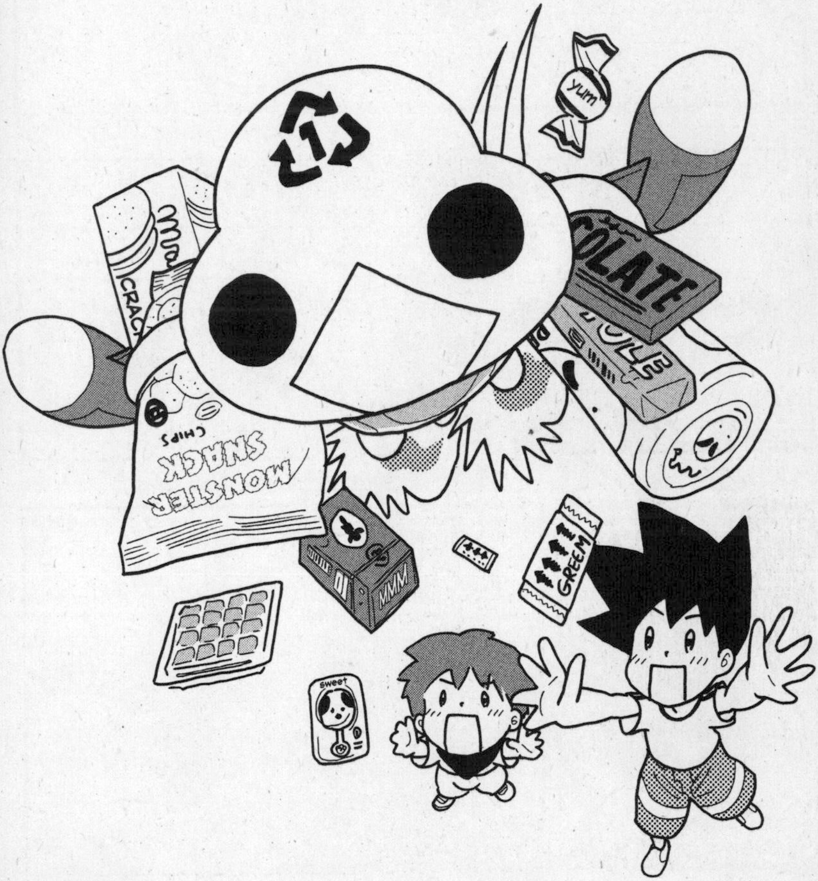
yum
COLATE
MONSTER SNACK
CHIPS
GREEM
MMM
sweet

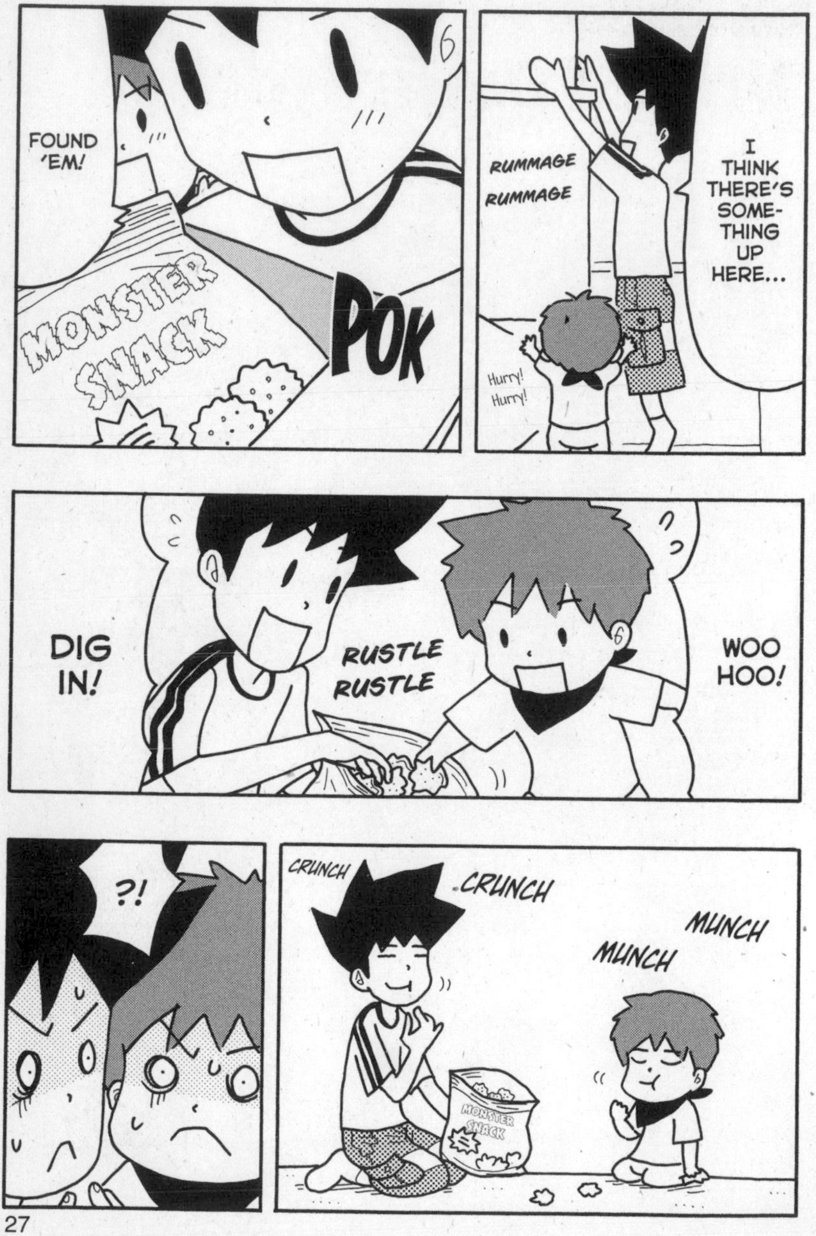
I THINK THERE'S SOME-THING UP HERE...
RUMMAGE
RUMMAGE
Hurry!
Hurry!
FOUND 'EM!
POK
MONSTER SNACK
WOO HOO!
RUSTLE
RUSTLE
DIG IN!
MUNCH
MUNCH
CRUNCH
CRUNCH
MONSTER SNACK
?!

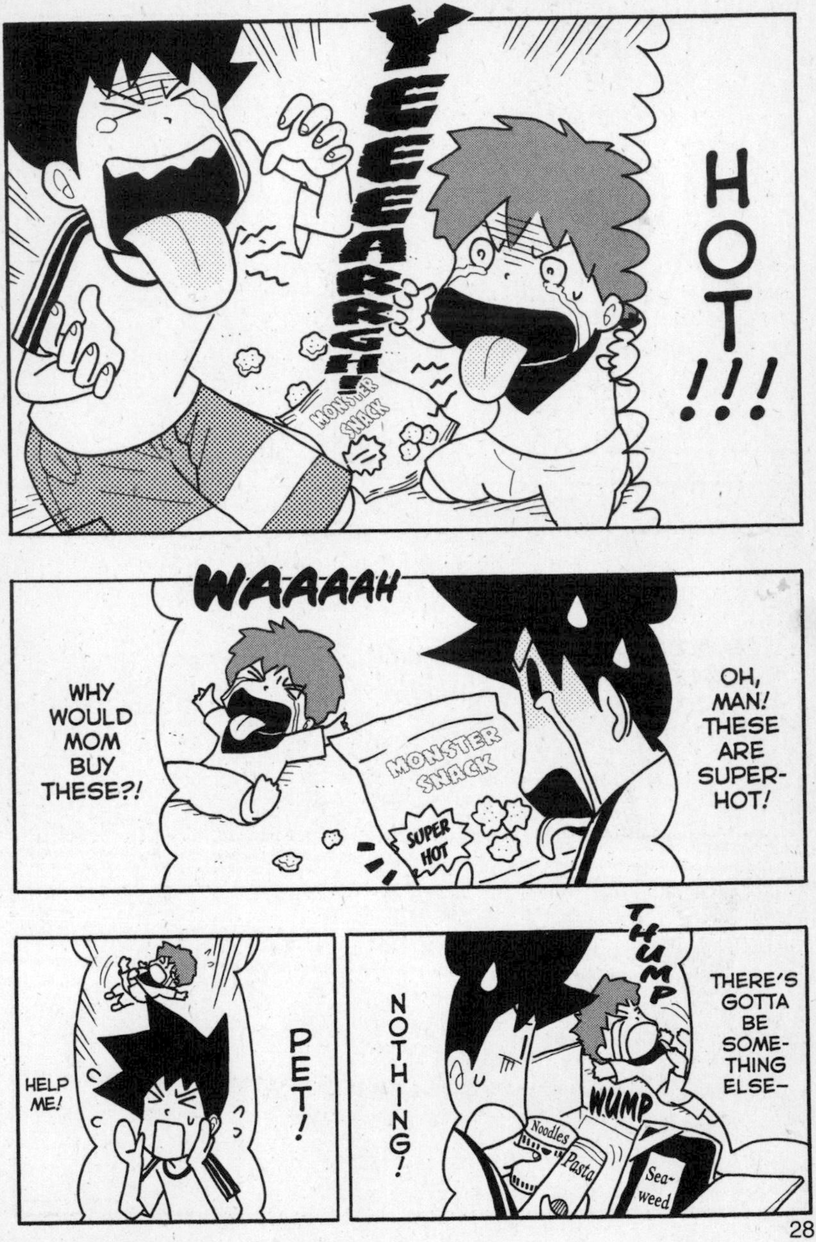
HOT!!!
YEEEEARRGH!!
MONSTER SNACK
WAAAAH
OH, MAN! THESE ARE SUPER-HOT!
WHY WOULD MOM BUY THESE?!
MONSTER SNACK
SUPER HOT
THUMP
THERE'S GOTTA BE SOMETHING ELSE—
NOTHING!
WUMP
Noodles
Pasta
Sea-weed
PET!
HELP ME!

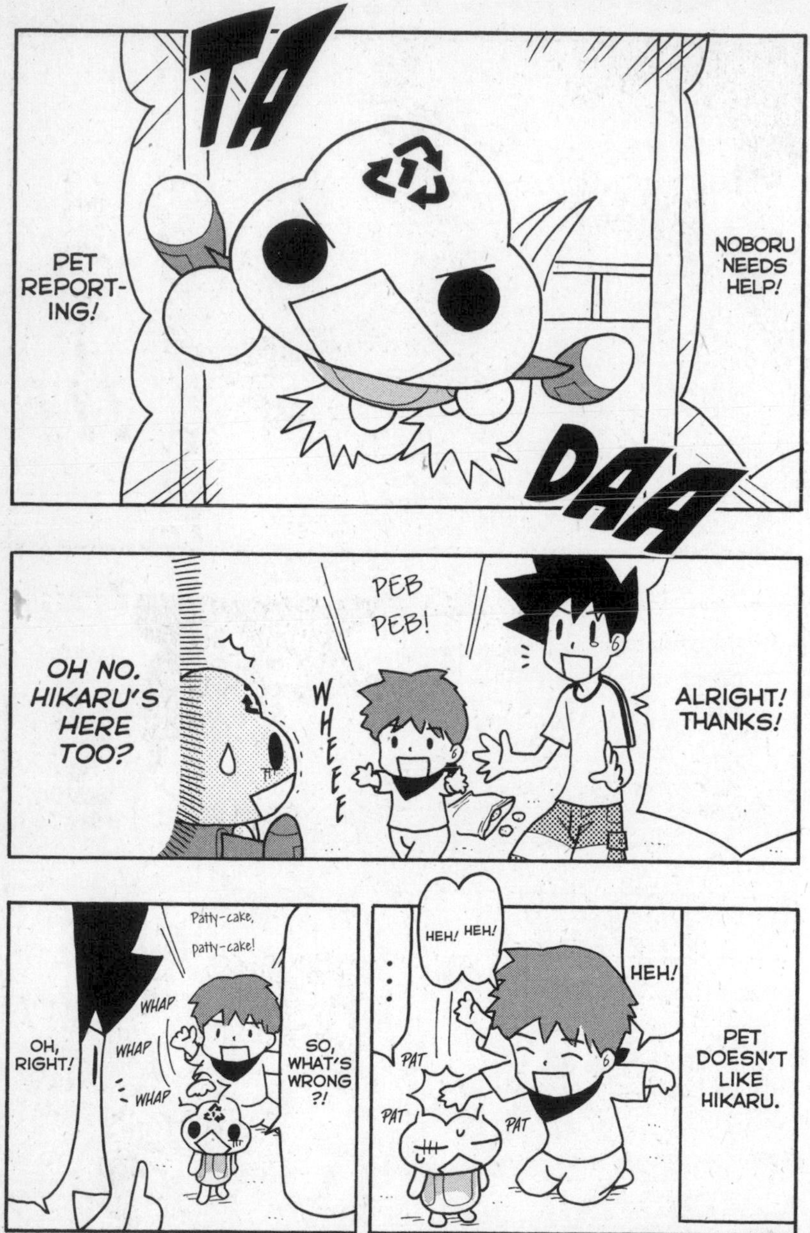
NOBORU NEEDS HELP!
TA
PET REPORTING!
DAA
ALRIGHT! THANKS!
PEB PEB!
WHEEE
OH NO. HIKARU'S HERE TOO?
HEH!
HEH! HEH!
PET DOESN'T LIKE HIKARU.
PAT
PAT
PAT
Patty-cake, patty-cake!
SO, WHAT'S WRONG?!
WHAP
WHAP
WHAP
OH, RIGHT!

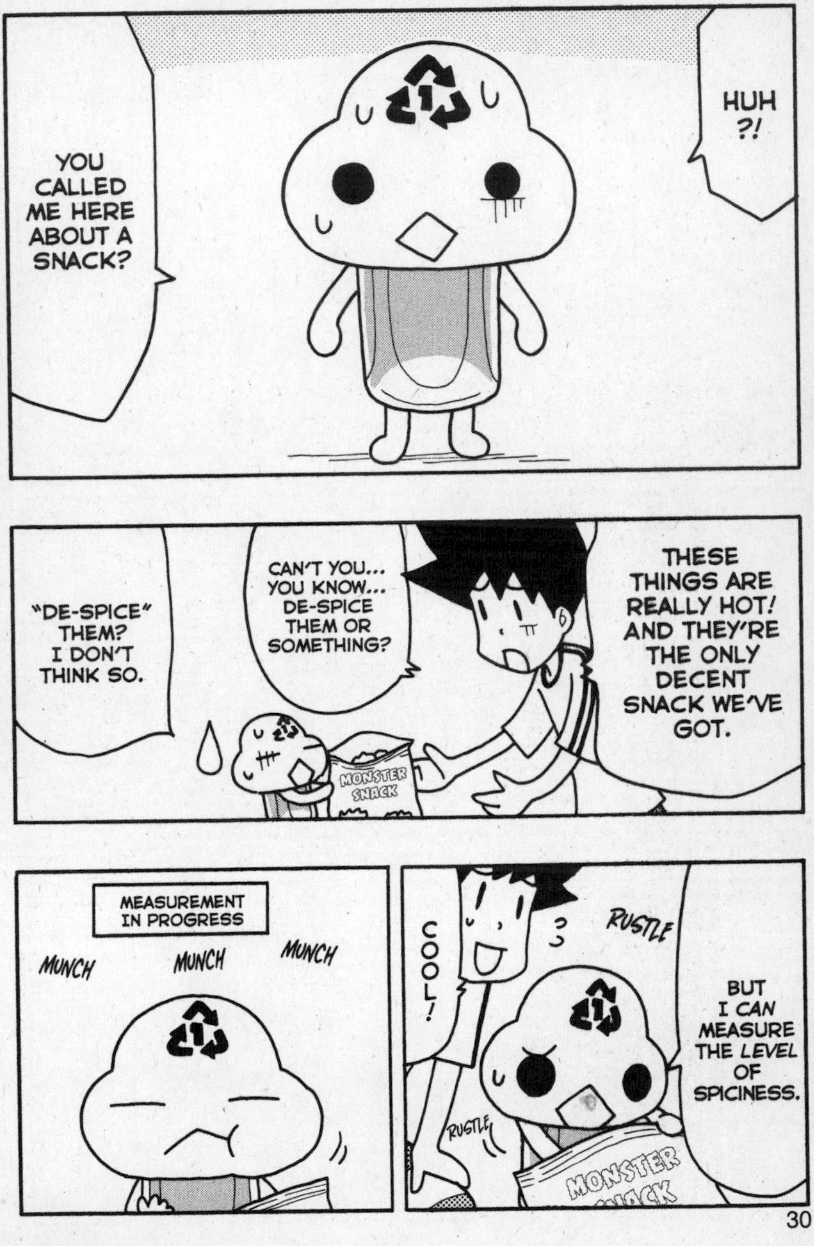
HUH ?!
YOU CALLED ME HERE ABOUT A SNACK?
THESE THINGS ARE REALLY HOT! AND THEY'RE THE ONLY DECENT SNACK WE'VE GOT.
CAN'T YOU... YOU KNOW... DE-SPICE THEM OR SOMETHING?
MONSTER SNACK
"DE-SPICE" THEM? I DON'T THINK SO.
BUT I *CAN* MEASURE THE *LEVEL* OF SPICINESS.
RUSTLE
COOL!
RUSTLE
MEASUREMENT IN PROGRESS
MUNCH
MUNCH
MUNCH

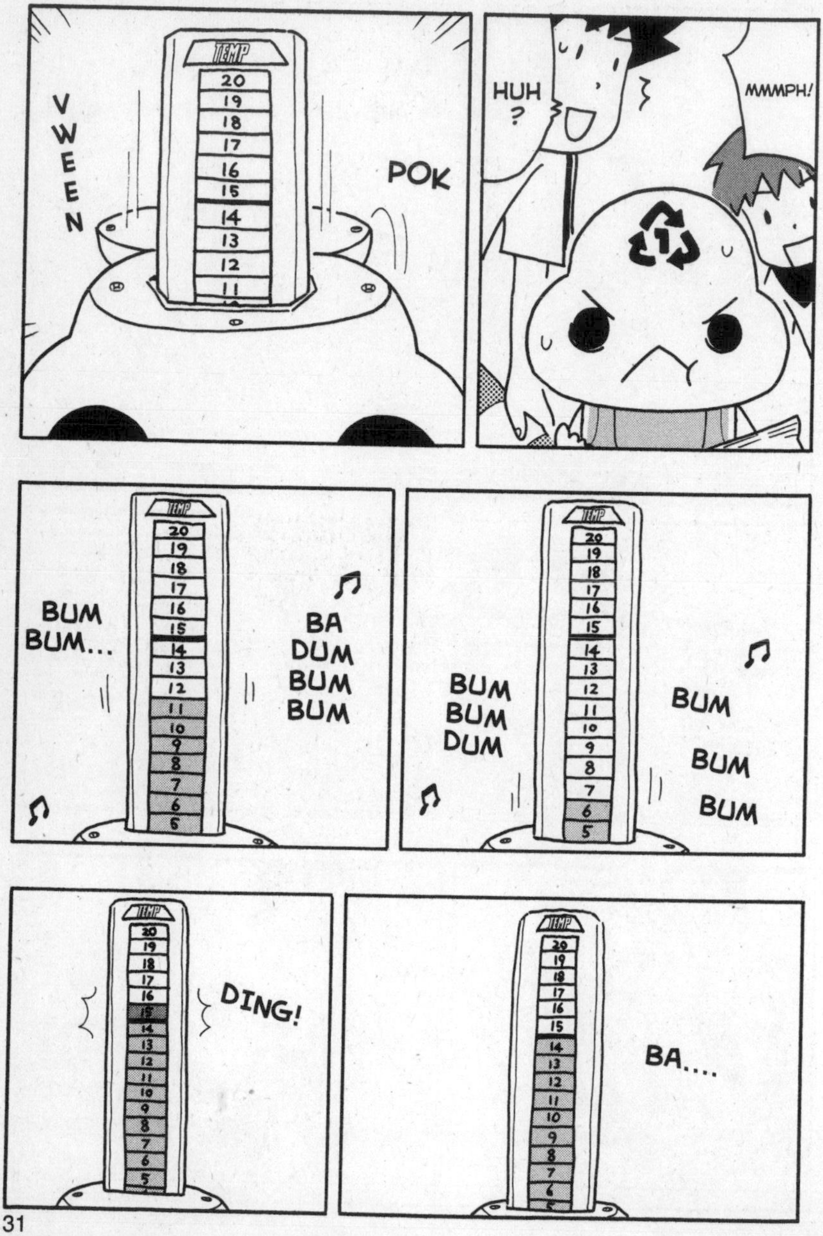
MMMPH!
HUH?
POK
VWEEN
BUM
BUM
BUM
BUM
BUM
DUM
BA
DUM
BUM
BUM
BUM
BUM...
BA....
DING!

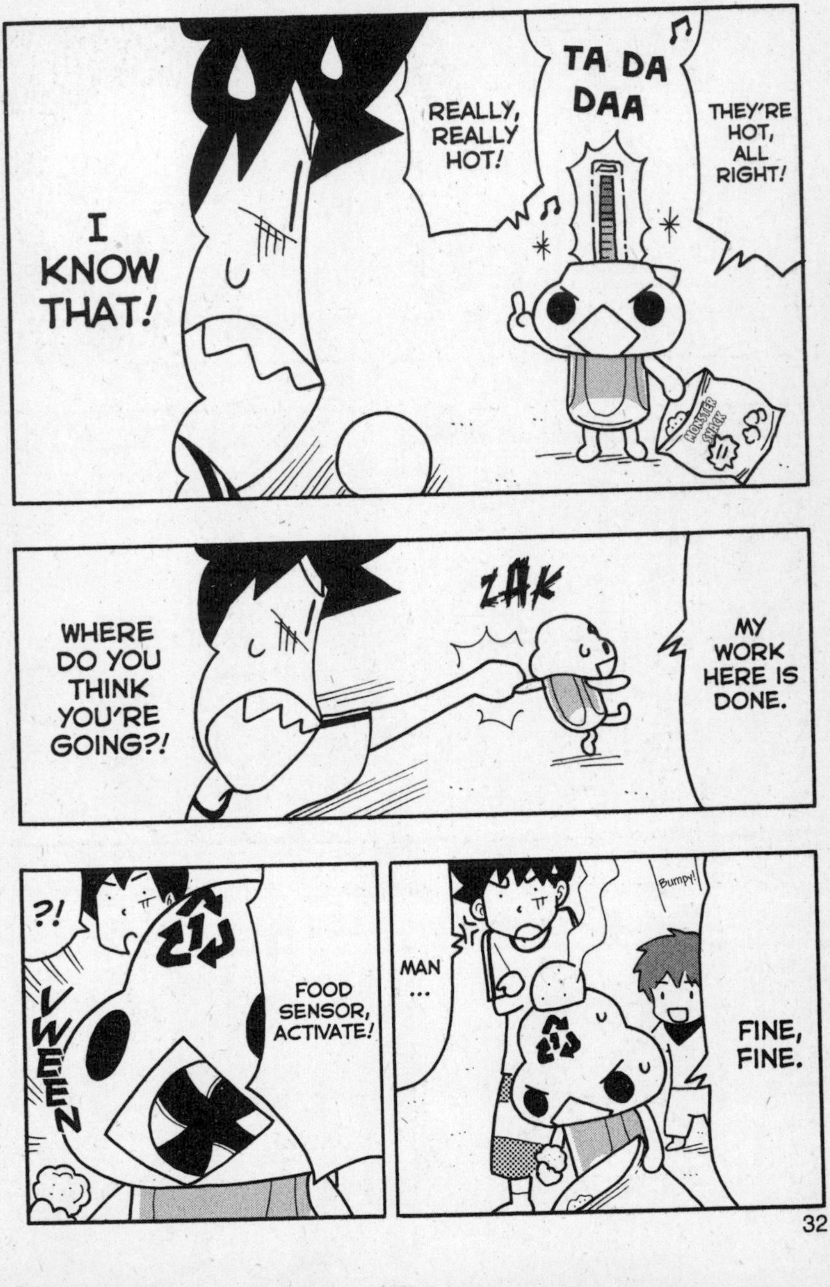
THEY'RE HOT, ALL RIGHT!
TA DA DAA
REALLY, REALLY HOT!
MONSTER SNACK
I KNOW THAT!
MY WORK HERE IS DONE.
ZAK
WHERE DO YOU THINK YOU'RE GOING?!
Bumpy!
FINE, FINE.
MAN ...
FOOD SENSOR, ACTIVATE!
VWEEN
?!

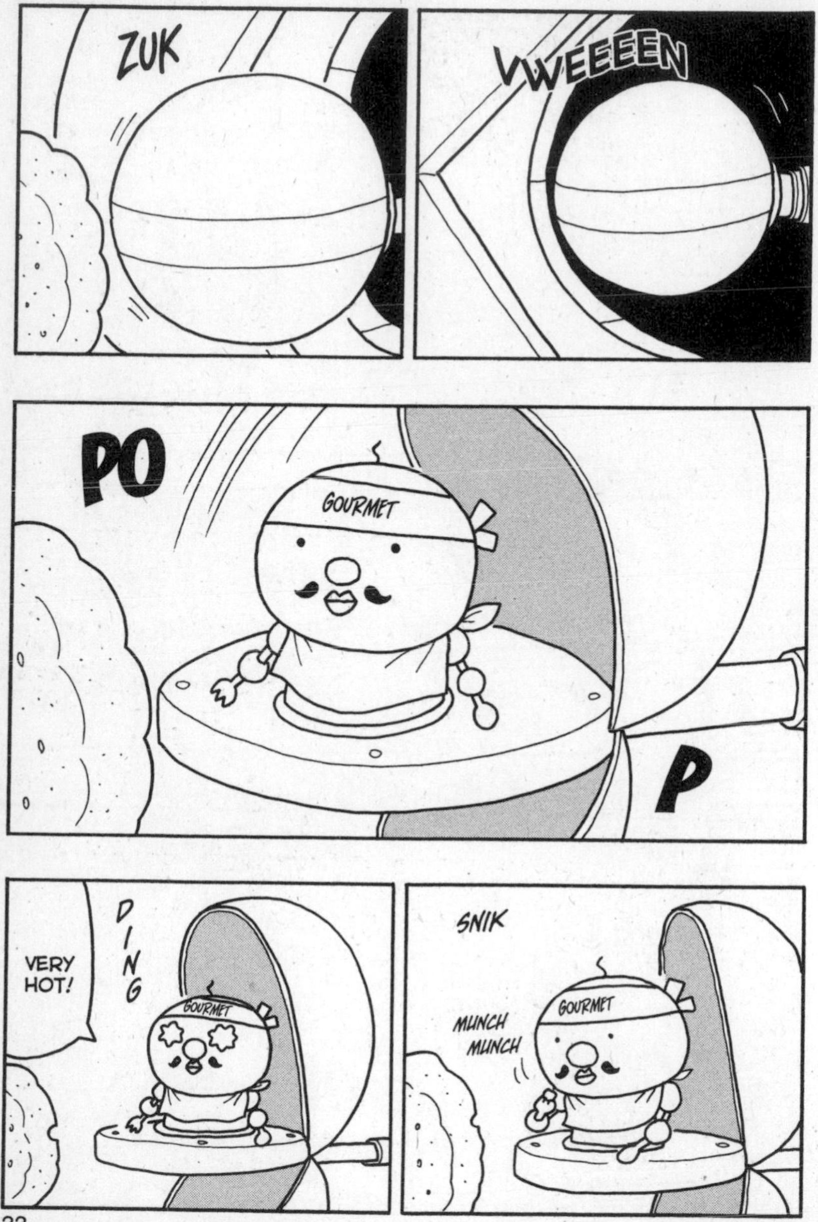
VWEEEEN
ZUK
PO
GOURMET
P
SNIK
GOURMET
MUNCH
MUNCH
DING
VERY HOT!
GOURMET

EXPERTS AGREE! THESE ARE HOT!
YEESH
MONSTER SNACK
Completely unsafe for kids!
UM... WHO WAS THAT LITTLE MAN?
I HAVE AN IDEA! WHY DON'T I TRADE YOU YOUR CHIPS FOR SOME OF MY SNACKS?
HUH?
REALLY?!
TA DAAA
YUM
PET Snack
OIL
Robo-riffic!
500ml
PET Snack
BATTERY Fluid
Robo-riffic!
300ml

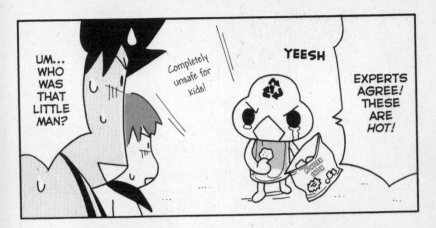

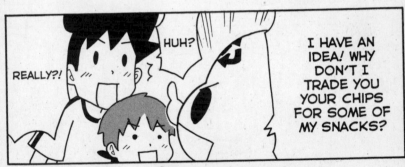

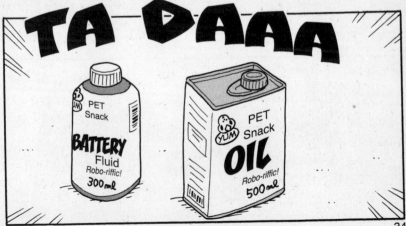

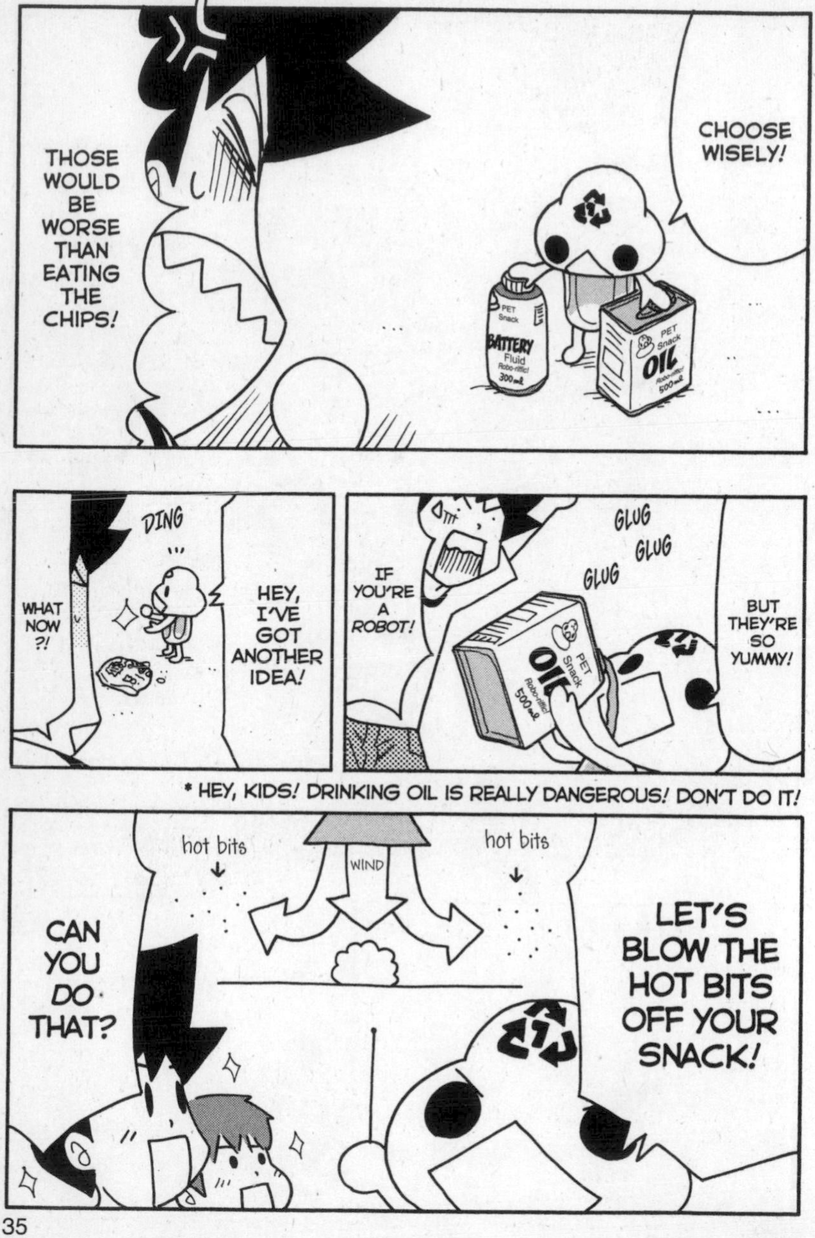
CHOOSE WISELY!
PET Snack OIL Robo-riffic! 500ml
PET Snack BATTERY Fluid Robo-riffic! 300ml
THOSE WOULD BE WORSE THAN EATING THE CHIPS!
BUT THEY'RE SO YUMMY!
GLUG GLUG GLUG
IF YOU'RE A ROBOT!
HEY, I'VE GOT ANOTHER IDEA!
DING
WHAT NOW?!
* HEY, KIDS! DRINKING OIL IS REALLY DANGEROUS! DON'T DO IT!
LET'S BLOW THE HOT BITS OFF YOUR SNACK!
hot bits
WIND
hot bits
CAN YOU DO THAT?

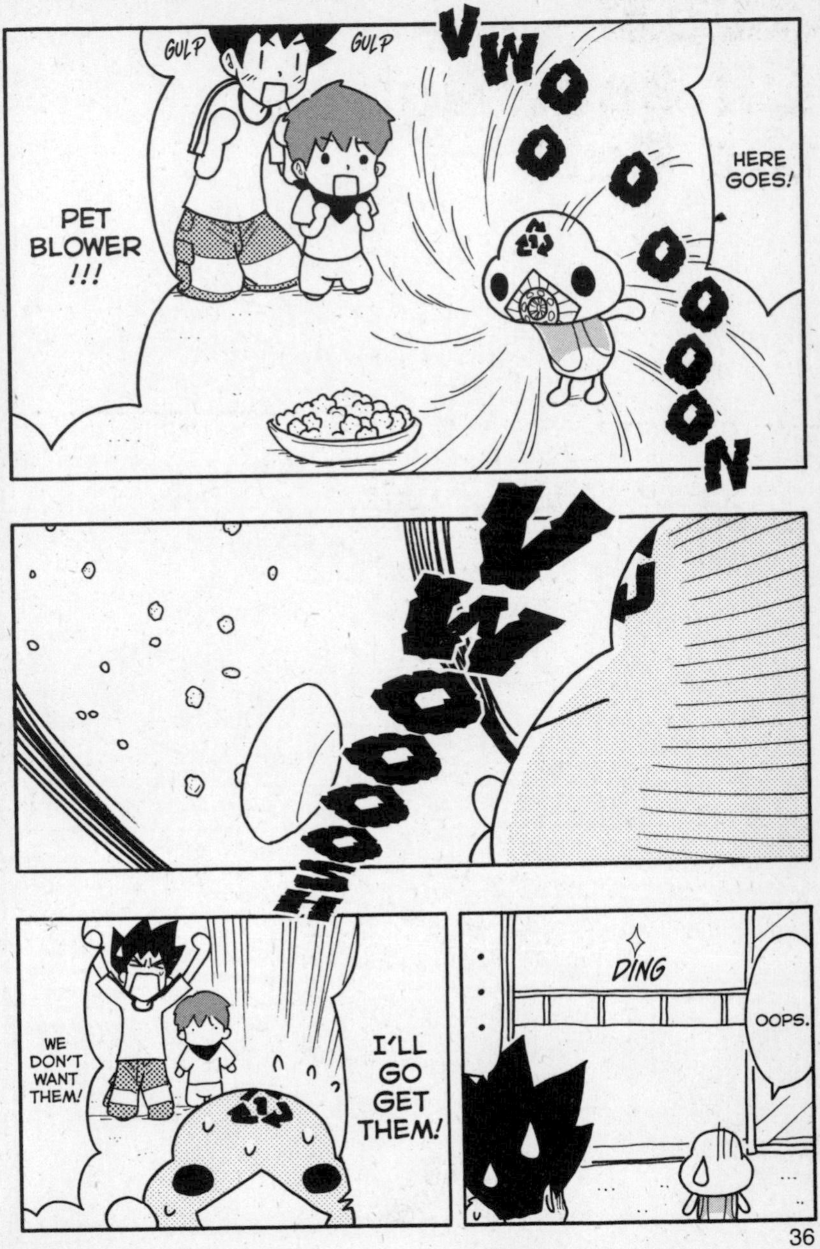
HERE GOES!
VWOOOOOOOON
GULP
GULP
PET BLOWER !!!
VWOOOOOOSH!
DING
OOPS.
I'LL GO GET THEM!
WE DON'T WANT THEM!

## CHAPTER 4

# L'il Bagz Raises the Bar!

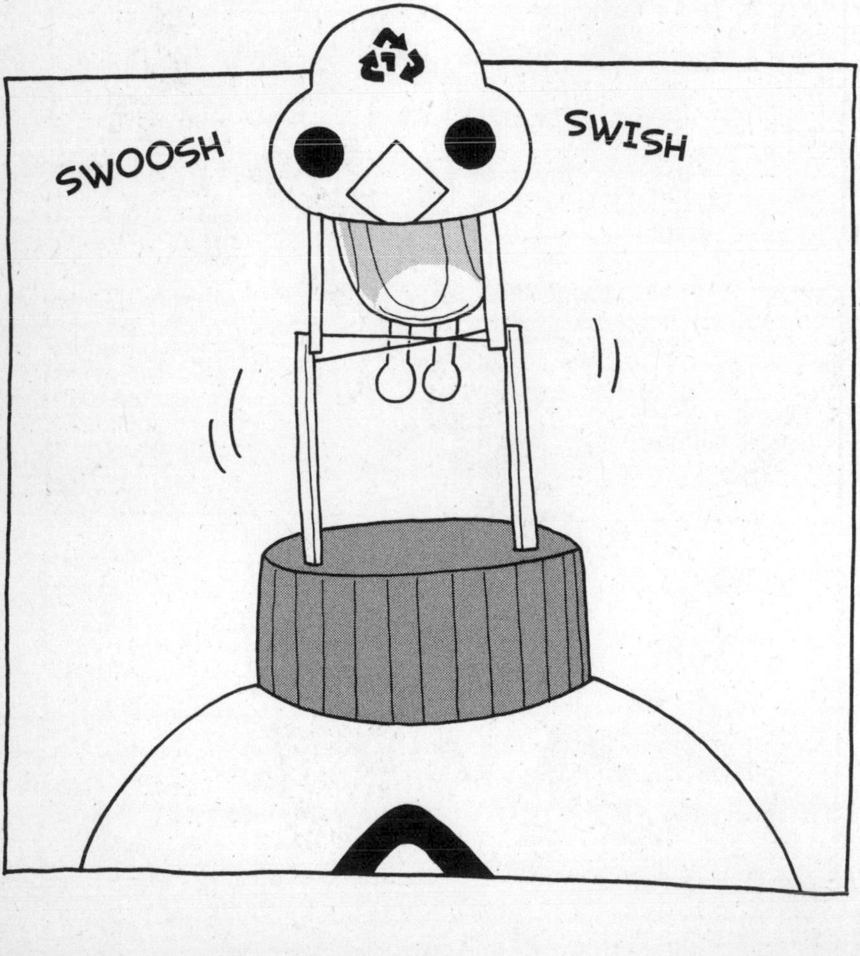
SWISH
SWOOSH

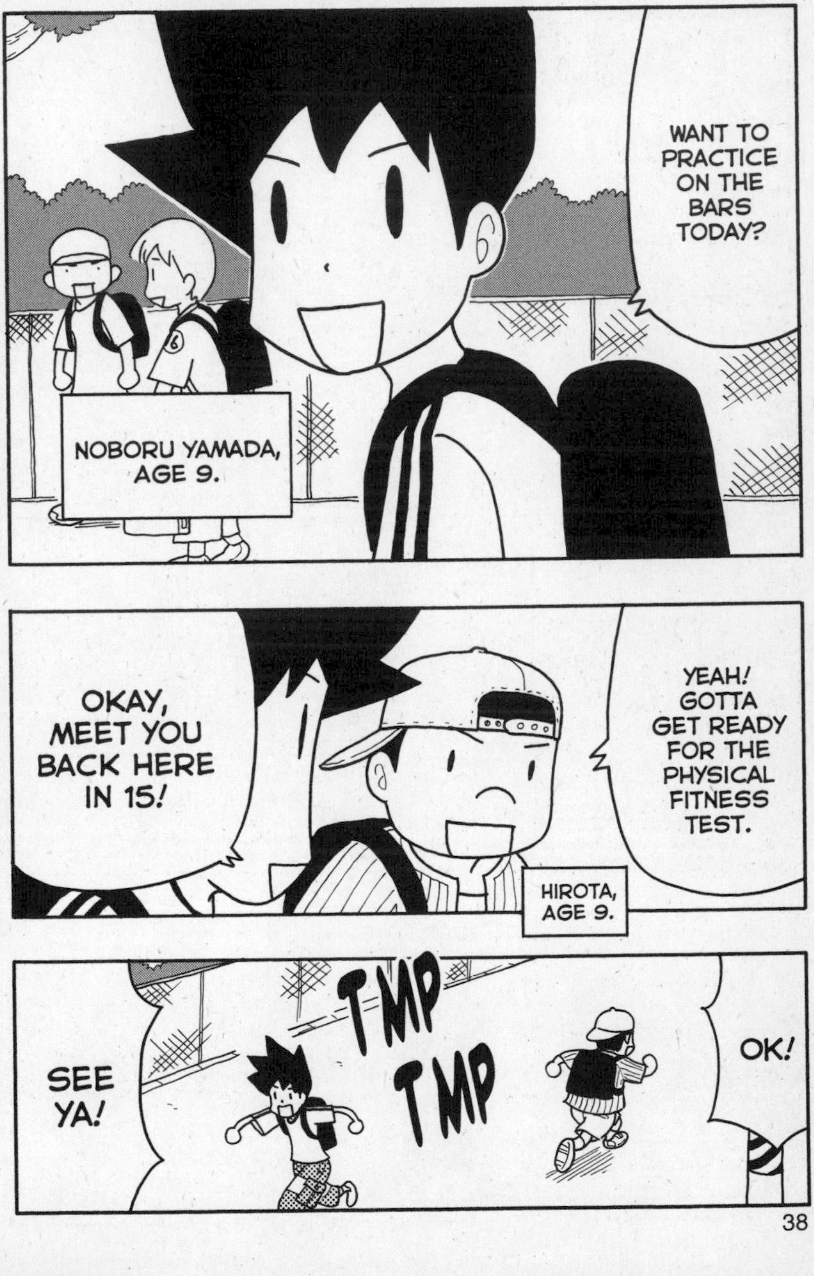
WANT TO PRACTICE ON THE BARS TODAY?
NOBORU YAMADA, AGE 9.
YEAH! GOTTA GET READY FOR THE PHYSICAL FITNESS TEST.
OKAY, MEET YOU BACK HERE IN 15!
HIROTA, AGE 9.
OK!
TMP TMP
SEE YA!

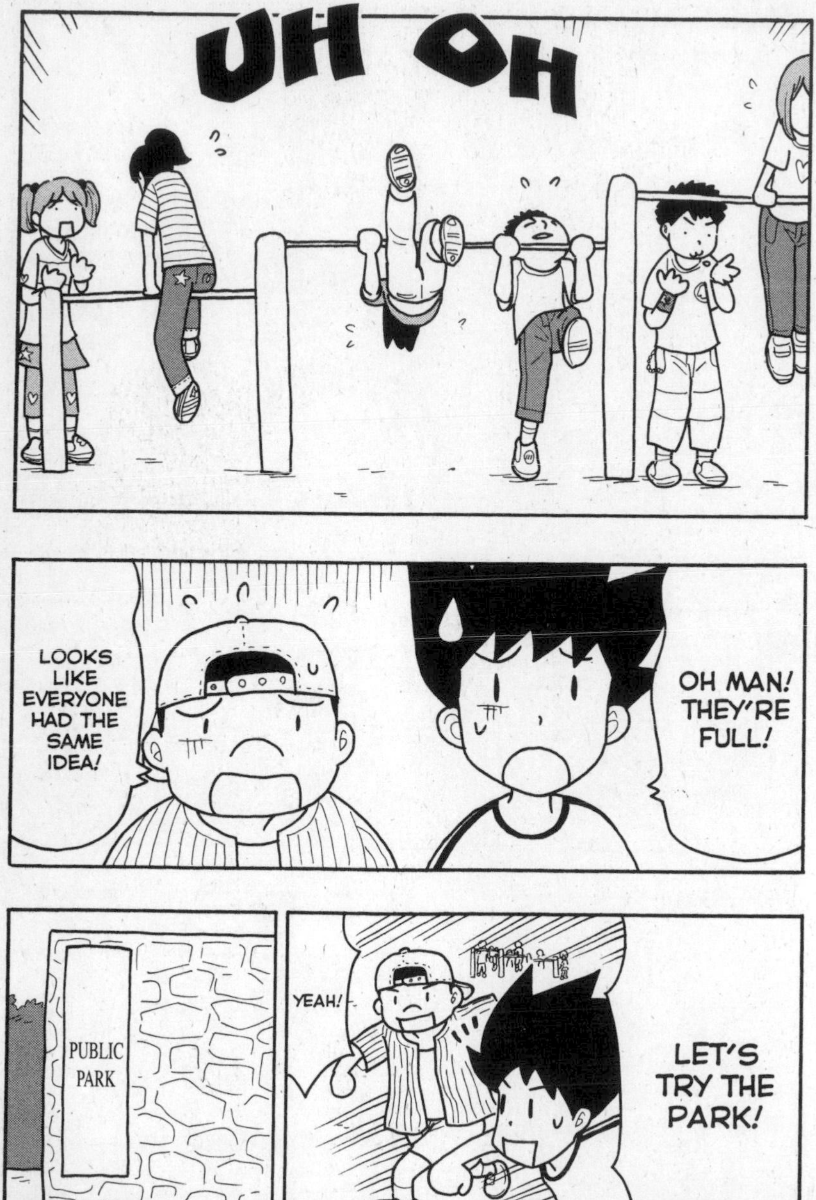
UH OH
OH MAN! THEY'RE FULL!
LOOKS LIKE EVERYONE HAD THE SAME IDEA!
LET'S TRY THE PARK!
YEAH!
PUBLIC PARK

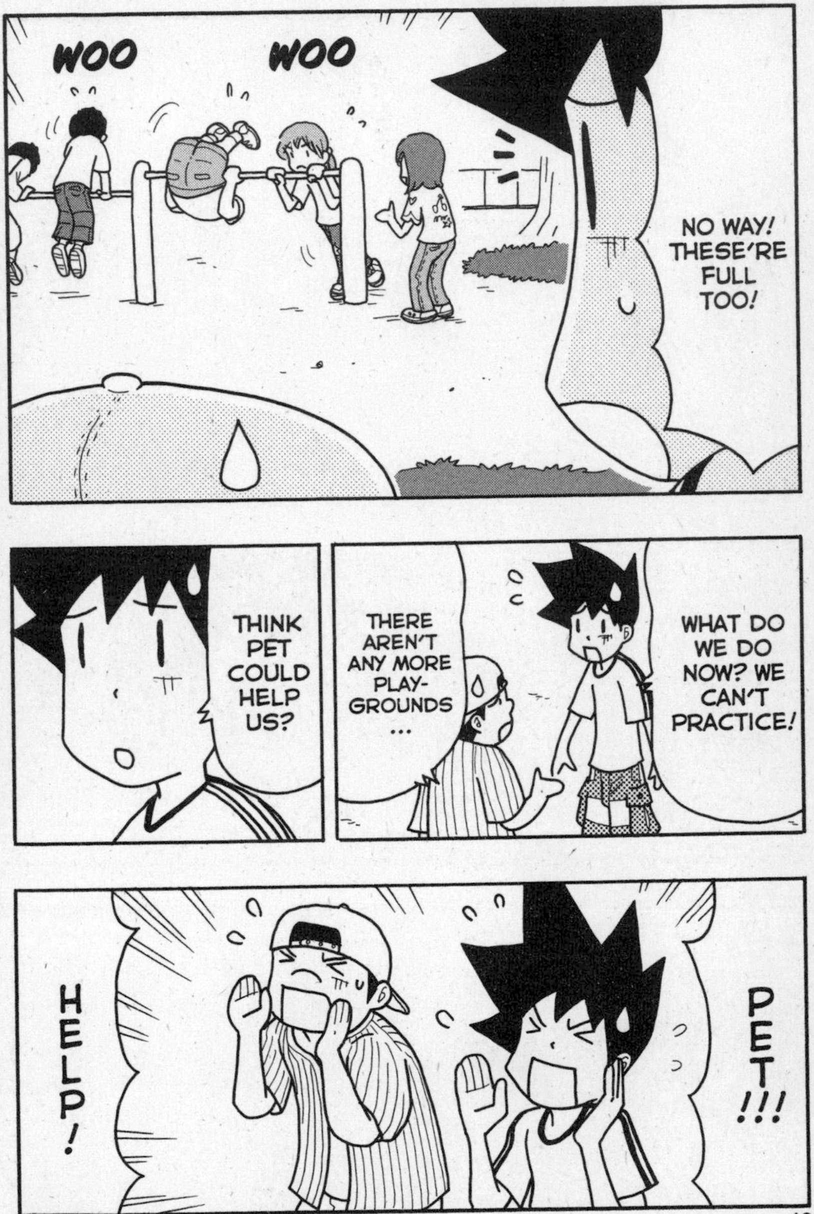
WOO
WOO
NO WAY! THESE'RE FULL TOO!
WHAT DO WE DO NOW? WE CAN'T PRACTICE!
THERE AREN'T ANY MORE PLAY-GROUNDS...
THINK PET COULD HELP US?
PET!!!
HELP!

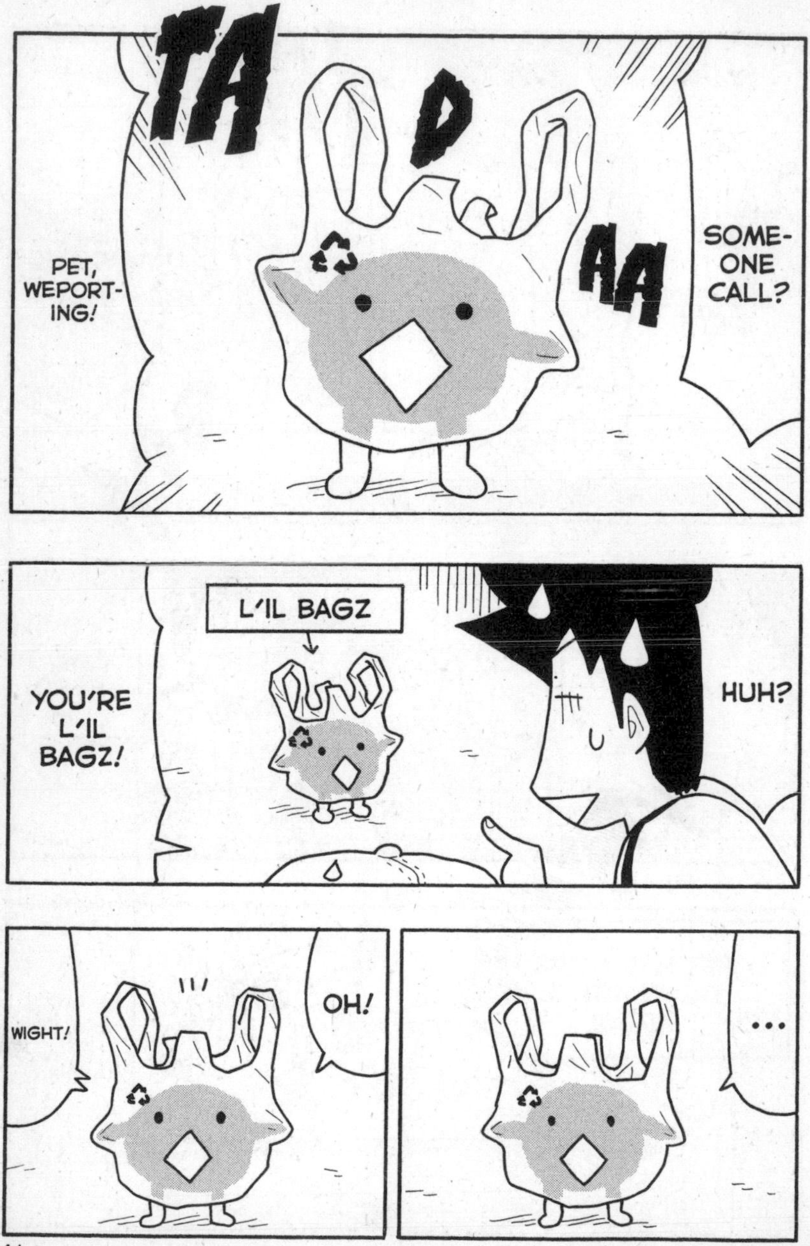
SOME-ONE CALL?
TA D AA
PET, WEPORT-ING!
HUH?
L'IL BAGZ
YOU'RE L'IL BAGZ!
...
OH!
WIGHT!

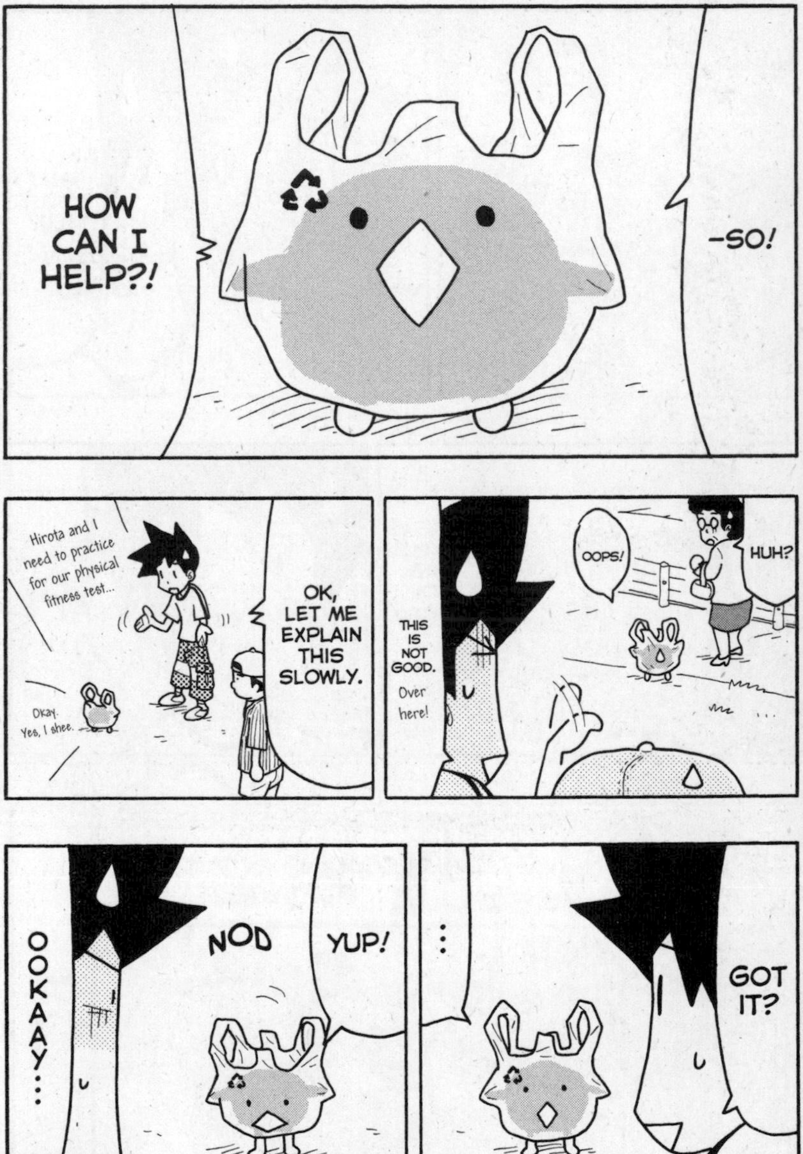
-SO!
HOW CAN I HELP?!
HUH?
OOPS!
THIS IS NOT GOOD.
Over here!
OK, LET ME EXPLAIN THIS SLOWLY.
Hirota and I need to practice for our physical fitness test...
Okay. Yes, I shee.
GOT IT?
...
YUP!
NOD
OOKAAY...

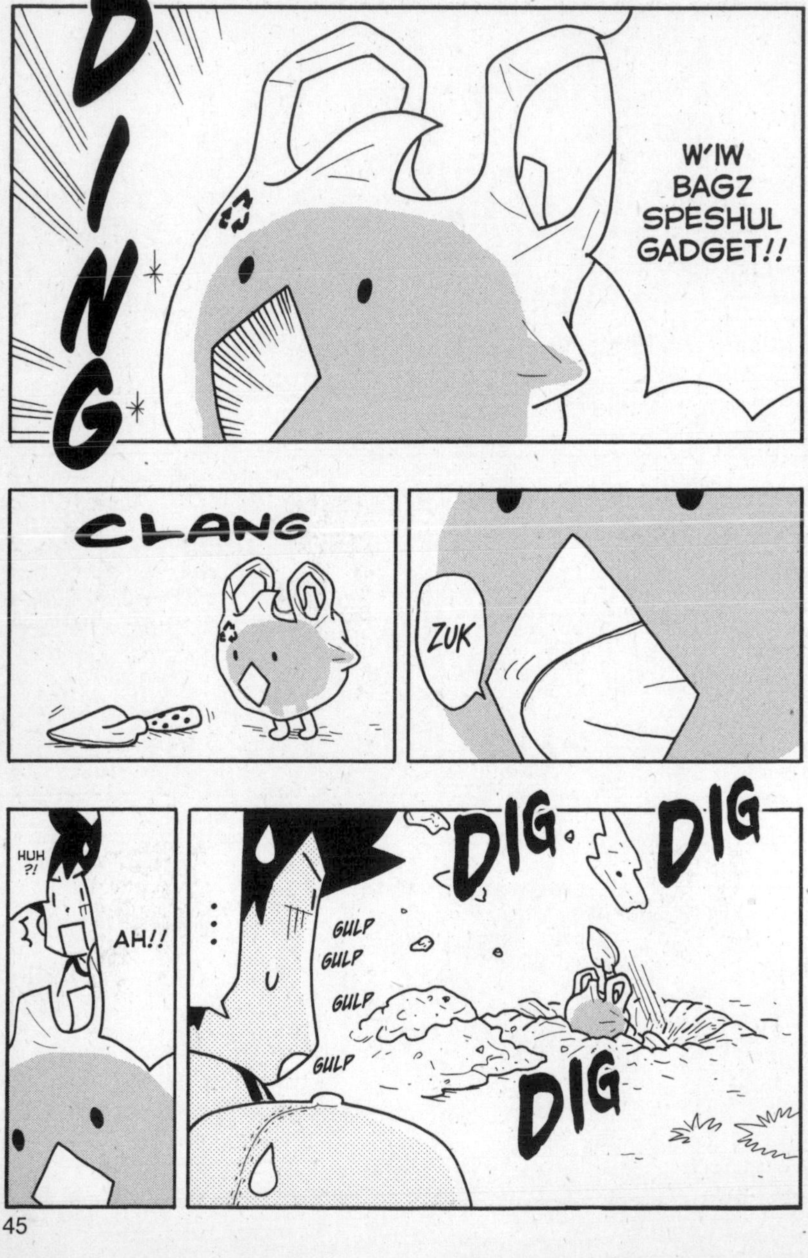

W'IW BAGZ SPESHUL GADGET!!
DING
ZUK
CLANG
DIG DIG
...
GULP
GULP
GULP
GULP
DIG
HUH ?!
AH!!

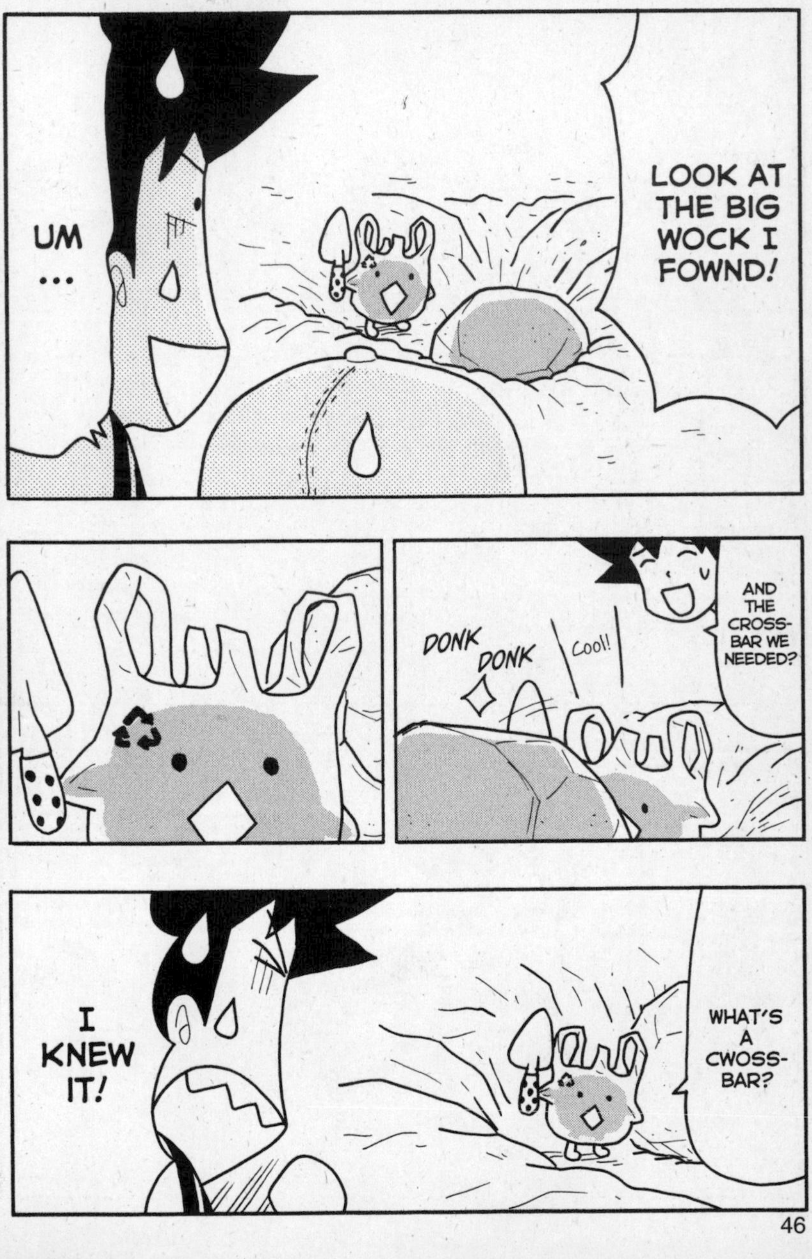
LOOK AT THE BIG WOCK I FOWND!
UM ...
AND THE CROSS-BAR WE NEEDED?
Cool!
DONK DONK
WHAT'S A CWOSS-BAR?
I KNEW IT!

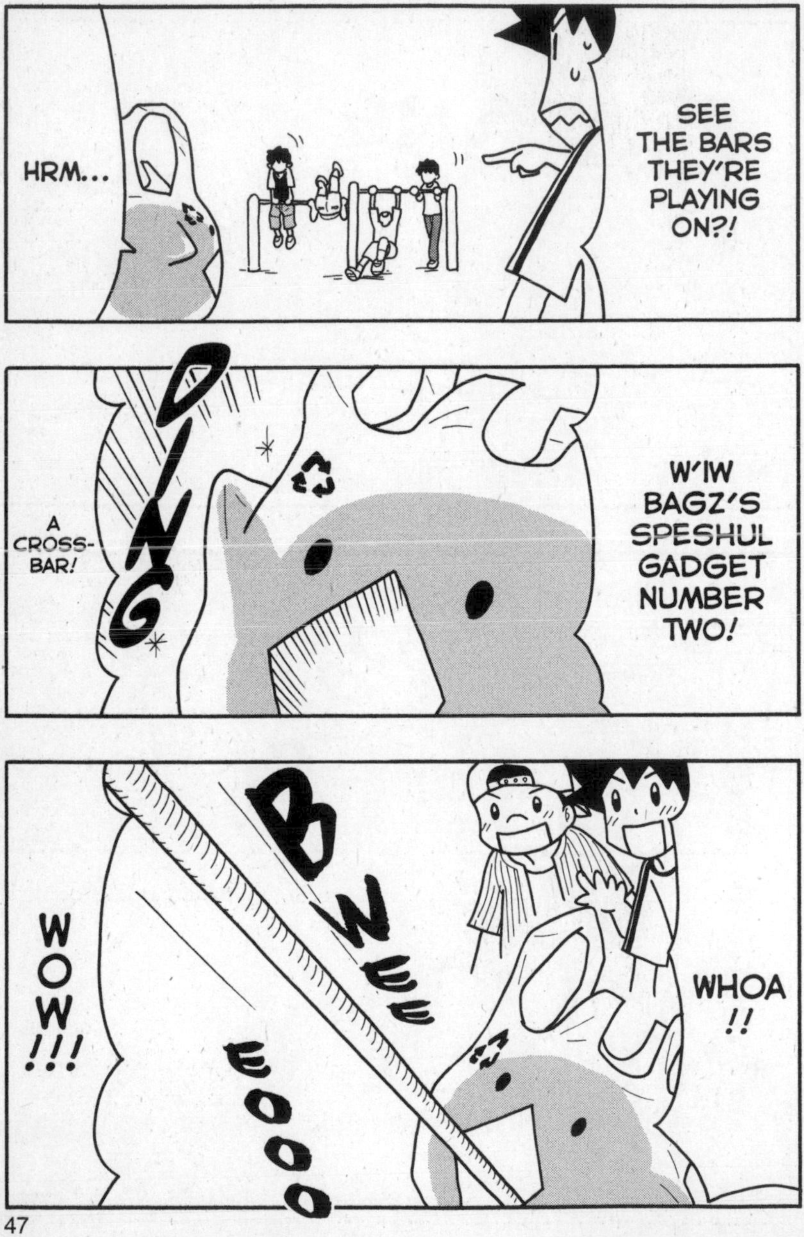
SEE THE BARS THEY'RE PLAYING ON?!
HRM...
W'IW BAGZ'S SPESHUL GADGET NUMBER TWO!
DING
A CROSS-BAR!
WHOA!!
BWEEEEOOO
WOW!!!

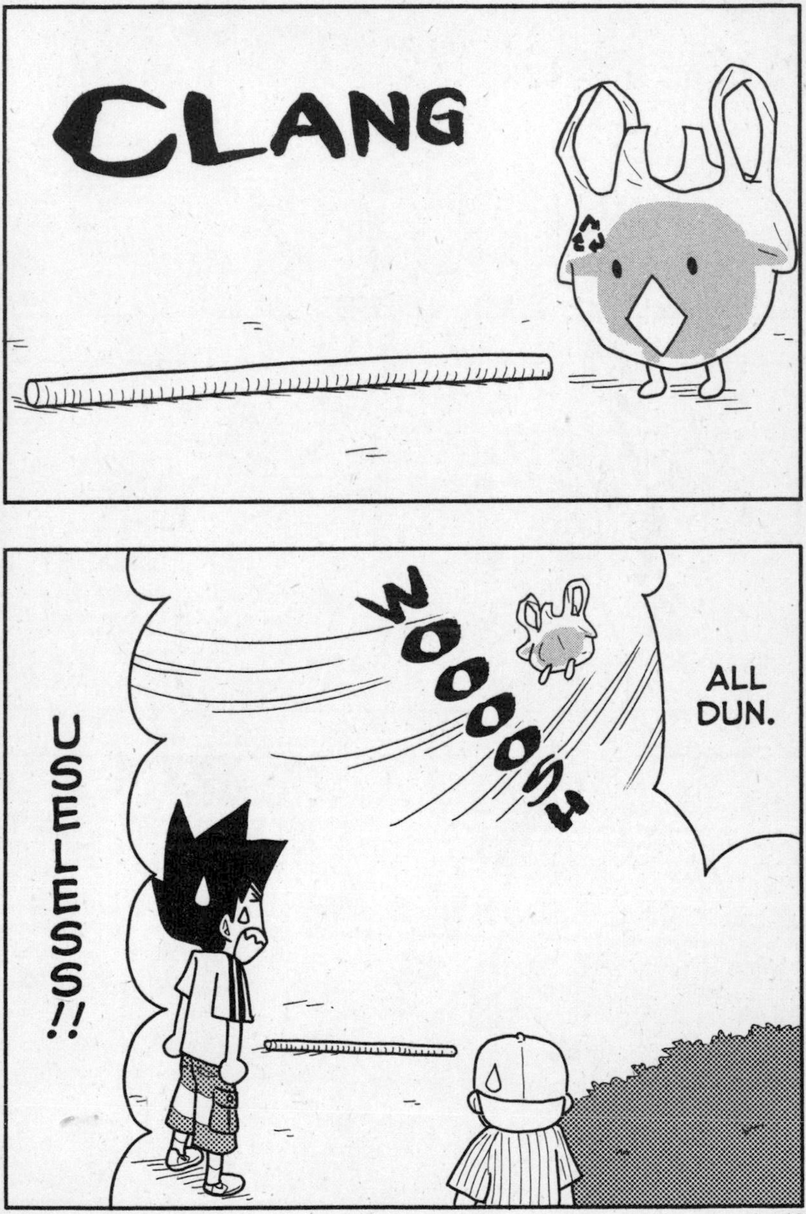
CLANG
ALL DUN.
WOOOOSH
USELESS!!

CHAPTER 5

# Anti-viral PET

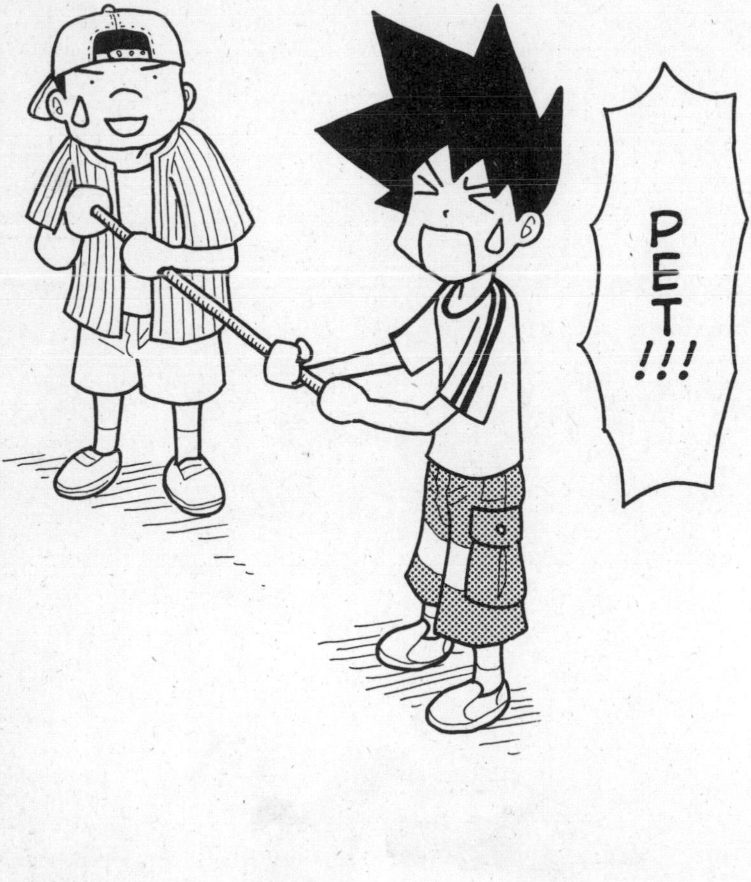
PET!!!

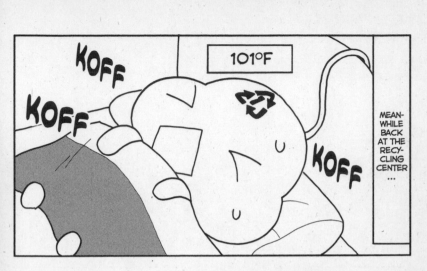

101°F

KOFF
KOFF
KOFF

MEAN-WHILE BACK AT THE RECY-CLING CENTER ...

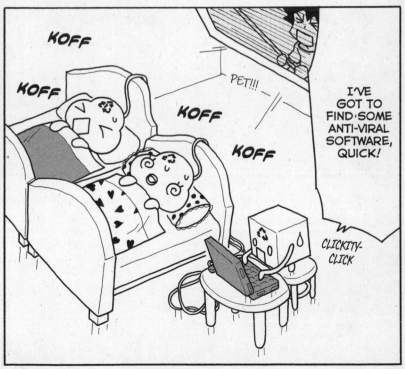

KOFF
KOFF
KOFF
KOFF

PET!!!

I'VE GOT TO FIND SOME ANTI-VIRAL SOFTWARE, QUICK!

CLICKITY-CLICK

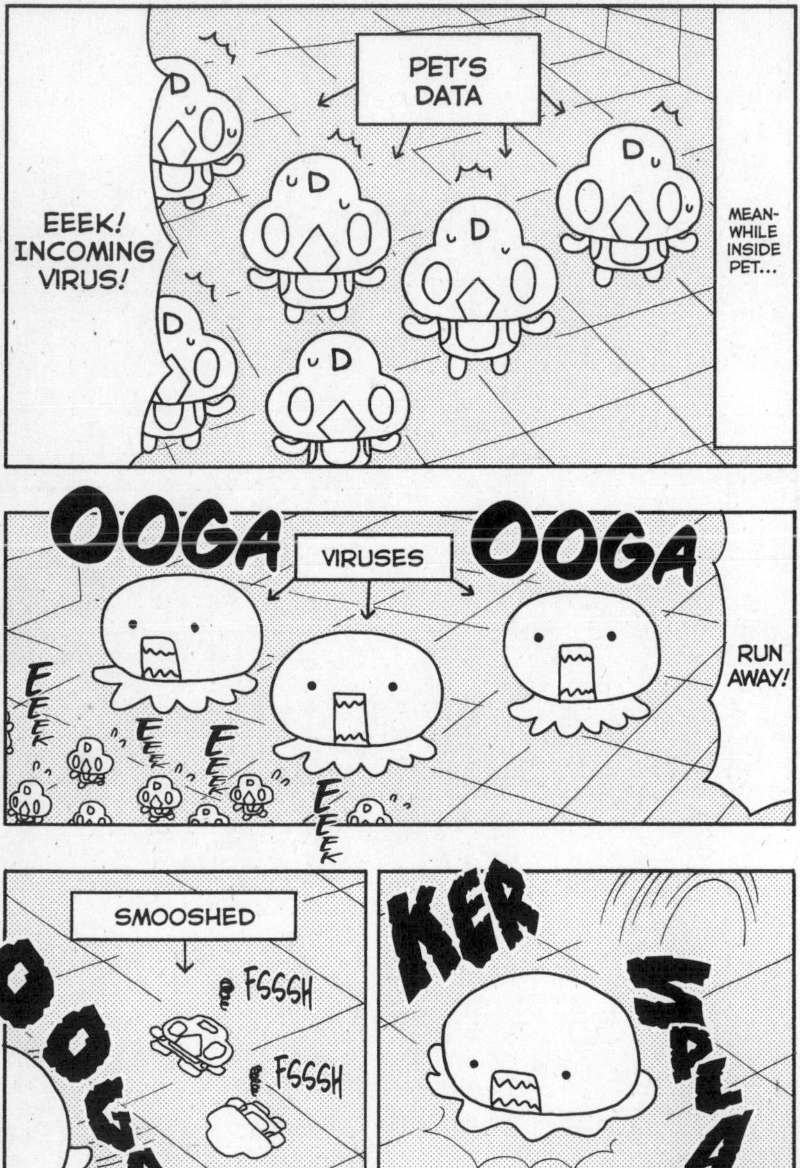
MEAN-WHILE INSIDE PET...
PET'S DATA
EEEK! INCOMING VIRUS!
RUN AWAY!
OOGA
VIRUSES
OOGA
EEEEK
EEEEK
EEEEK
EEEEK
EEEEK
KER SPLAT
SMOOSHED
FSSSH
FSSSH
OOGA

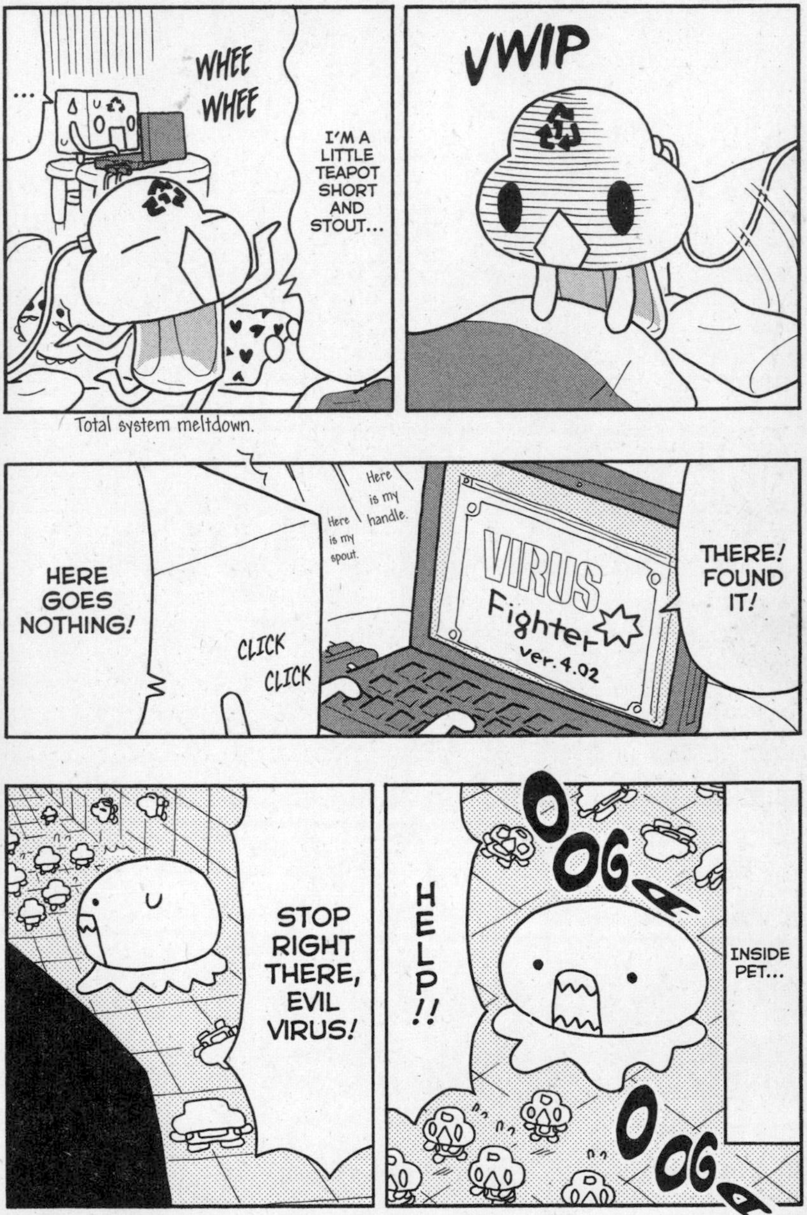
VWIP
...
I'M A LITTLE TEAPOT SHORT AND STOUT...
WHEE WHEE
Total system meltdown.
THERE! FOUND IT!
Here is my handle.
Here is my spout.
VIRUS Fighter ver. 4.02
CLICK CLICK
HERE GOES NOTHING!
INSIDE PET...
OOGA
OOGA
HELP!!
STOP RIGHT THERE, EVIL VIRUS!

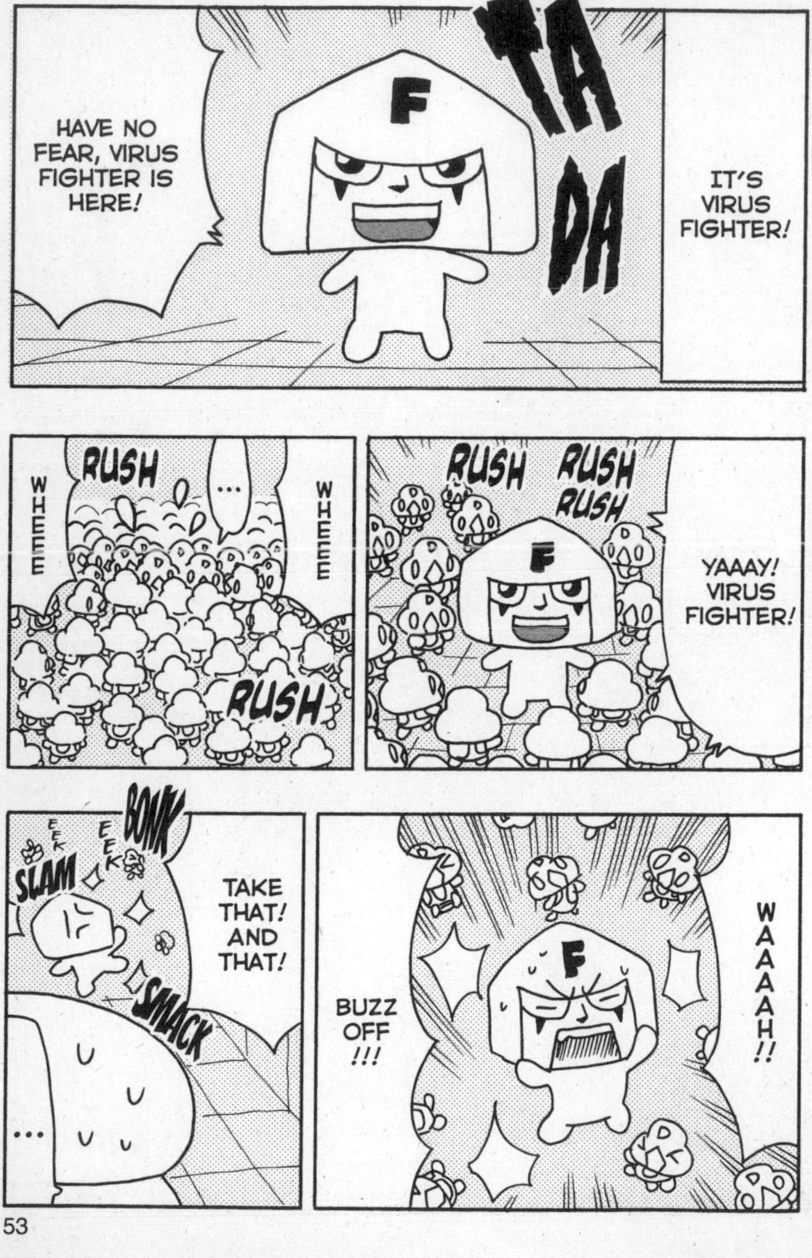
IT'S VIRUS FIGHTER!
TA DA
HAVE NO FEAR, VIRUS FIGHTER IS HERE!
RUSH RUSH RUSH
YAAAY! VIRUS FIGHTER!
WHEEE
...
RUSH
WHEEE
RUSH
WAAAAH!!
BUZZ OFF!!!
TAKE THAT! AND THAT!
BONK
EEK
EEK
SLAM
SMACK
...

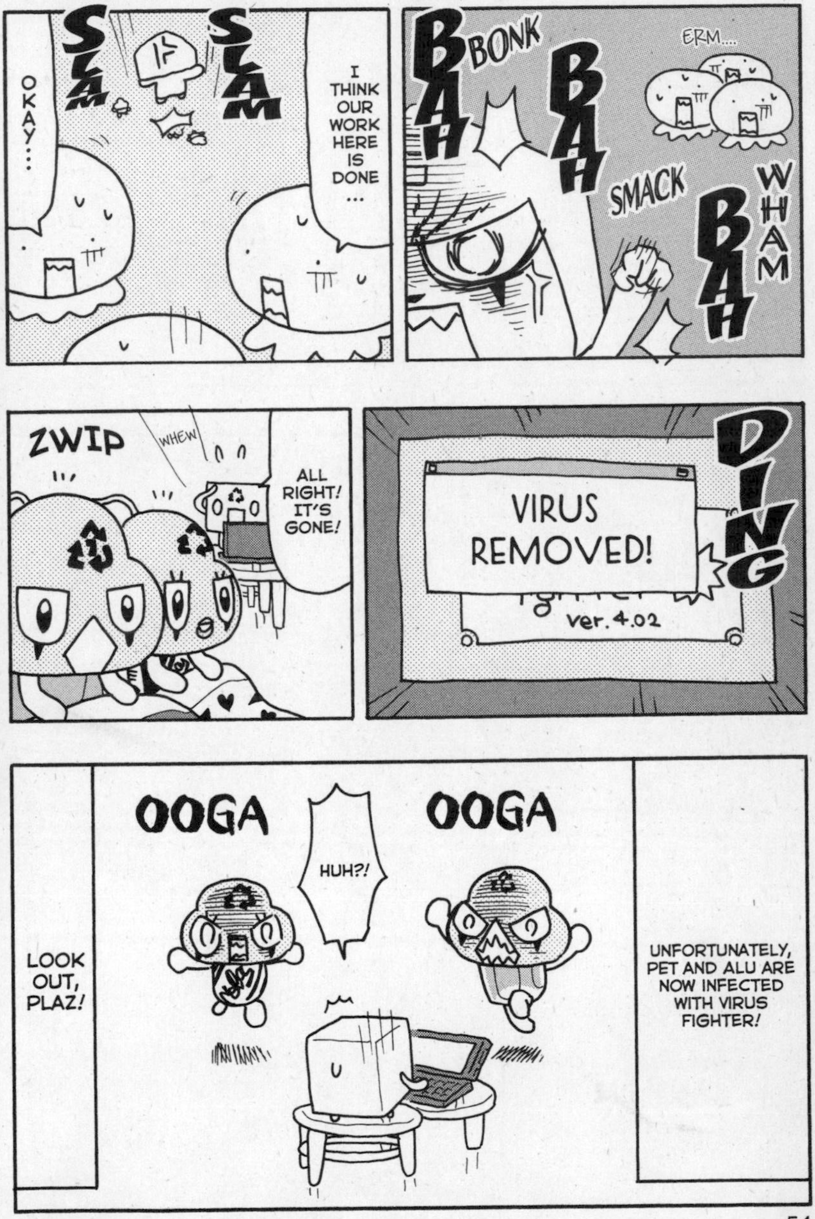
BAH
BONK
BAH
ERM...
SMACK
WHAM
BAH
SLAM
SLAM
I THINK OUR WORK HERE IS DONE ...
OKAY...
VIRUS REMOVED!
Ver. 4.02
DING
ZWIP
WHEW
ALL RIGHT! IT'S GONE!
UNFORTUNATELY, PET AND ALU ARE NOW INFECTED WITH VIRUS FIGHTER!
OOGA
OOGA
HUH?!
LOOK OUT, PLAZ!

CHAPTER 6

# Vitabot, Reporting!

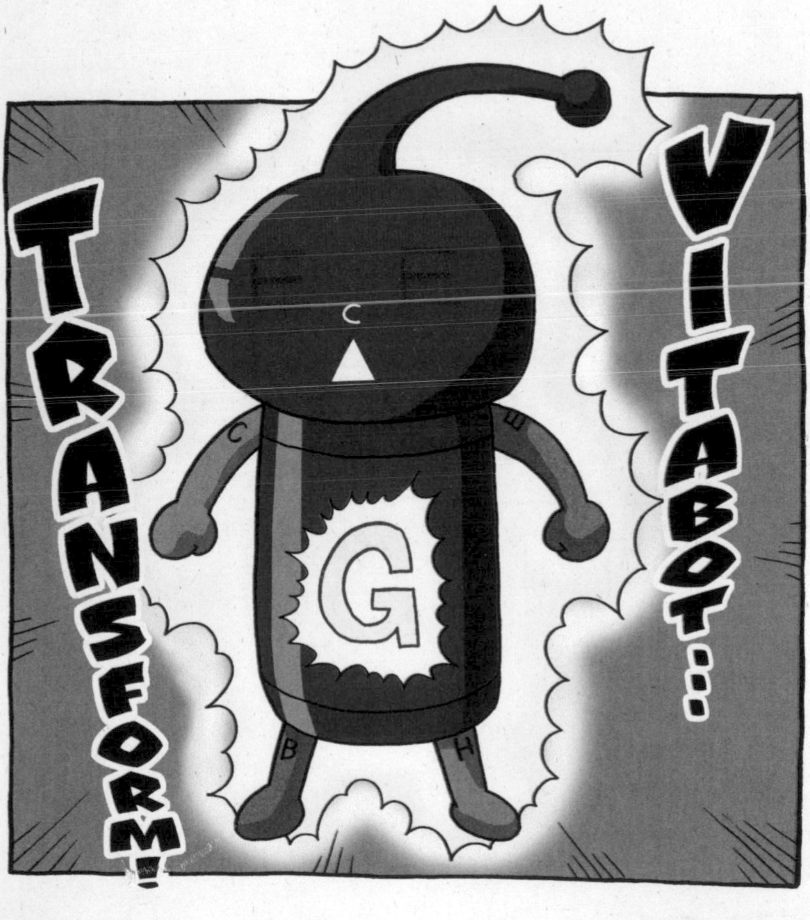
VITABOT...
TRANSFORM!

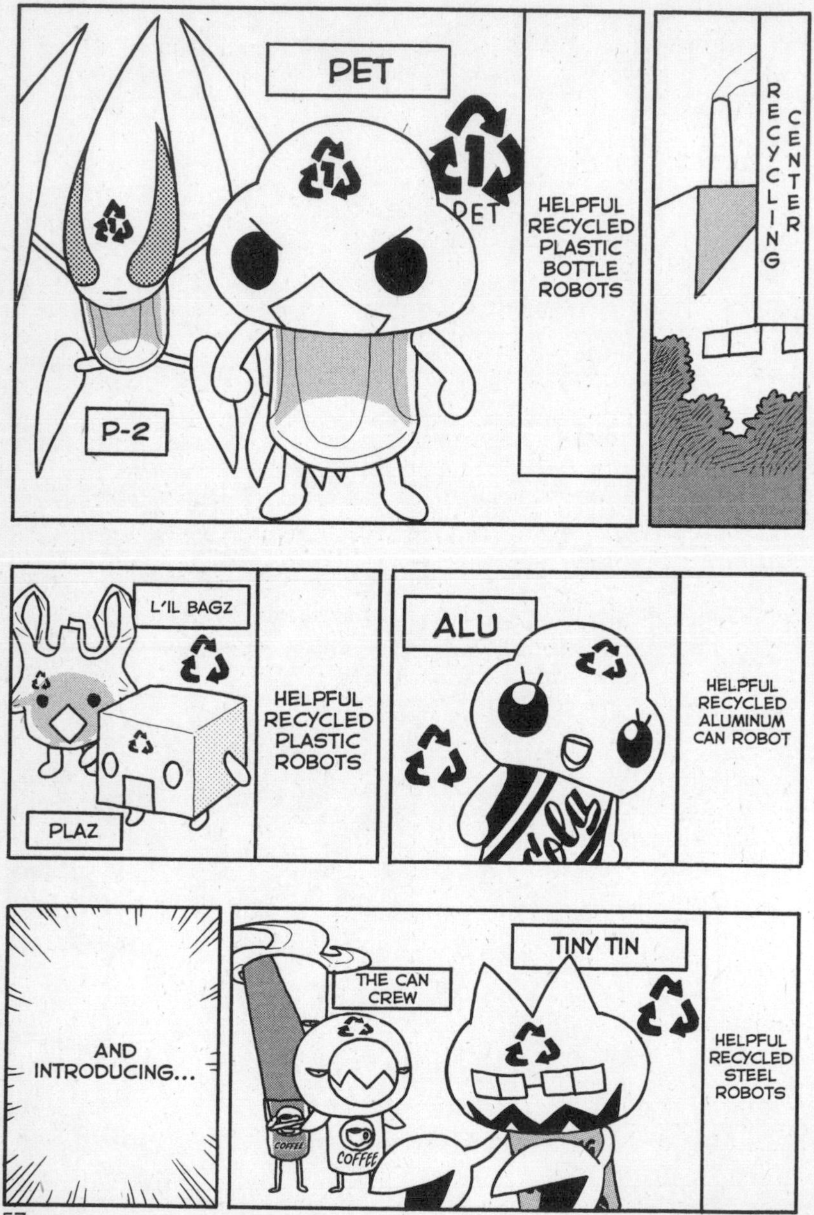
RECYCLING CENTER
HELPFUL RECYCLED PLASTIC BOTTLE ROBOTS
PET
PET
P-2
HELPFUL RECYCLED ALUMINUM CAN ROBOT
ALU
HELPFUL RECYCLED PLASTIC ROBOTS
L'IL BAGZ
PLAZ
HELPFUL RECYCLED STEEL ROBOTS
TINY TIN
THE CAN CREW
COFFEE
COFFEE
AND INTRODUCING...

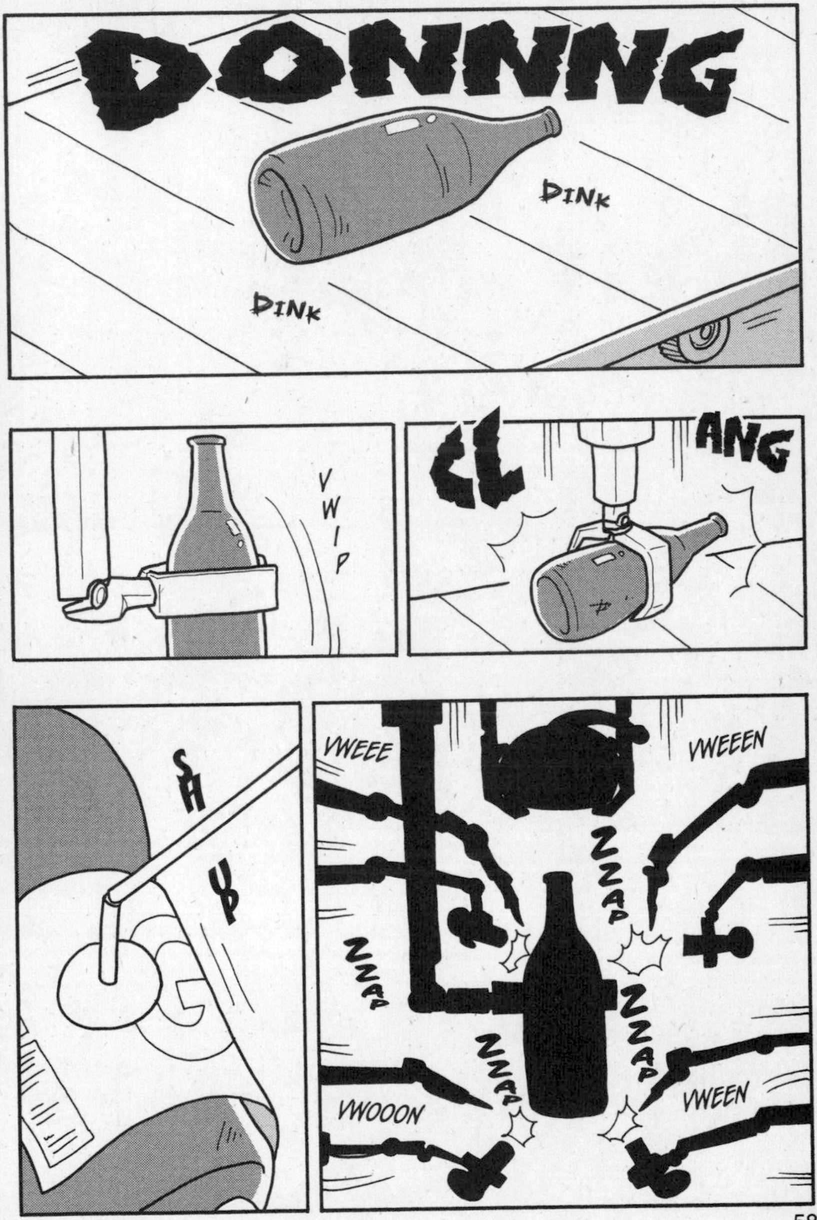
DONNNG
DINK
DINK
CLANG
VWIP
VWEEEN
ZZAP
VWEEE
ZZAP
ZZAP
ZZAP
VWEEN
VWOOON
SHUP

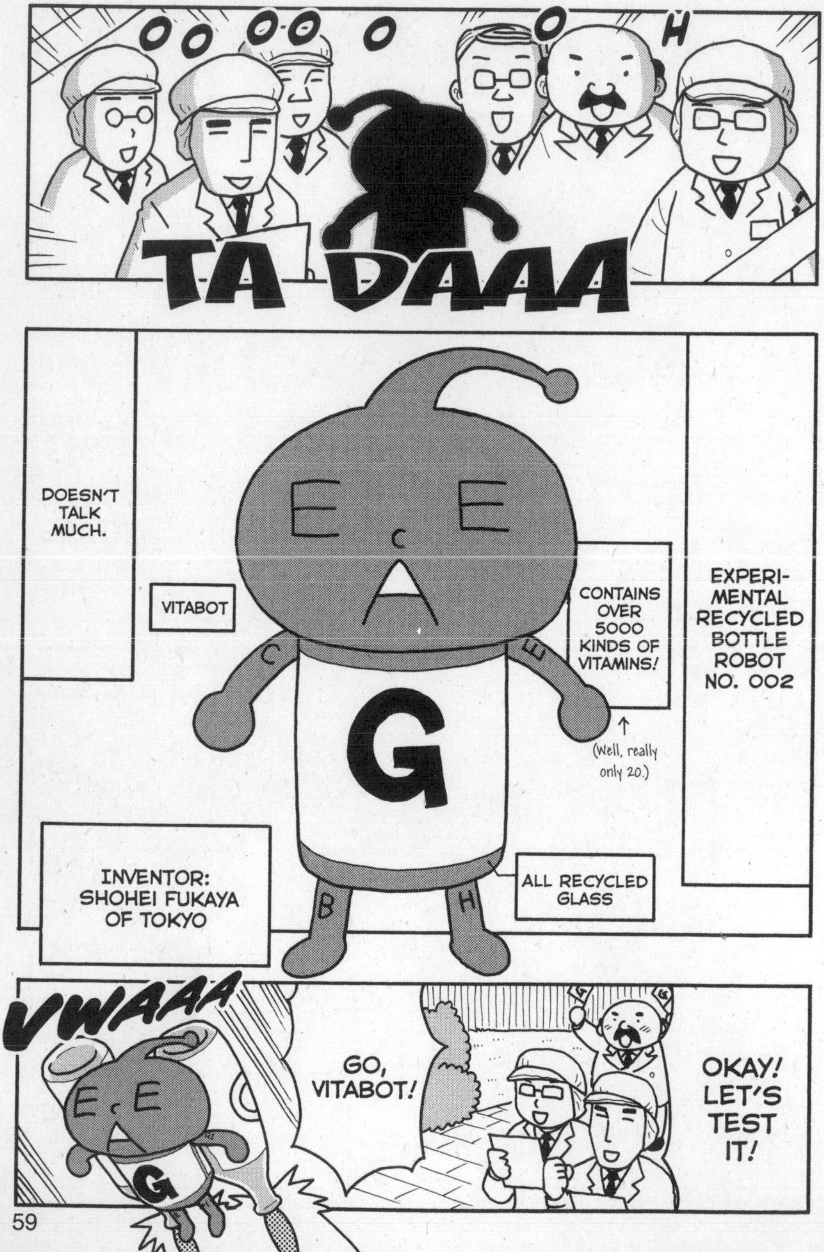
OOOOOOOH
TA DAAA
EXPERIMENTAL RECYCLED BOTTLE ROBOT NO. 002
CONTAINS OVER 5000 KINDS OF VITAMINS!
(Well, really only 20.)
DOESN'T TALK MUCH.
VITABOT
ALL RECYCLED GLASS
INVENTOR: SHOHEI FUKAYA OF TOKYO
OKAY! LET'S TEST IT!
GO, VITABOT!
VWAAA

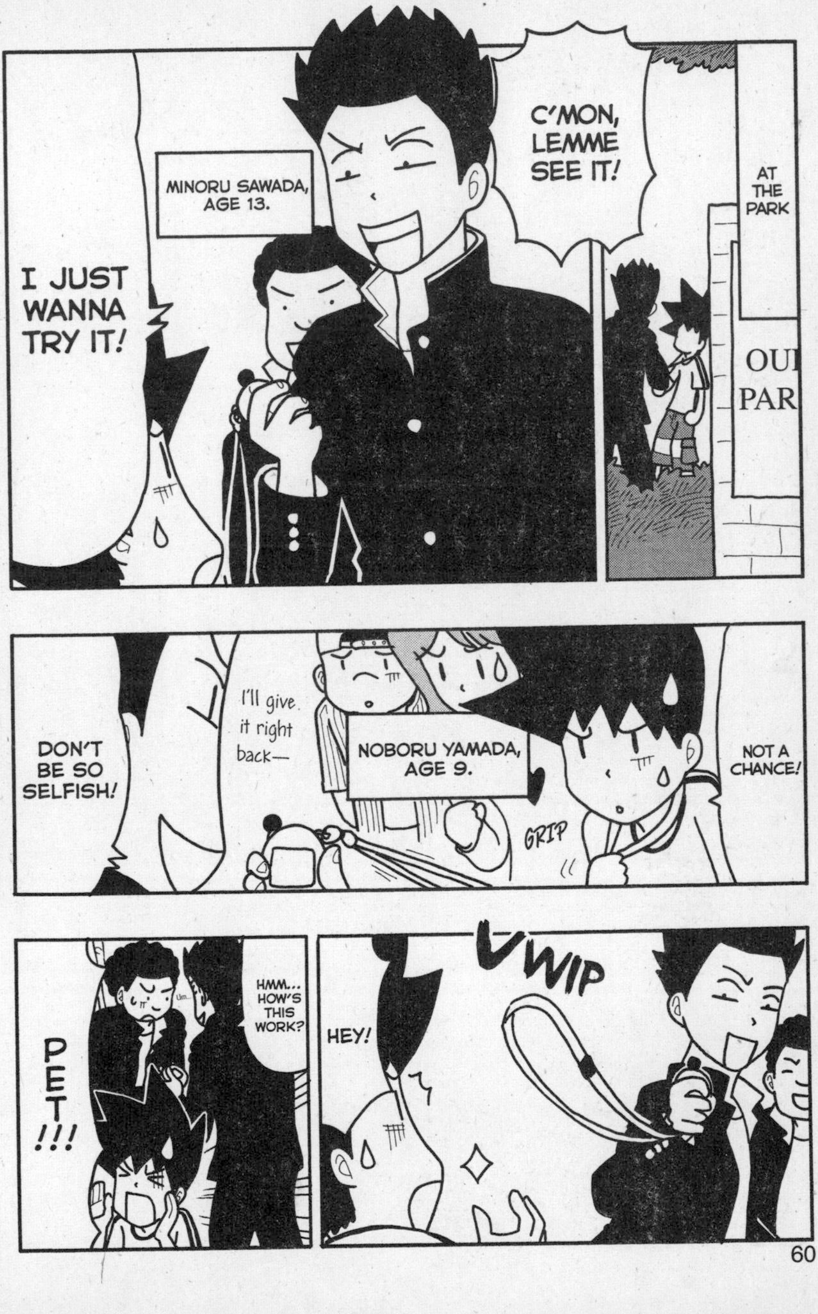
AT THE PARK
C'MON, LEMME SEE IT!
MINORU SAWADA, AGE 13.
I JUST WANNA TRY IT!
NOT A CHANCE!
NOBORU YAMADA, AGE 9.
GRIP
I'll give it right back—
DON'T BE SO SELFISH!
WIP
HEY!
HMM... HOW'S THIS WORK?
Um...
PET!!!

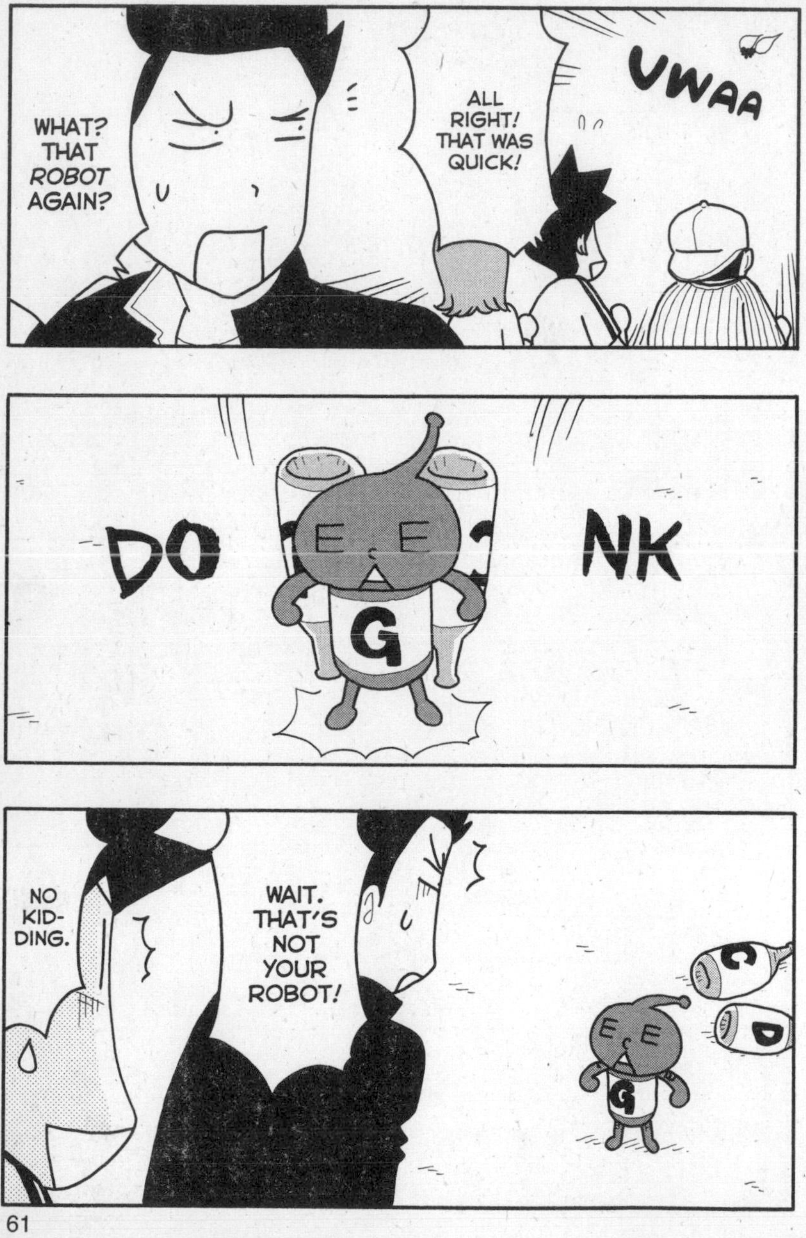
UWAA
ALL RIGHT! THAT WAS QUICK!
WHAT? THAT *ROBOT* AGAIN?
DO
NK
WAIT. THAT'S NOT YOUR ROBOT!
NO KID-DING.

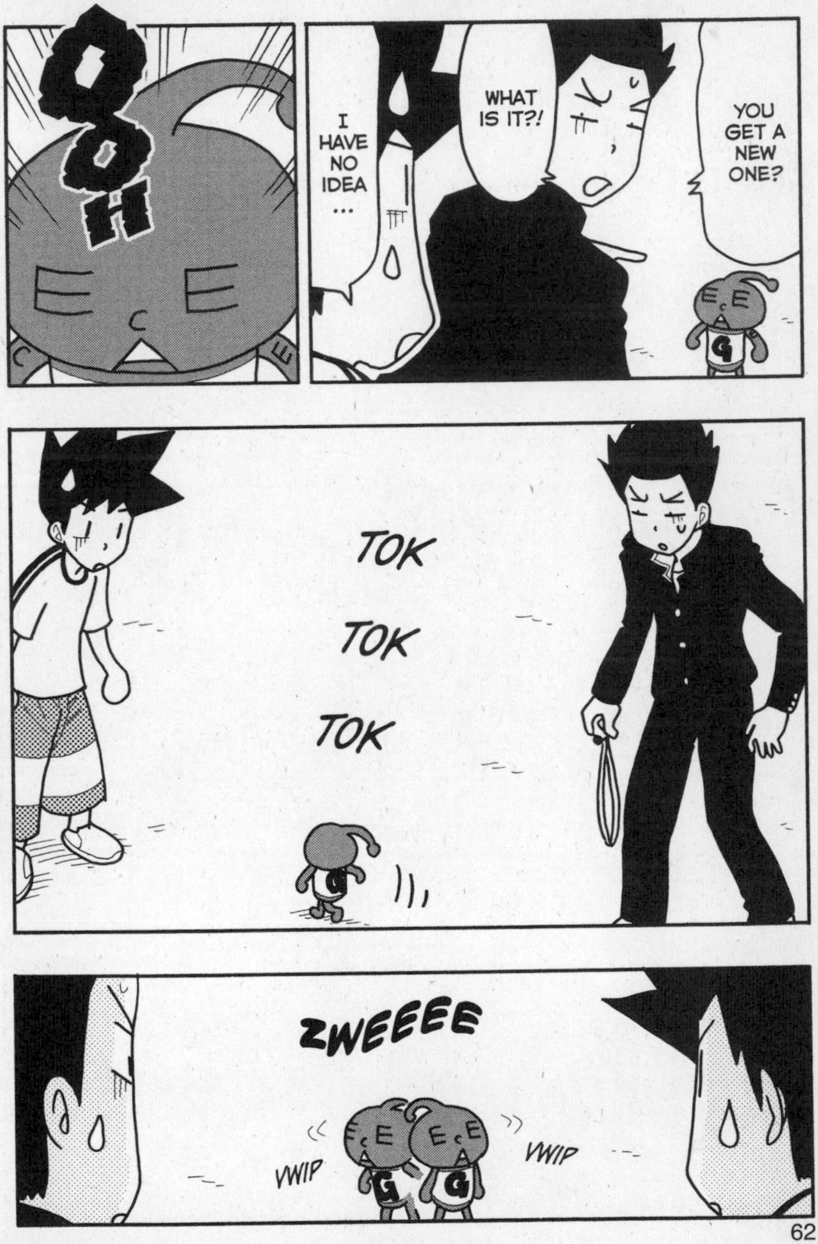
YOU GET A NEW ONE?
WHAT IS IT?!
I HAVE NO IDEA ...
OH
TOK
TOK
TOK
ZWEEEE
VWIP
VWIP

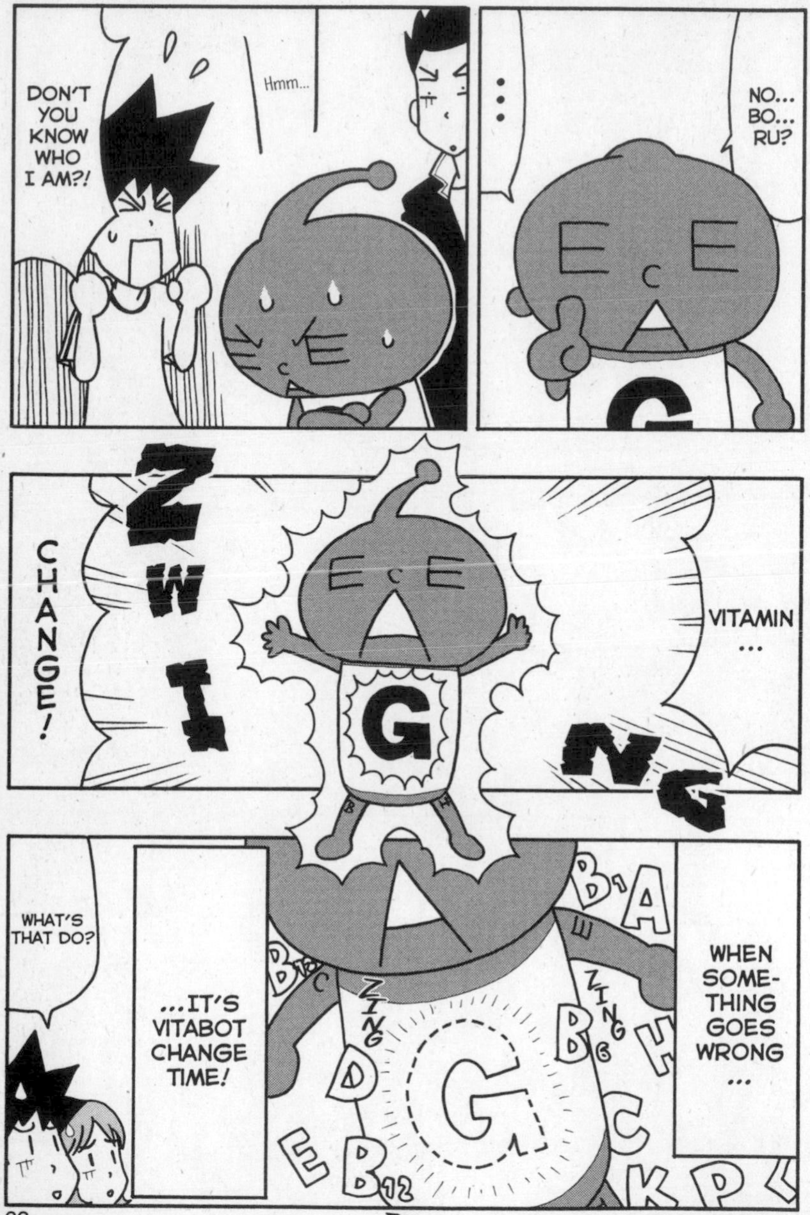

NO... BO... RU?
...
Hmm...
DON'T YOU KNOW WHO I AM?!
VITAMIN ...
ZWING
CHANGE!
WHEN SOMETHING GOES WRONG ...
...IT'S VITABOT CHANGE TIME!
WHAT'S THAT DO?
ZING
ZING
ZING

VITAMIN...
TA
DAAA
P!!!
UM, IS THERE A VITAMIN P?
THERE IS!
ZWING
VITABOT SENDS A VITA-SIGNAL TO THE RECYCLING CENTER!
WHOA!!!

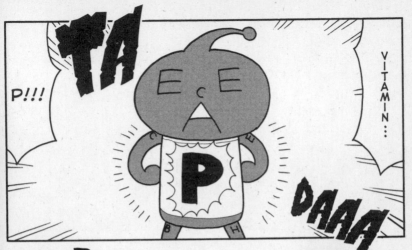

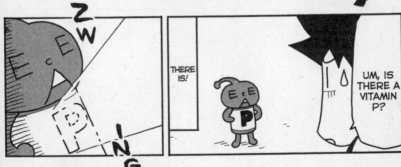

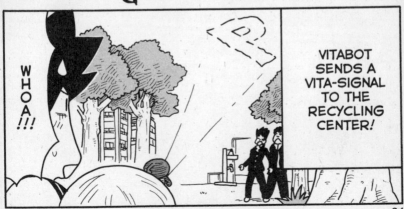

ZWIK

UM... WHAT DOES "P" MEAN?

OH GREAT.

P

"PLEASE SEND HELP"

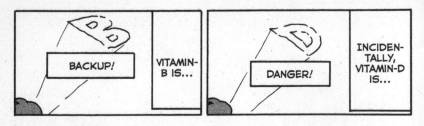

BACKUP!

VITAMIN-B IS...

DANGER!

INCIDENTALLY, VITAMIN-D IS...

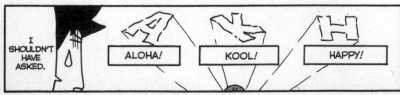

I SHOULDN'T HAVE ASKED.

ALOHA!

KOOL!

HAPPY!

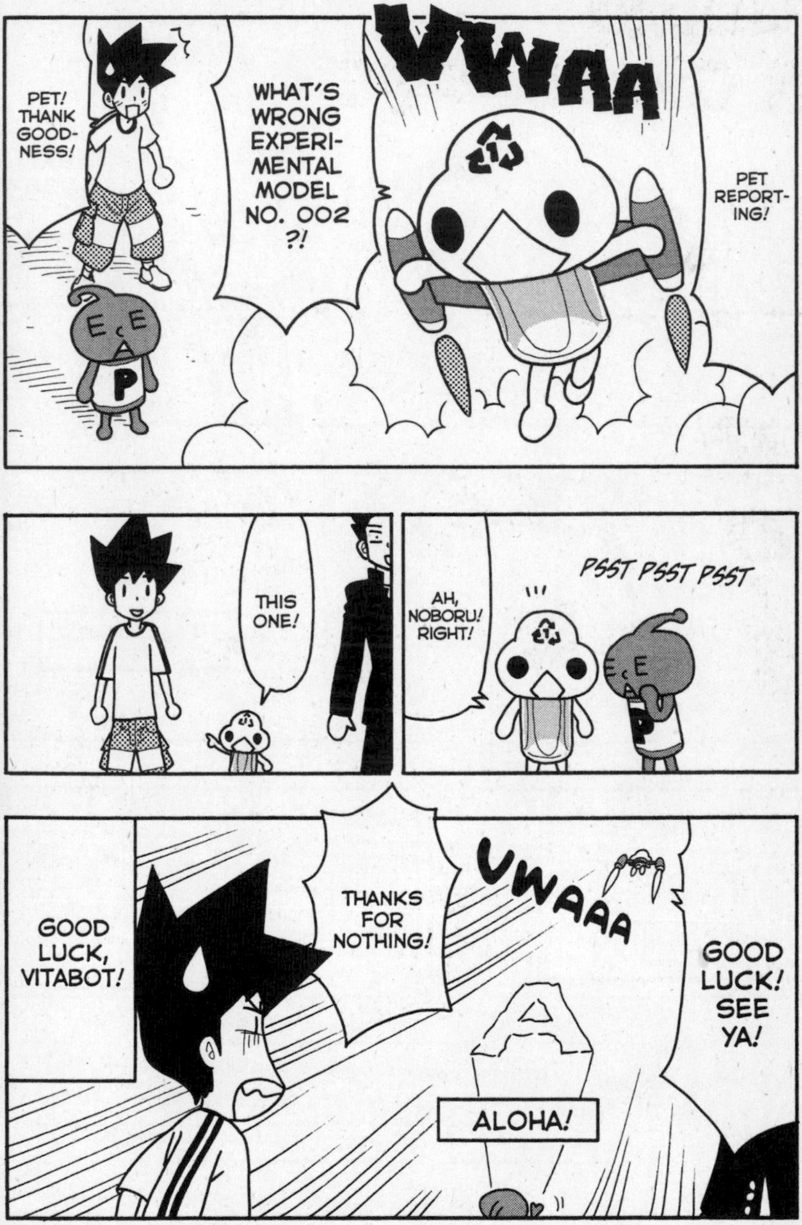
VWAA
PET REPORTING!
WHAT'S WRONG EXPERIMENTAL MODEL NO. 002 ?!
PET! THANK GOODNESS!
PSST PSST PSST
AH, NOBORU! RIGHT!
THIS ONE!
GOOD LUCK! SEE YA!
UWAAA
THANKS FOR NOTHING!
ALOHA!
GOOD LUCK, VITABOT!

CHAPTER 7

# A Gift for PET

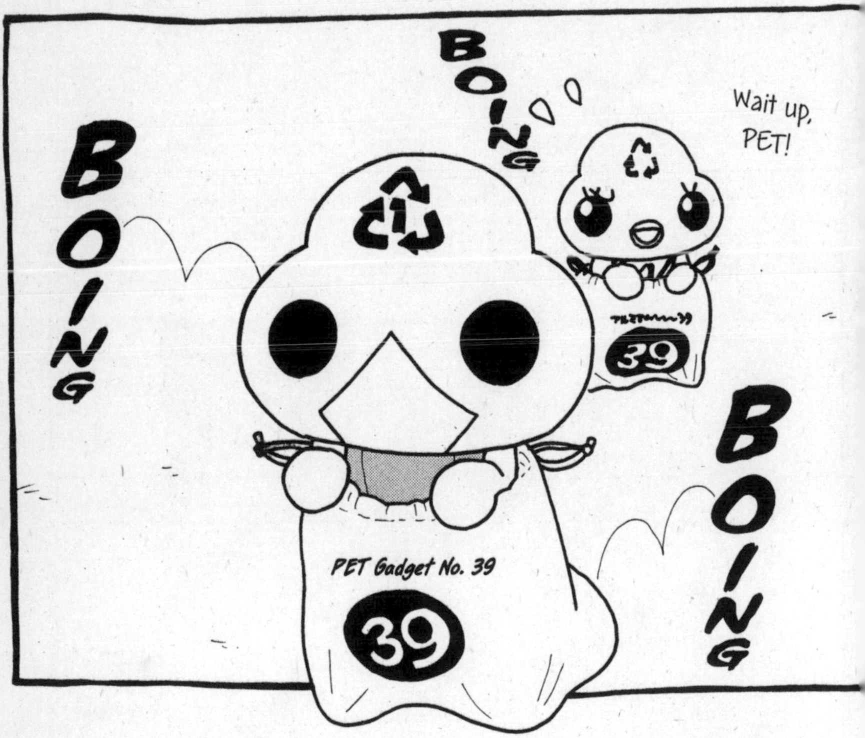
Wait up, PET!
BOING
BOING
BOING
PET Gadget No. 39
39
39

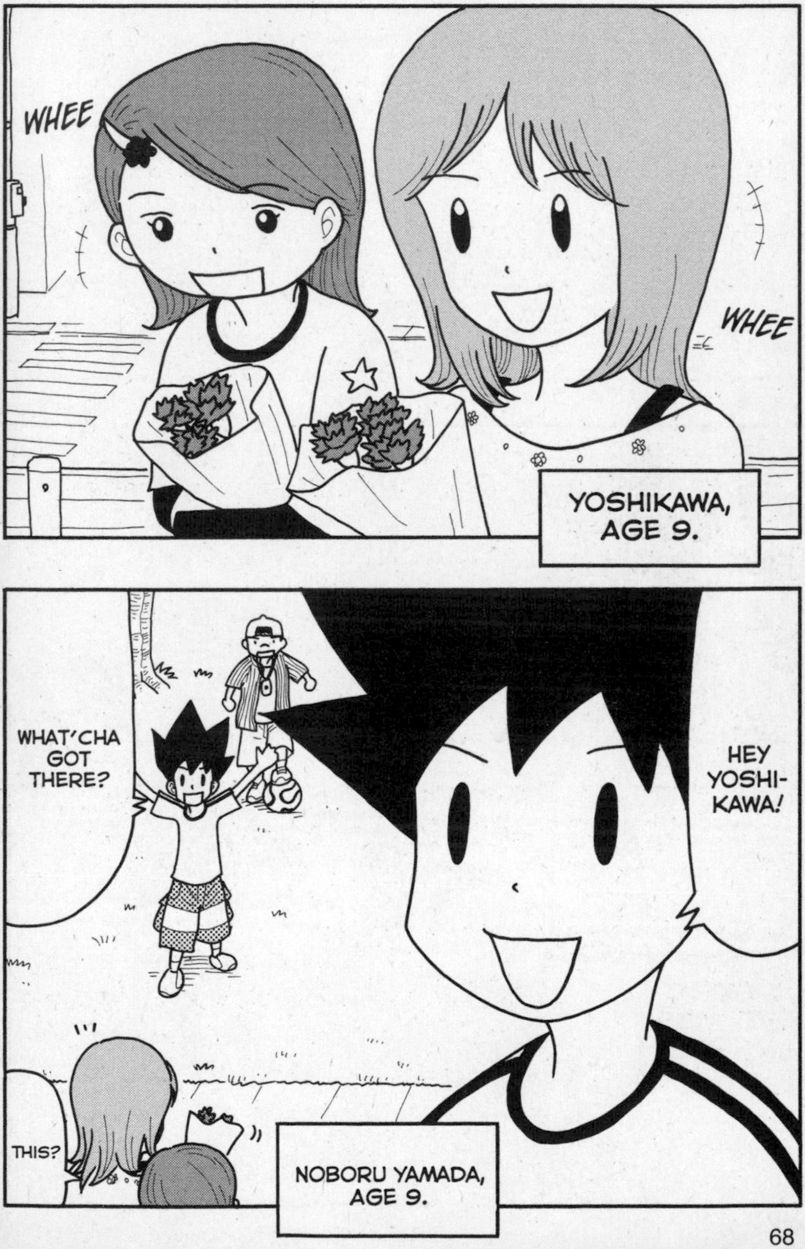
WHEE
WHEE
YOSHIKAWA, AGE 9.
HEY YOSHI-KAWA!
WHAT'CHA GOT THERE?
THIS?
NOBORU YAMADA, AGE 9.

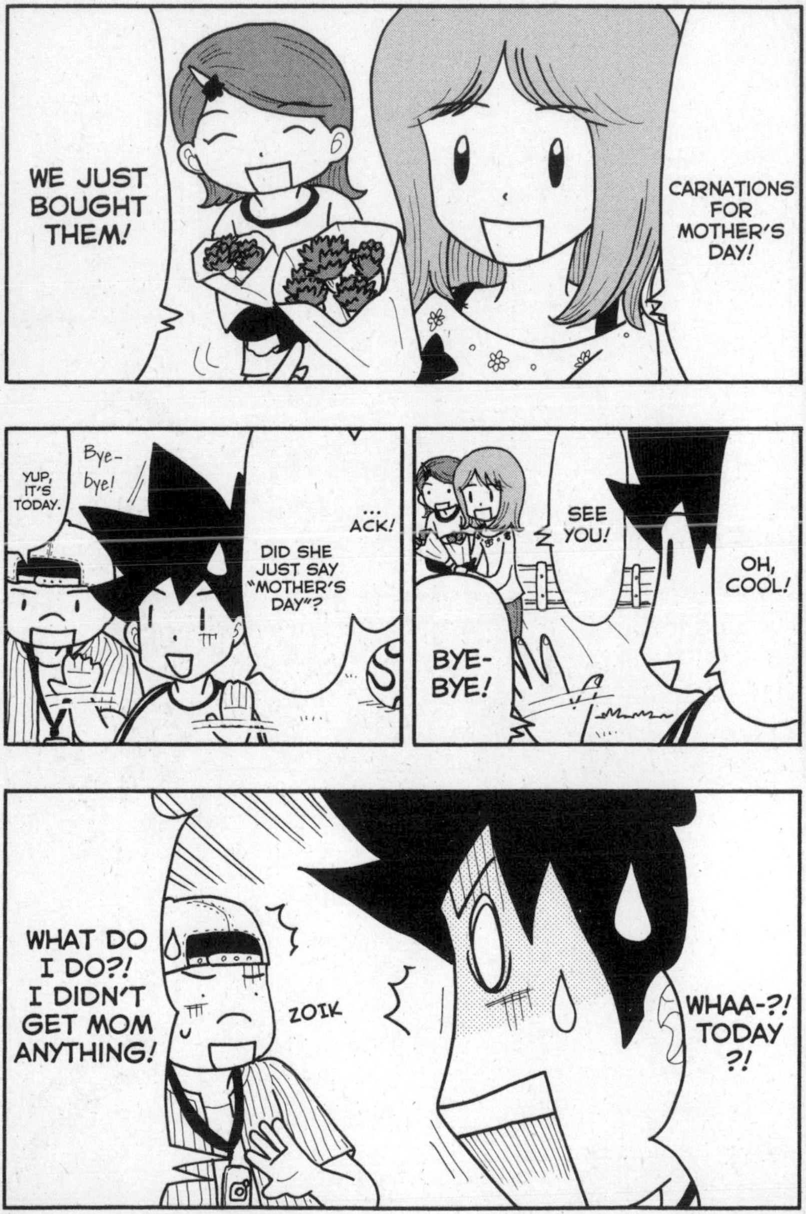
CARNATIONS FOR MOTHER'S DAY!
WE JUST BOUGHT THEM!
OH, COOL!
SEE YOU!
BYE-BYE!
... ACK!
DID SHE JUST SAY "MOTHER'S DAY"?
Bye-bye!
YUP, IT'S TODAY.
WHAA-?! TODAY ?!
ZOIK
WHAT DO I DO?! I DIDN'T GET MOM ANYTHING!

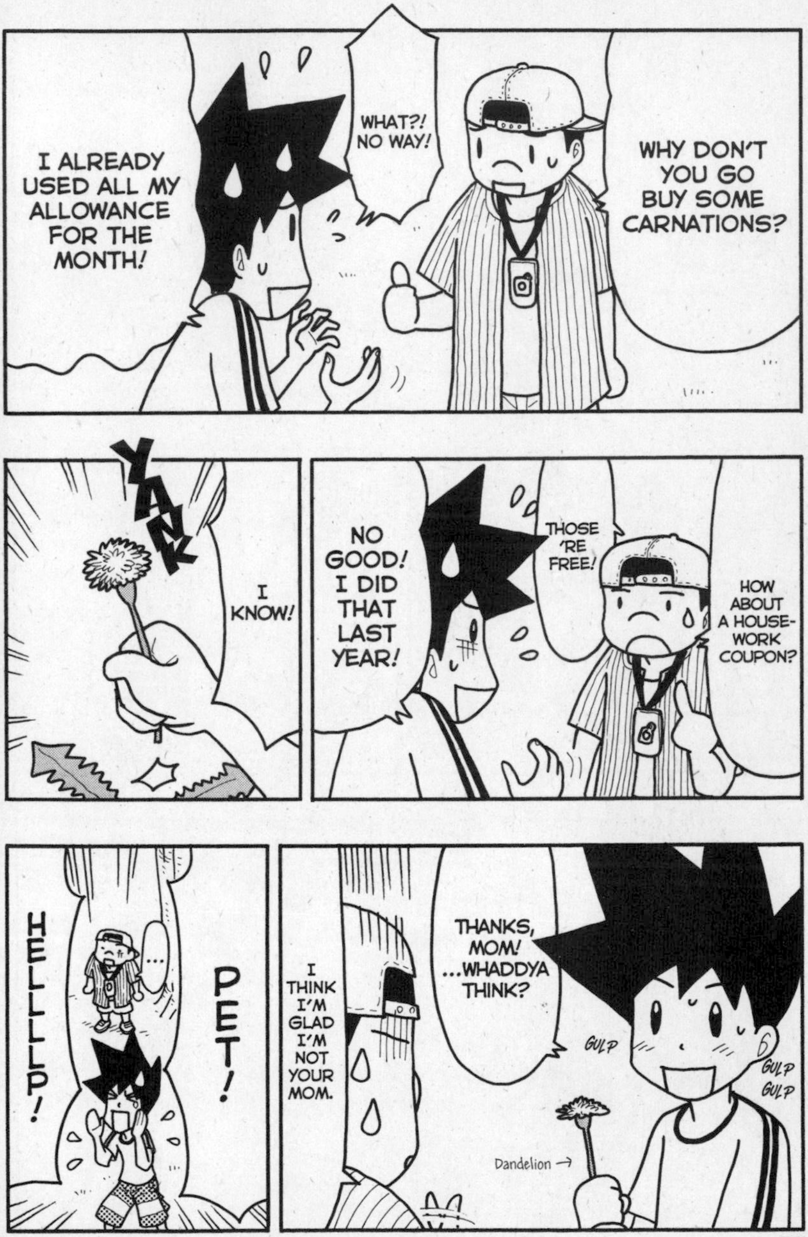
WHY DON'T YOU GO BUY SOME CARNATIONS?
WHAT?! NO WAY!
I ALREADY USED ALL MY ALLOWANCE FOR THE MONTH!
HOW ABOUT A HOUSE-WORK COUPON?
THOSE 'RE FREE!
NO GOOD! I DID THAT LAST YEAR!
I KNOW!
YANK
THANKS, MOM! ...WHADDYA THINK?
GULP
GULP GULP
Dandelion →
I THINK I'M GLAD I'M NOT YOUR MOM.
...
PET!
HELLLLP!

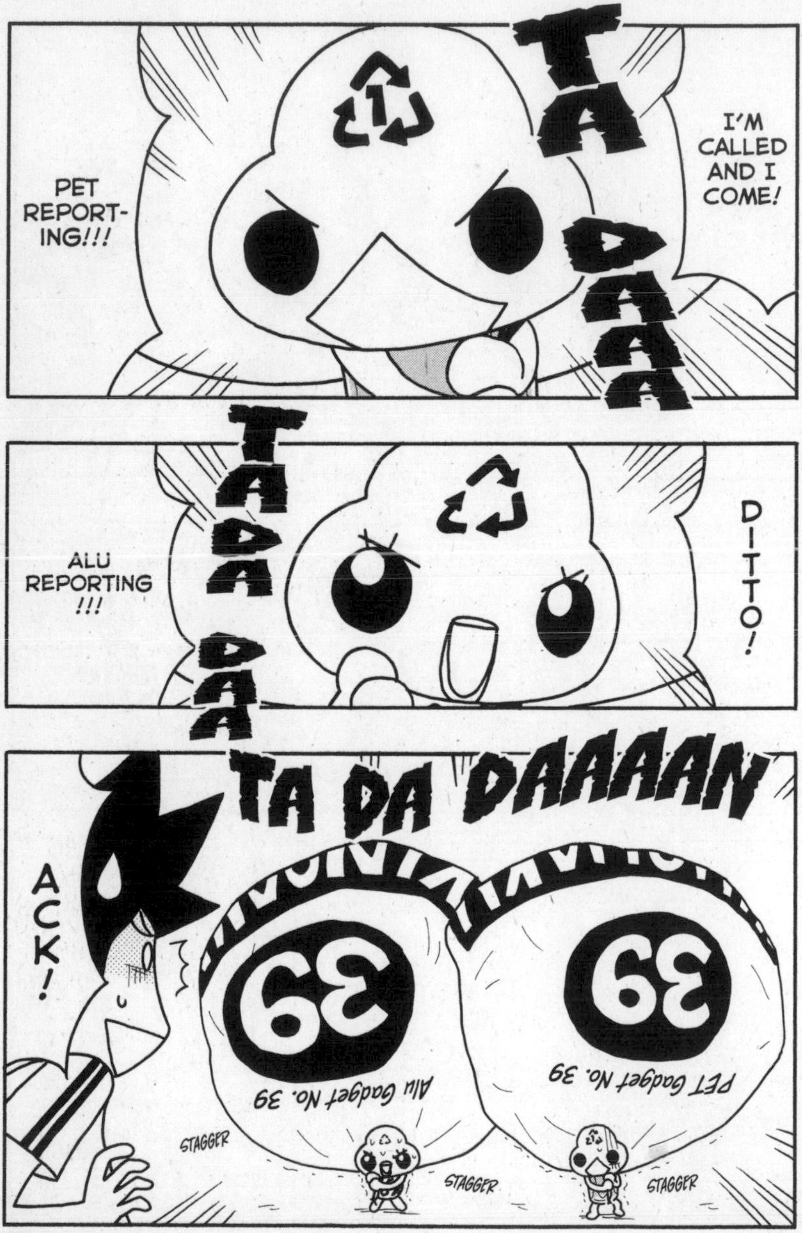
I'M CALLED AND I COME!
TA DAAA
PET REPORTING!!!
DITTO!
TA DA DAA
ALU REPORTING!!!
TA DA DAAAAN
ACK!
39
PET Gadget No. 39
STAGGER
39
Alu Gadget No. 39
STAGGER
STAGGER

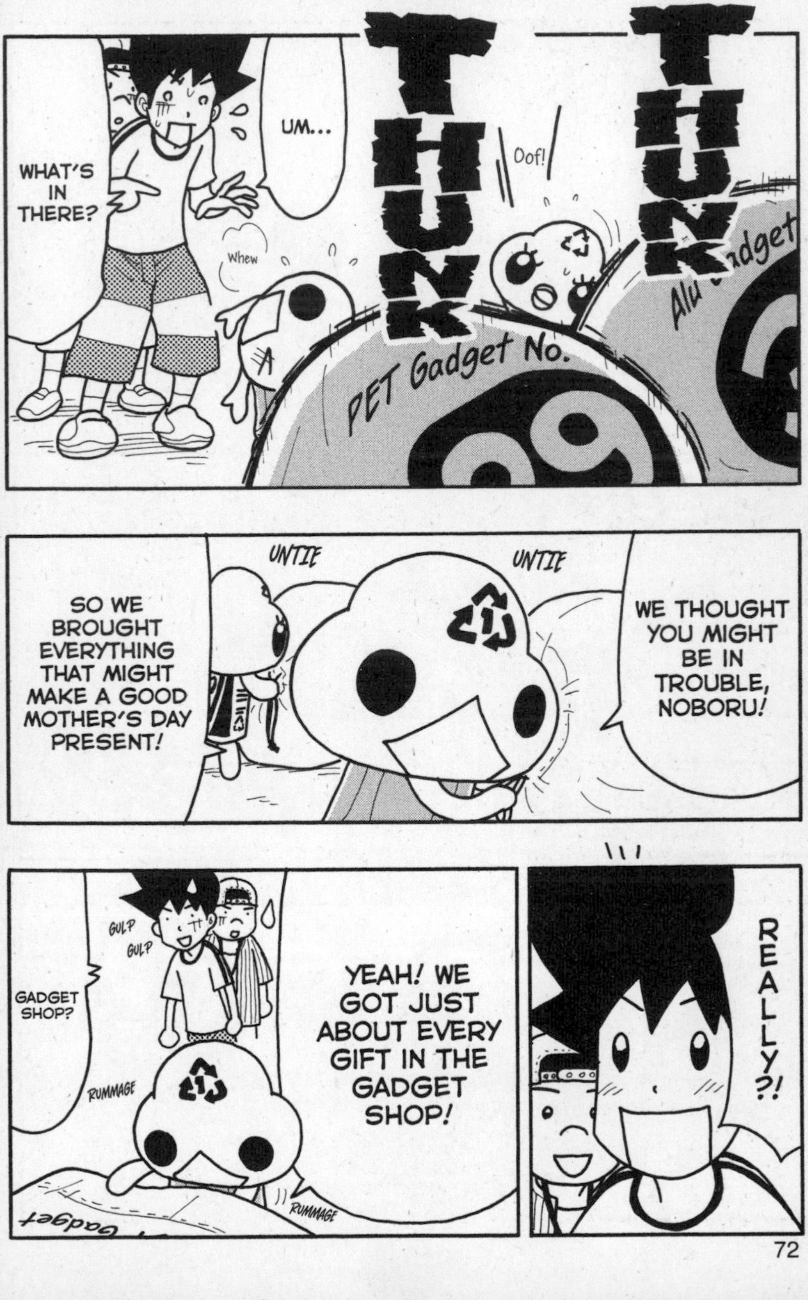

THUNK
THUNK
Oof!
PET Gadget No.
UM...
Whew
WHAT'S IN THERE?
WE THOUGHT YOU MIGHT BE IN TROUBLE, NOBORU!
UNTIE
UNTIE
SO WE BROUGHT EVERYTHING THAT MIGHT MAKE A GOOD MOTHER'S DAY PRESENT!
REALLY?!
YEAH! WE GOT JUST ABOUT EVERY GIFT IN THE GADGET SHOP!
GULP
GULP
GADGET SHOP?
RUMMAGE
RUMMAGE

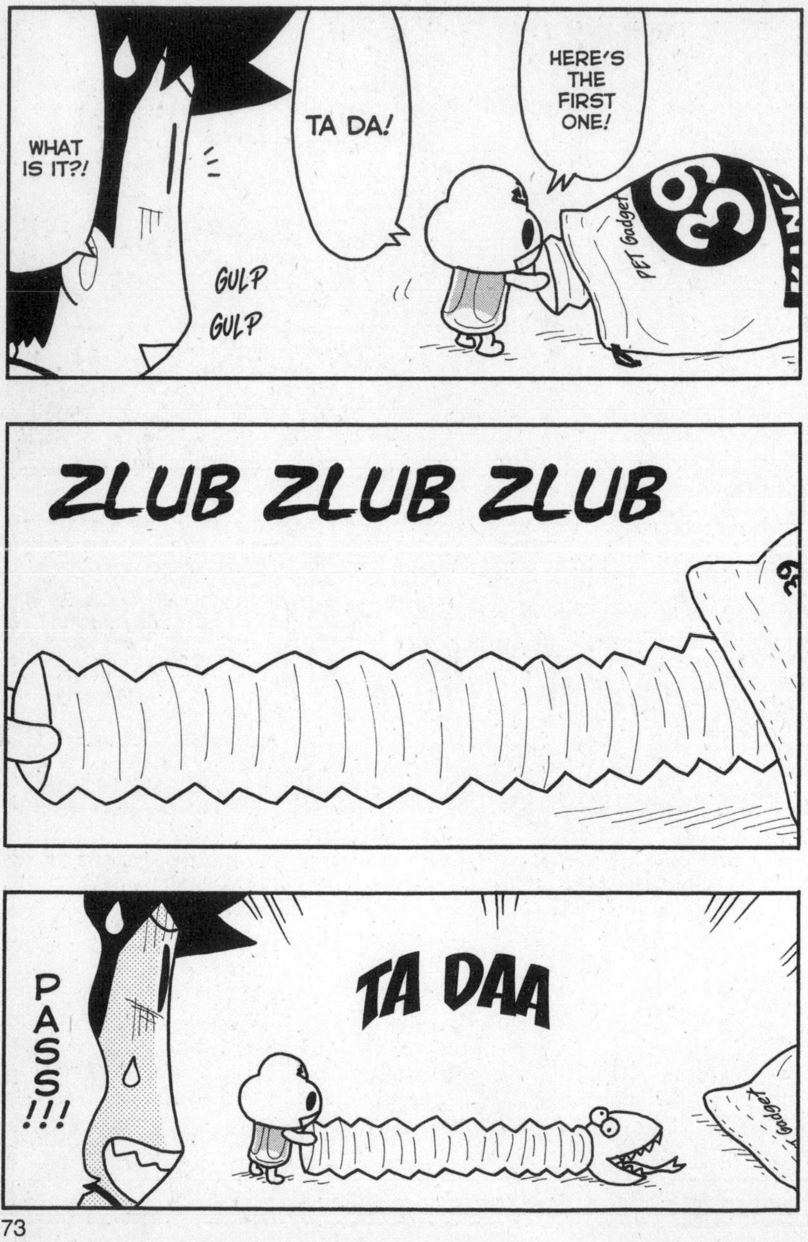
HERE'S THE FIRST ONE!
PET Gadget
TA DA!
GULP
GULP
WHAT IS IT?!
ZLUB ZLUB ZLUB
TA DAA
Gadget
PASS!!!

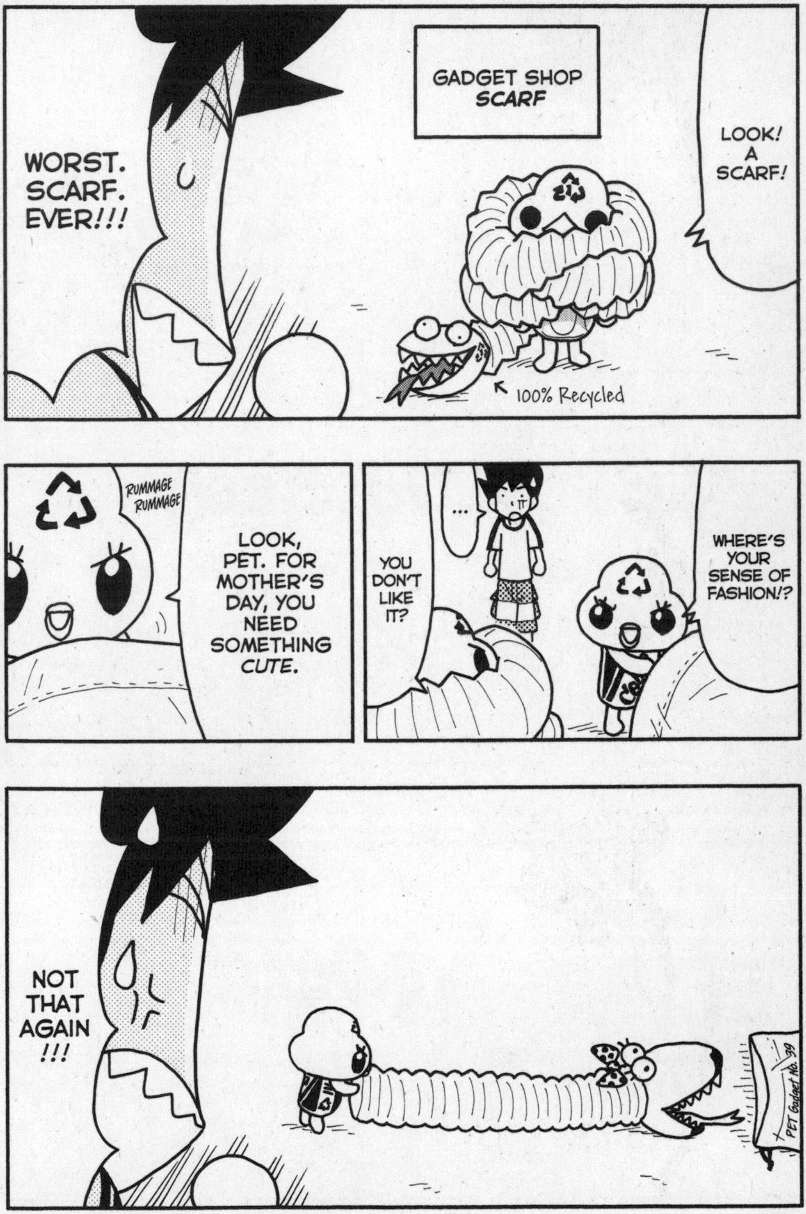
LOOK! A SCARF!
GADGET SHOP SCARF
100% Recycled
WORST. SCARF. EVER!!!
WHERE'S YOUR SENSE OF FASHION!?
...
YOU DON'T LIKE IT?
LOOK, PET. FOR MOTHER'S DAY, YOU NEED SOMETHING CUTE.
RUMMAGE RUMMAGE
PET Gadget No. 39
NOT THAT AGAIN!!!

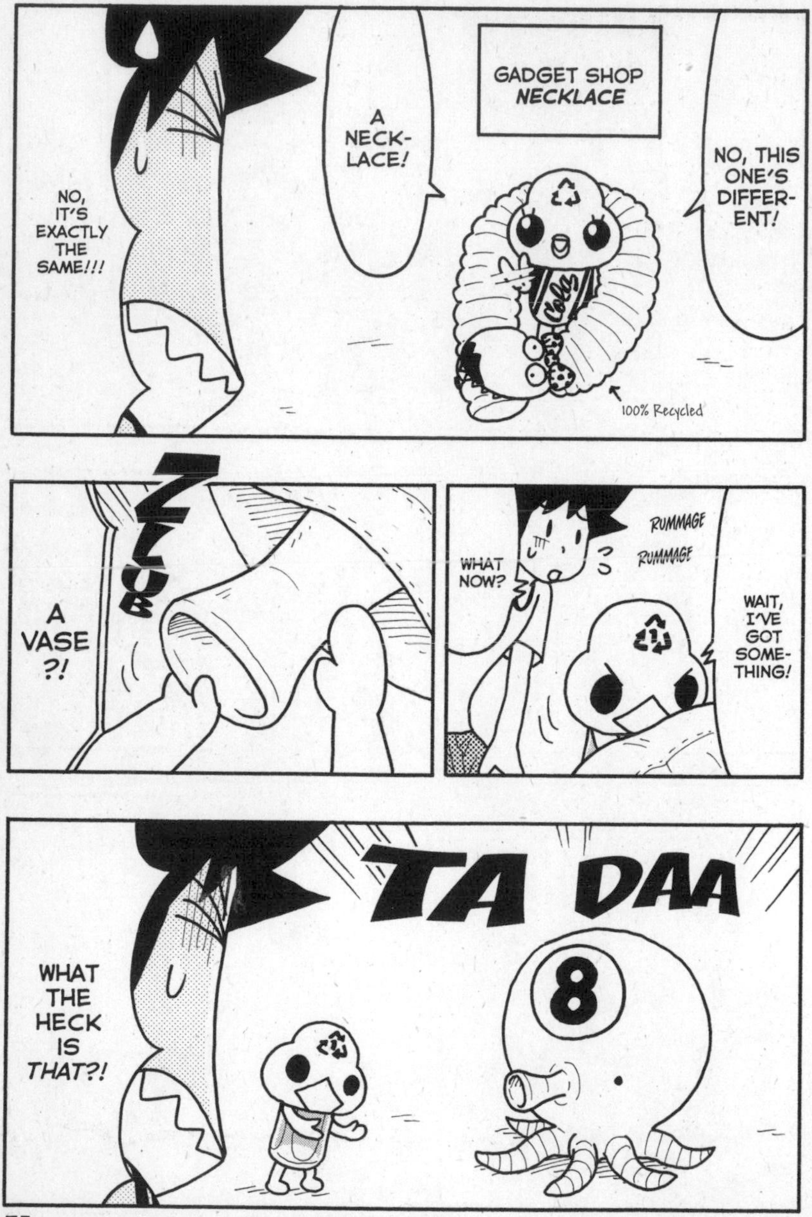
NO, THIS ONE'S DIFFERENT!
GADGET SHOP *NECKLACE*
A NECKLACE!
100% Recycled
NO, IT'S EXACTLY THE SAME!!!
WAIT, I'VE GOT SOMETHING!
RUMMAGE
RUMMAGE
WHAT NOW?
ZLUB
A VASE?!
TA DAA
8
WHAT THE HECK IS *THAT*?!

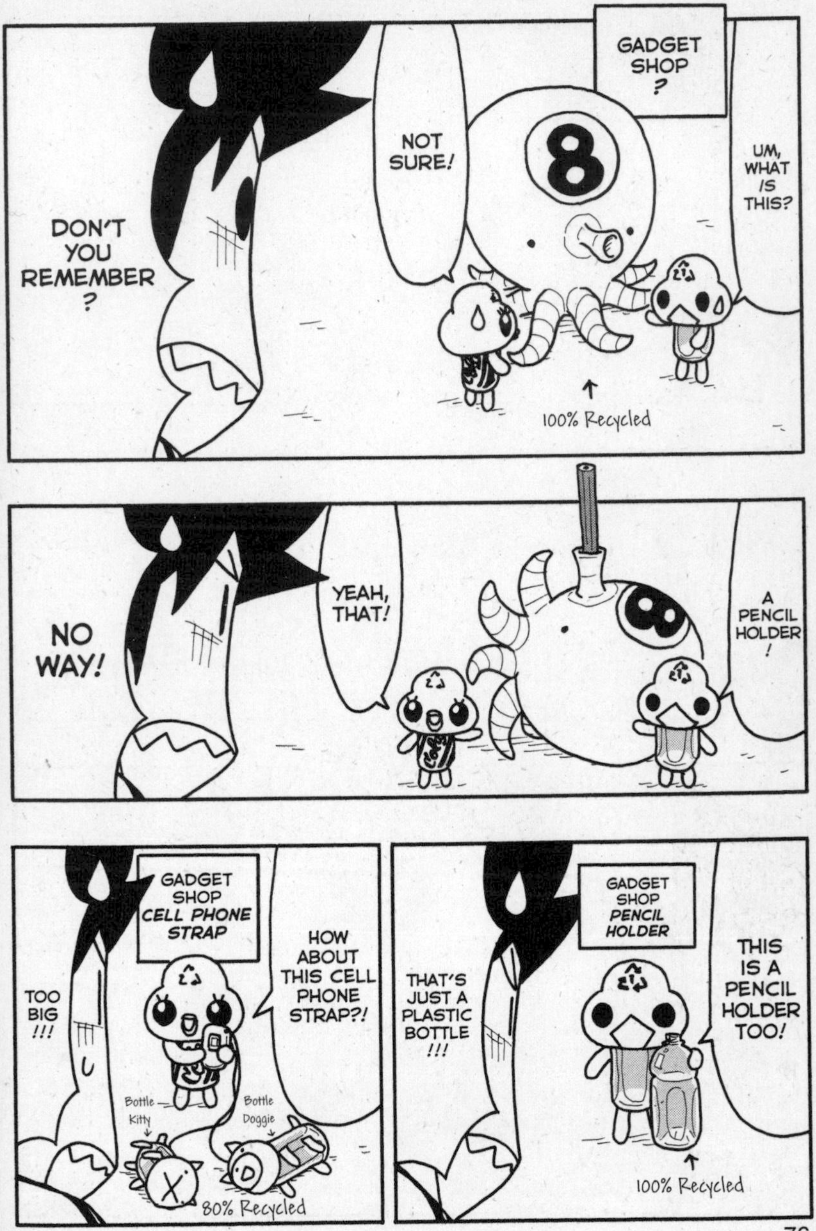
GADGET SHOP ?
UM, WHAT IS THIS?
NOT SURE!
100% Recycled
DON'T YOU REMEMBER ?
A PENCIL HOLDER!
YEAH, THAT!
NO WAY!
GADGET SHOP PENCIL HOLDER
THIS IS A PENCIL HOLDER TOO!
THAT'S JUST A PLASTIC BOTTLE!!!
100% Recycled
GADGET SHOP CELL PHONE STRAP
HOW ABOUT THIS CELL PHONE STRAP?!
TOO BIG!!!
Bottle Doggie
Bottle Kitty
80% Recycled

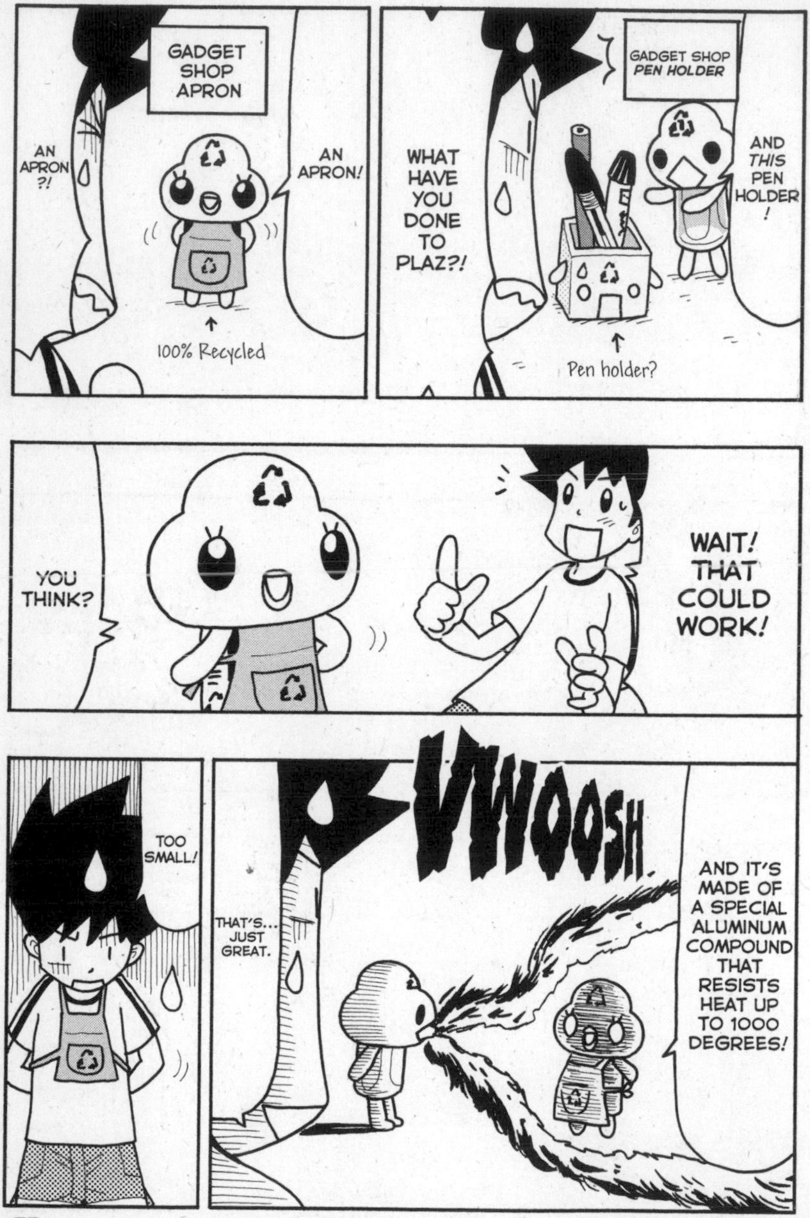
GADGET SHOP *PEN HOLDER*
AND *THIS* PEN HOLDER!
WHAT HAVE YOU DONE TO PLAZ?!
Pen holder?
GADGET SHOP APRON
AN APRON!
AN APRON?!
100% Recycled
WAIT! THAT COULD WORK!
YOU THINK?
VWOOSH
AND IT'S MADE OF A SPECIAL ALUMINUM COMPOUND THAT RESISTS HEAT UP TO 1000 DEGREES!
THAT'S... JUST GREAT.
TOO SMALL!

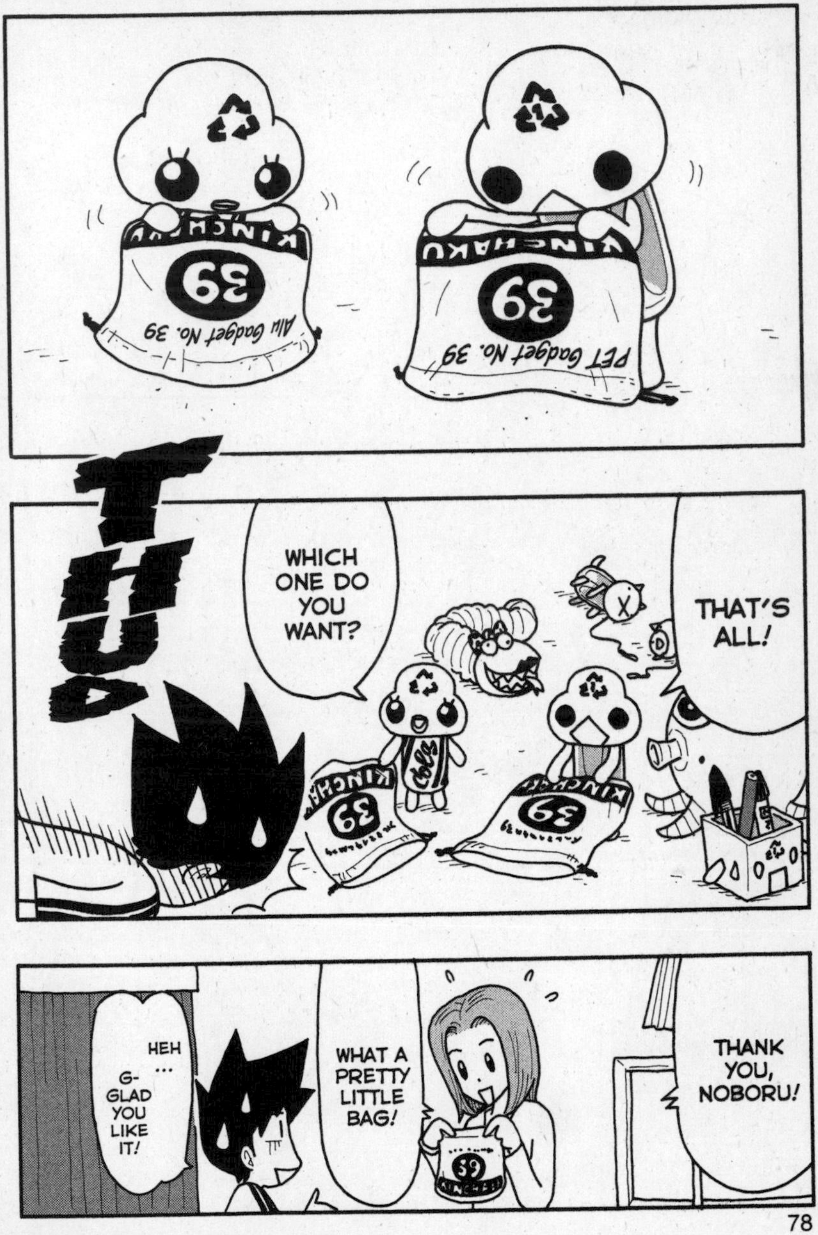
KINCHAKU
PET Gadget No. 39
KINCHAKU
Alu Gadget No. 39
THAT'S ALL!
WHICH ONE DO YOU WANT?
THUD
THANK YOU, NOBORU!
WHAT A PRETTY LITTLE BAG!
HEH ... G-GLAD YOU LIKE IT!

# CHAPTER 8
# Plaz Takes a Nap

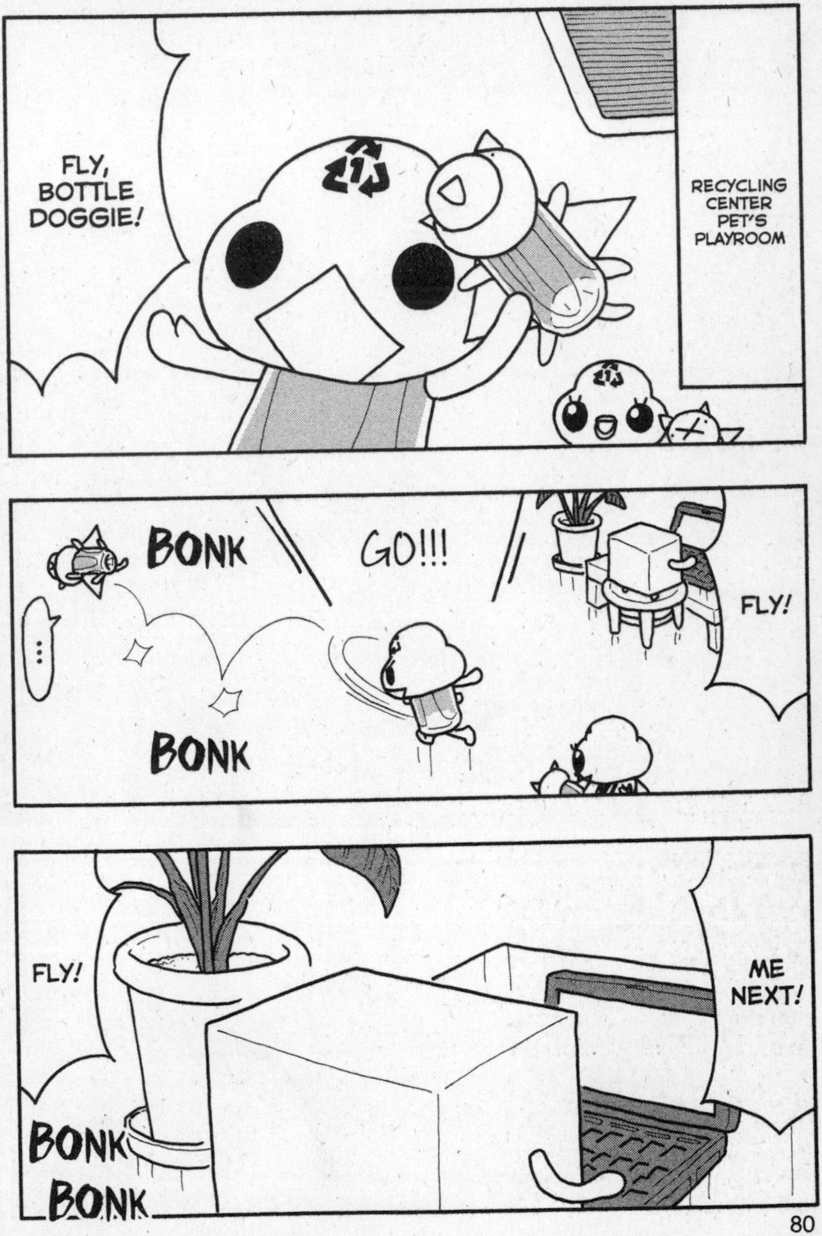
RECYCLING CENTER PET'S PLAYROOM
FLY, BOTTLE DOGGIE!
FLY!
GO!!!
BONK
...
BONK
ME NEXT!
FLY!
BONK
BONK

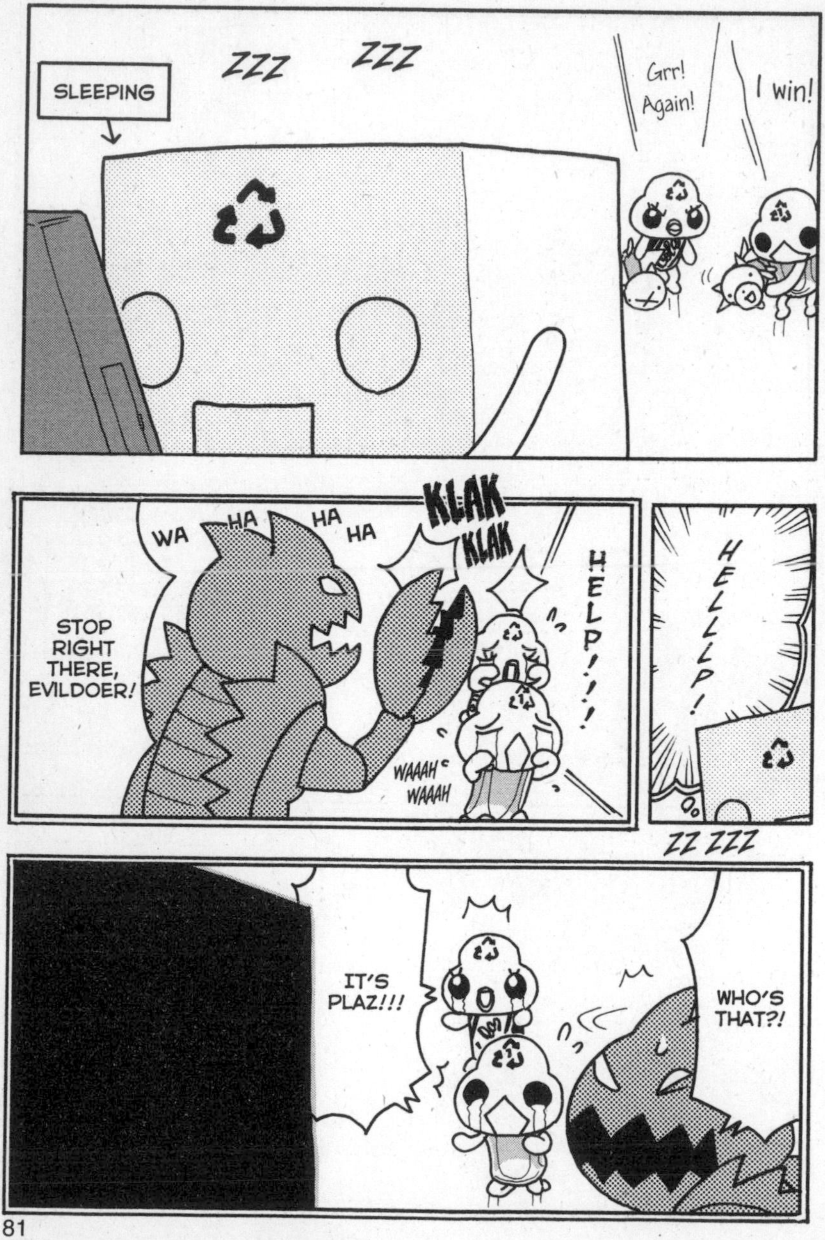
I win!
Grr! Again!
ZZZ ZZZ
SLEEPING
HELLLP!
ZZ ZZZ
KLAK KLAK
HELP!!!
WA HA HA HA
STOP RIGHT THERE, EVILDOER!
WAAAH WAAAH
WHO'S THAT?!
IT'S PLAZ!!!

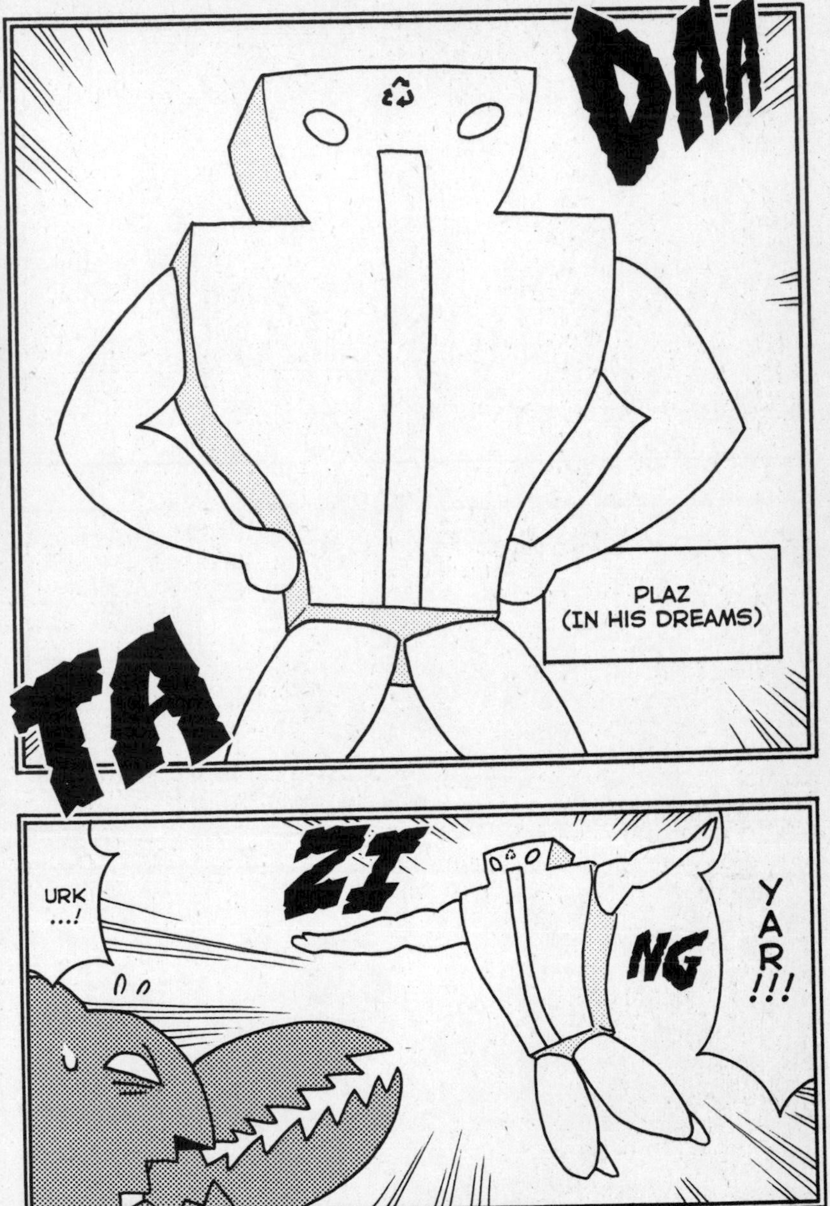
DAA
PLAZ
(IN HIS DREAMS)
TA
YAR!!!
ZI
NG
URK ...!

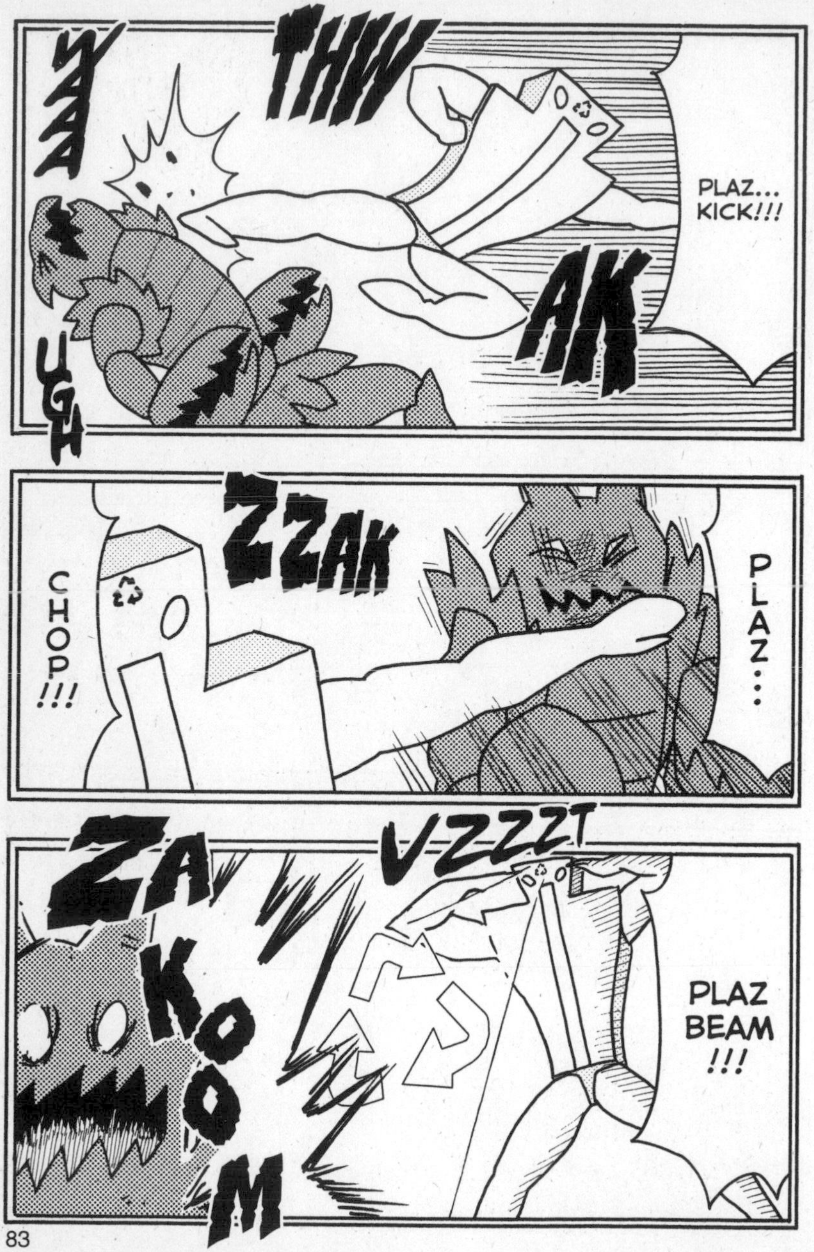
PLAZ...
KICK!!!
THW
AK
UGH
PLAZ...
ZZAK
CHOP!!!
PLAZ
BEAM
!!!
VZZZT
ZA
KOOM

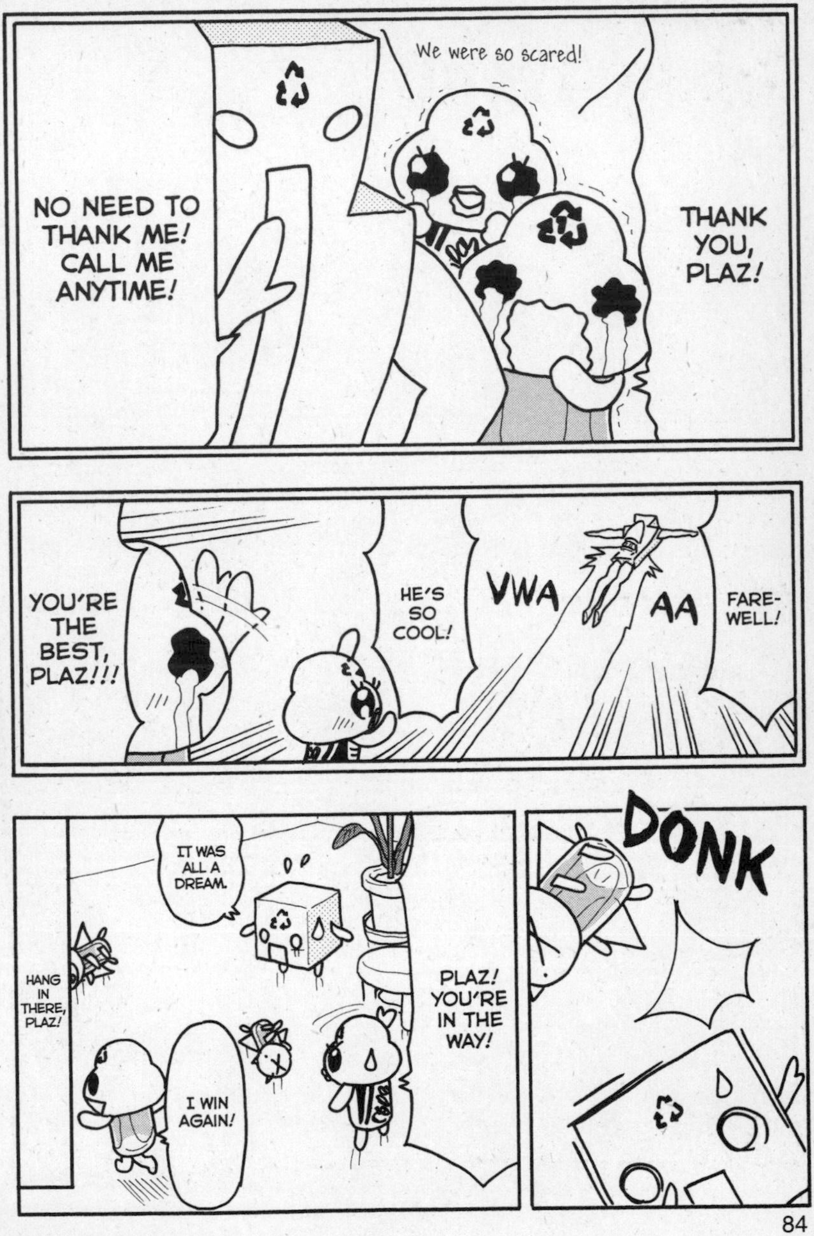
THANK YOU, PLAZ!
We were so scared!
NO NEED TO THANK ME! CALL ME ANYTIME!
FARE-WELL!
VWA AA
HE'S SO COOL!
YOU'RE THE BEST, PLAZ!!!
DONK
PLAZ! YOU'RE IN THE WAY!
IT WAS ALL A DREAM.
I WIN AGAIN!
HANG IN THERE, PLAZ!

## CHAPTER 9

# Topsy Turvy

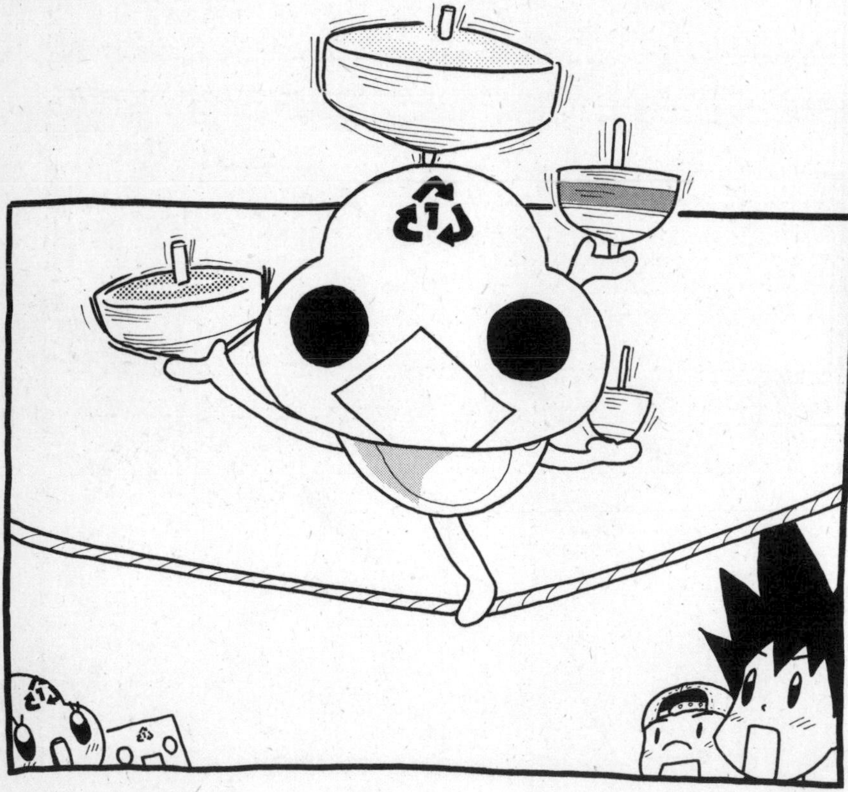

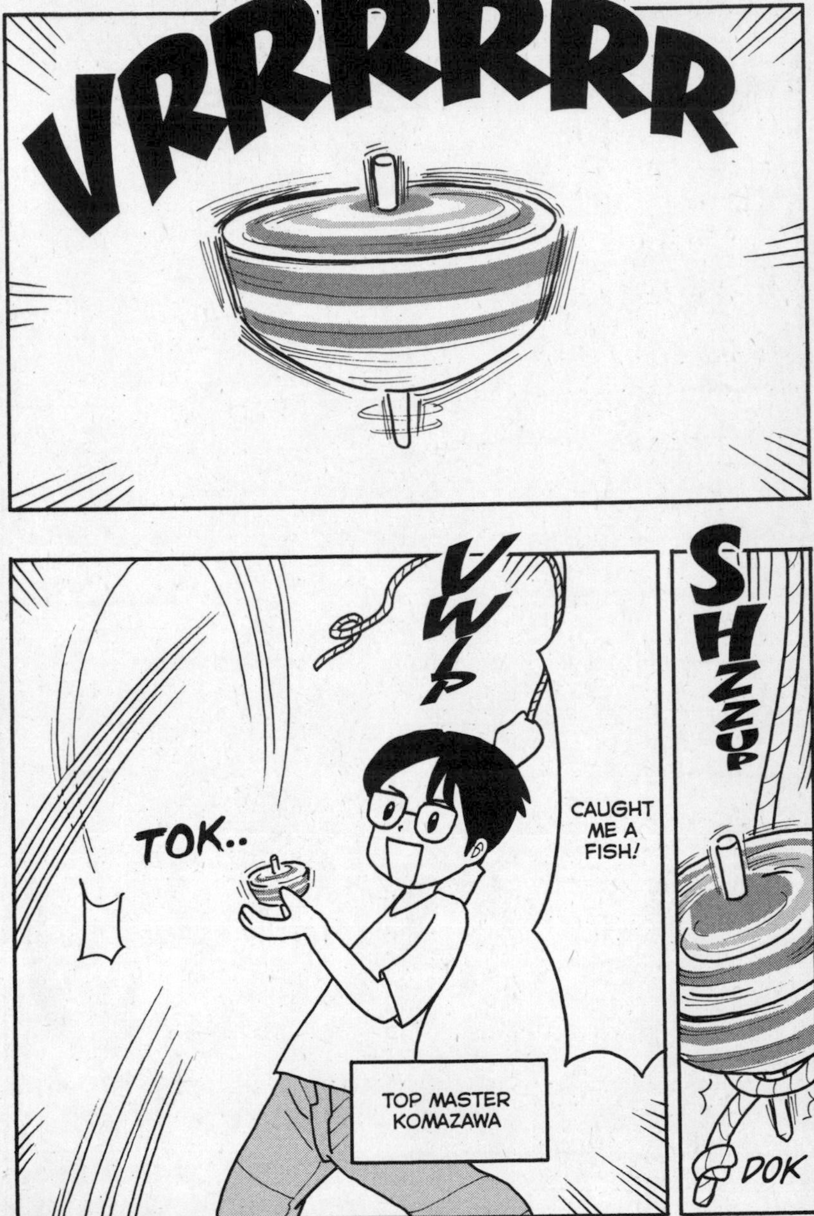
VRRRRRRR
SHZZUP
DOK
VWIP
CAUGHT ME A FISH!
TOK..
TOP MASTER KOMAZAWA

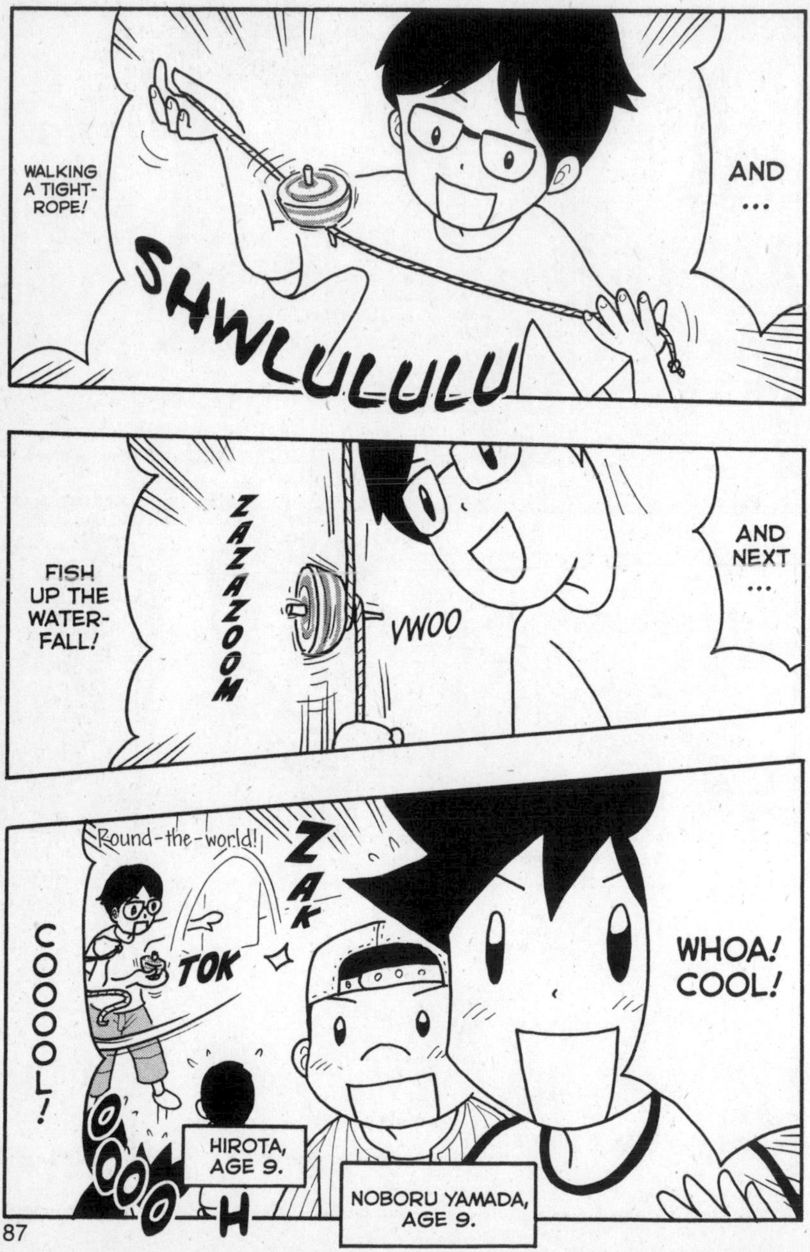
AND ...
WALKING A TIGHT-ROPE!
SHWLULULU
AND NEXT ...
VWOO
ZAZAZOOM
FISH UP THE WATER-FALL!
WHOA! COOL!
ZAK
TOK
Round-the-world!
NOBORU YAMADA, AGE 9.
HIROTA, AGE 9.
COOOOOL!
OOOOOH

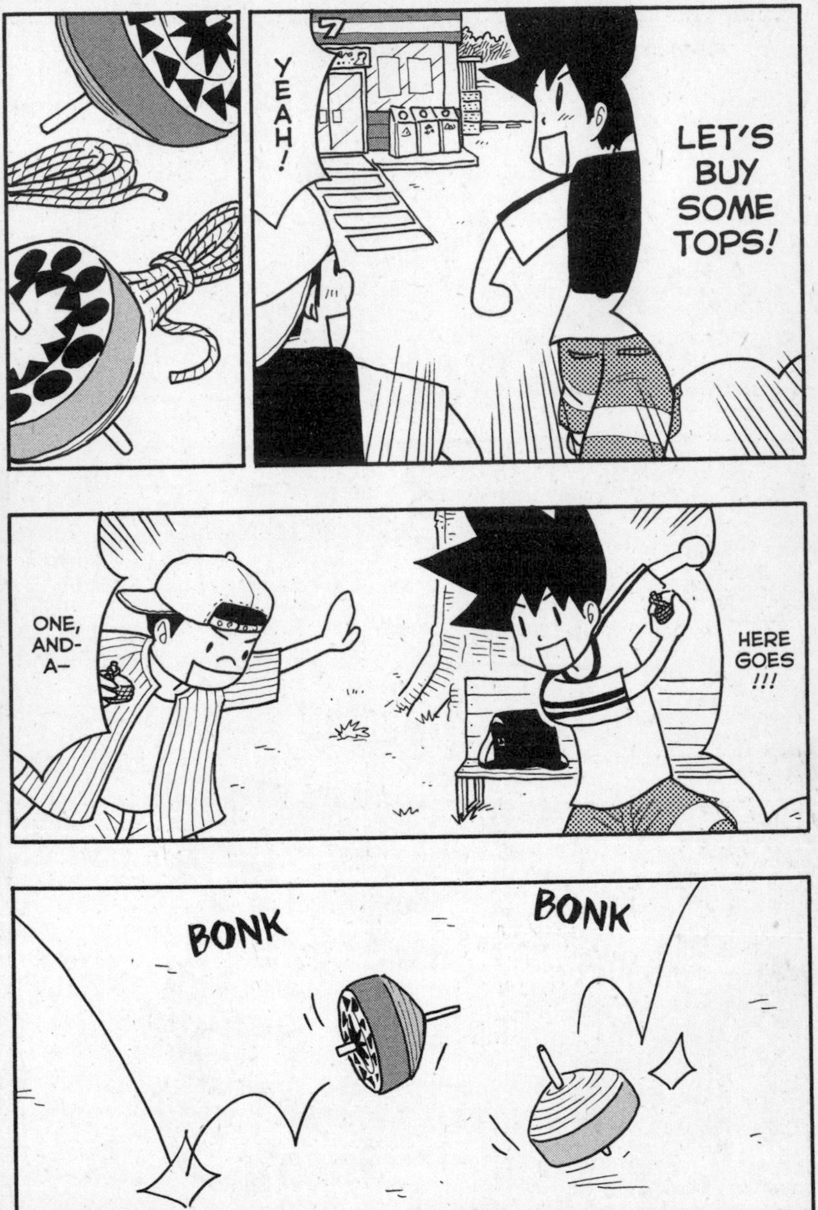
LET'S BUY SOME TOPS!
YEAH!
HERE GOES!!!
ONE, AND-A-
BONK
BONK

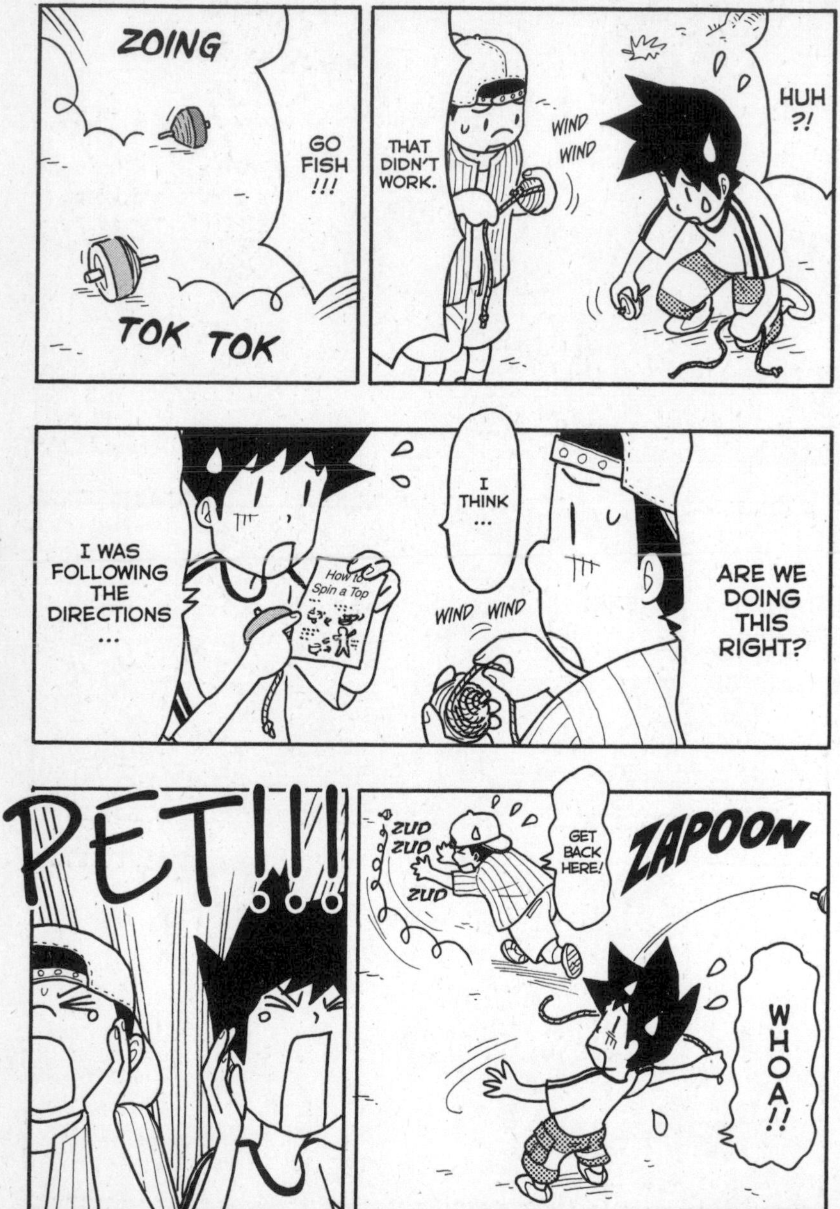
HUH ?!
WIND WIND
THAT DIDN'T WORK.
GO FISH !!!
ZOING
TOK TOK
ARE WE DOING THIS RIGHT?
I THINK ...
WIND WIND
I WAS FOLLOWING THE DIRECTIONS ...
How to Spin a Top
ZAPOON
GET BACK HERE!
ZUD ZUD ZUD
WHOA!!
PET!!!

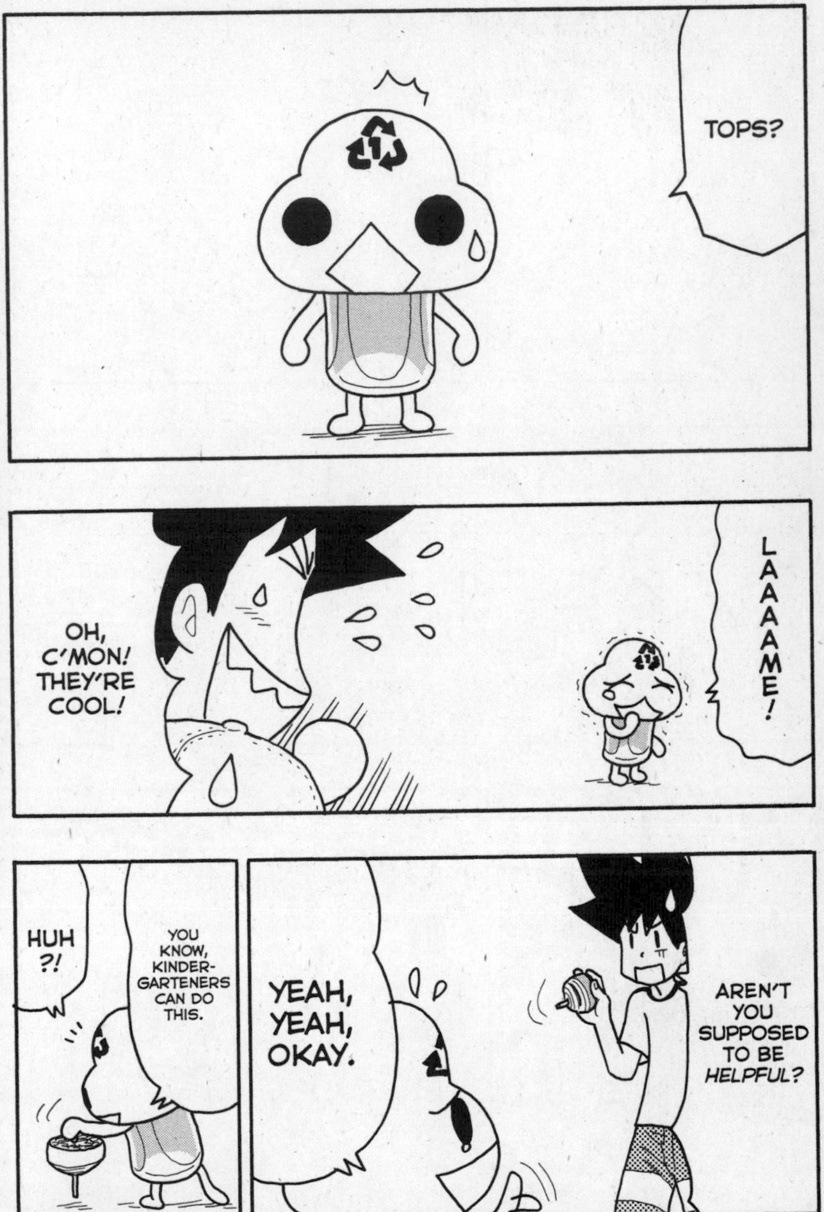
TOPS?
LAAAAAME!
OH, C'MON! THEY'RE COOL!
AREN'T YOU SUPPOSED TO BE *HELPFUL*?
YEAH, YEAH, OKAY.
YOU KNOW, KINDER-GARTENERS CAN DO THIS.
HUH?!

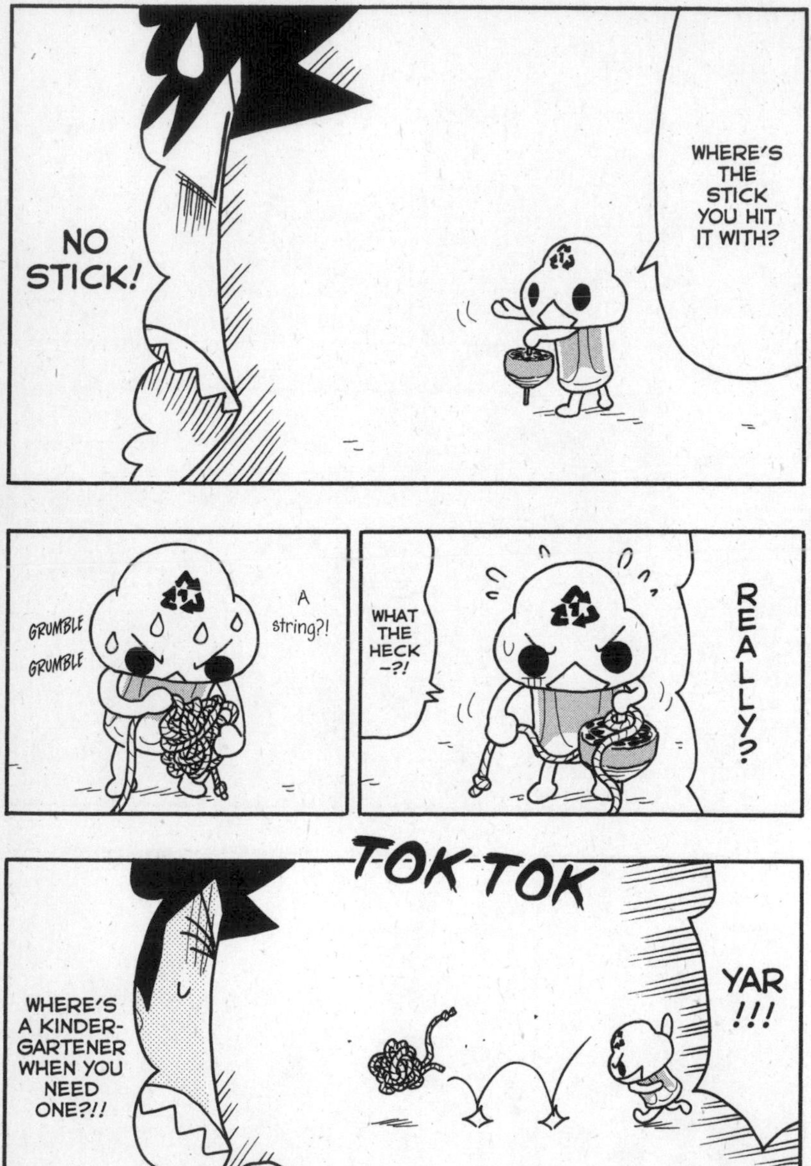
WHERE'S THE STICK YOU HIT IT WITH?
NO STICK!
REALLY?
WHAT THE HECK -?!
A string?!
GRUMBLE
GRUMBLE
TOK TOK
YAR !!!
WHERE'S A KINDER-GARTENER WHEN YOU NEED ONE?!!

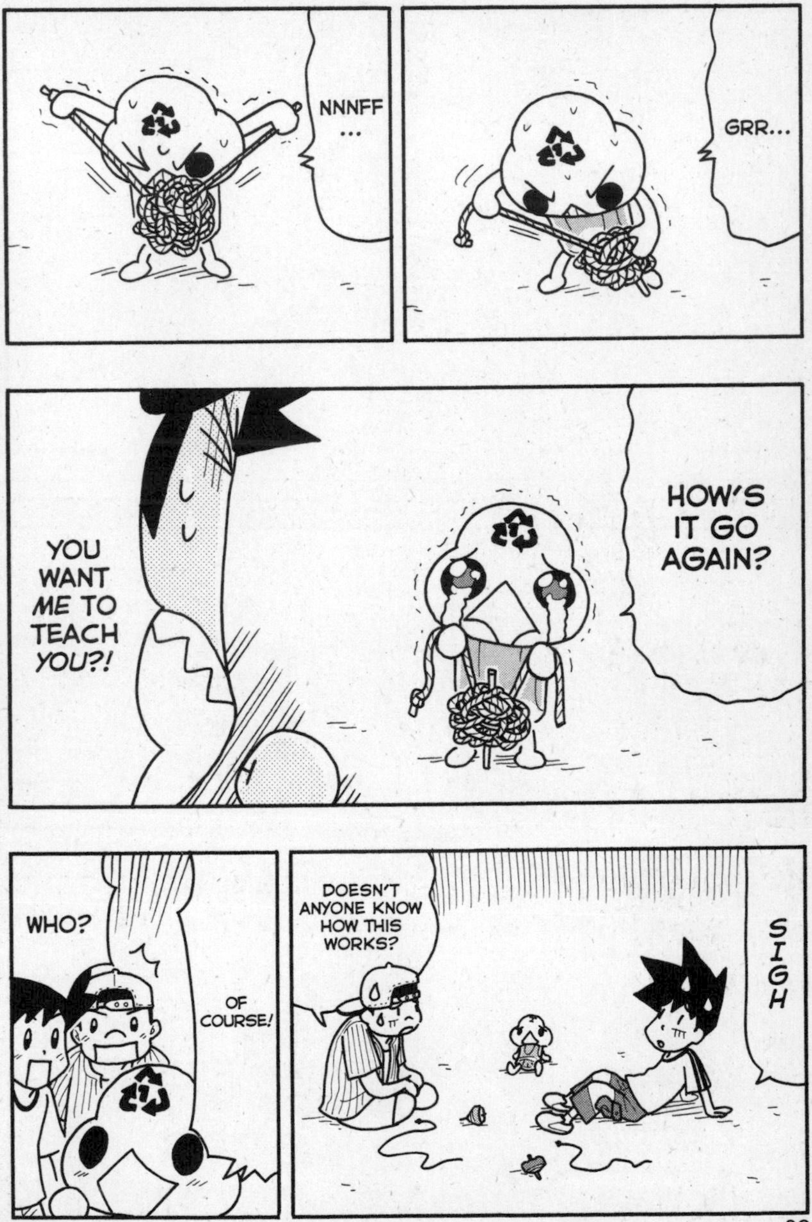
GRR...
NNNFF ...
HOW'S IT GO AGAIN?
YOU WANT *ME* TO TEACH *YOU*?!
SIGH
DOESN'T ANYONE KNOW HOW THIS WORKS?
WHO?
OF COURSE!

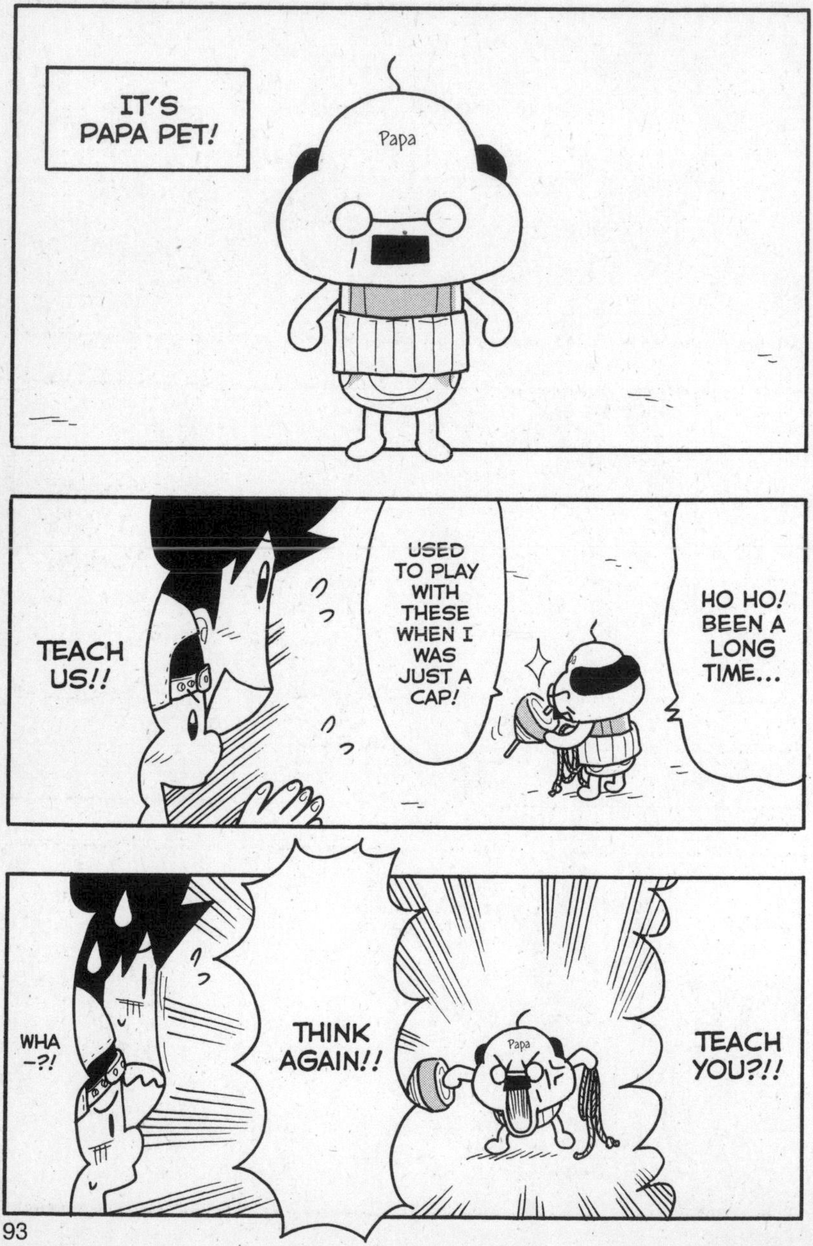
IT'S PAPA PET!
Papa
HO HO! BEEN A LONG TIME...
USED TO PLAY WITH THESE WHEN I WAS JUST A CAP!
TEACH US!!
TEACH YOU?!!
Papa
THINK AGAIN!!
WHA—?!

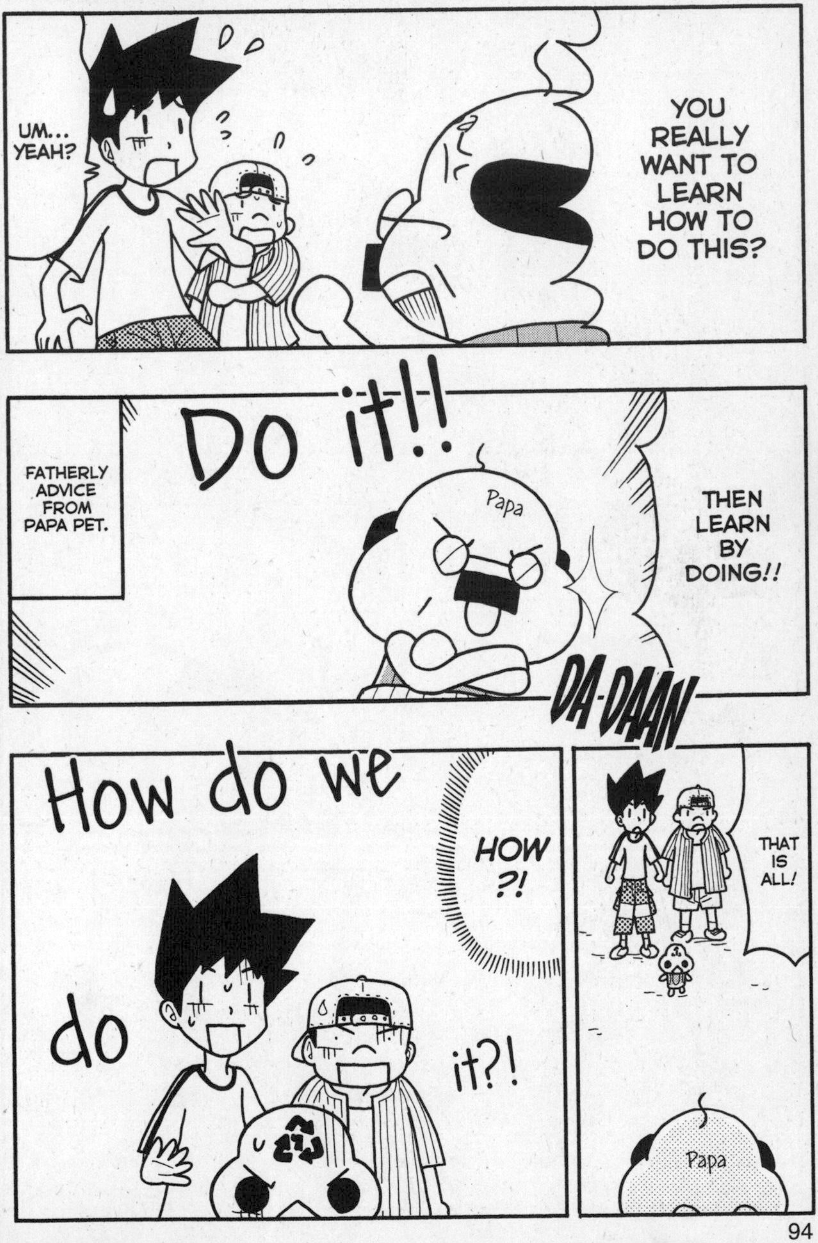
YOU REALLY WANT TO LEARN HOW TO DO THIS?
UM... YEAH?
THEN LEARN BY DOING!!
Do it!!
Papa
FATHERLY ADVICE FROM PAPA PET.
DA-DAAN
THAT IS ALL!
Papa
HOW ?!
How do we do it?!

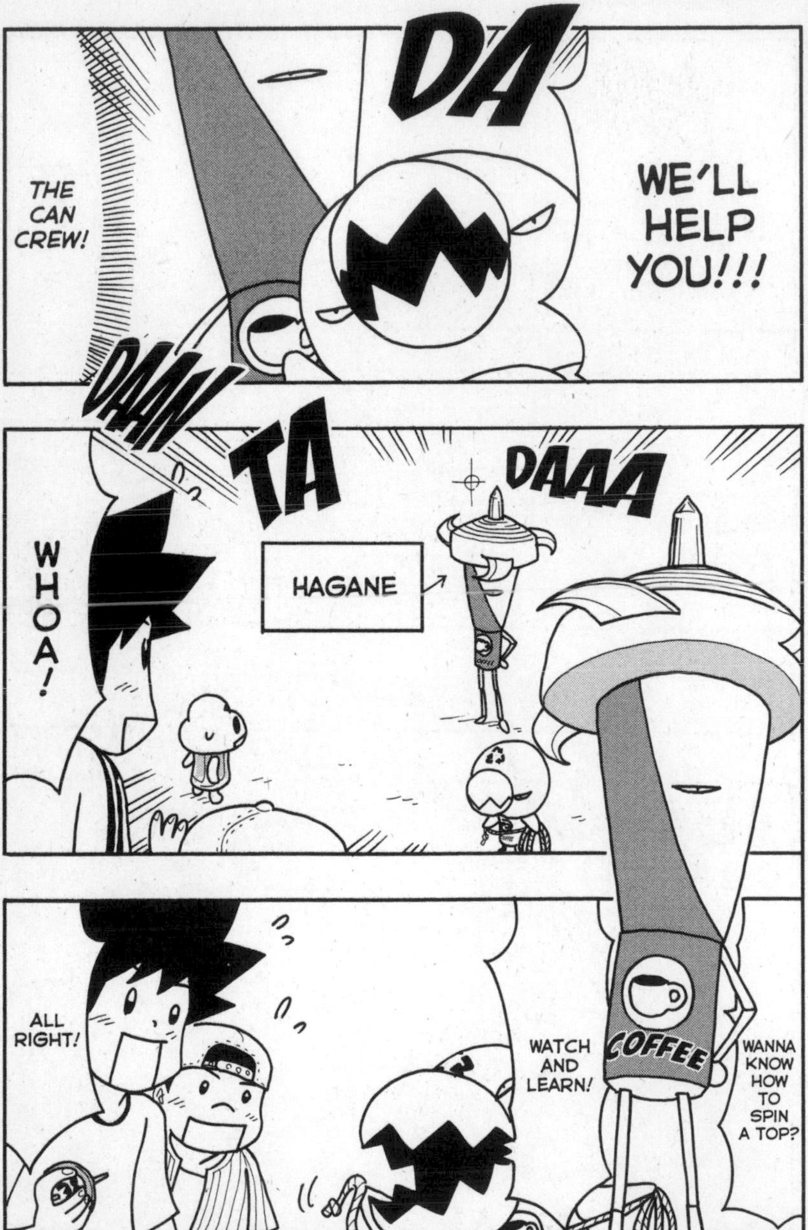

DA
WE'LL HELP YOU!!!
THE CAN CREW!
DAAN
DAAAA
TA
HAGANE
WHOA!
WANNA KNOW HOW TO SPIN A TOP?
COFFEE
WATCH AND LEARN!
ALL RIGHT!

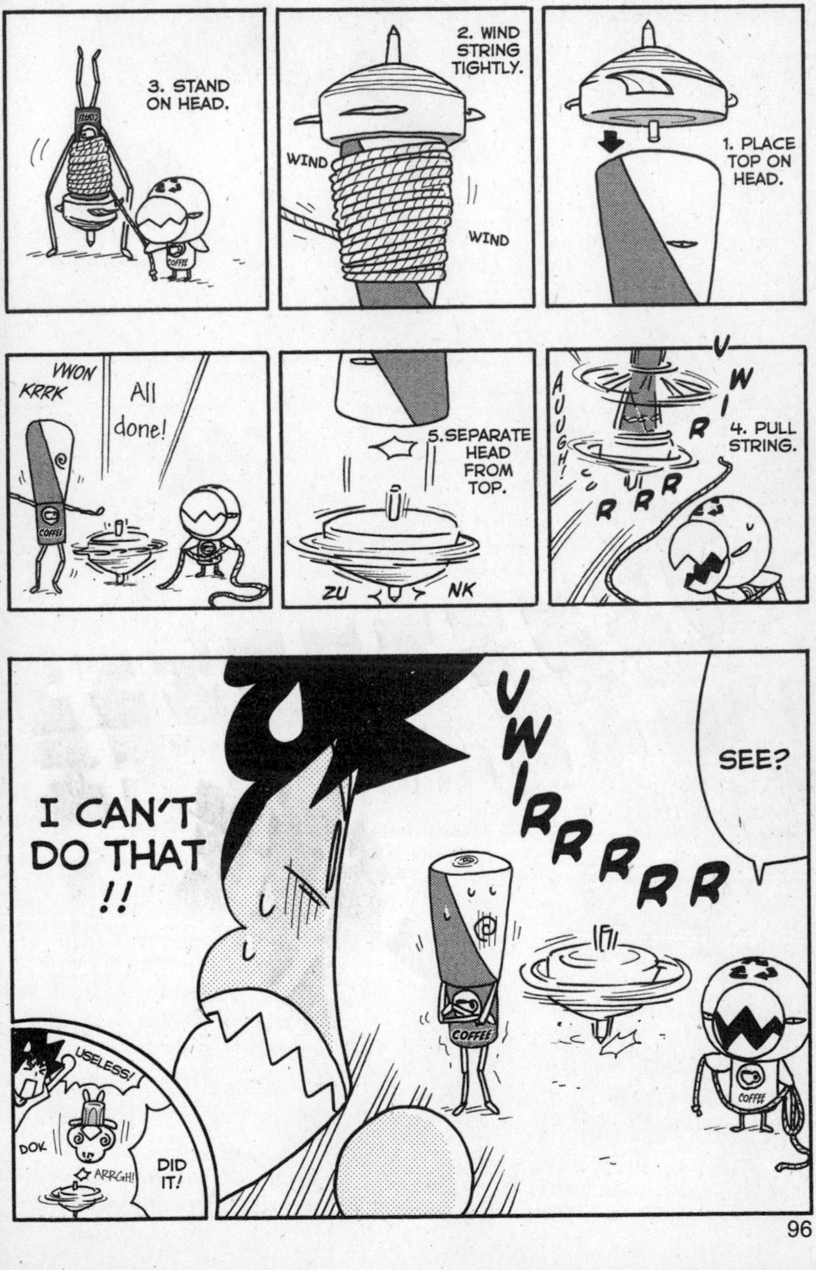
1. PLACE TOP ON HEAD.
2. WIND STRING TIGHTLY.
WIND
WIND
3. STAND ON HEAD.
4. PULL STRING.
UWIRRRR
AUUGH!
5.SEPARATE HEAD FROM TOP.
ZU NK
VWON
KRRK
All done!
SEE?
UWIRRRRRR
I CAN'T DO THAT!!
USELESS!
DID IT!
DOK
ARRGH!

# CHAPTER 10
# PET Mark 2, Reporting!

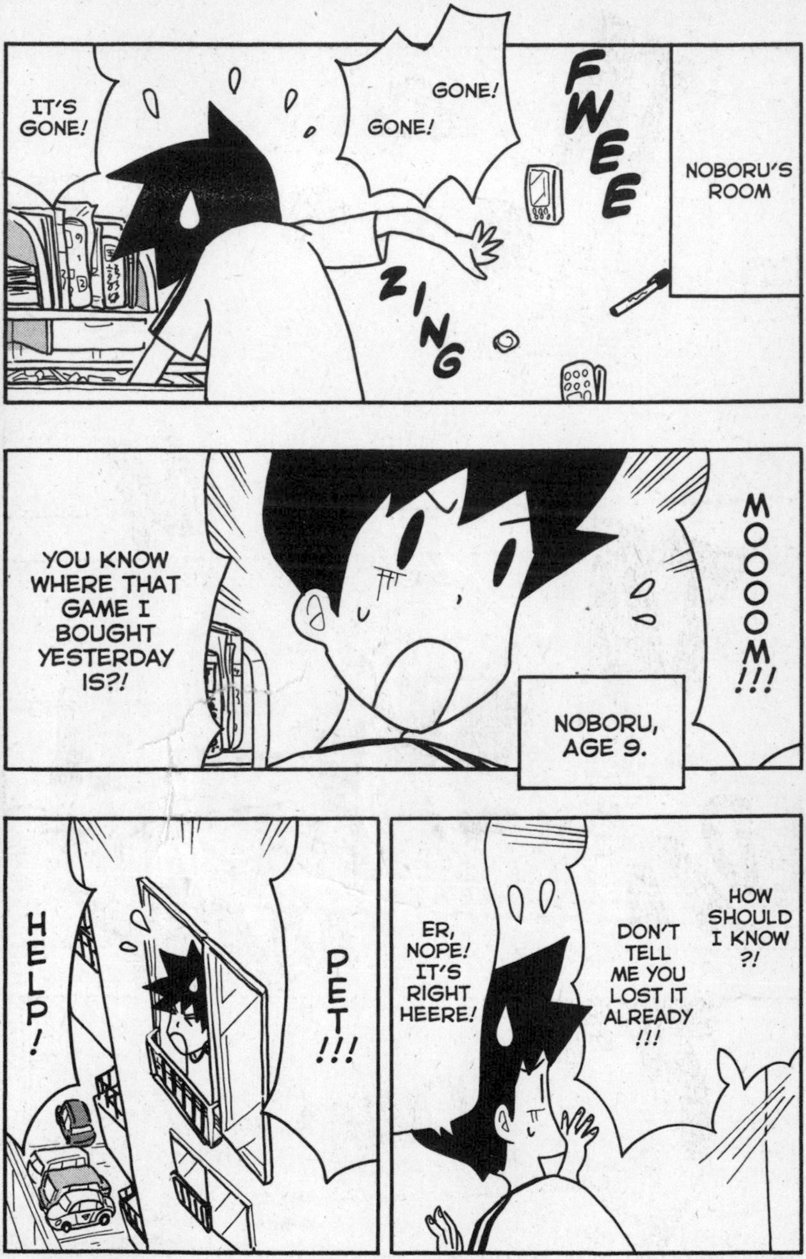
NOBORU'S ROOM
FWEE
GONE!
GONE!
IT'S GONE!
ZING
MOOOOOM!!!
NOBORU, AGE 9.
YOU KNOW WHERE THAT GAME I BOUGHT YESTERDAY IS?!
HOW SHOULD I KNOW?!
DON'T TELL ME YOU LOST IT ALREADY!!!
ER, NOPE! IT'S RIGHT HEERE!
PET!!!
HELP!

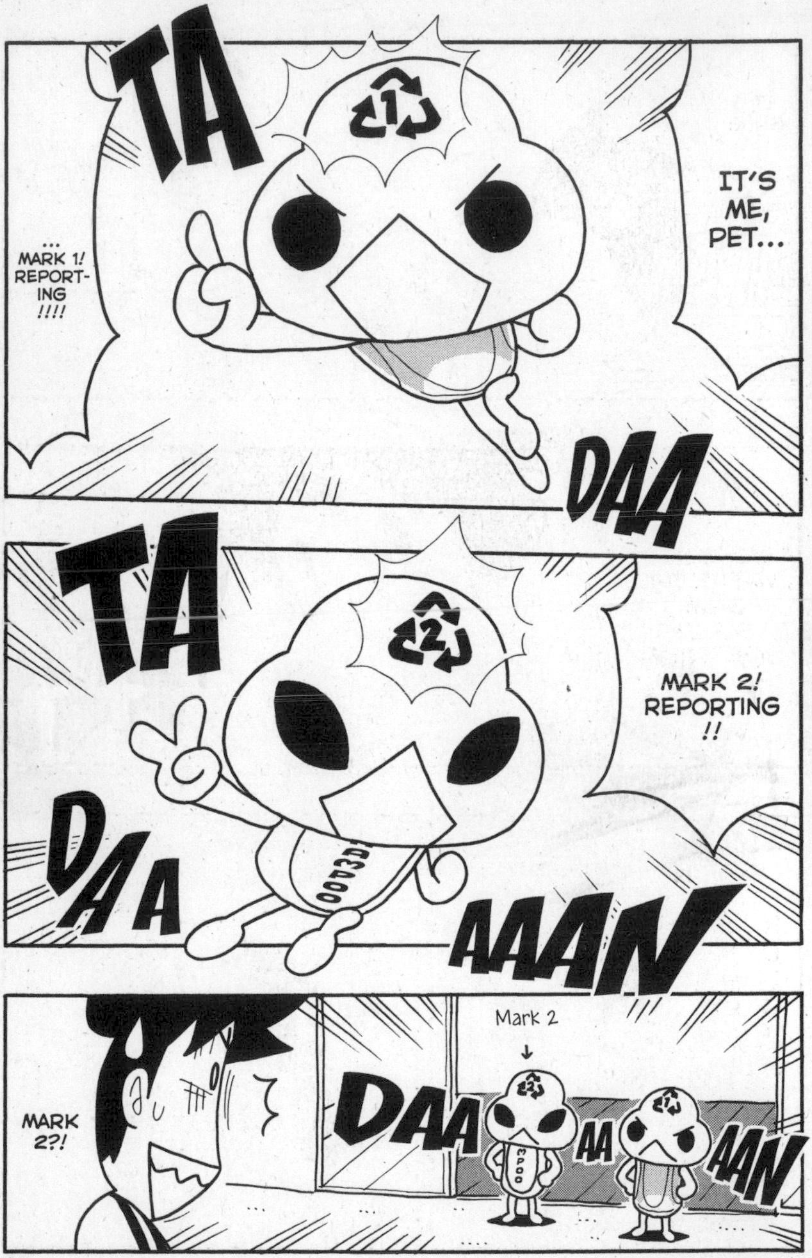
IT'S ME, PET...
TA
... MARK 1! REPORTING !!!!
DAA
MARK 2! REPORTING !!
TA
DAA
AAAN
Mark 2
DAA
AA
AAN
MARK 2?!

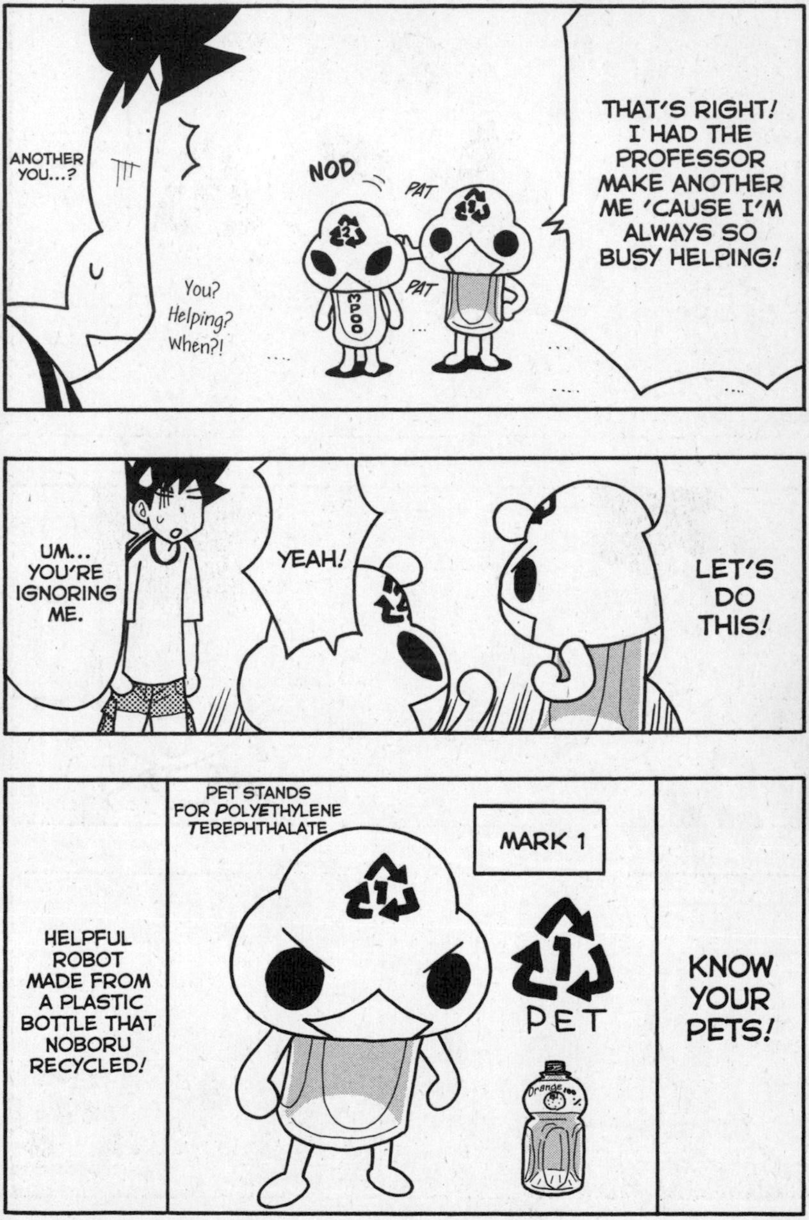
THAT'S RIGHT! I HAD THE PROFESSOR MAKE ANOTHER ME 'CAUSE I'M ALWAYS SO BUSY HELPING!
NOD
PAT
PAT
You? Helping? When?!
ANOTHER YOU...?
LET'S DO THIS!
YEAH!
UM... YOU'RE IGNORING ME.
KNOW YOUR PETS!
MARK 1
PET STANDS FOR POLYETHYLENE TEREPHTHALATE
PET
HELPFUL ROBOT MADE FROM A PLASTIC BOTTLE THAT NOBORU RECYCLED!

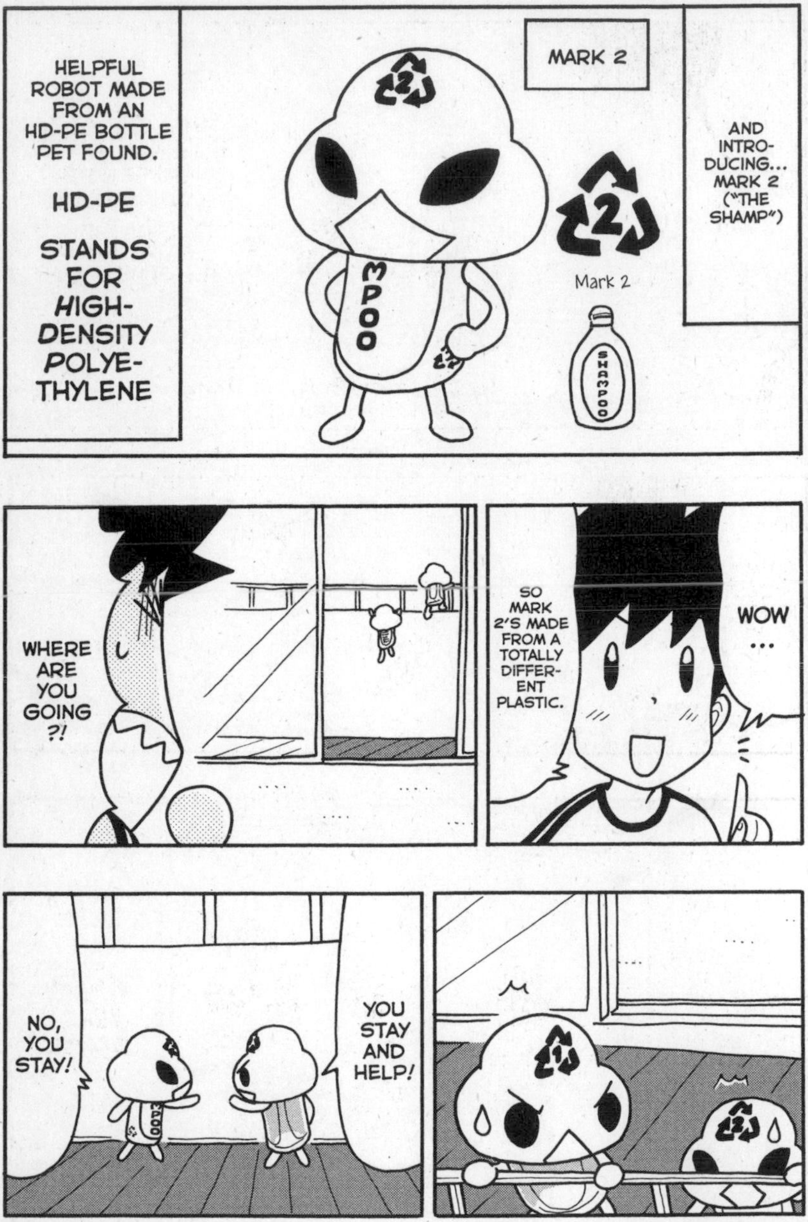
AND INTRODUCING... MARK 2 ("THE SHAMP")
MARK 2
Mark 2
SHAMPOO
MPOO
HELPFUL ROBOT MADE FROM AN HD-PE BOTTLE PET FOUND.
HD-PE
STANDS FOR HIGH-DENSITY POLYETHYLENE
WOW ...
SO MARK 2'S MADE FROM A TOTALLY DIFFERENT PLASTIC.
WHERE ARE YOU GOING ?!
YOU STAY AND HELP!
NO, YOU STAY!

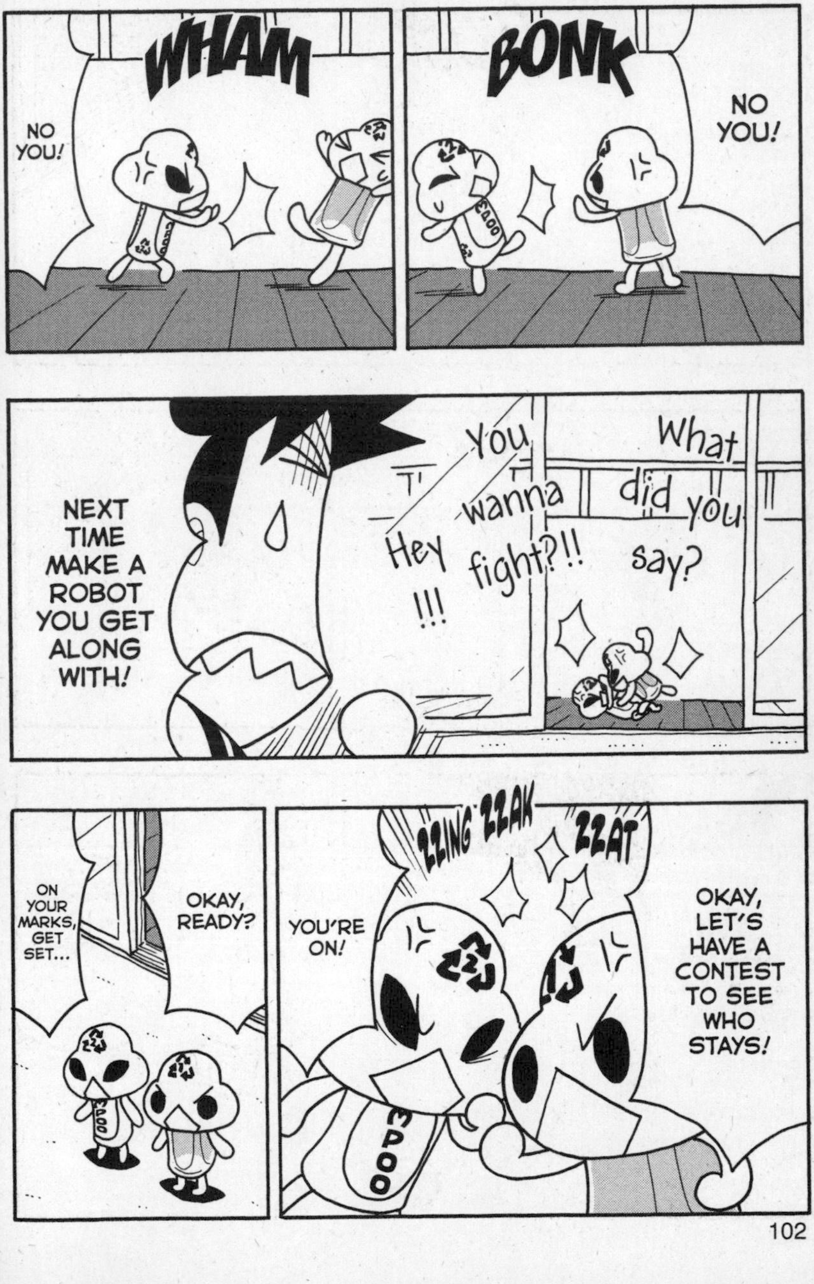
BONK
NO YOU!
WHAM
NO YOU!
What did you say?
You wanna fight?!!
Hey !!!
NEXT TIME MAKE A ROBOT YOU GET ALONG WITH!
OKAY, LET'S HAVE A CONTEST TO SEE WHO STAYS!
ZZAT
ZZAK
ZZING
YOU'RE ON!
OKAY, READY?
ON YOUR MARKS, GET SET...

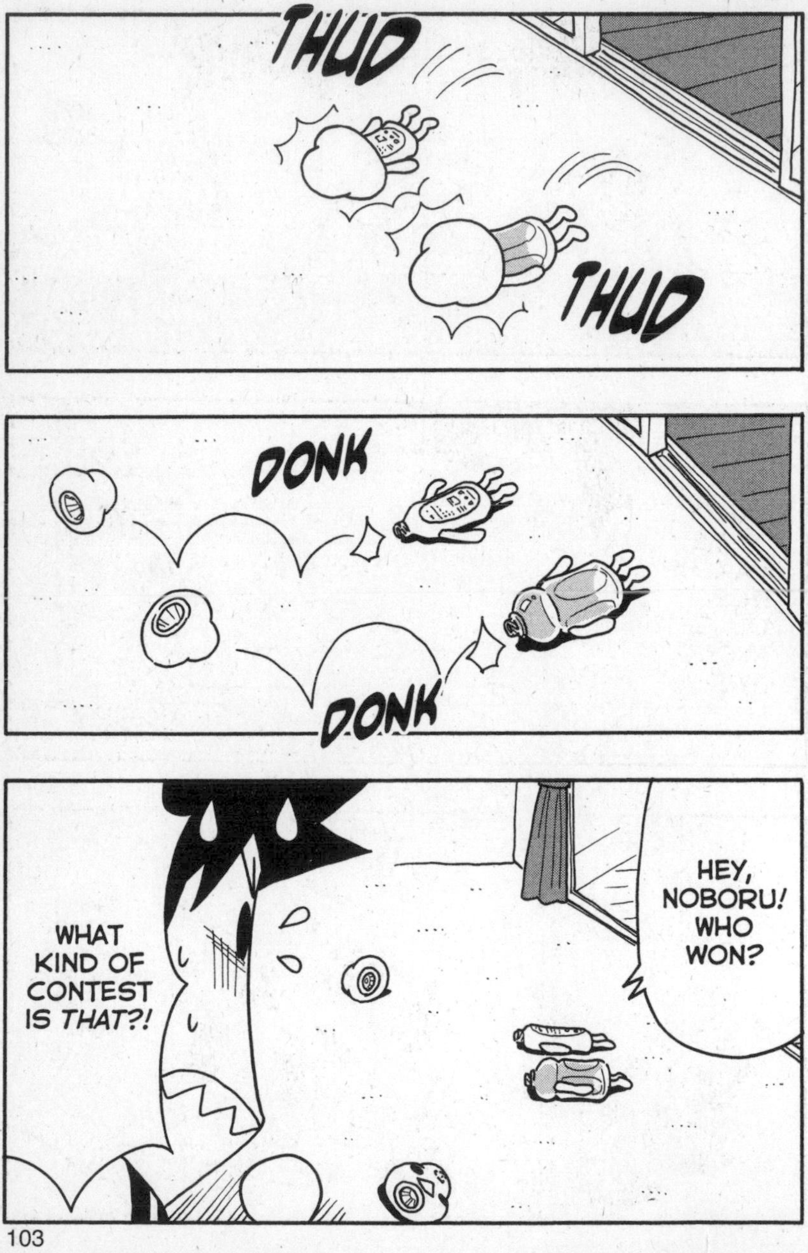
THUD
THUD
DONK
DONK
HEY, NOBORU! WHO WON?
WHAT KIND OF CONTEST IS *THAT?!*

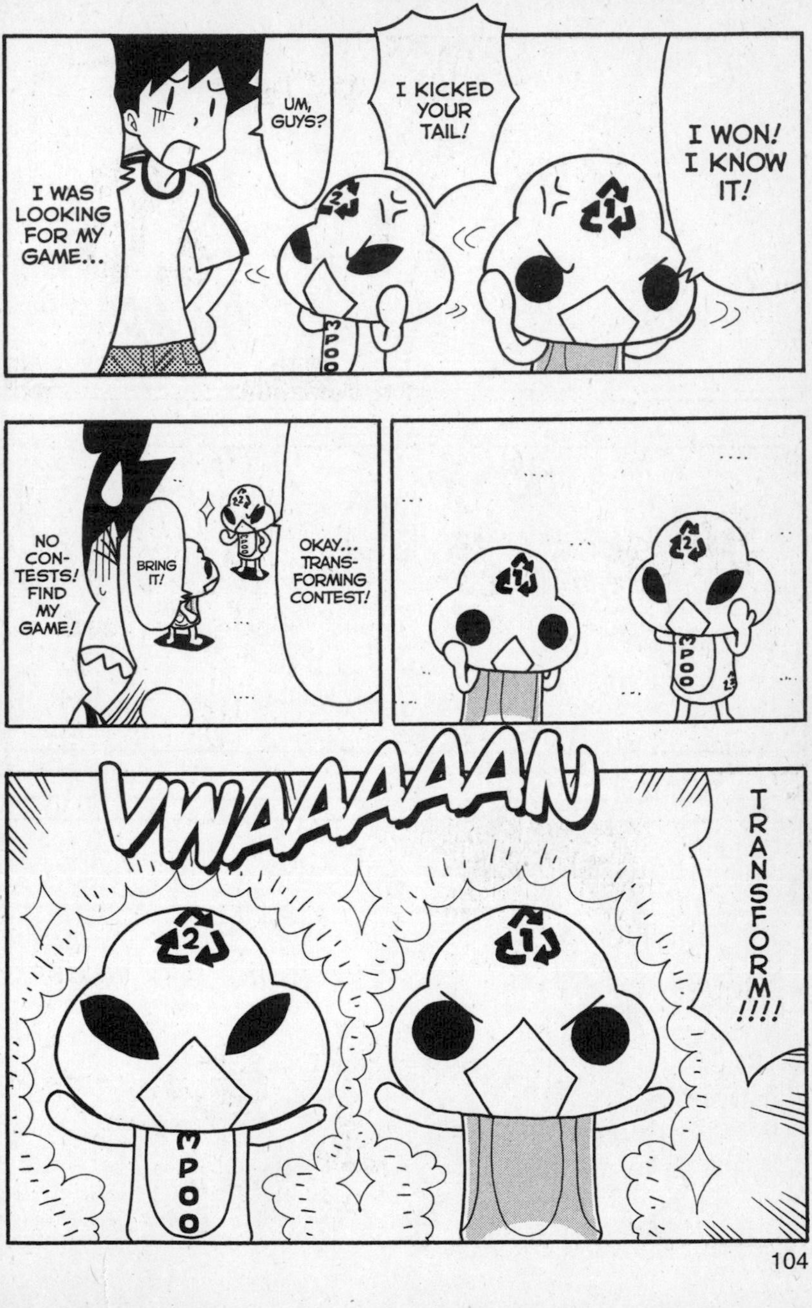
I WON! I KNOW IT!
I KICKED YOUR TAIL!
UM, GUYS?
I WAS LOOKING FOR MY GAME...
OKAY... TRANS-FORMING CONTEST!
BRING IT!
NO CON-TESTS! FIND MY GAME!
TRANSFORM!!!!
VWAAAAAN

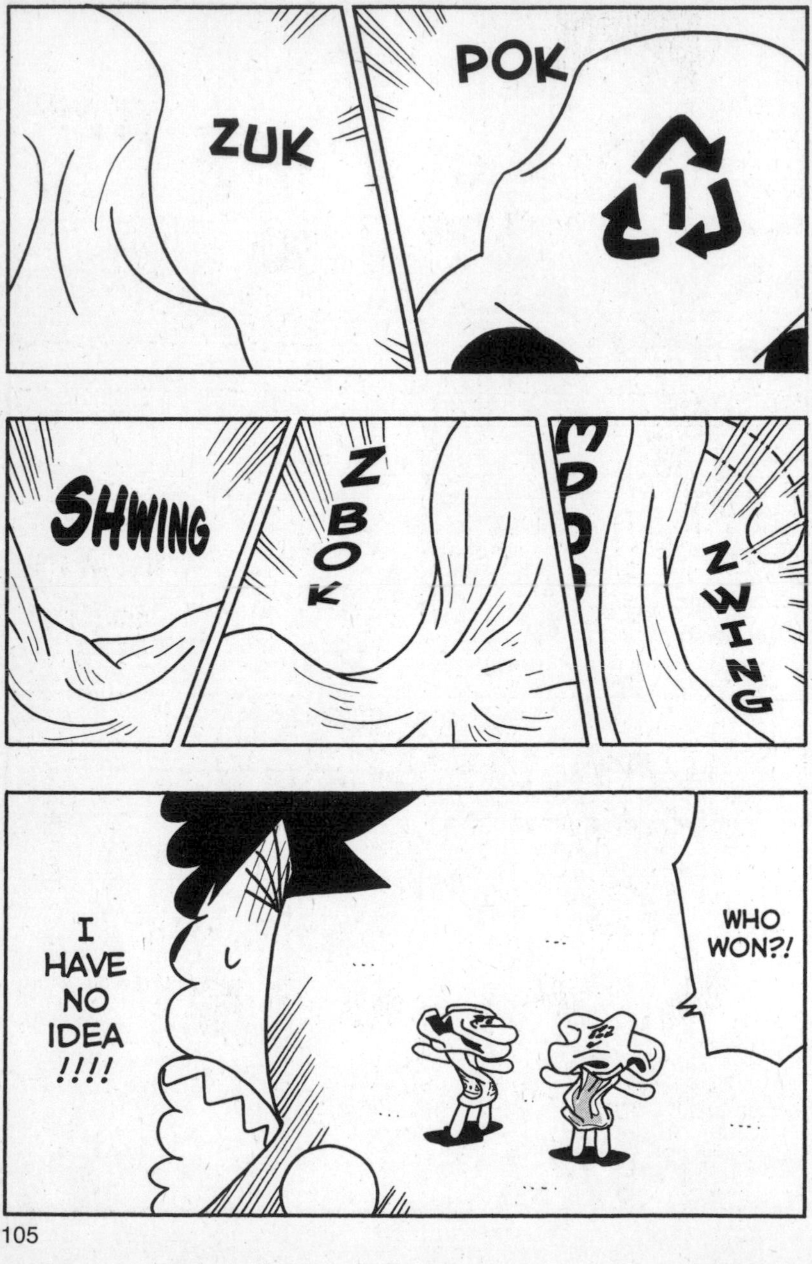
POK
ZUK
ZWING
ZBOK
SHWING
WHO WON?!
...
...
I HAVE NO IDEA !!!!

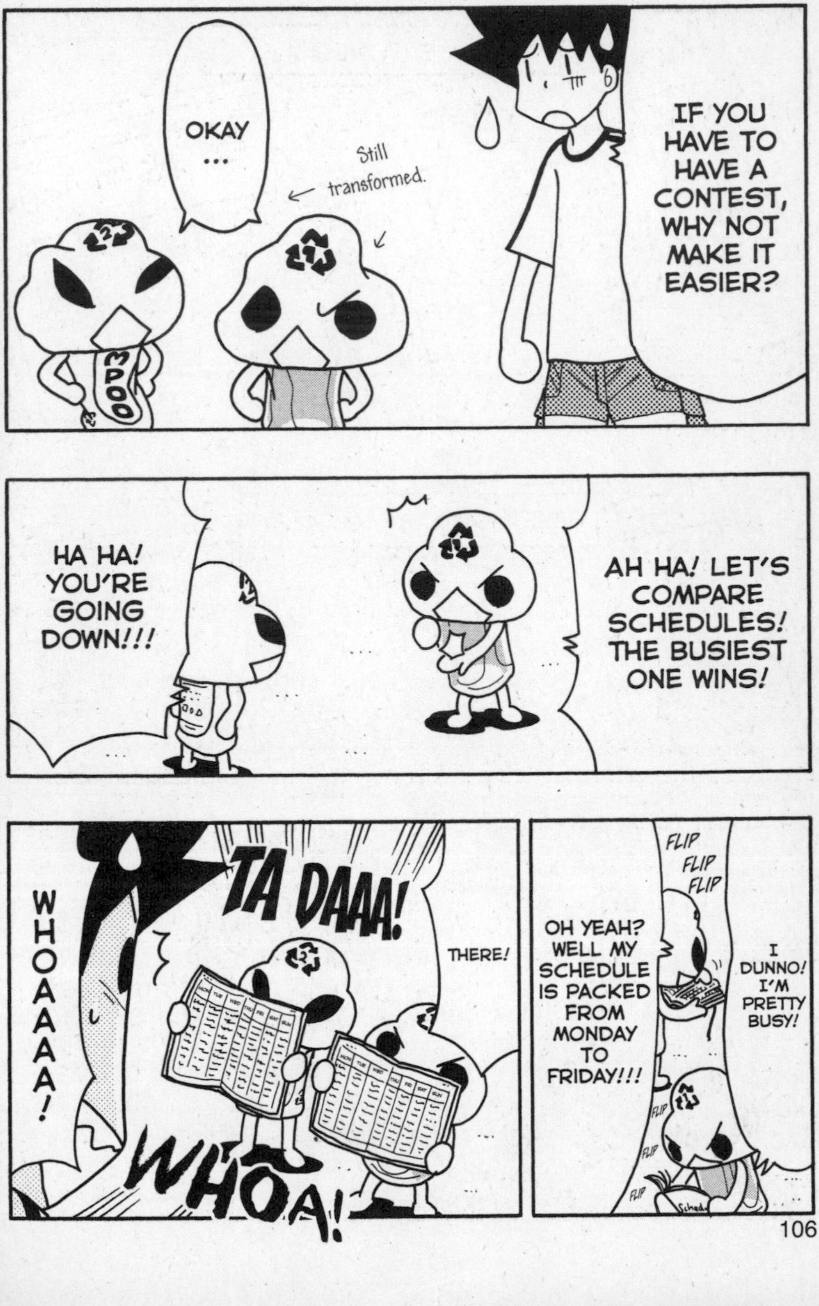
IF YOU HAVE TO HAVE A CONTEST, WHY NOT MAKE IT EASIER?
OKAY ...
Still transformed.
AH HA! LET'S COMPARE SCHEDULES! THE BUSIEST ONE WINS!
HA HA! YOU'RE GOING DOWN!!!
FLIP FLIP FLIP
I DUNNO! I'M PRETTY BUSY!
OH YEAH? WELL MY SCHEDULE IS PACKED FROM MONDAY TO FRIDAY!!!
FLIP FLIP FLIP
TA DAAA!
THERE!
WHOAAAA!
WHOA!

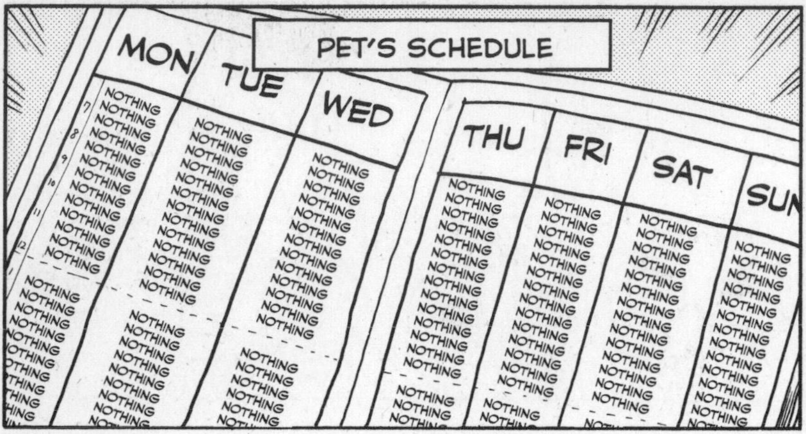
PET'S SCHEDULE
MON
TUE
WED
THU
FRI
SAT
SUN
7
8
9
10
11
12
NOTHING

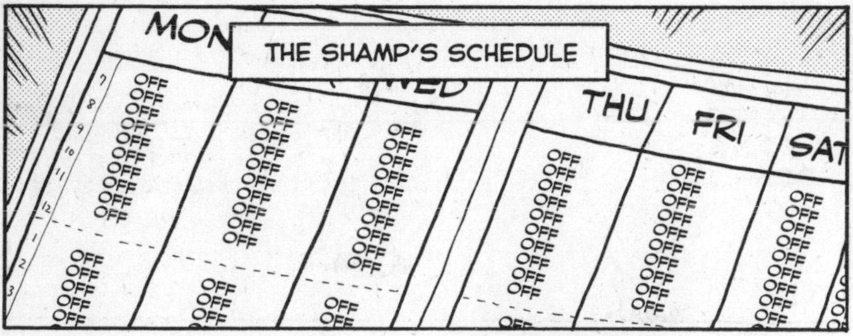
THE SHAMP'S SCHEDULE
MON
WED
THU
FRI
SAT
7
8
9
10
11
12
1
2
3
OFF

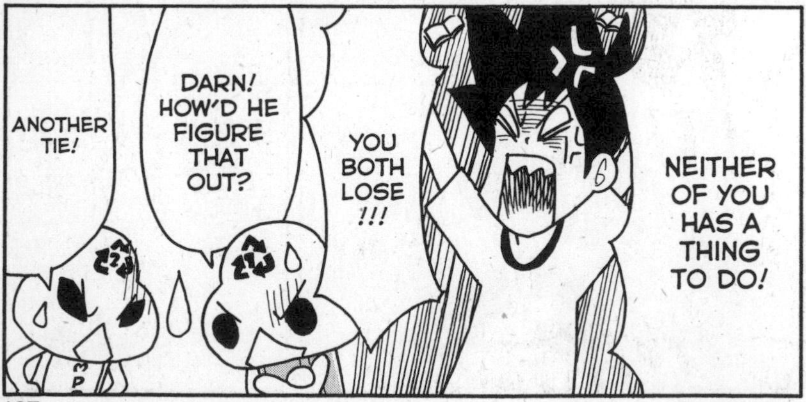
NEITHER OF YOU HAS A THING TO DO!
YOU BOTH LOSE!!!
DARN! HOW'D HE FIGURE THAT OUT?
ANOTHER TIE!

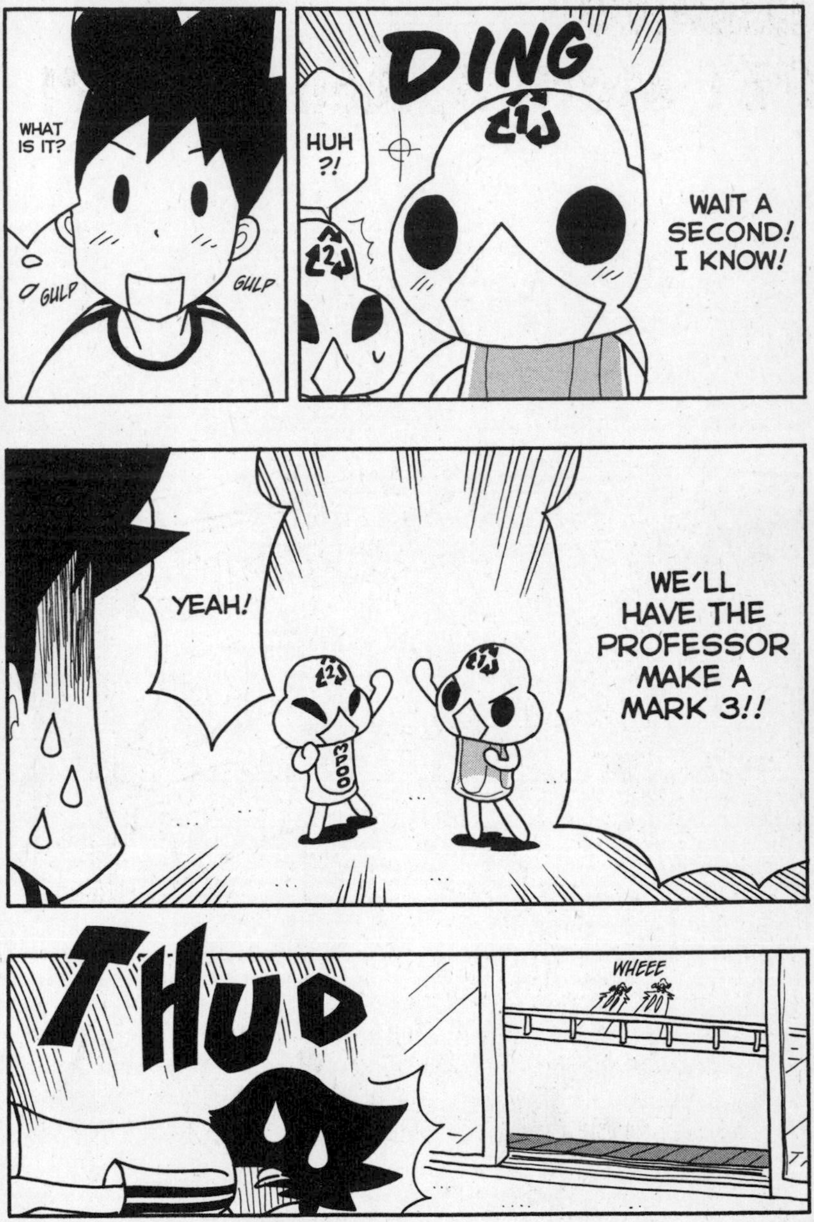
DING
WAIT A SECOND! I KNOW!
HUH ?!
WHAT IS IT?
GULP
GULP
WE'LL HAVE THE PROFESSOR MAKE A MARK 3!!
YEAH!
MPOO
WHEEE
THUD

## CHAPTER 11

# PET Mark 3, Reporting?!

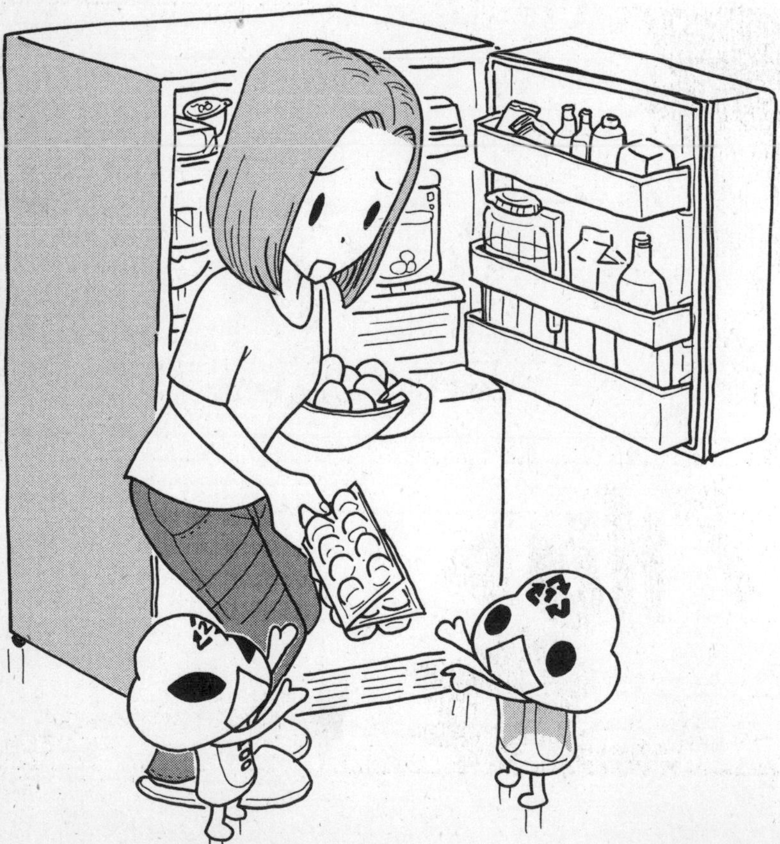

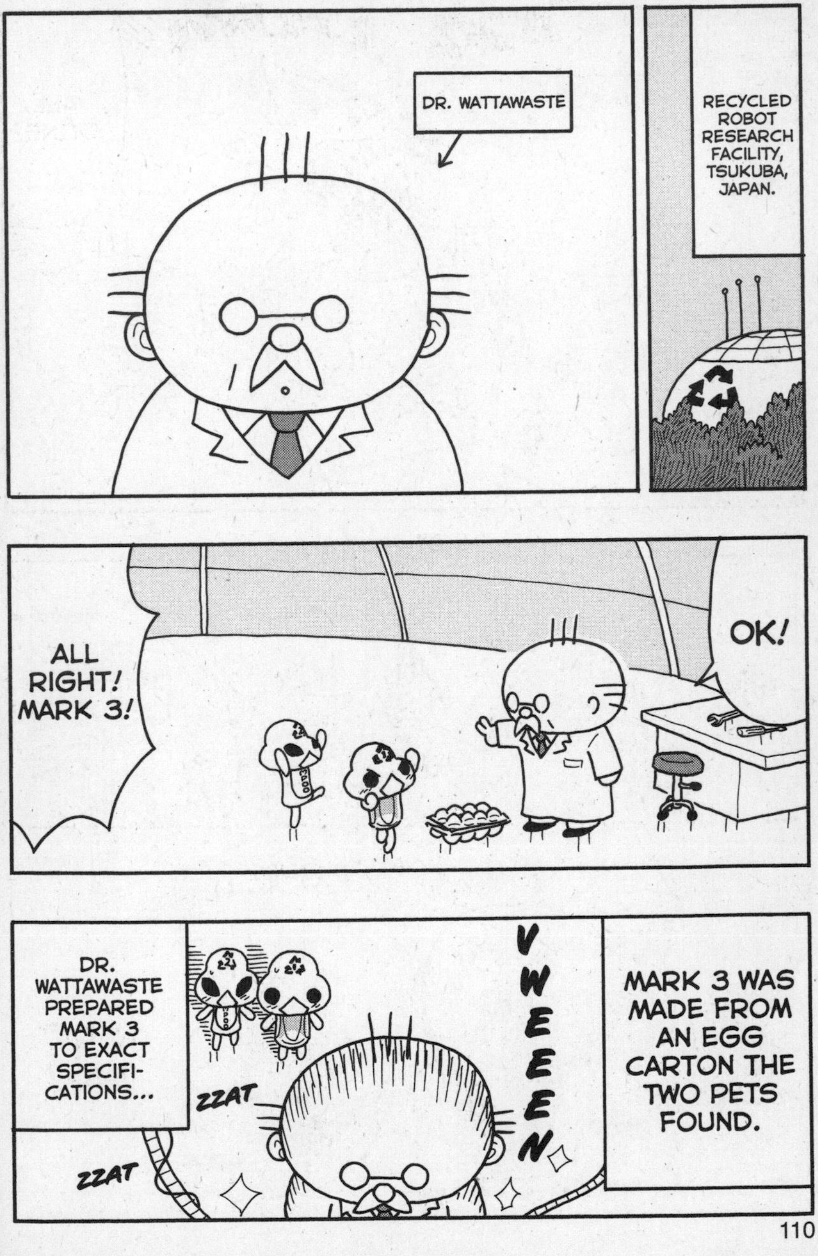
RECYCLED ROBOT RESEARCH FACILITY, TSUKUBA, JAPAN.
DR. WATTAWASTE
ALL RIGHT! MARK 3!
OK!
MARK 3 WAS MADE FROM AN EGG CARTON THE TWO PETS FOUND.
VWEEEN
ZZAT
DR. WATTAWASTE PREPARED MARK 3 TO EXACT SPECIFI-CATIONS...
ZZAT

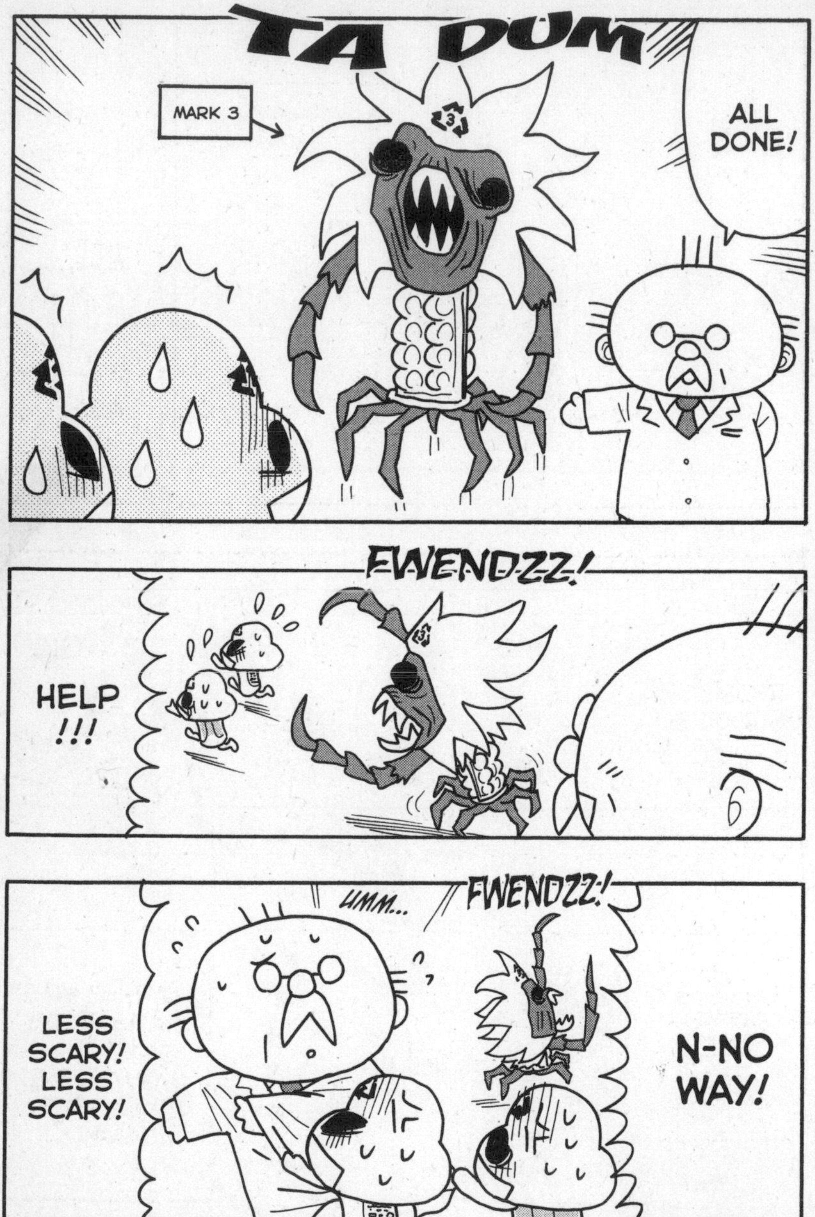
TA DUM
ALL DONE!
MARK 3
FWENDZZ!
HELP!!!
N-NO WAY!
FWENDZZ!
UMM...
LESS SCARY! LESS SCARY!

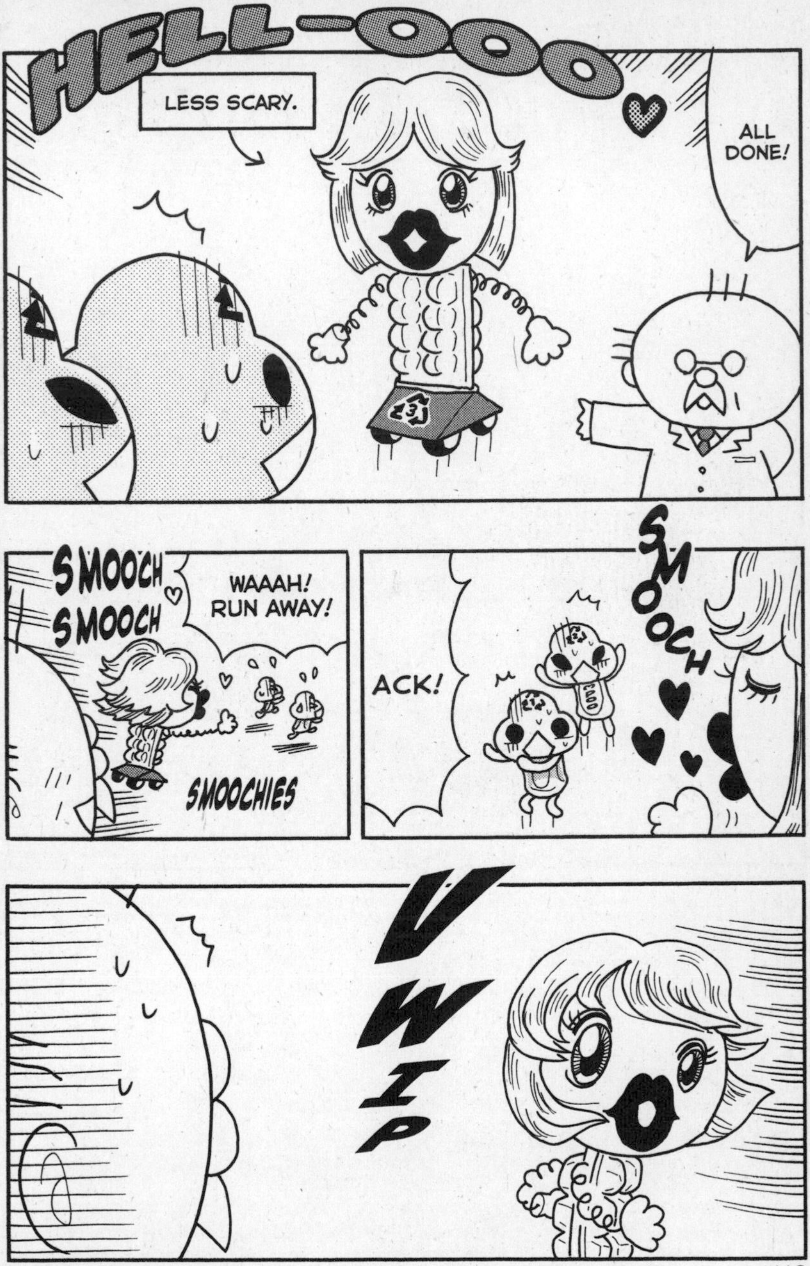
ALL DONE!
HELL-OOO ♥
LESS SCARY.
SMOOCH
ACK!
WAAAH! RUN AWAY!
SMOOCH SMOOCH
SMOOCHIES
VWIP

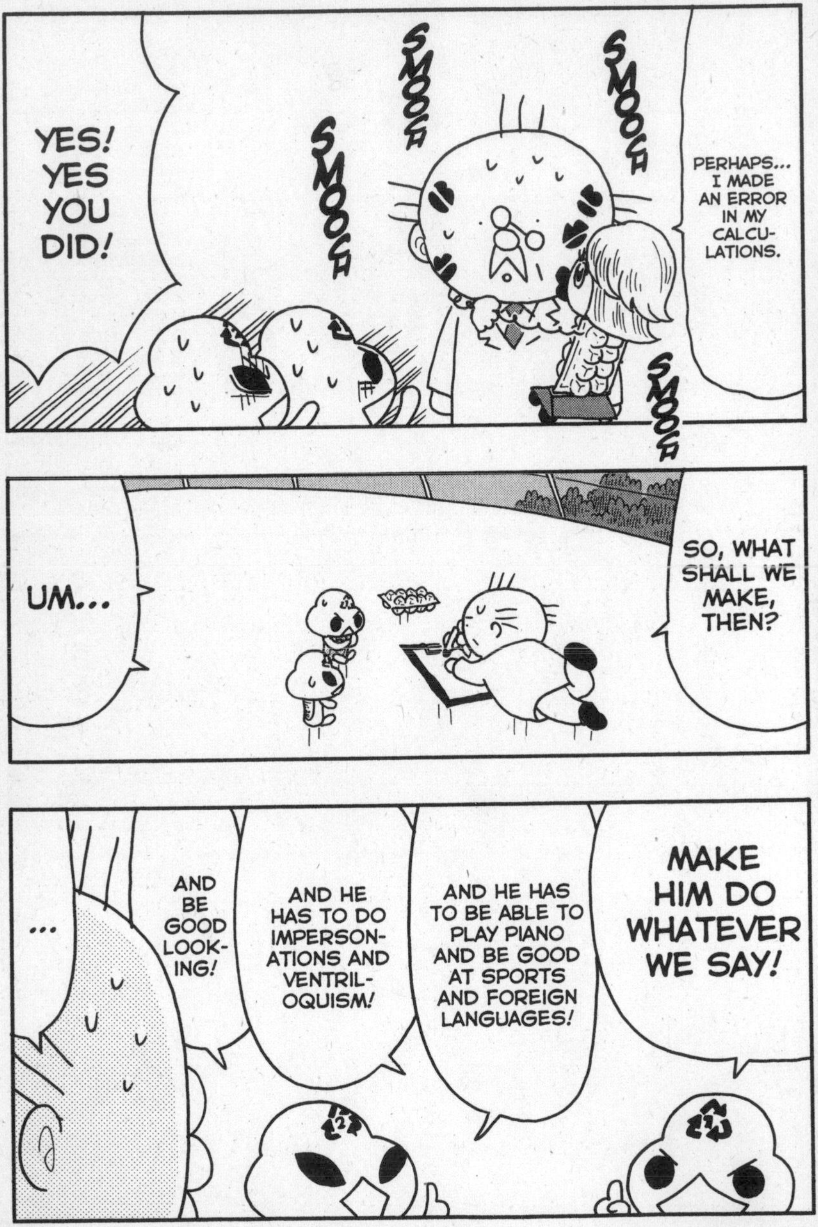
PERHAPS... I MADE AN ERROR IN MY CALCU-LATIONS.
SMOOCH
SMOOCH
SMOOCH
SMOOCH
YES! YES YOU DID!
SO, WHAT SHALL WE MAKE, THEN?
UM...
MAKE HIM DO WHATEVER WE SAY!
AND HE HAS TO BE ABLE TO PLAY PIANO AND BE GOOD AT SPORTS AND FOREIGN LANGUAGES!
AND HE HAS TO DO IMPERSON-ATIONS AND VENTRIL-OQUISM!
AND BE GOOD LOOK-ING!
...

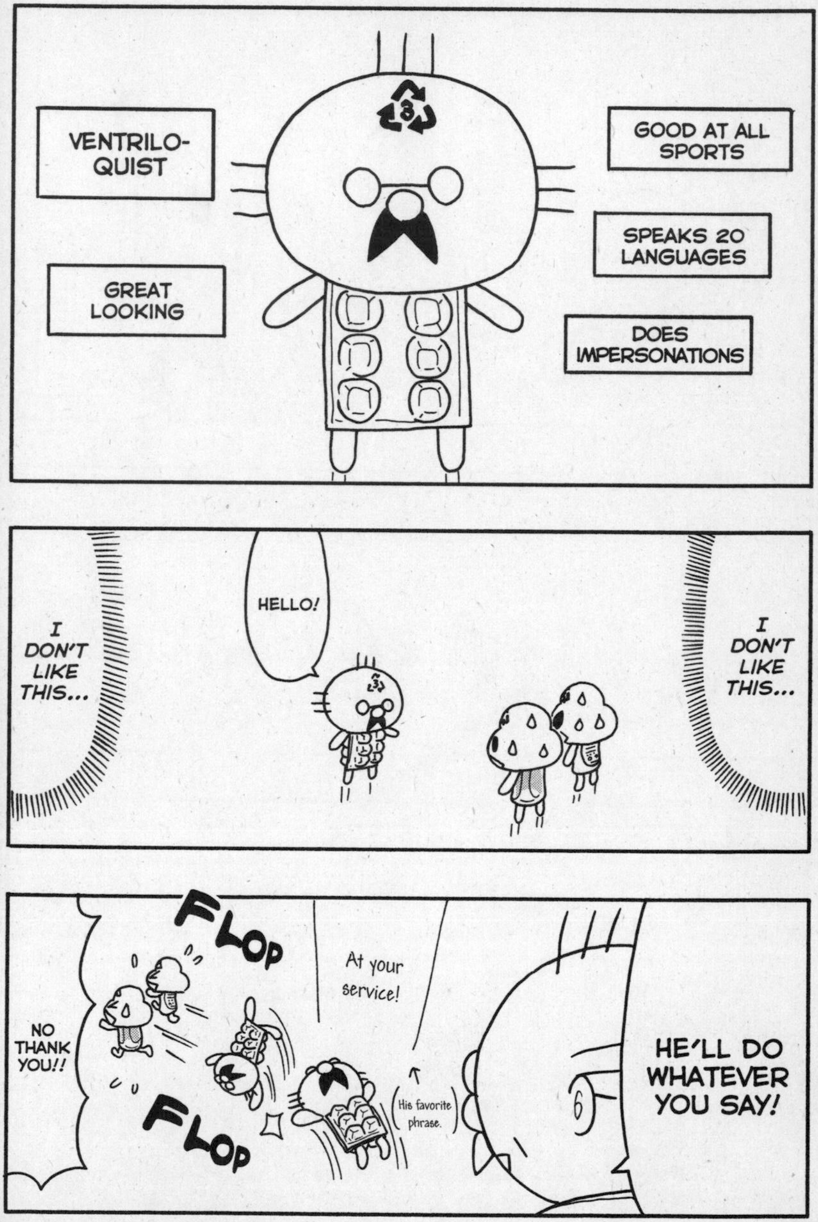
GOOD AT ALL SPORTS
SPEAKS 20 LANGUAGES
DOES IMPERSONATIONS
VENTRILO-QUIST
GREAT LOOKING
I DON'T LIKE THIS...
HELLO!
I DON'T LIKE THIS...
HE'LL DO WHATEVER YOU SAY!
His favorite phrase.
At your service!
FLOP
FLOP
NO THANK YOU!!

# CHAPTER 12 It's Soccer Time, PET!

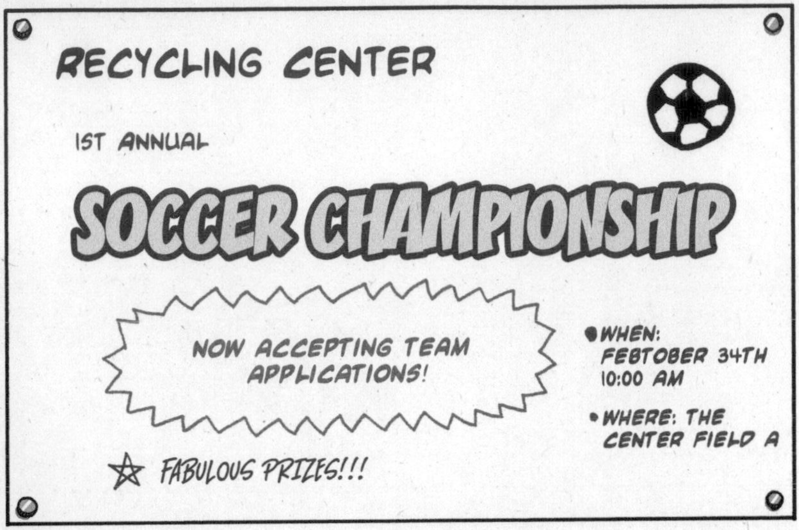
RECYCLING CENTER
1ST ANNUAL
SOCCER CHAMPIONSHIP
NOW ACCEPTING TEAM APPLICATIONS!
• WHEN: FEBTOBER 34TH 10:00 AM
• WHERE: THE CENTER FIELD A
FABULOUS PRIZES!!!

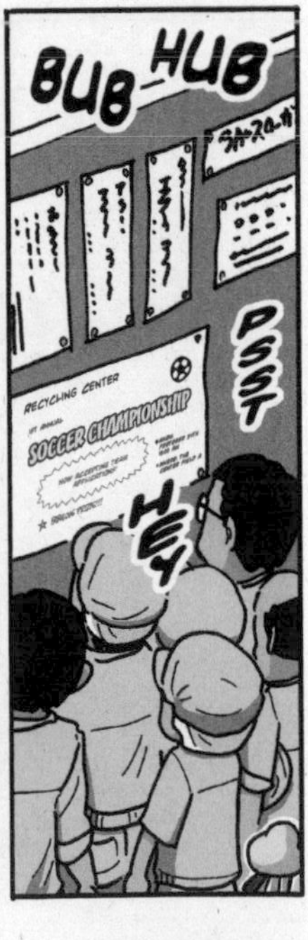
BUB HUB
RECYCLING CENTER
SOCCER CHAMPIONSHIP
PSST
HEY

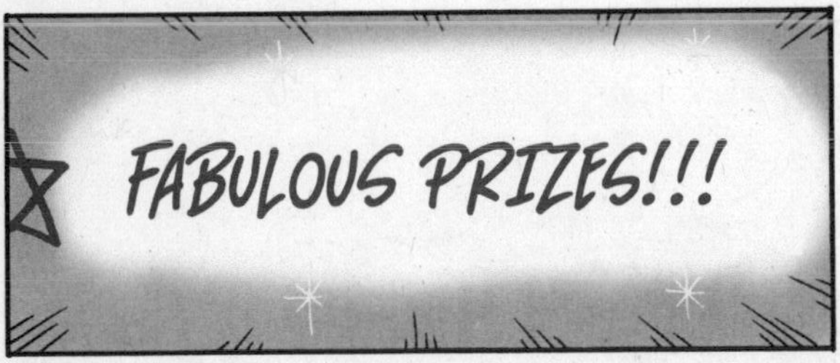
FABULOUS PRIZES!!!

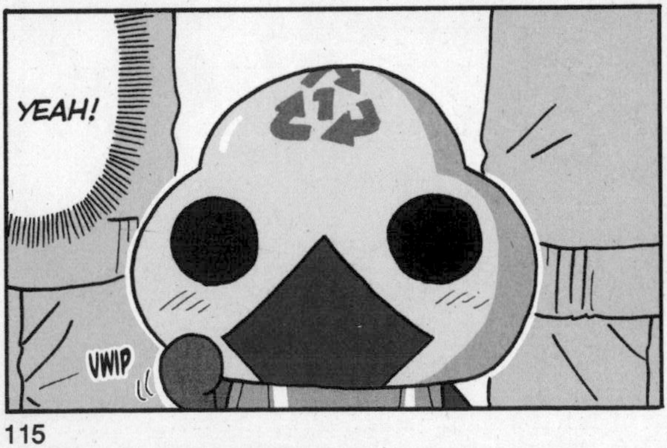
YEAH!
VWIP

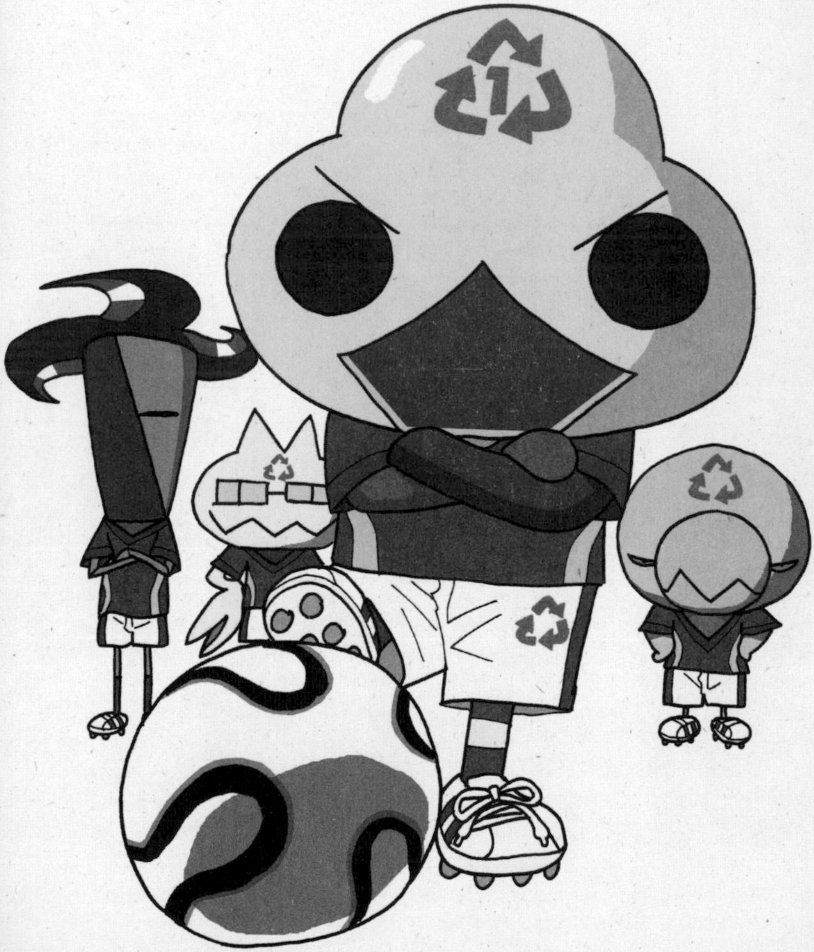

CHAPTER 12

# It's Soccer Time, PET!

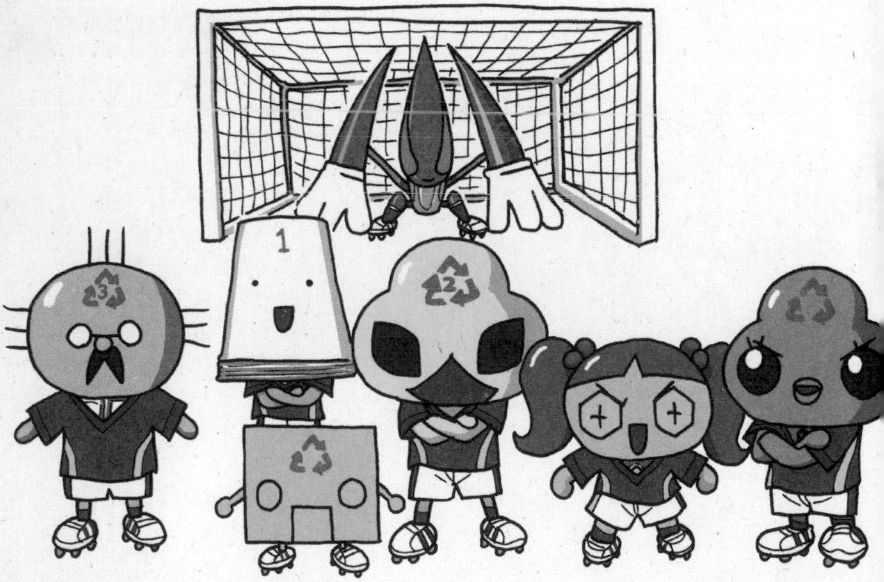

1

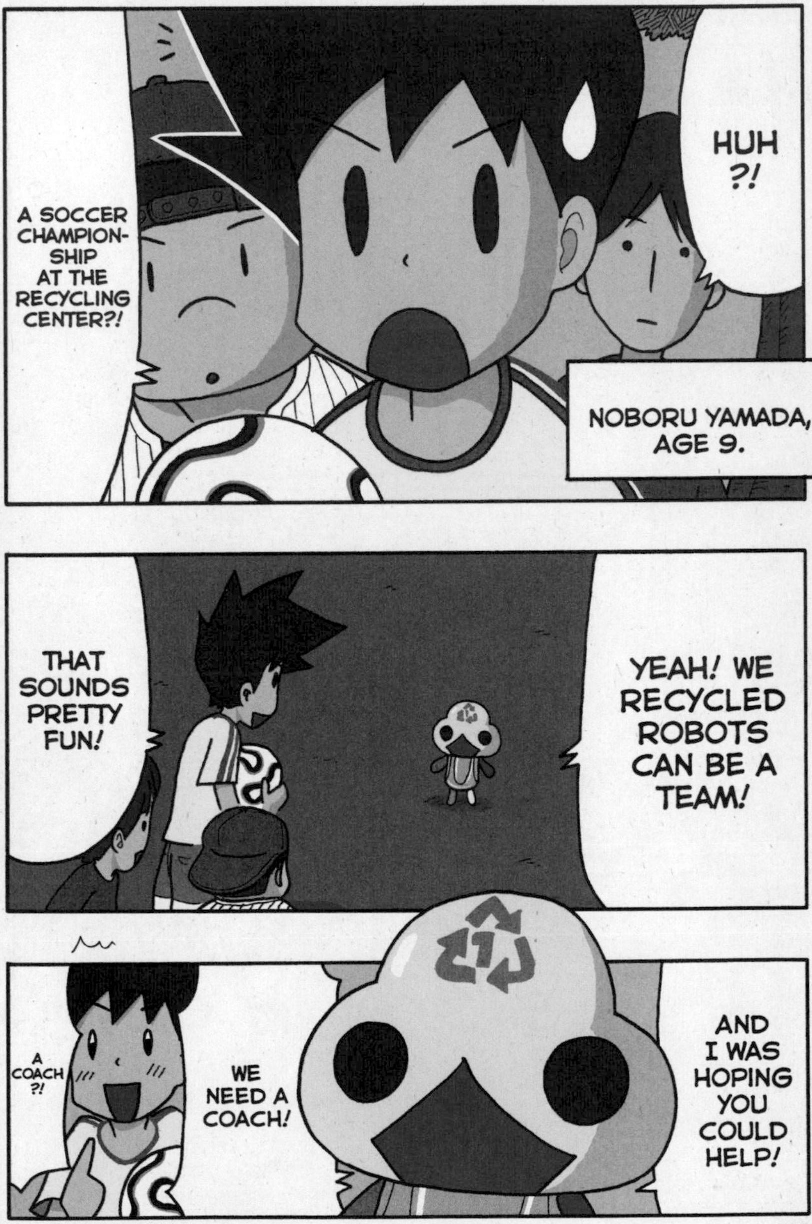
HUH ?!
NOBORU YAMADA, AGE 9.
A SOCCER CHAMPIONSHIP AT THE RECYCLING CENTER?!
YEAH! WE RECYCLED ROBOTS CAN BE A TEAM!
THAT SOUNDS PRETTY FUN!
AND I WAS HOPING YOU COULD HELP!
WE NEED A COACH!
A COACH ?!

I GUESS WE COULD DO THAT...
GUYS?
YEAH!
RIGHT! WE CAN BE HELPFUL FOR A CHANGE!
HEH
YAAHOO!
FABULOUS PRIZES !!!!
PRIZES?
OH, ER, NOTHING !!
SO... DO YOU HAVE A TEAM?
'COURSE!
VWIP

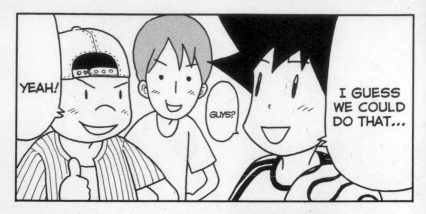

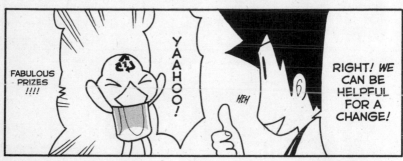

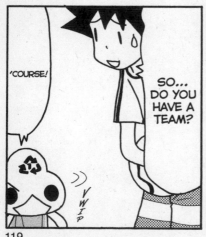

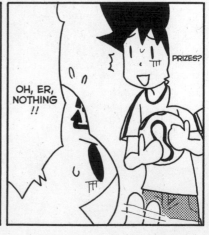

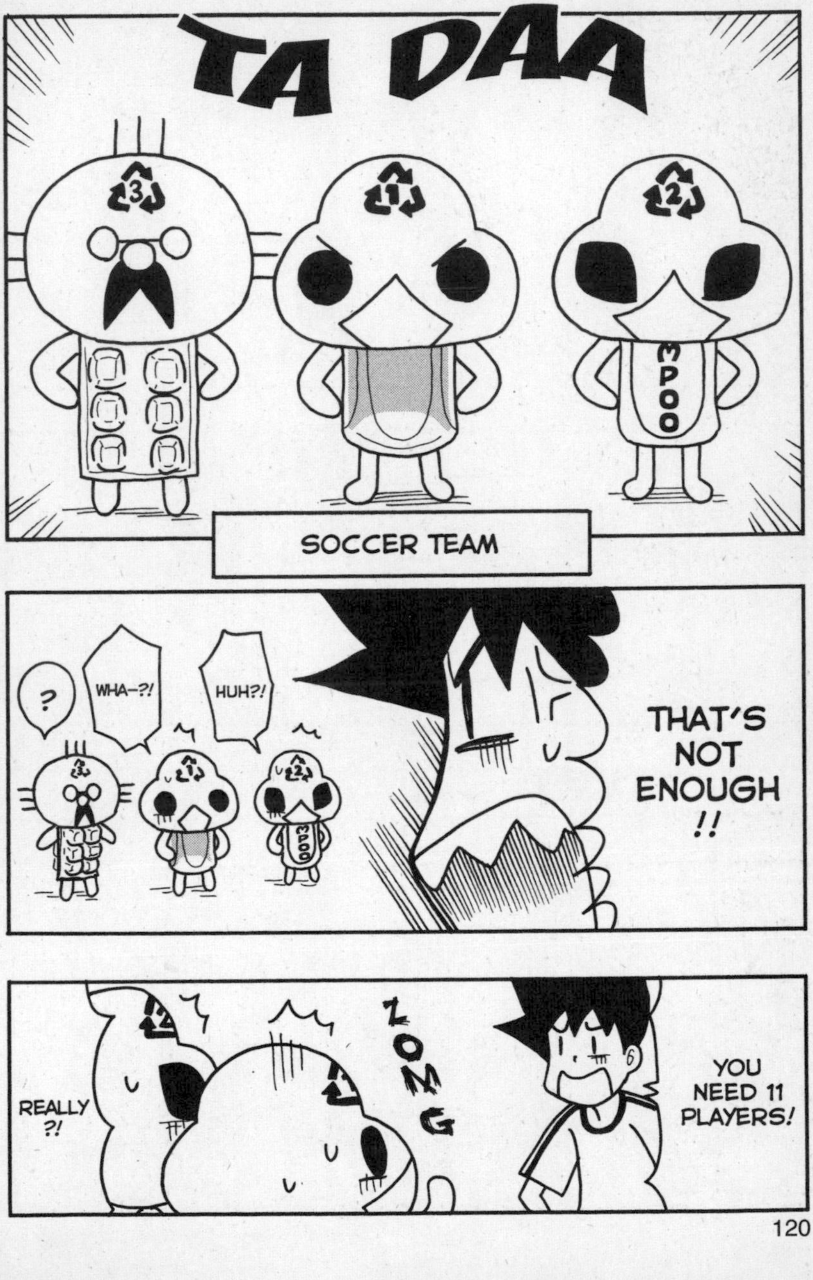
TA DAA
SOCCER TEAM
THAT'S NOT ENOUGH !!
HUH?!
WHA-?!
?
YOU NEED 11 PLAYERS!
ZOMG
REALLY ?!

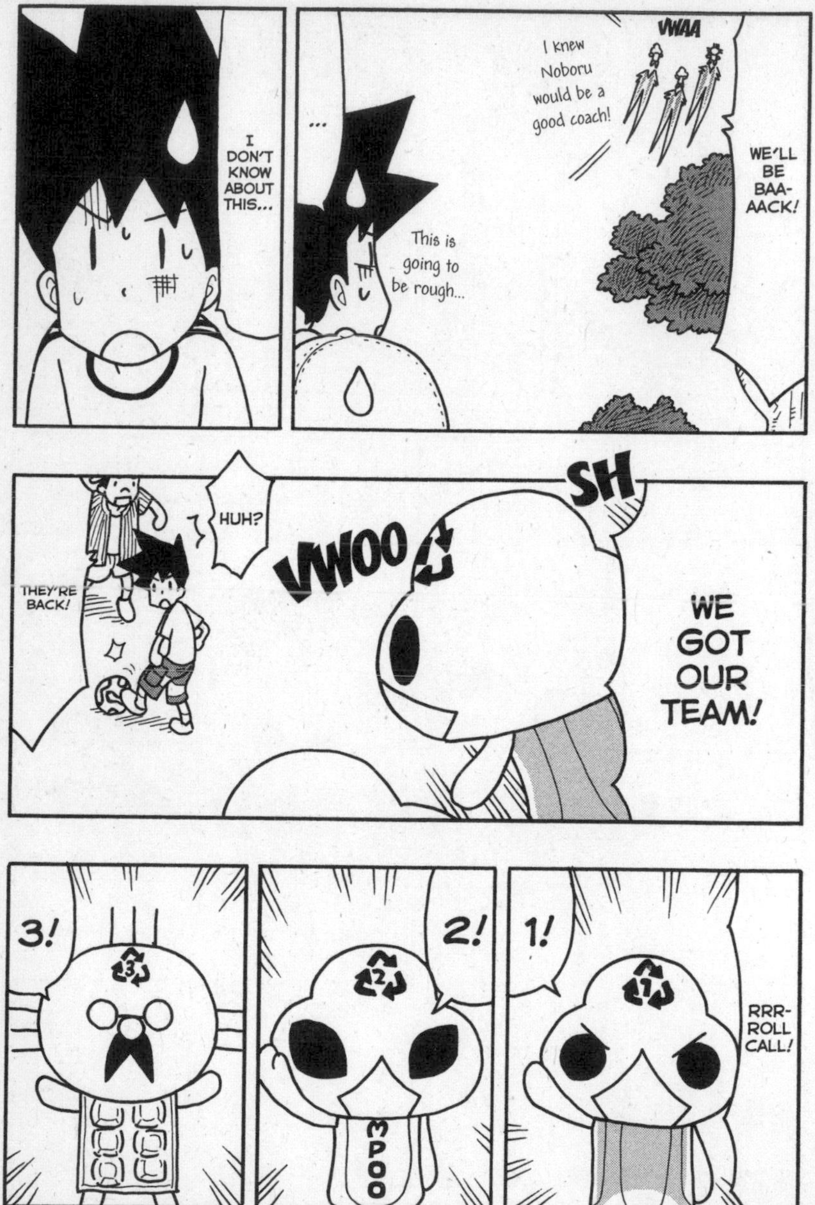
VWAA
WE'LL BE BAA-AACK!
I knew Noboru would be a good coach!
...
This is going to be rough...
I DON'T KNOW ABOUT THIS...
SH
VWOO
WE GOT OUR TEAM!
HUH?
THEY'RE BACK!
RRR-ROLL CALL!
1!
2!
MPOO
3!

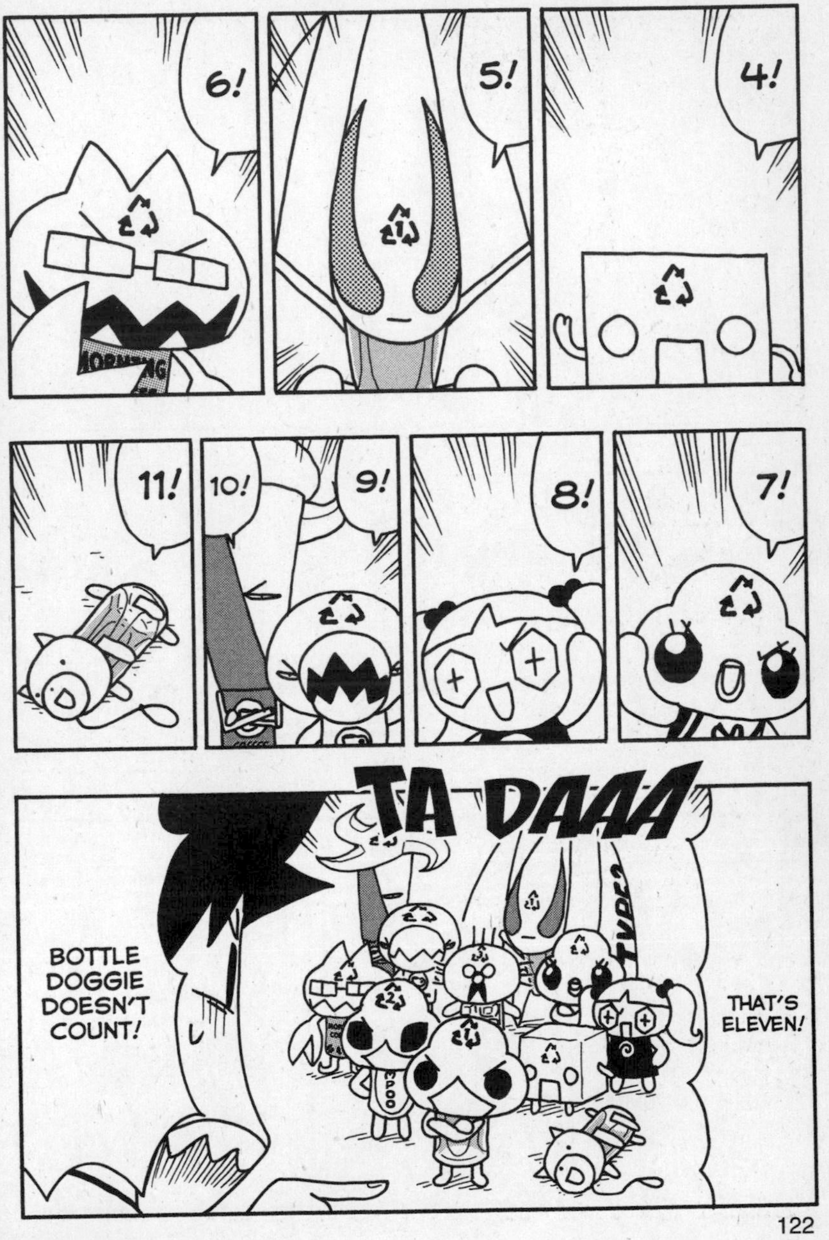
4!
5!
6!
7!
8!
9!
10!
11!
TA DAAA
THAT'S ELEVEN!
BOTTLE DOGGIE DOESN'T COUNT!

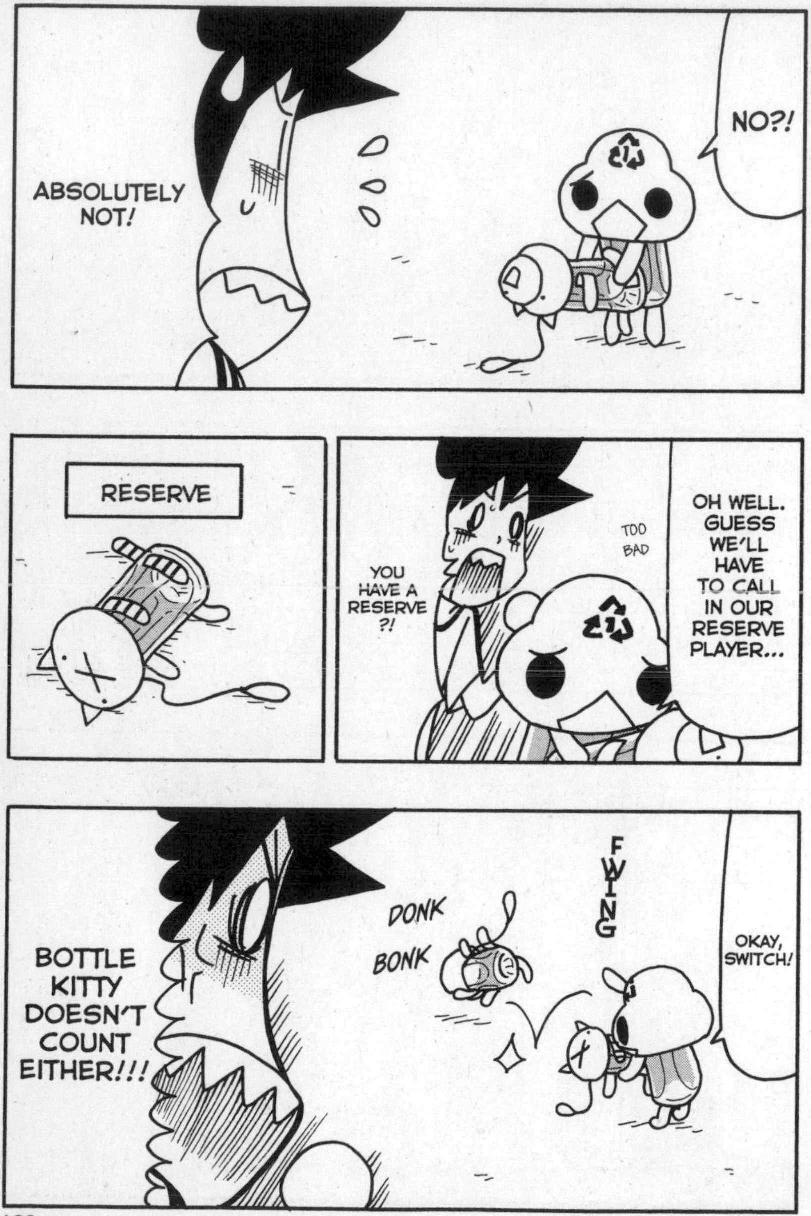
NO?!
ABSOLUTELY NOT!
OH WELL. GUESS WE'LL HAVE TO CALL IN OUR RESERVE PLAYER...
TOO BAD
YOU HAVE A RESERVE?!
RESERVE
OKAY, SWITCH!
FWING
DONK
BONK
BOTTLE KITTY DOESN'T COUNT EITHER!!!

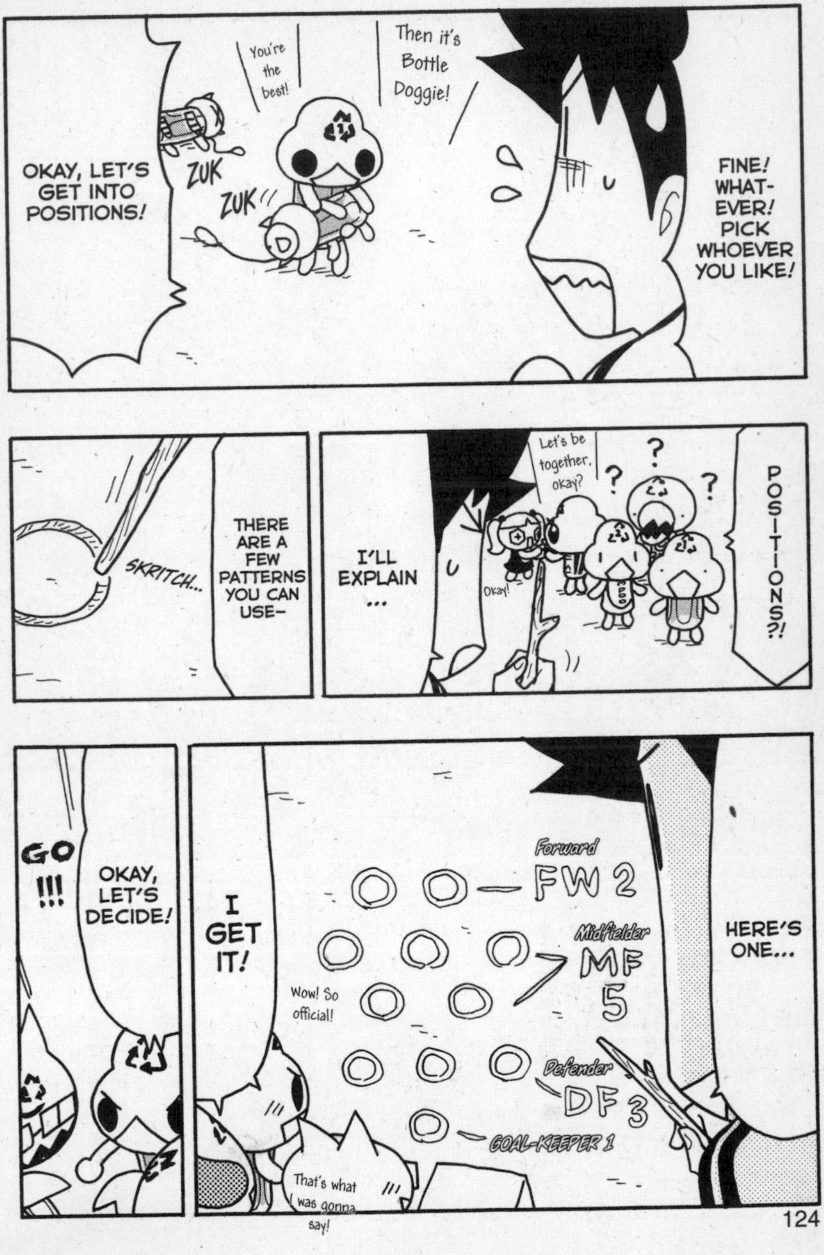

FINE! WHAT-EVER! PICK WHOEVER YOU LIKE!
Then it's Bottle Doggie!
You're the best!
ZUK
ZUK
OKAY, LET'S GET INTO POSITIONS!
POSITIONS?!
?
?
?
Let's be together, okay?
Okay!
I'LL EXPLAIN...
THERE ARE A FEW PATTERNS YOU CAN USE-
SKRITCH...
HERE'S ONE...
Forward
FW 2
Midfielder
MF 5
Defender
DF 3
GOAL-KEEPER 1
I GET IT!
Wow! So official!
That's what I was gonna say!
OKAY, LET'S DECIDE!
GO!!!

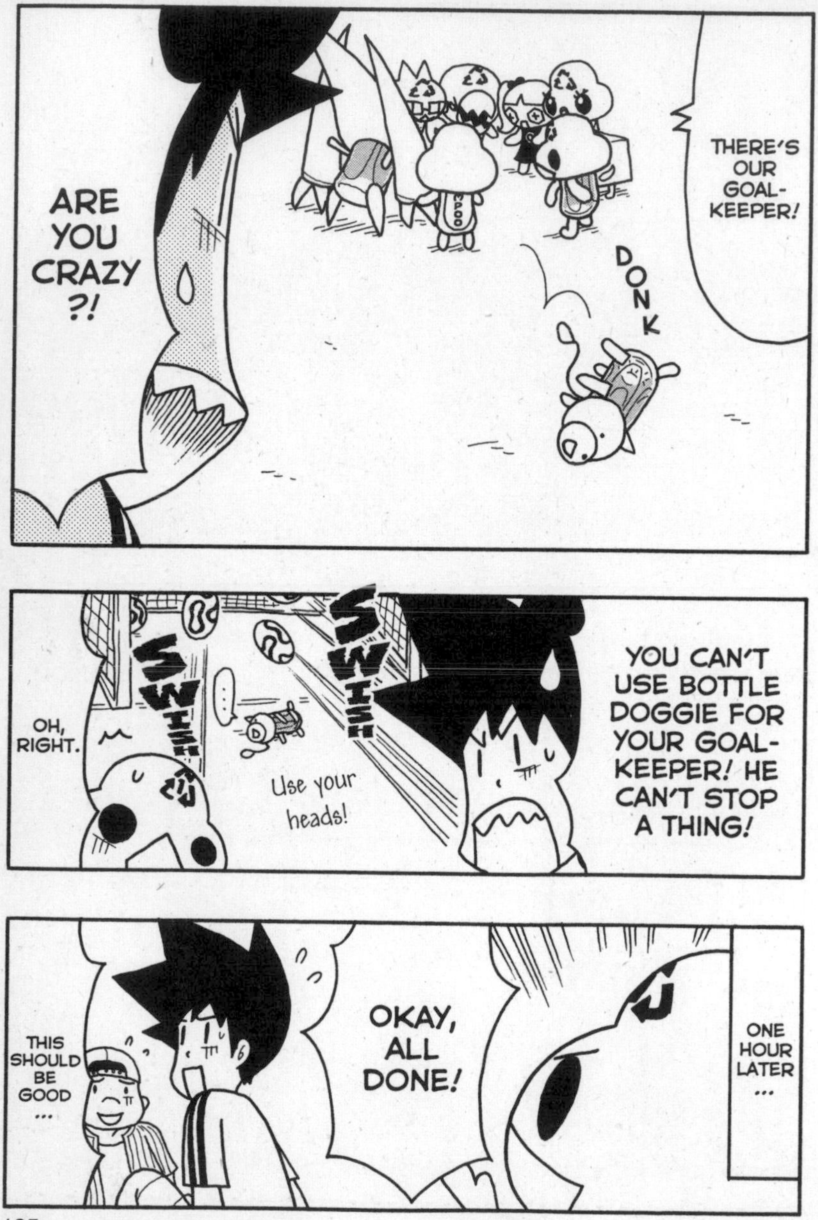
THERE'S OUR GOAL-KEEPER!
DONK
ARE YOU CRAZY?!
YOU CAN'T USE BOTTLE DOGGIE FOR YOUR GOAL-KEEPER! HE CAN'T STOP A THING!
SWISH
SWISH
...
Use your heads!
OH, RIGHT.
ONE HOUR LATER ...
OKAY, ALL DONE!
THIS SHOULD BE GOOD ...

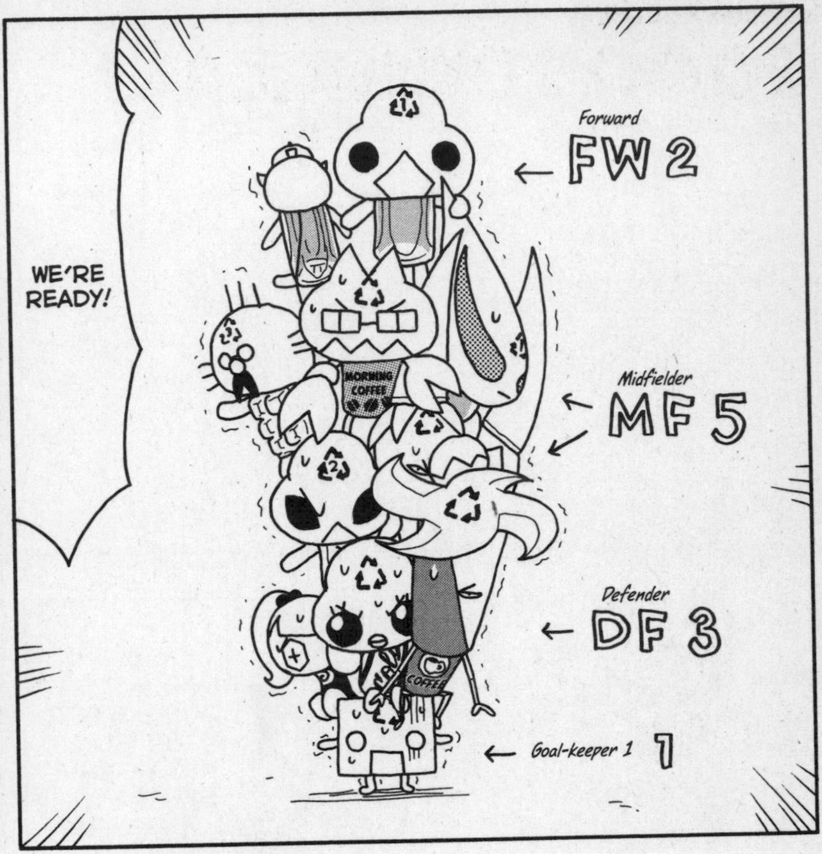
WE'RE READY!
Forward
FW 2
Midfielder
MF 5
Defender
DF 3
Goal-keeper 1
1

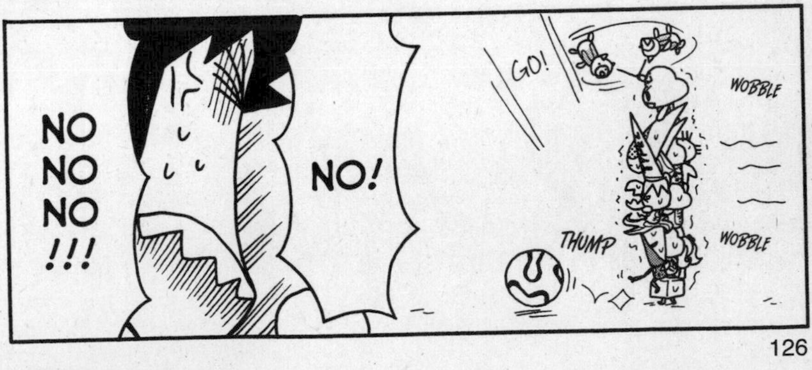
GO!
WOBBLE
WOBBLE
THUMP
NO!
NO NO NO !!!

# CHAPTER 13
# GOOOOOOAAAAL!

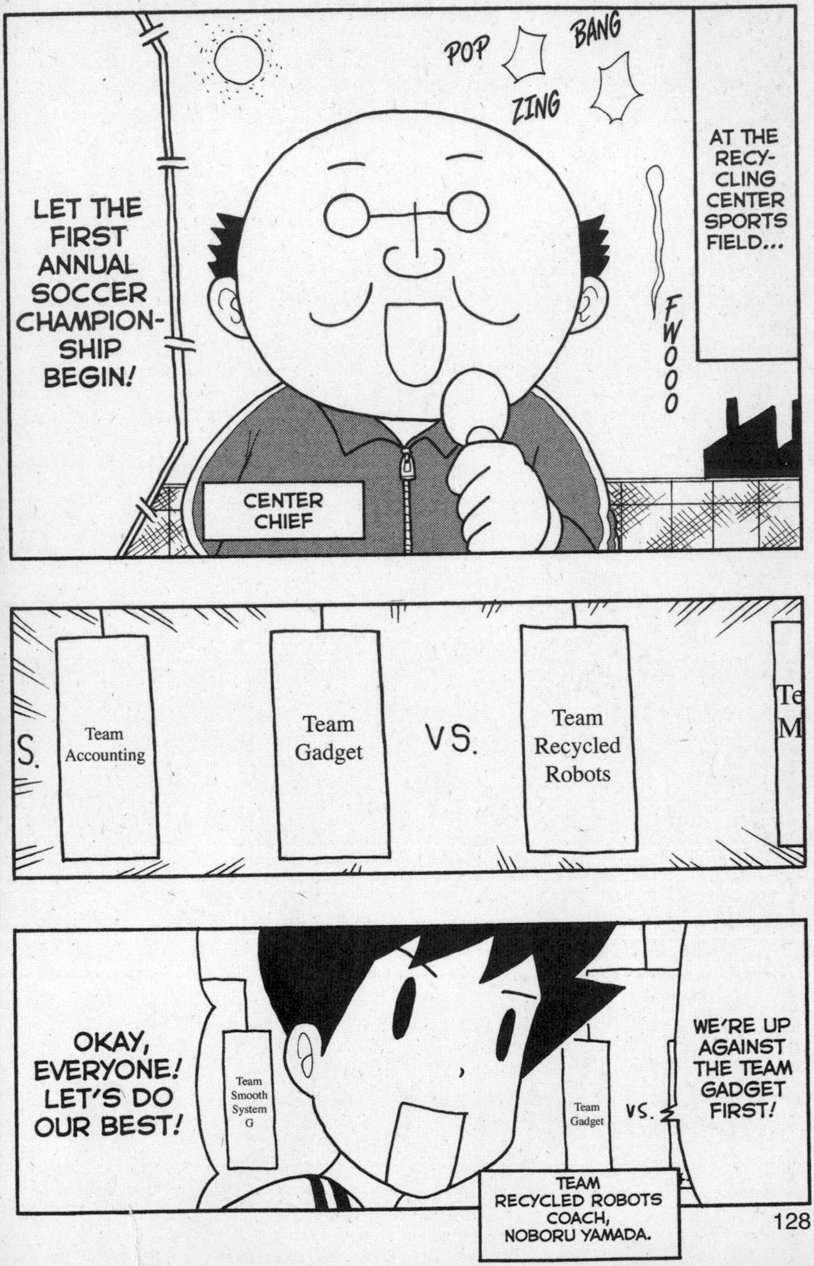
AT THE RECYCLING CENTER SPORTS FIELD...
BANG
POP
ZING
FWOOO
LET THE FIRST ANNUAL SOCCER CHAMPIONSHIP BEGIN!
CENTER CHIEF
Team Recycled Robots
VS.
Team Gadget
Team Accounting
WE'RE UP AGAINST THE TEAM GADGET FIRST!
VS.
Team Gadget
Team Smooth System G
OKAY, EVERYONE! LET'S DO OUR BEST!
TEAM RECYCLED ROBOTS COACH, NOBORU YAMADA.

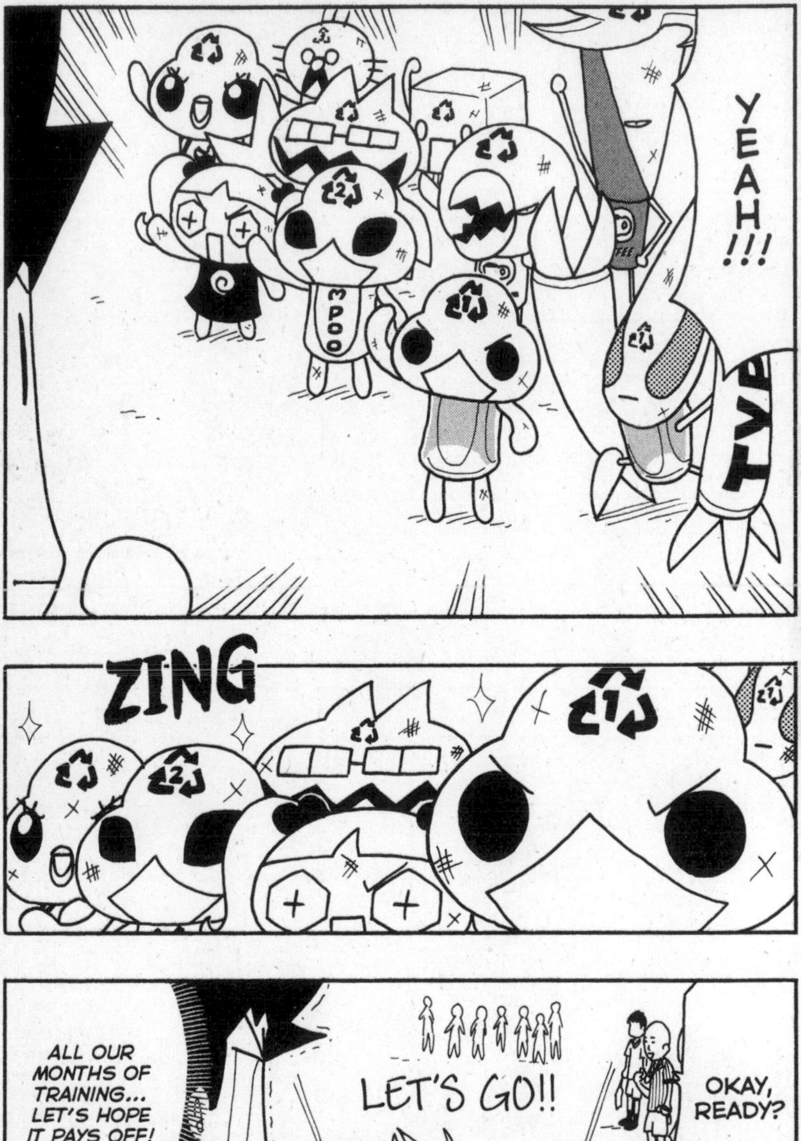
YEAH!!!
ZING
OKAY, READY?
LET'S GO!!
ALL OUR MONTHS OF TRAINING... LET'S HOPE IT PAYS OFF!

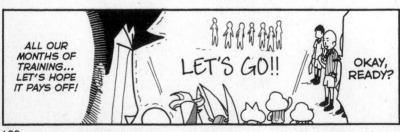

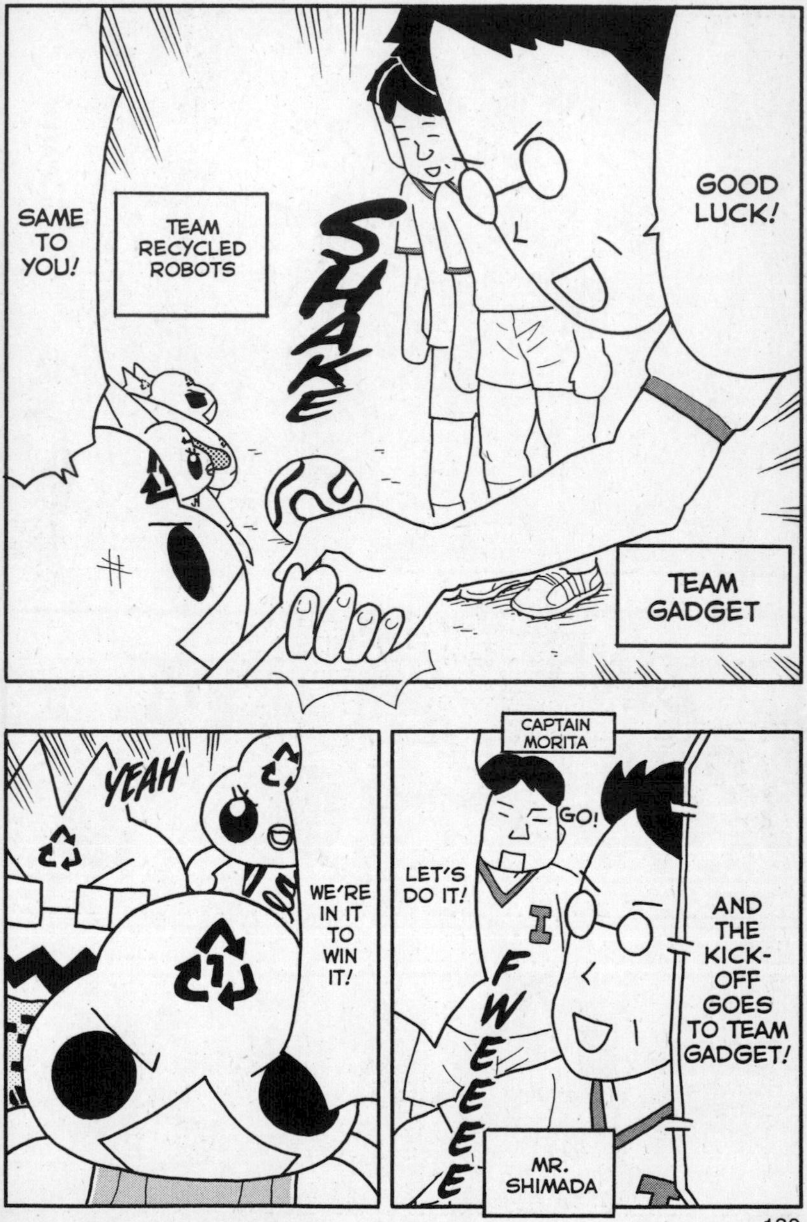
GOOD LUCK!
SHAKE
TEAM RECYCLED ROBOTS
SAME TO YOU!
TEAM GADGET
CAPTAIN MORITA
AND THE KICK-OFF GOES TO TEAM GADGET!
GO!
LET'S DO IT!
FWEEEEEE
MR. SHIMADA
YEAH
WE'RE IN IT TO WIN IT!

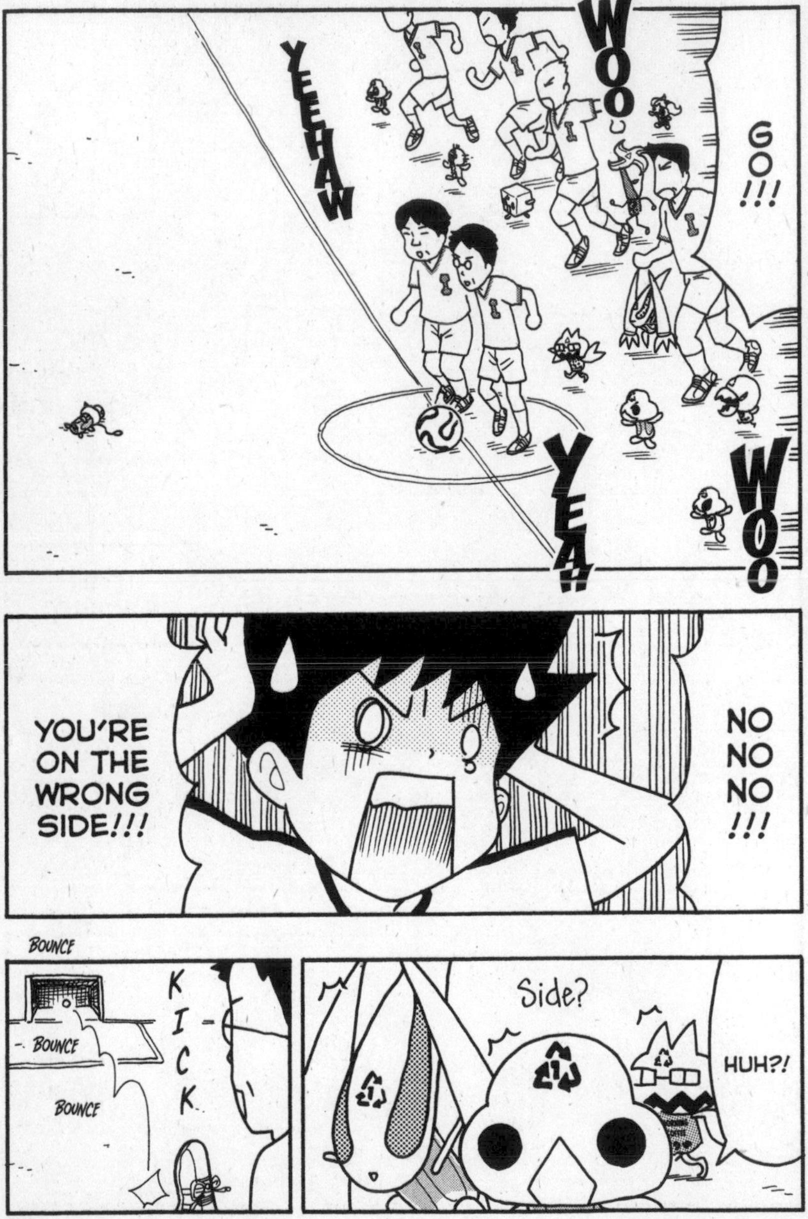
GO!!!
WOO
YEEHAW
WOO
YEA!!
NO NO NO!!!
YOU'RE ON THE WRONG SIDE!!!
HUH?!
Side?
BOUNCE
KICK
BOUNCE
BOUNCE

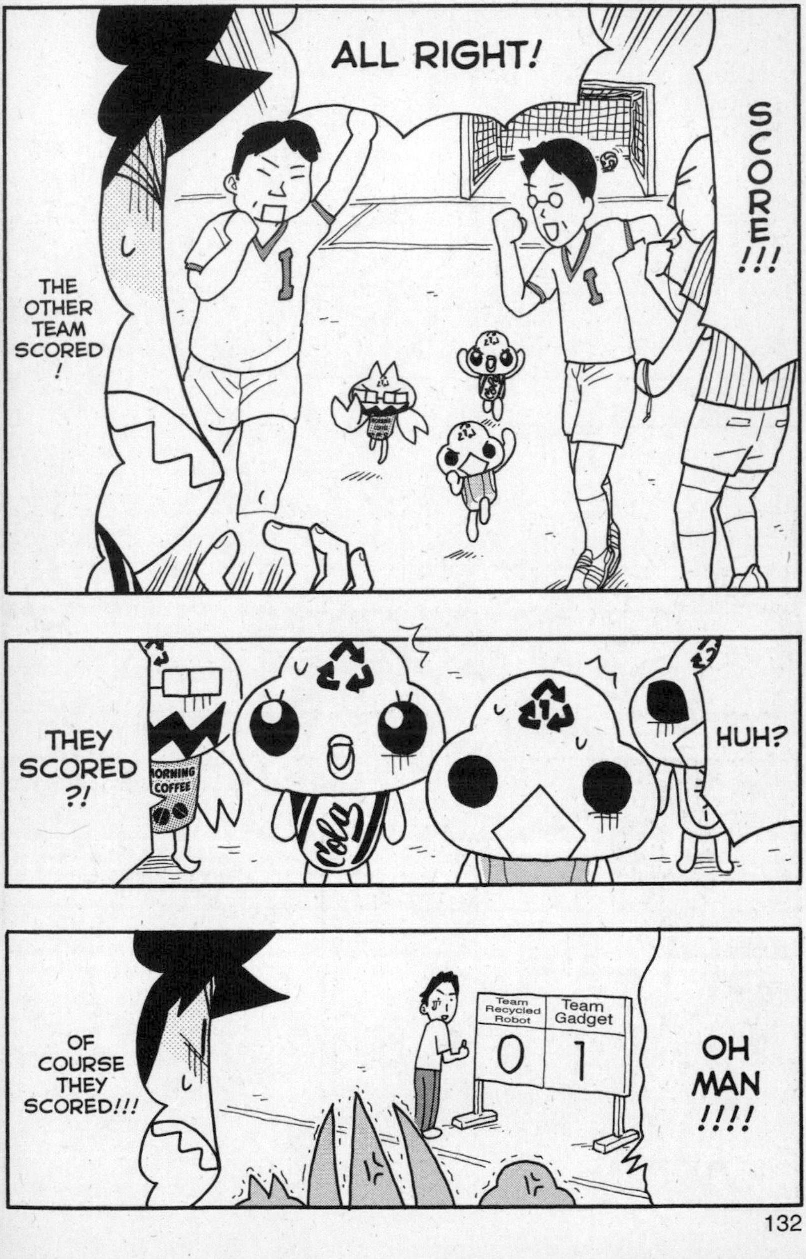
ALL RIGHT!
SCORE!!!
THE OTHER TEAM SCORED!
HUH?
THEY SCORED?!
OH MAN!!!!
Team Gadget
1
Team Recycled Robot
0
OF COURSE THEY SCORED!!!

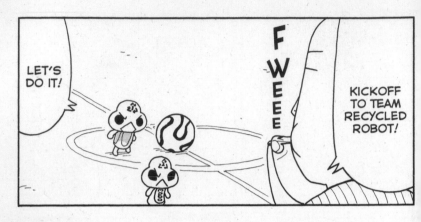

KICKOFF TO TEAM RECYCLED ROBOT!
FWEEE
LET'S DO IT!
KICK KICK
KICK KICK
WAP
I'LL KICK IT!
WAP WAP
NO, ME!
You want a piece of this?!
C'mon!
DECIDE THAT *BEFORE* THE KICK-OFF!

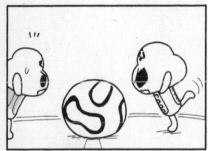

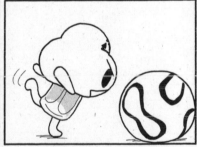

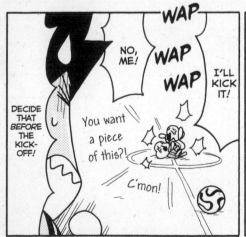

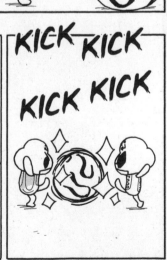

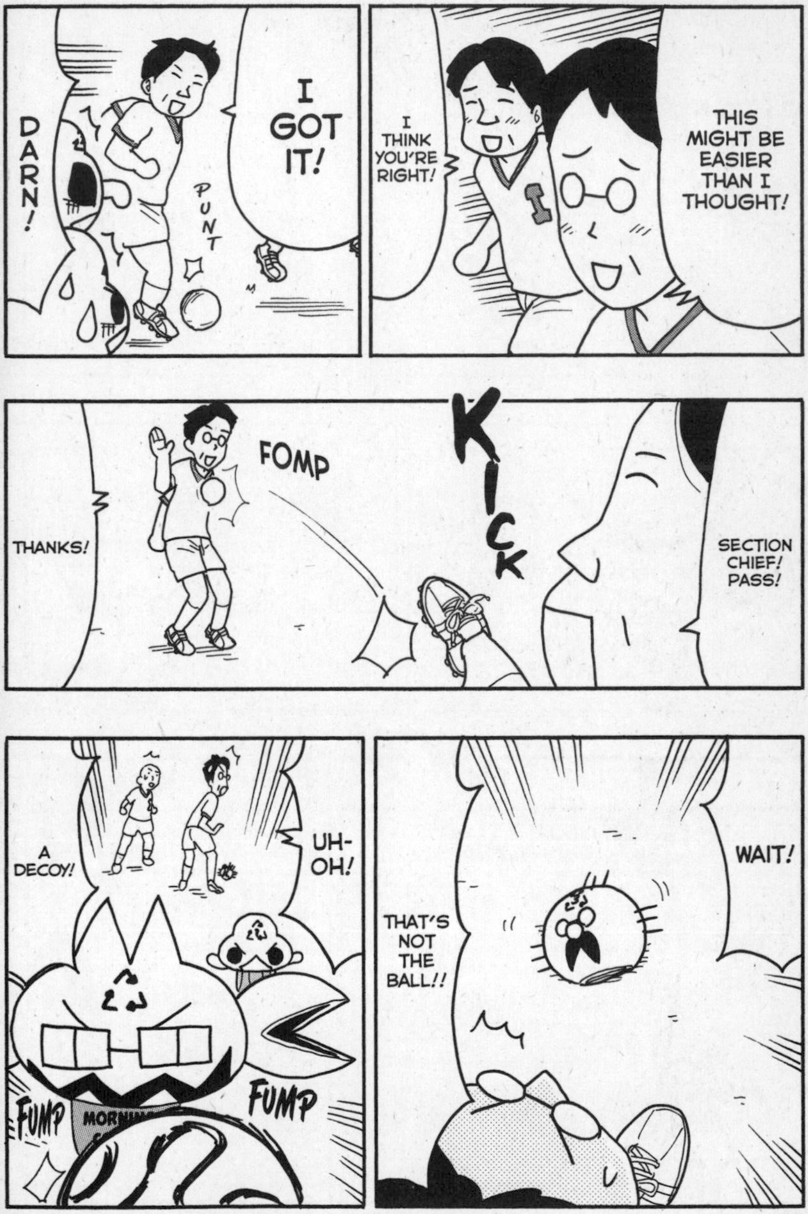
THIS MIGHT BE EASIER THAN I THOUGHT!
I THINK YOU'RE RIGHT!
I GOT IT!
PUNT
DARN!
SECTION CHIEF! PASS!
KICK
FOMP
THANKS!
WAIT!
THAT'S NOT THE BALL!!
UH-OH!
A DECOY!
FUMP
FUMP

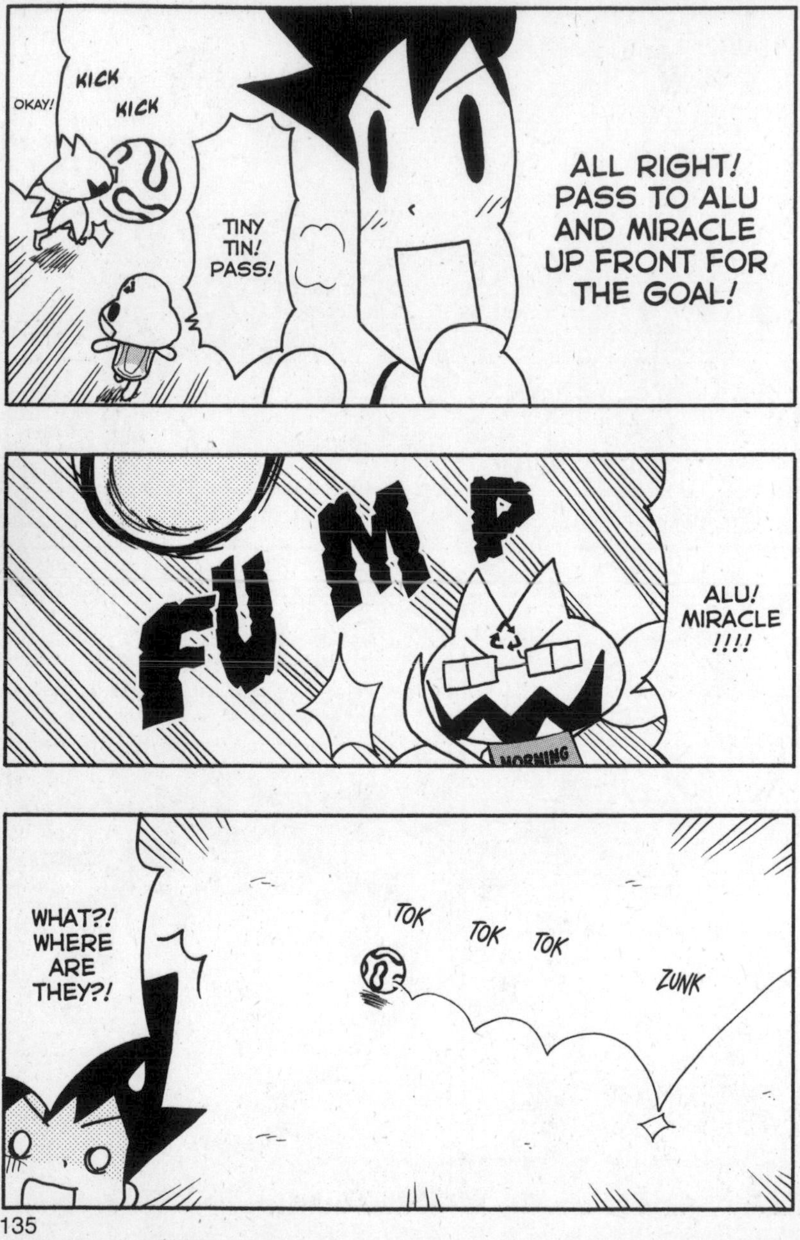
ALL RIGHT! PASS TO ALU AND MIRACLE UP FRONT FOR THE GOAL!
TINY TIN! PASS!
KICK
KICK
OKAY!
ALU! MIRACLE !!!!
FUMP
MORNING
ZUNK
TOK
TOK
TOK
WHAT?! WHERE ARE THEY?!

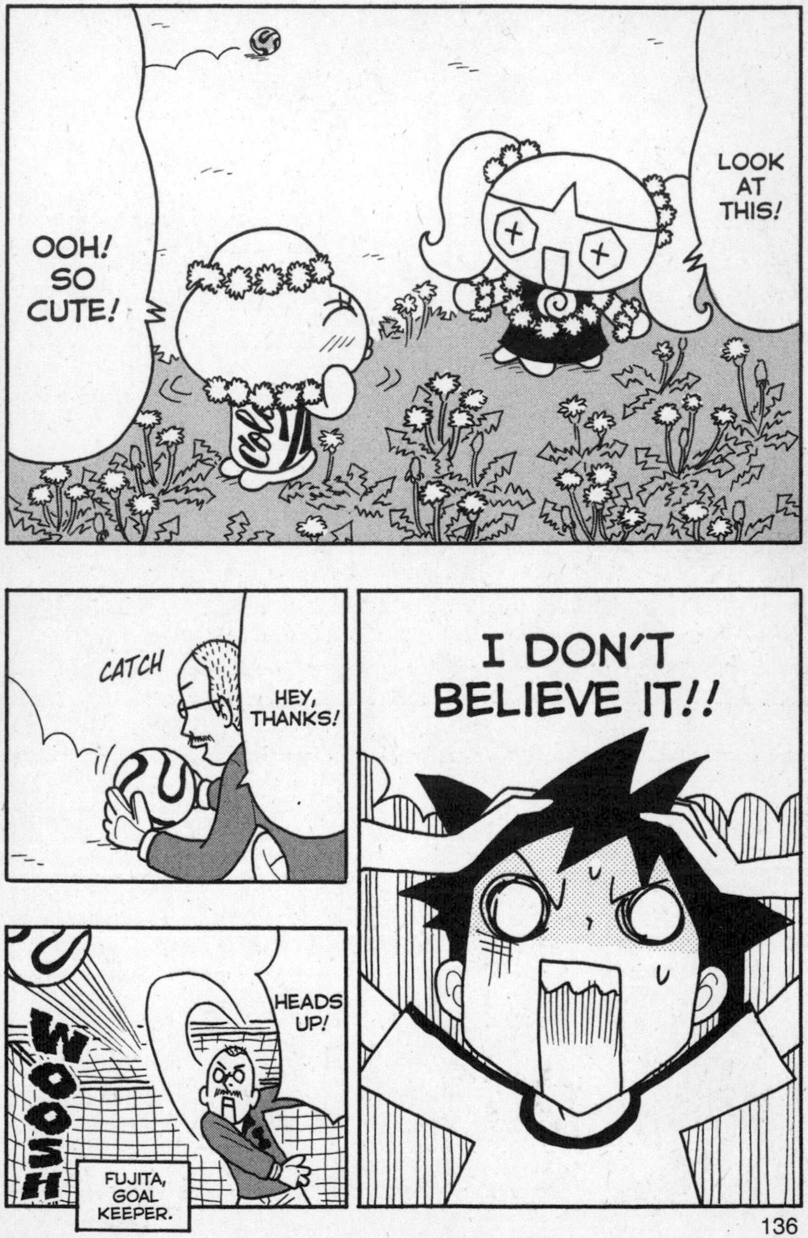
LOOK AT THIS!
OOH! SO CUTE!
I DON'T BELIEVE IT!!
HEY, THANKS!
CATCH
HEADS UP!
WOOSH
FUJITA, GOAL KEEPER.

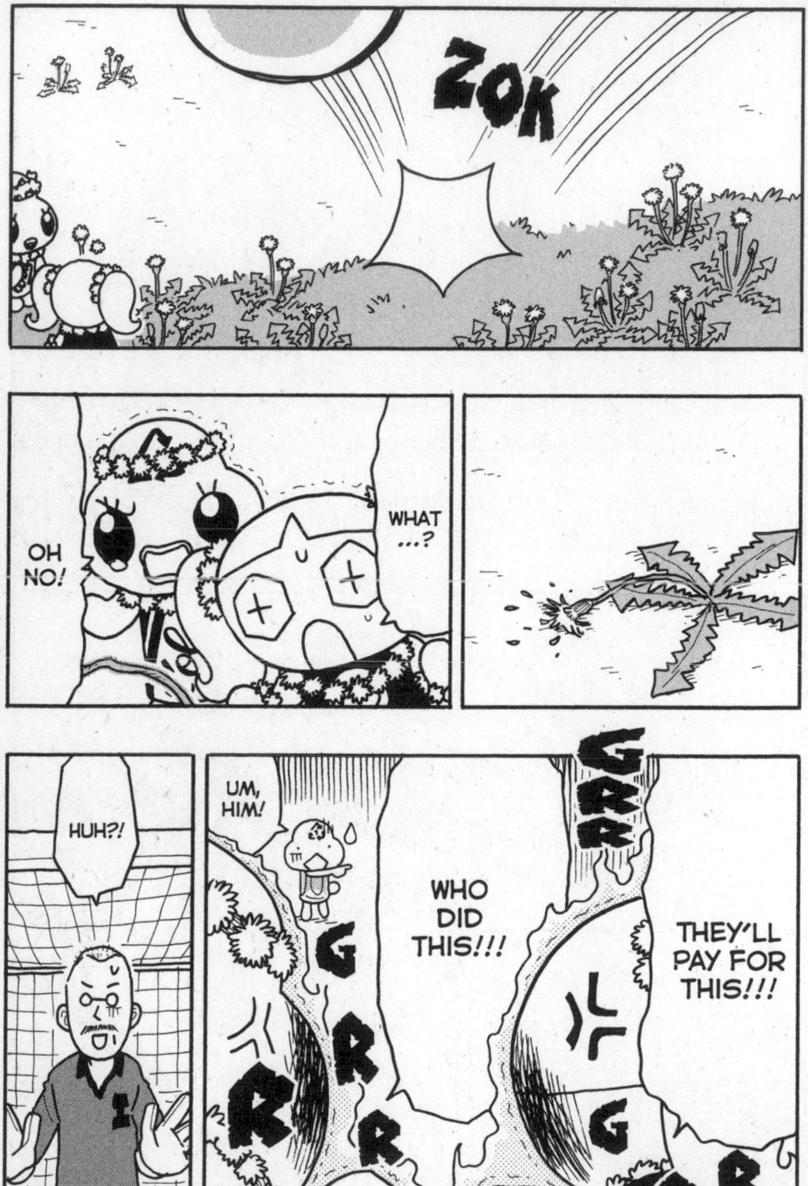
ZOK
WHAT ...?
OH NO!
GRR
THEY'LL PAY FOR THIS!!!
GRRR
WHO DID THIS!!!
UM, HIM!
GRRR
HUH?!

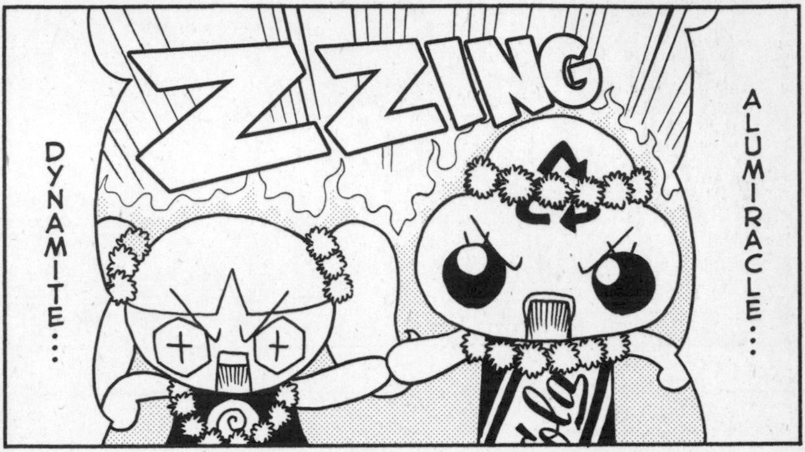
ALUMIRACLE...
ZZING
DYNAMITE...

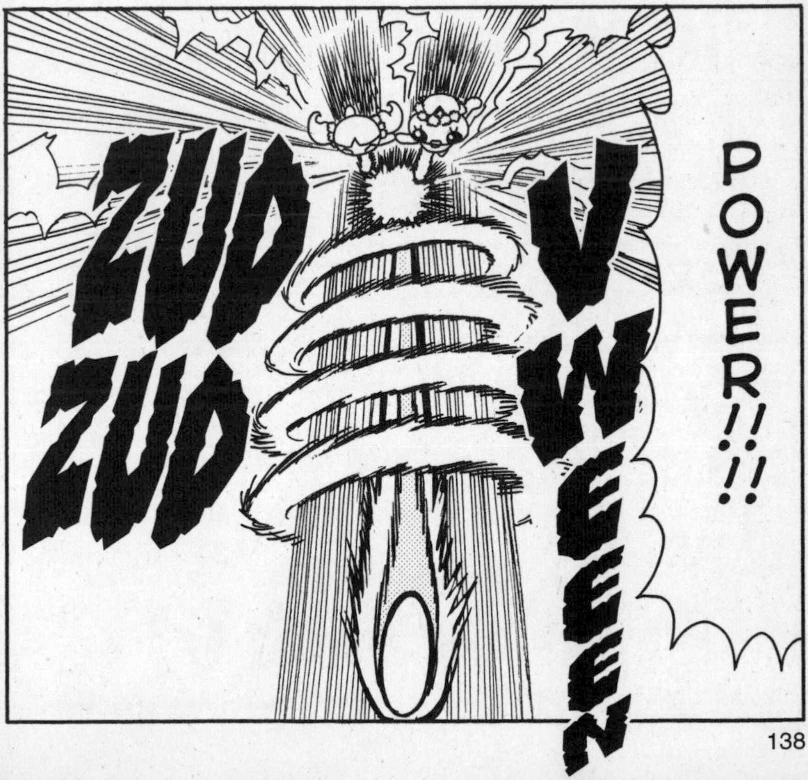
POWER!!!!
VWEEEN
ZUD ZUD

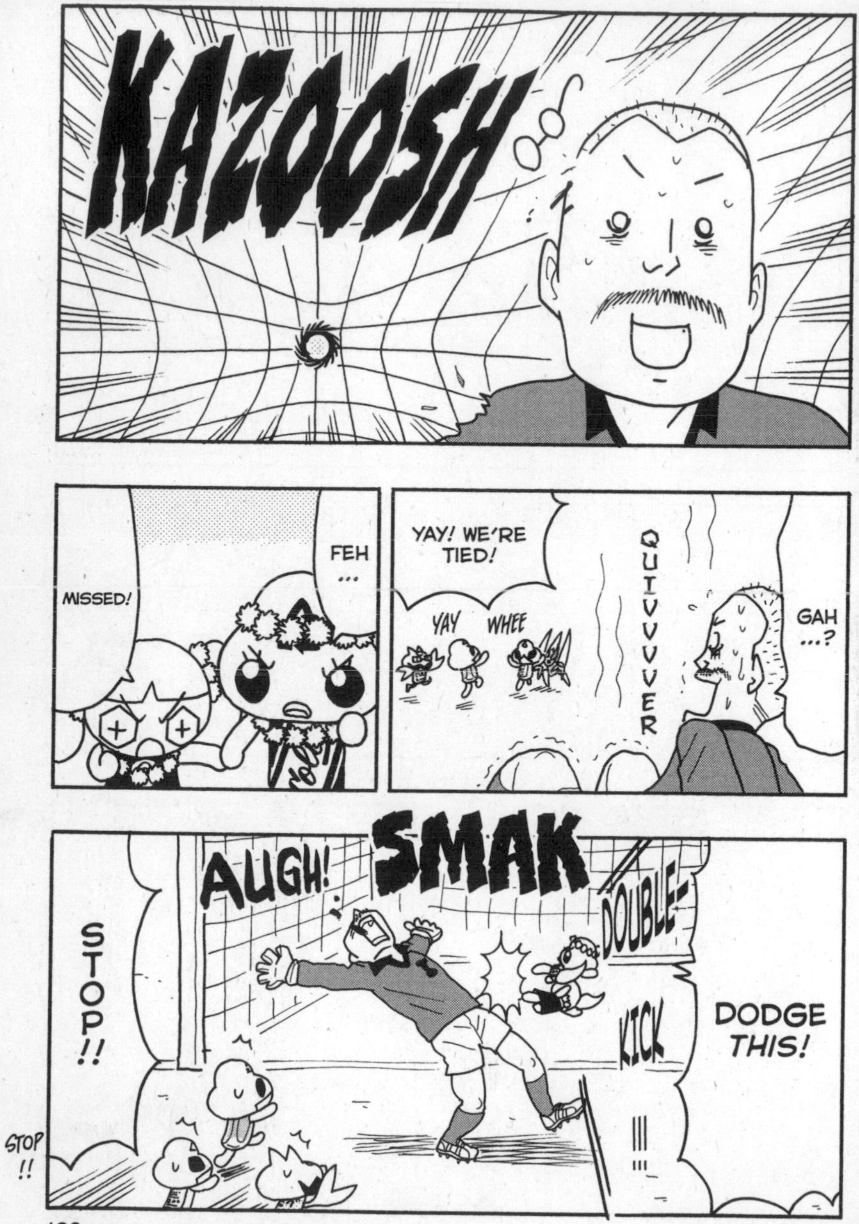
KAZOOSH
GAH ...?
QUIVVVVER
YAY! WE'RE TIED!
WHEE
YAY
FEH ...
MISSED!
DODGE THIS!
DOUBLE-KICK
!!!
SMAK
AUGH!
STOP!!
STOP !!

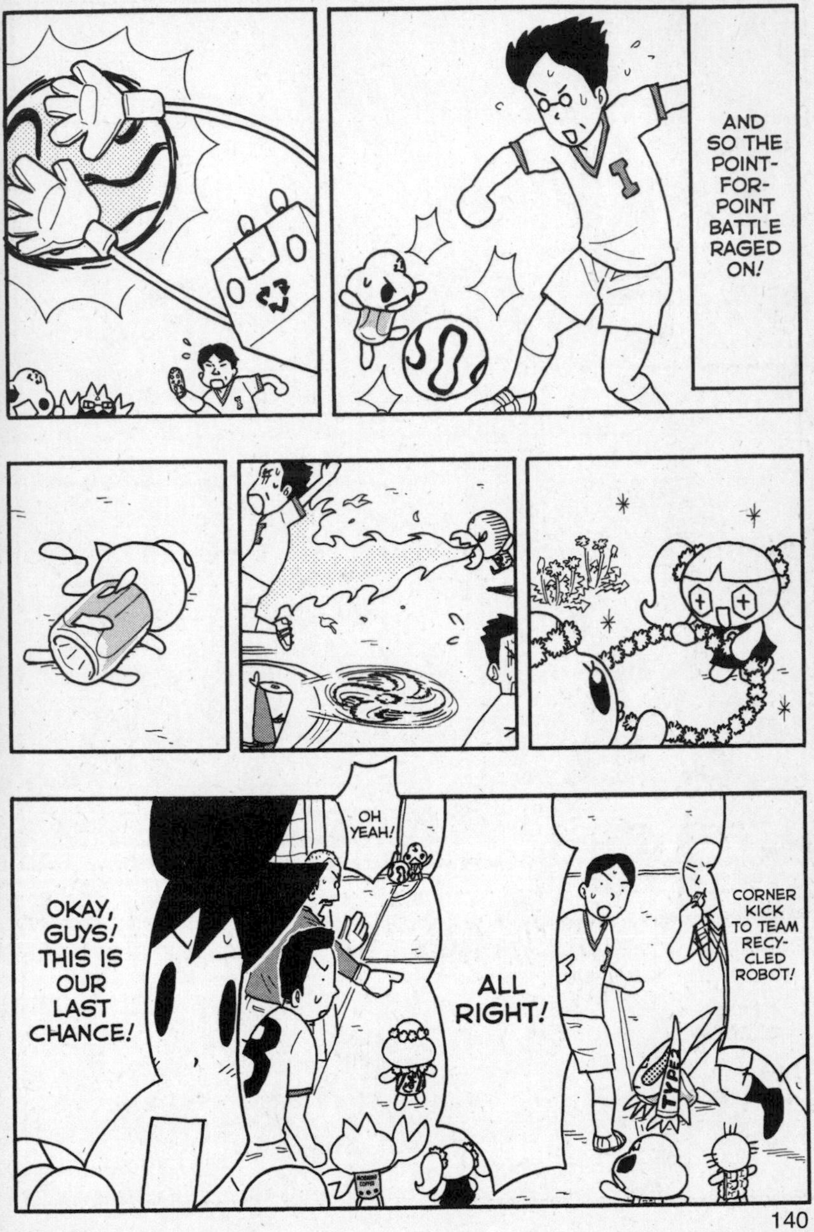
AND SO THE POINT-FOR-POINT BATTLE RAGED ON!
CORNER KICK TO TEAM RECYCLED ROBOT!
ALL RIGHT!
OH YEAH!
OKAY, GUYS! THIS IS OUR LAST CHANCE!

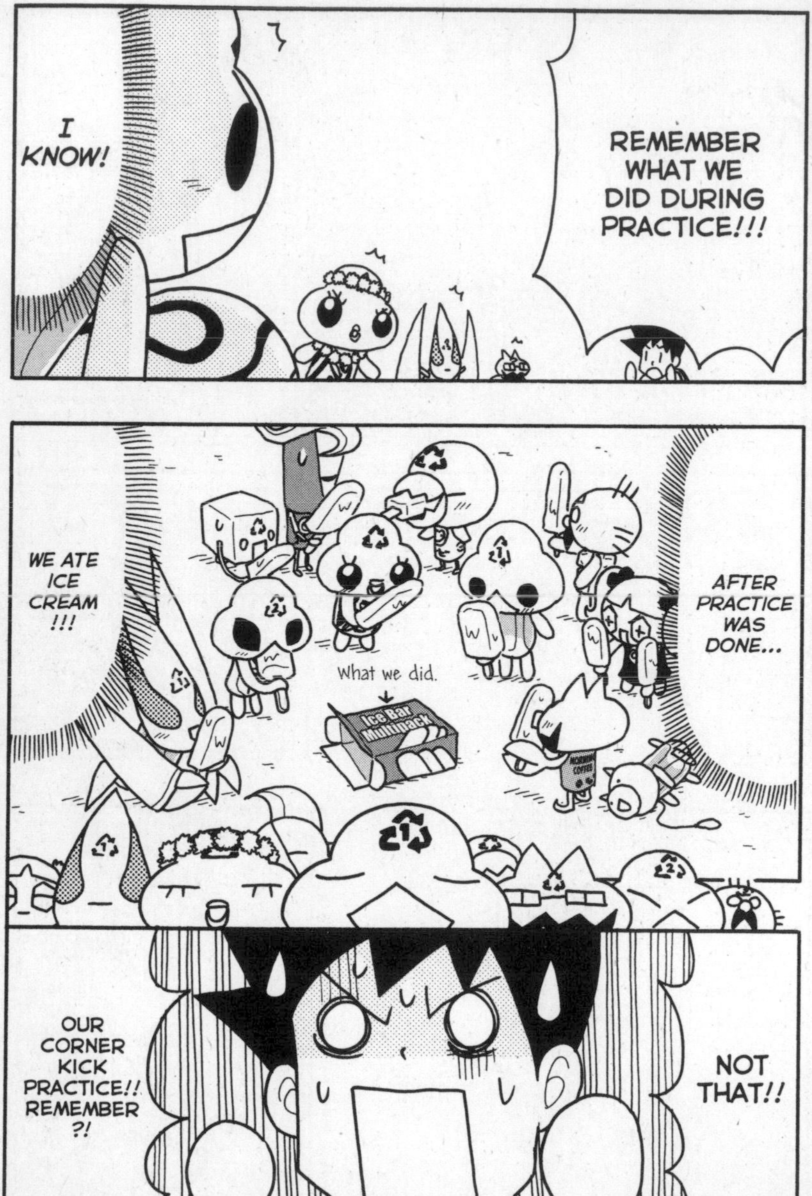
REMEMBER WHAT WE DID DURING PRACTICE!!!
I KNOW!
AFTER PRACTICE WAS DONE...
WE ATE ICE CREAM!!!
What we did.
Ice Bar Multipack
NOT THAT!!
OUR CORNER KICK PRACTICE!! REMEMBER?!

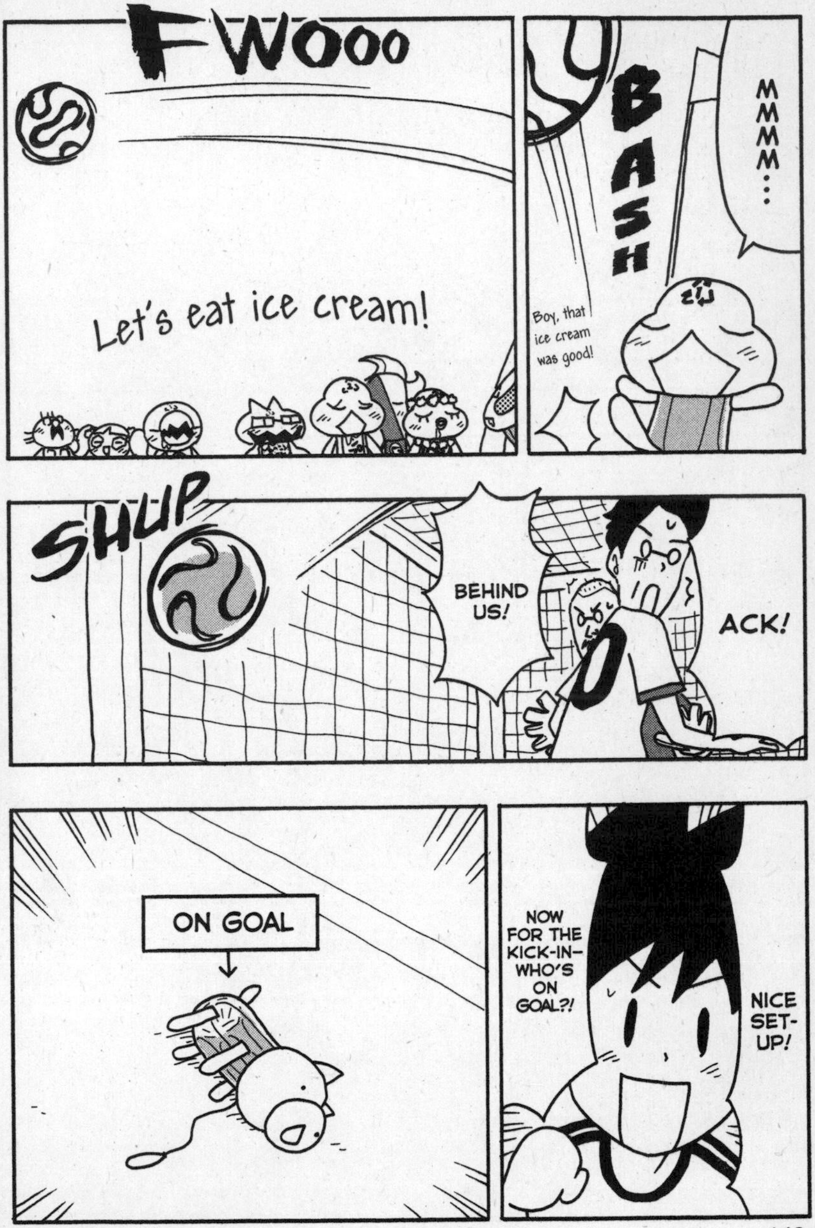
MMMM...
BASH
Boy, that ice cream was good!
FWOOO
Let's eat ice cream!
ACK!
BEHIND US!
SHUP
NICE SET-UP!
NOW FOR THE KICK-IN—WHO'S ON GOAL?!
ON GOAL

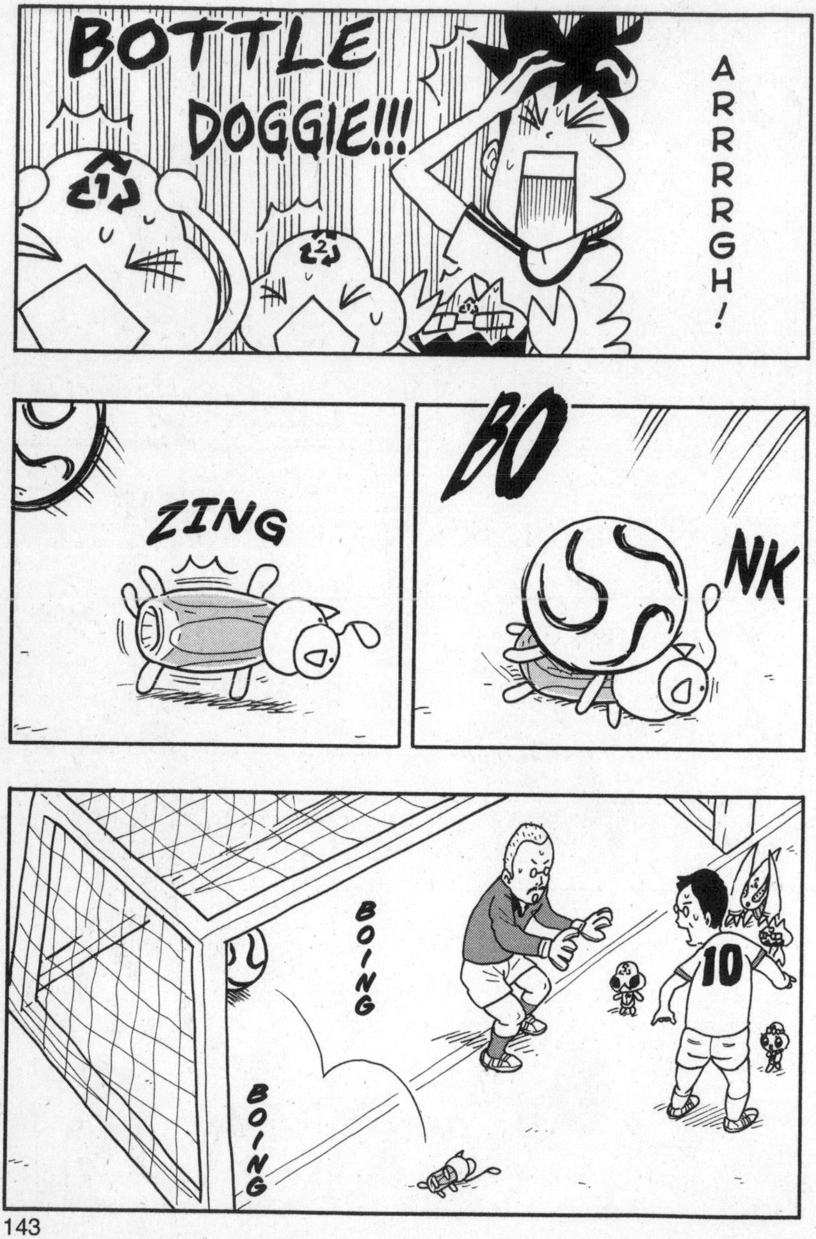
ARRRRGH!
BOTTLE DOGGIE!!!
BO NK
ZING
BOING
BOING

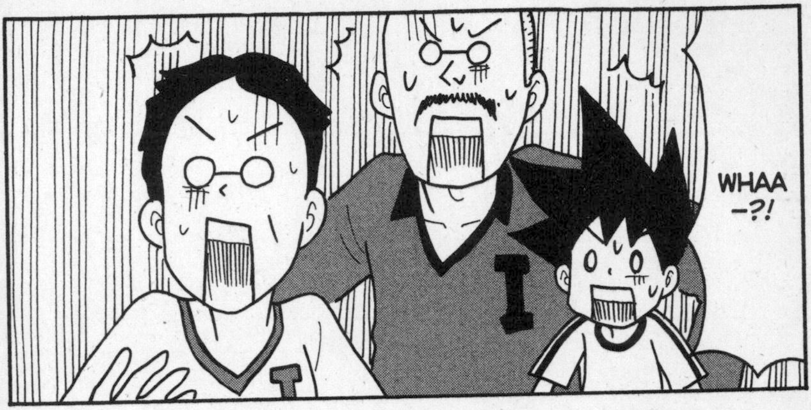
WHAA
-?!

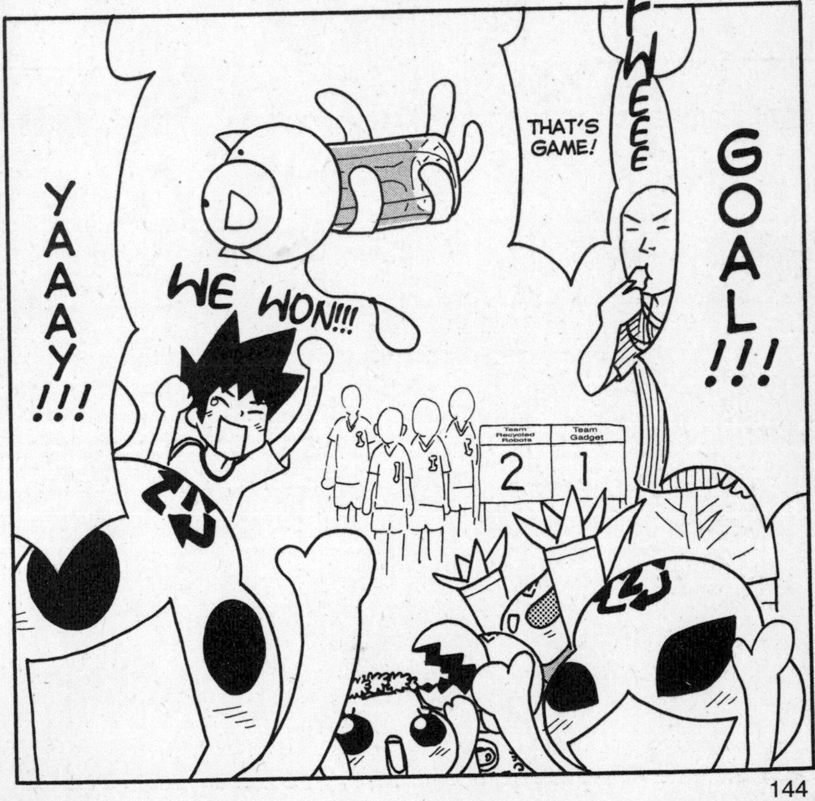
GOAL!!!
FWEEE
THAT'S GAME!
Team Recycled Robots
2
Team Gadget
1
WE WON!!!
YAAAAY!!!

# CHAPTER 14 Leave It to GPS!

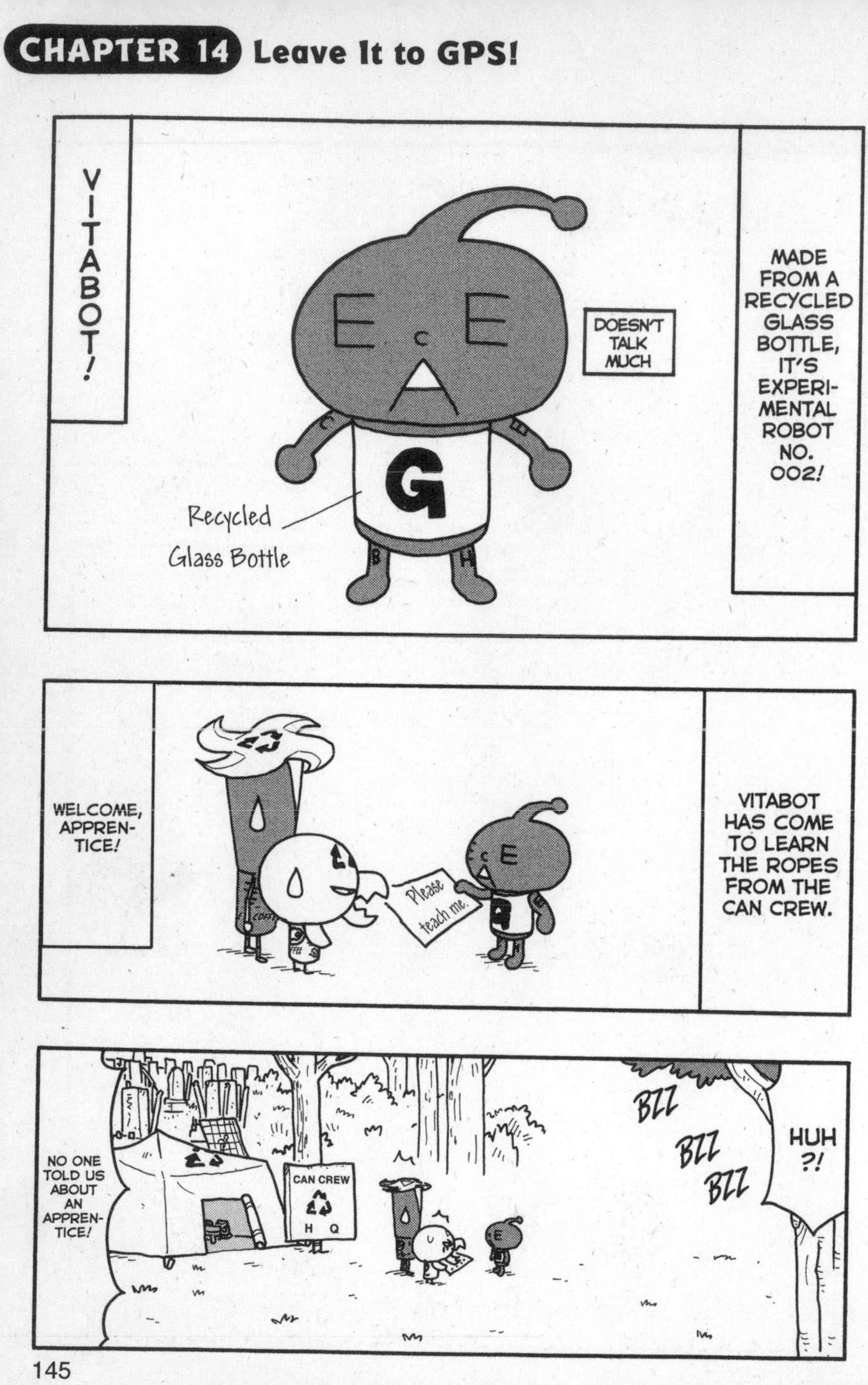
MADE FROM A RECYCLED GLASS BOTTLE, IT'S EXPERIMENTAL ROBOT NO. 002!
DOESN'T TALK MUCH
Recycled Glass Bottle
VITABOT!
VITABOT HAS COME TO LEARN THE ROPES FROM THE CAN CREW.
Please teach me.
WELCOME, APPRENTICE!
HUH ?!
BZZ
BZZ
BZZ
CAN CREW
H Q
NO ONE TOLD US ABOUT AN APPRENTICE!

## CHAPTER 14

# Leave It to GPS!

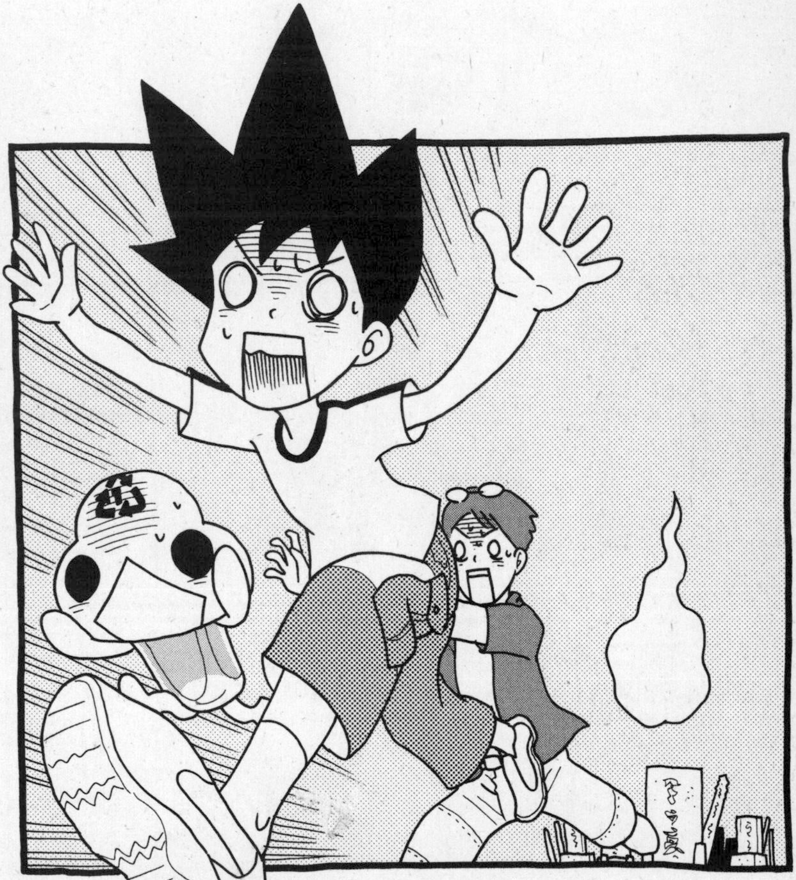

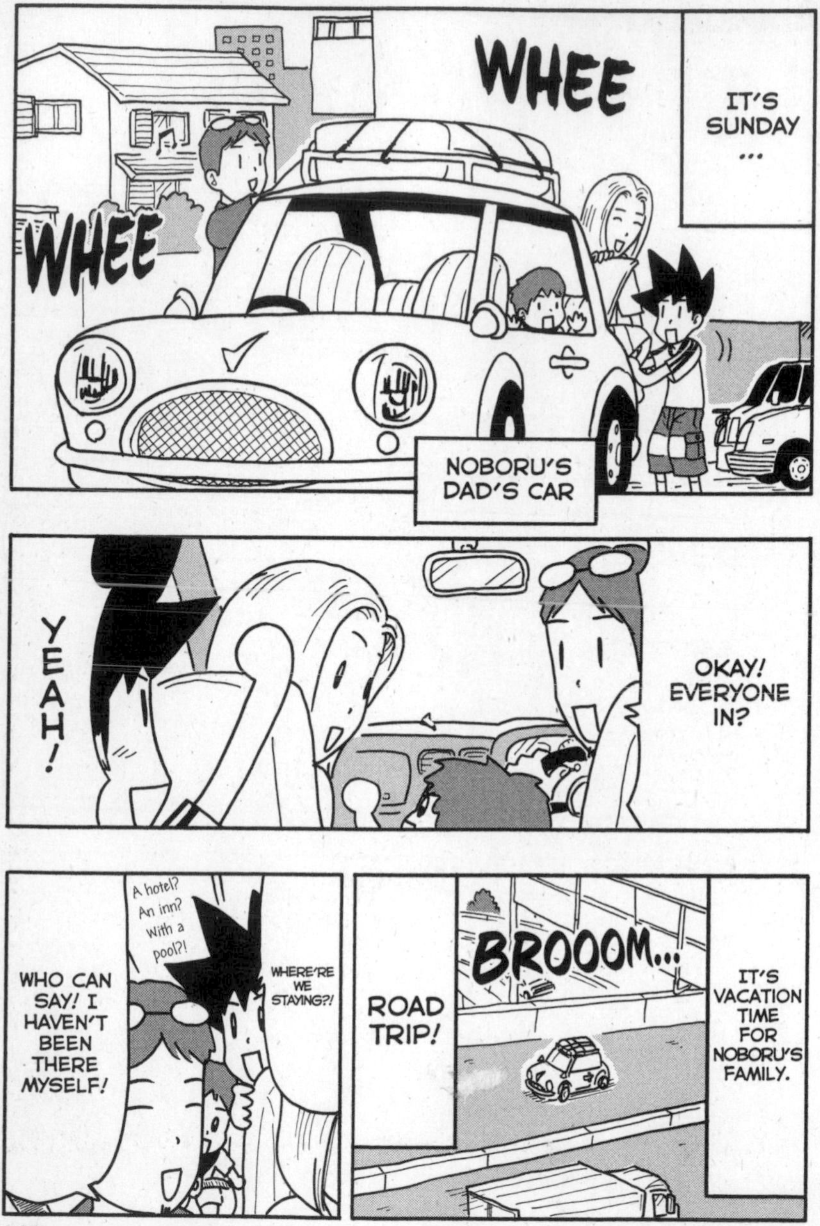
IT'S SUNDAY ...
WHEE
WHEE
NOBORU'S DAD'S CAR
OKAY! EVERYONE IN?
YEAH!
IT'S VACATION TIME FOR NOBORU'S FAMILY.
BROOOM...
ROAD TRIP!
WHERE'RE WE STAYING?!
A hotel? An inn? With a pool?!
WHO CAN SAY! I HAVEN'T BEEN THERE MYSELF!

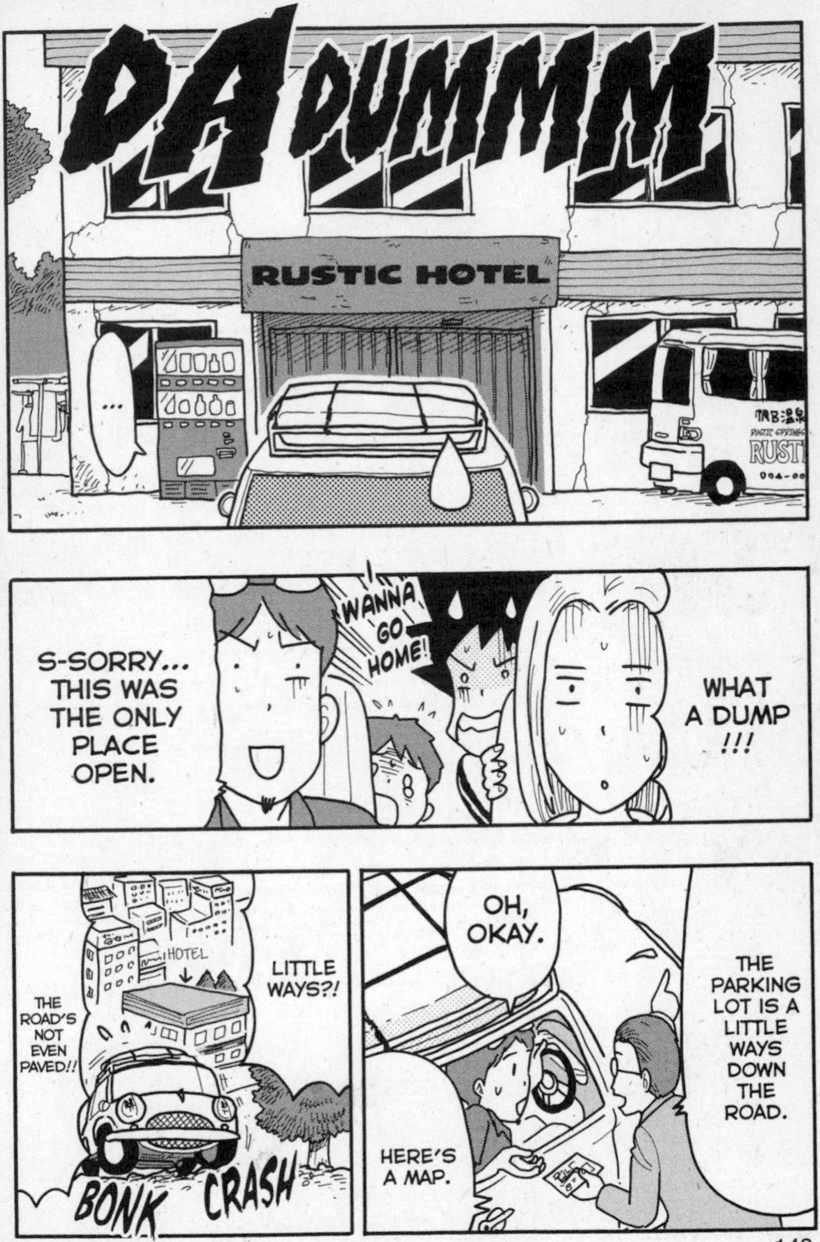
DA DUMMM
RUSTIC HOTEL
...
WHAT A DUMP!!!
I WANNA GO HOME!
S-SORRY... THIS WAS THE ONLY PLACE OPEN.
THE PARKING LOT IS A LITTLE WAYS DOWN THE ROAD.
OH, OKAY.
HERE'S A MAP.
LITTLE WAYS?!
HOTEL
THE ROAD'S NOT EVEN PAVED!!
CRASH
BONK

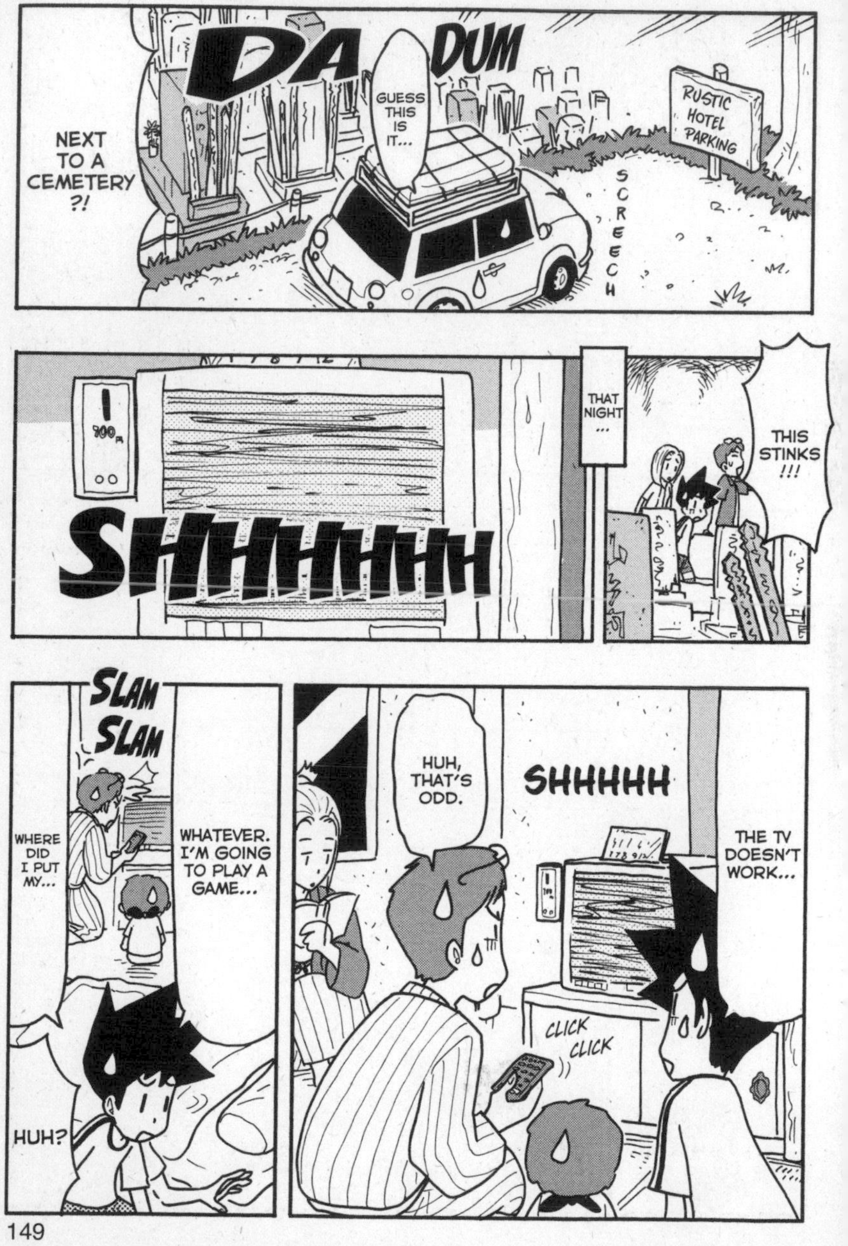
DA DUM
GUESS THIS IS IT...
RUSTIC HOTEL PARKING
SCREECH
NEXT TO A CEMETERY ?!
THIS STINKS !!!
THAT NIGHT ...
SHHHHHHH
THE TV DOESN'T WORK...
SHHHHH
HUH, THAT'S ODD.
CLICK CLICK
SLAM SLAM
WHATEVER. I'M GOING TO PLAY A GAME...
WHERE DID I PUT MY...
HUH?

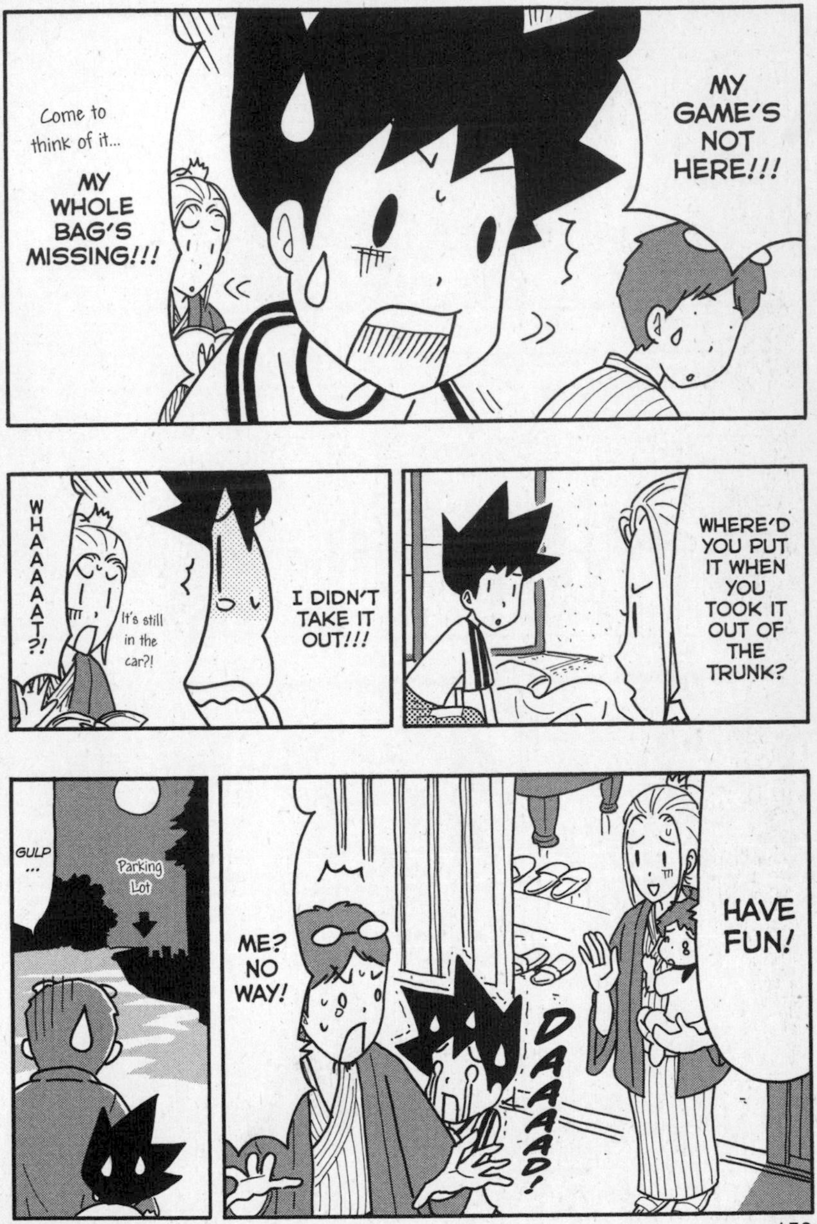
MY GAME'S NOT HERE!!!
Come to think of it...
MY WHOLE BAG'S MISSING!!!
WHERE'D YOU PUT IT WHEN YOU TOOK IT OUT OF THE TRUNK?
I DIDN'T TAKE IT OUT!!!
It's still in the car?!
WHAAAAAT?!
HAVE FUN!
DAAAAAD!
ME? NO WAY!
Parking Lot
GULP...

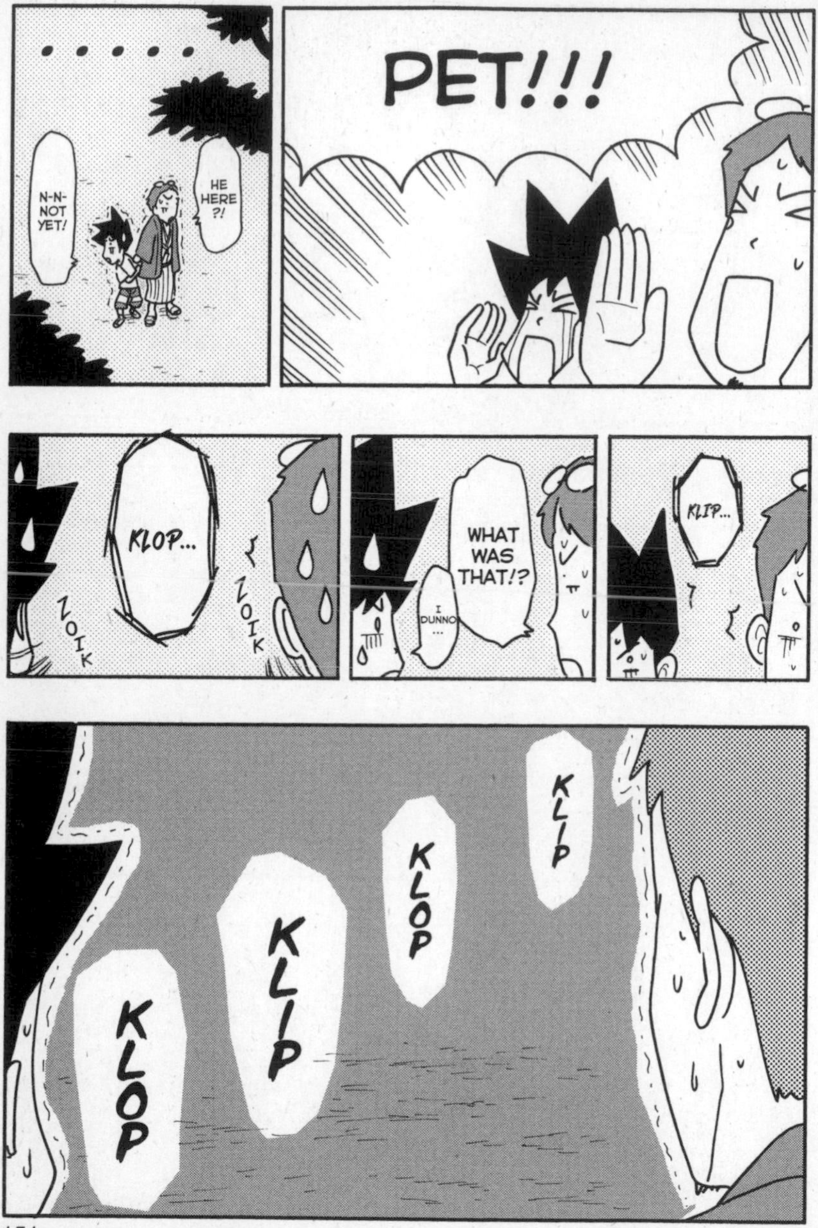
PET!!!
.....
HE HERE?!
N-N-NOT YET!
KLIP...
WHAT WAS THAT!?
I DUNNO...
KLOP...
ZOIK
ZOIK
KLIP
KLOP
KLIP
KLOP

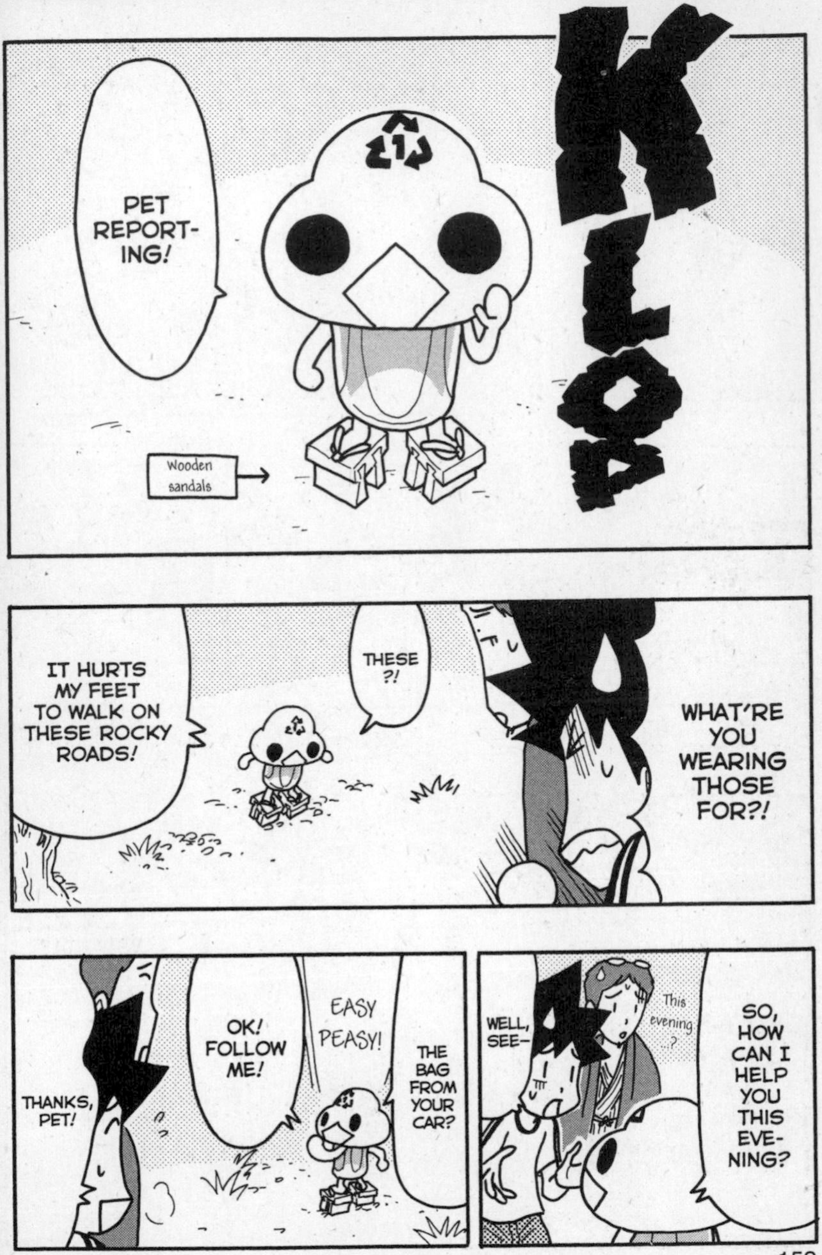
KLOP
PET REPORT-ING!
Wooden sandals
WHAT'RE YOU WEARING THOSE FOR?!
THESE?!
IT HURTS MY FEET TO WALK ON THESE ROCKY ROADS!
SO, HOW CAN I HELP YOU THIS EVE-NING?
This evening...?
WELL, SEE—
THE BAG FROM YOUR CAR?
EASY PEASY!
OK! FOLLOW ME!
THANKS, PET!

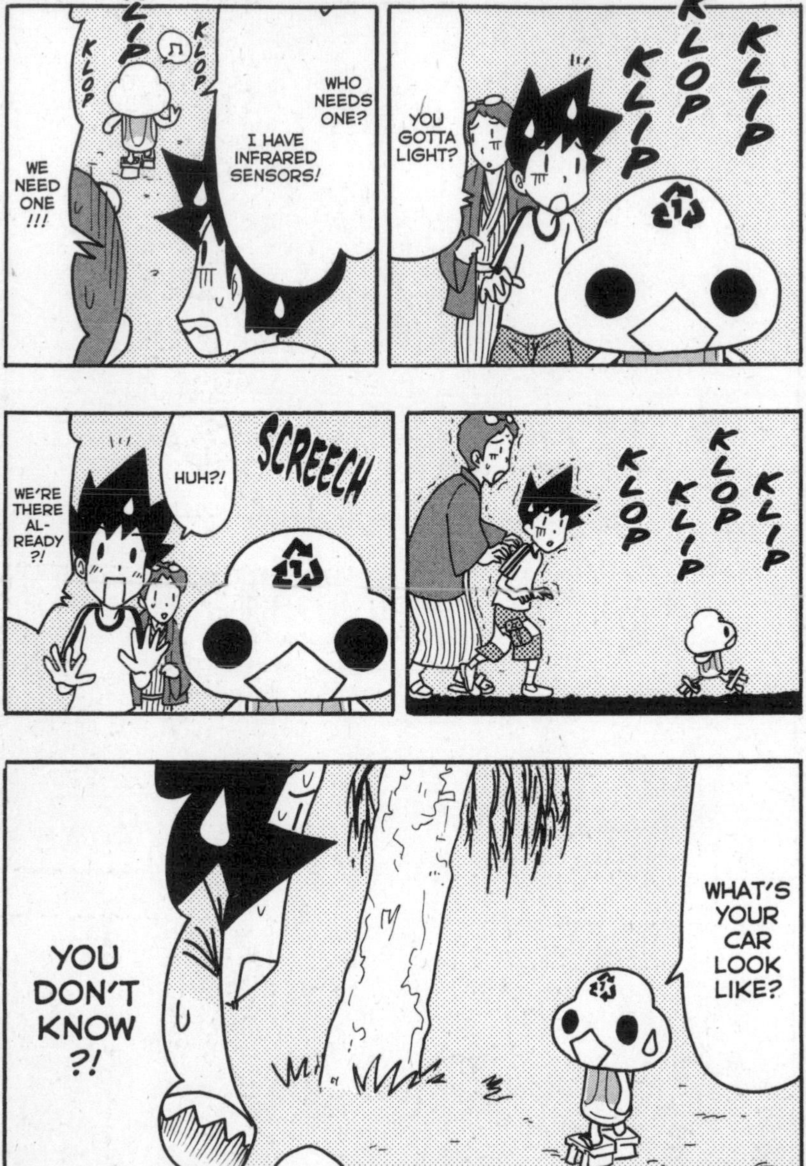
KLIP
KLOP
KLIP
YOU GOTTA LIGHT?
WHO NEEDS ONE?
I HAVE INFRARED SENSORS!
KLOP
KLIP
KLOP
WE NEED ONE!!!
KLIP
KLOP
KLIP
KLOP
SCREECH
HUH?!
WE'RE THERE AL-READY?!
WHAT'S YOUR CAR LOOK LIKE?
YOU DON'T KNOW?!

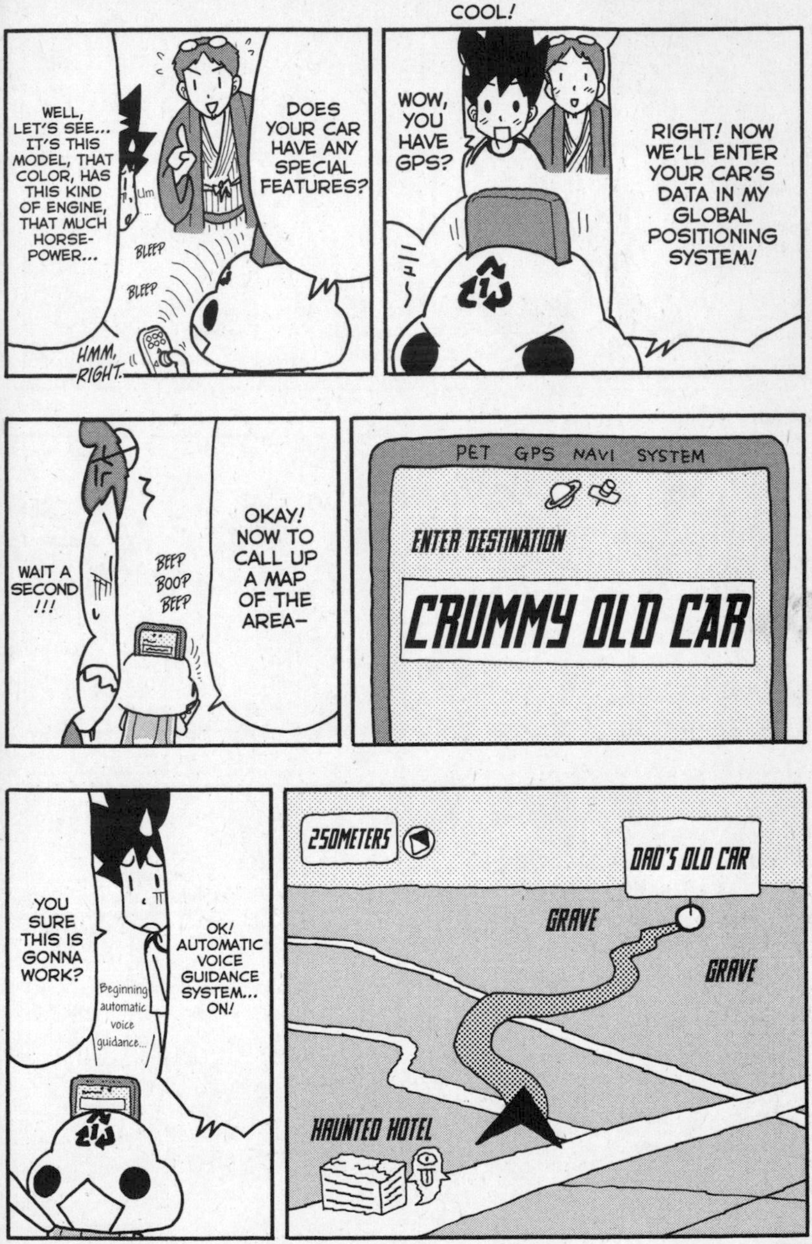
COOL!
RIGHT! NOW WE'LL ENTER YOUR CAR'S DATA IN MY GLOBAL POSITIONING SYSTEM!
WOW, YOU HAVE GPS?
DOES YOUR CAR HAVE ANY SPECIAL FEATURES?
WELL, LET'S SEE... IT'S THIS MODEL, THAT COLOR, HAS THIS KIND OF ENGINE, THAT MUCH HORSE-POWER...
Um ...
BLEEP
BLEEP
HMM, RIGHT.
PET GPS NAVI SYSTEM
ENTER DESTINATION
CRUMMY OLD CAR
OKAY! NOW TO CALL UP A MAP OF THE AREA–
BEEP BOOP BEEP
WAIT A SECOND !!!
250METERS
DAD'S OLD CAR
GRAVE
GRAVE
HAUNTED HOTEL
OK! AUTOMATIC VOICE GUIDANCE SYSTEM... ON!
YOU SURE THIS IS GONNA WORK?
Beginning automatic voice guidance...

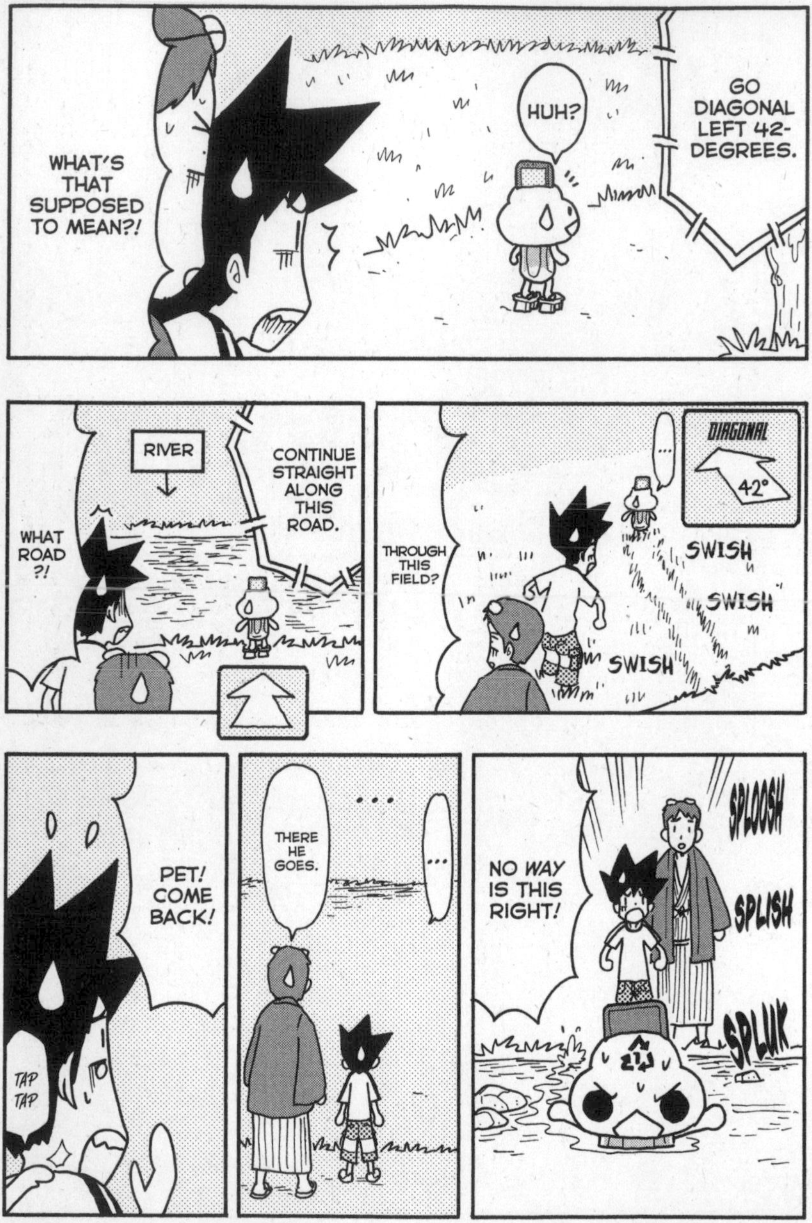
GO DIAGONAL LEFT 42-DEGREES.
HUH?
WHAT'S THAT SUPPOSED TO MEAN?!
DIAGONAL
42°
...
SWISH
SWISH
SWISH
THROUGH THIS FIELD?
CONTINUE STRAIGHT ALONG THIS ROAD.
RIVER
WHAT ROAD ?!
SPLOOSH
SPLISH
SPLUK
NO WAY IS THIS RIGHT!
...
• • •
THERE HE GOES.
PET! COME BACK!
TAP TAP

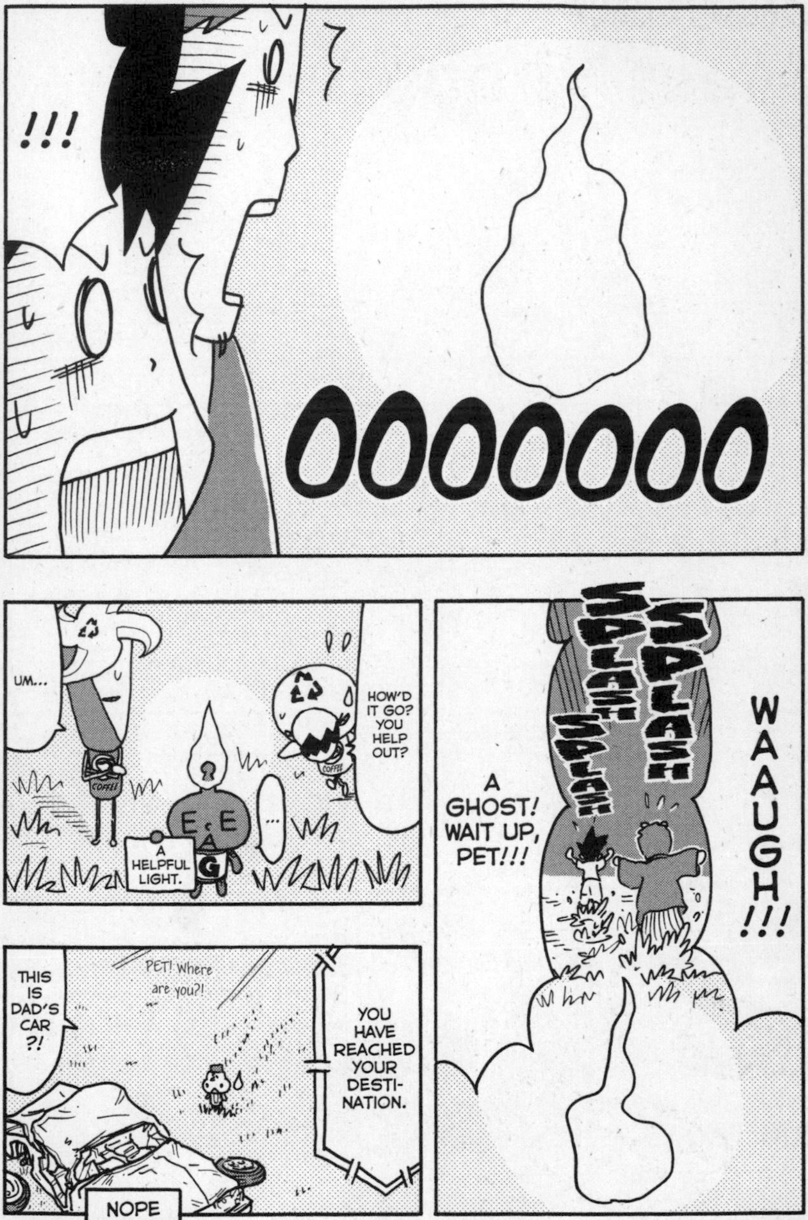
!!!
OOOOOOO
WAAUGH!!!
SPLASH
SPLASH
SPLASH
SPLASH
A GHOST! WAIT UP, PET!!!
HOW'D IT GO? YOU HELP OUT?
UM...
...
A HELPFUL LIGHT.
YOU HAVE REACHED YOUR DESTI-NATION.
PET! Where are you?!
THIS IS DAD'S CAR?!
NOPE

## CHAPTER 15

# Meet Vitabot!

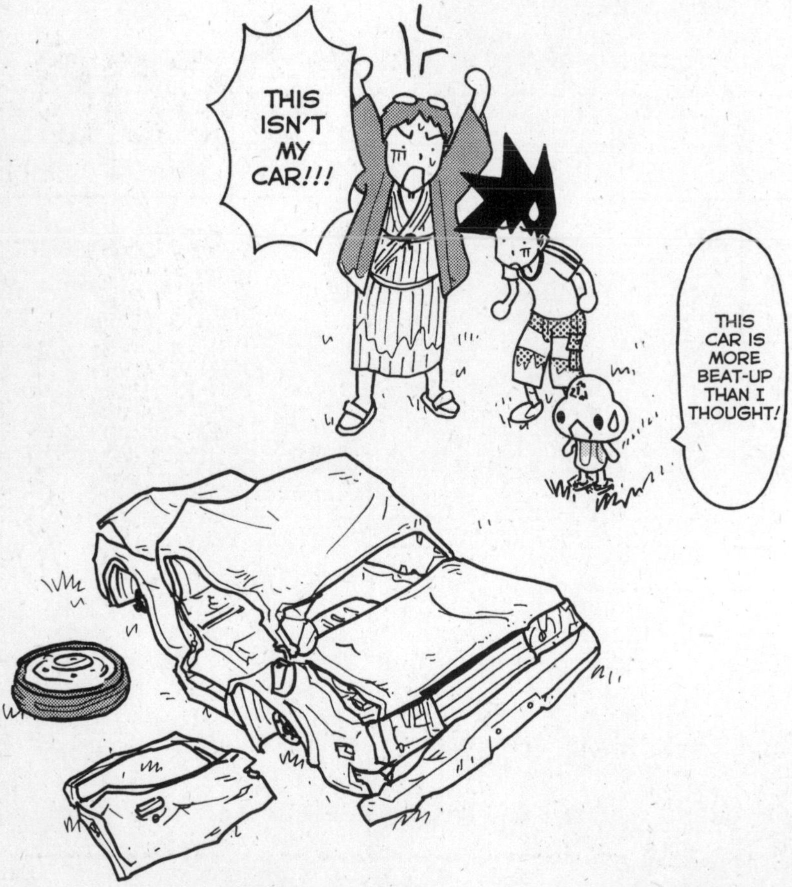
THIS CAR IS MORE BEAT-UP THAN I THOUGHT!
THIS ISN'T MY CAR!!!

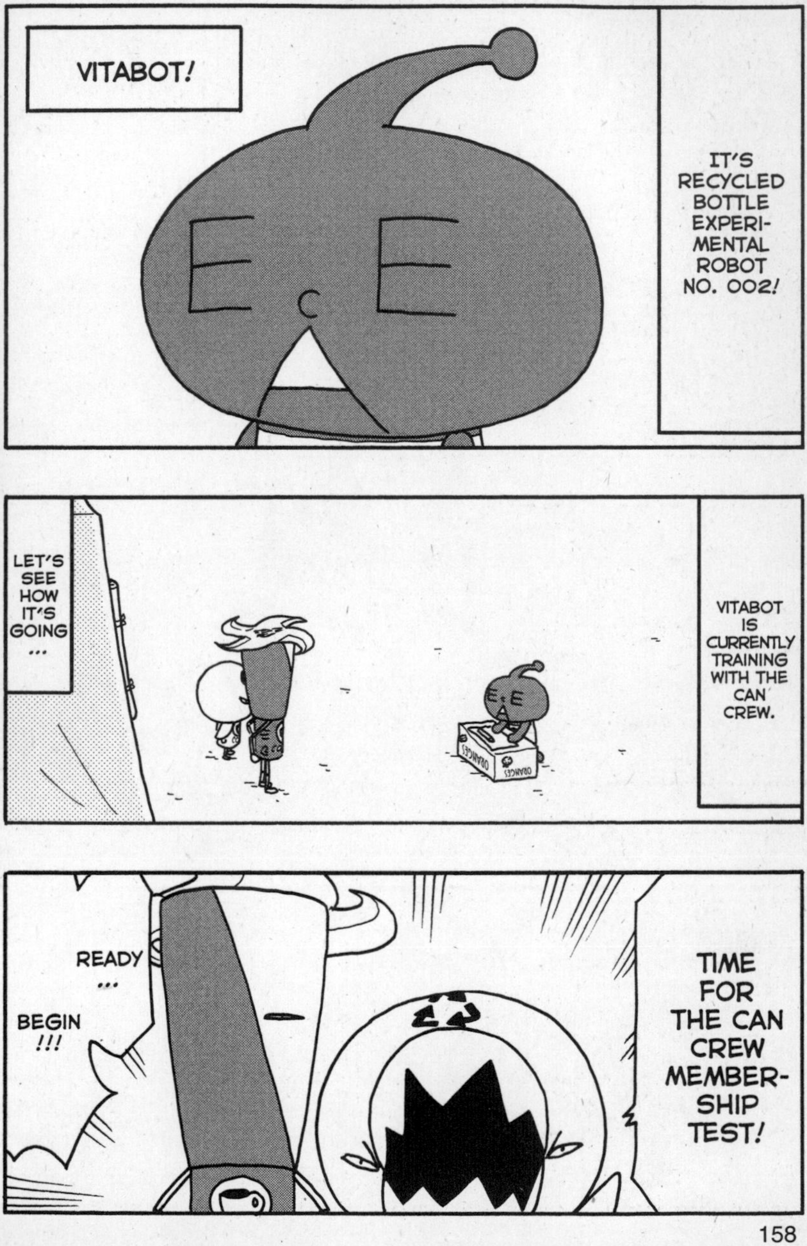
VITABOT!
IT'S RECYCLED BOTTLE EXPERI-MENTAL ROBOT NO. 002!
VITABOT IS CURRENTLY TRAINING WITH THE CAN CREW.
LET'S SEE HOW IT'S GOING...
TIME FOR THE CAN CREW MEMBER-SHIP TEST!
READY...
BEGIN!!!

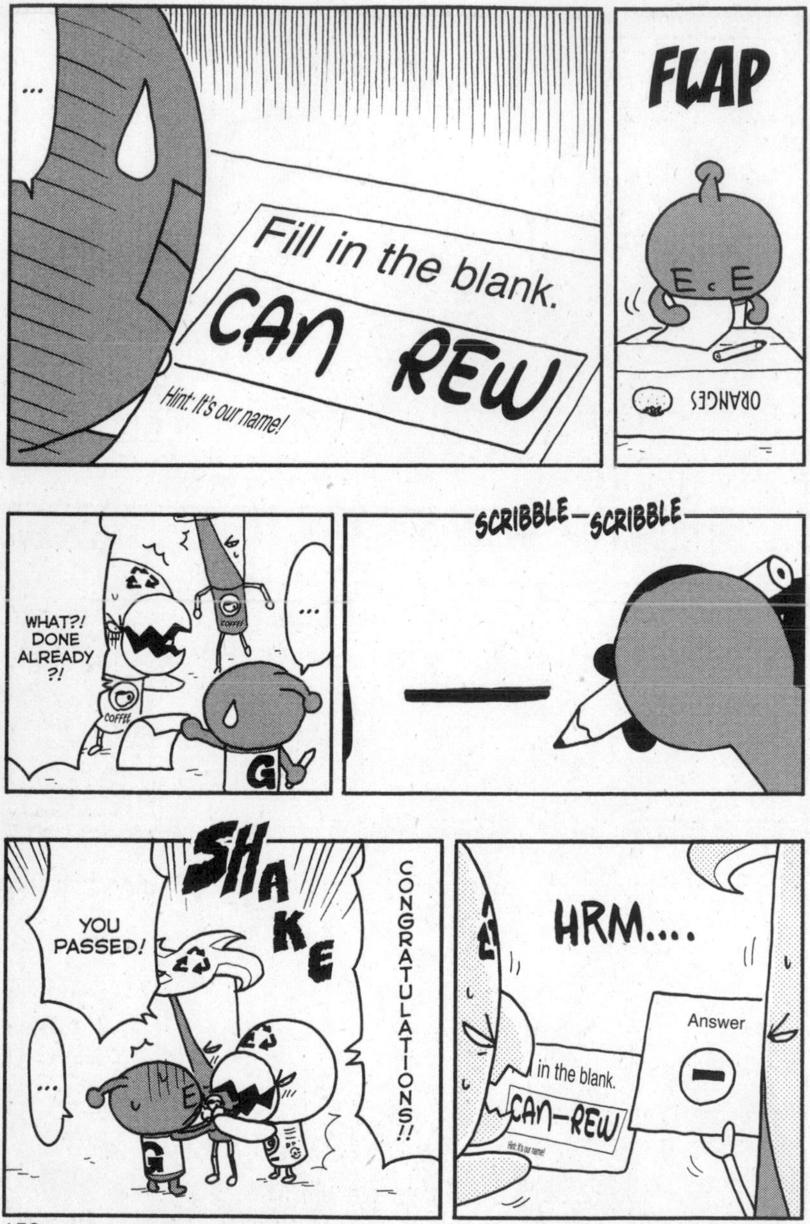
FLAP
ORANGES
...
Fill in the blank.
CAN REW
Hint: It's our name!
SCRIBBLE—SCRIBBLE
...
WHAT?! DONE ALREADY?!
COFFEE
HRM....
in the blank.
CAN—REW
Hint: It's our name!
Answer
CONGRATULATIONS!!
SHAKE
YOU PASSED!
...

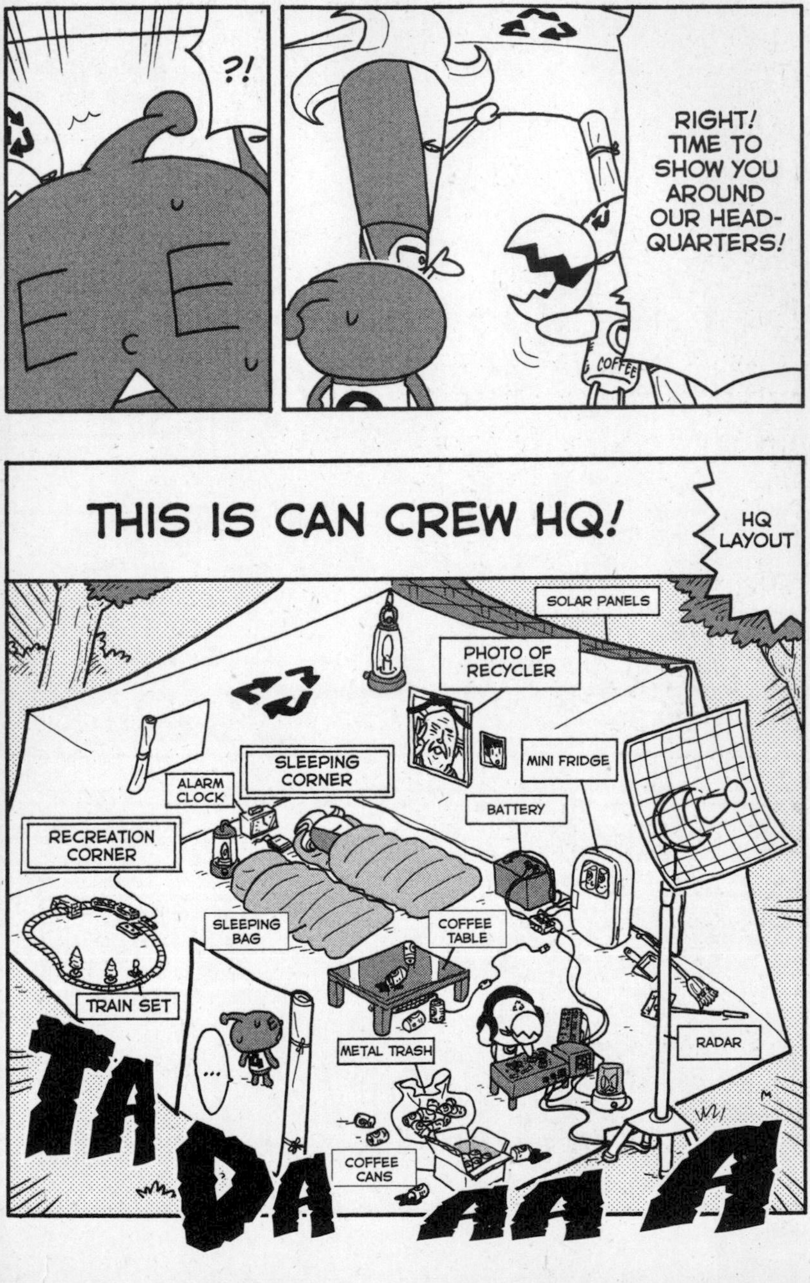
COFFEE
RIGHT! TIME TO SHOW YOU AROUND OUR HEAD-QUARTERS!
?!
HQ LAYOUT
THIS IS CAN CREW HQ!
SOLAR PANELS
PHOTO OF RECYCLER
MINI FRIDGE
SLEEPING CORNER
BATTERY
ALARM CLOCK
RECREATION CORNER
COFFEE TABLE
SLEEPING BAG
RADAR
TRAIN SET
METAL TRASH
...
COFFEE CANS
TA DA AA A

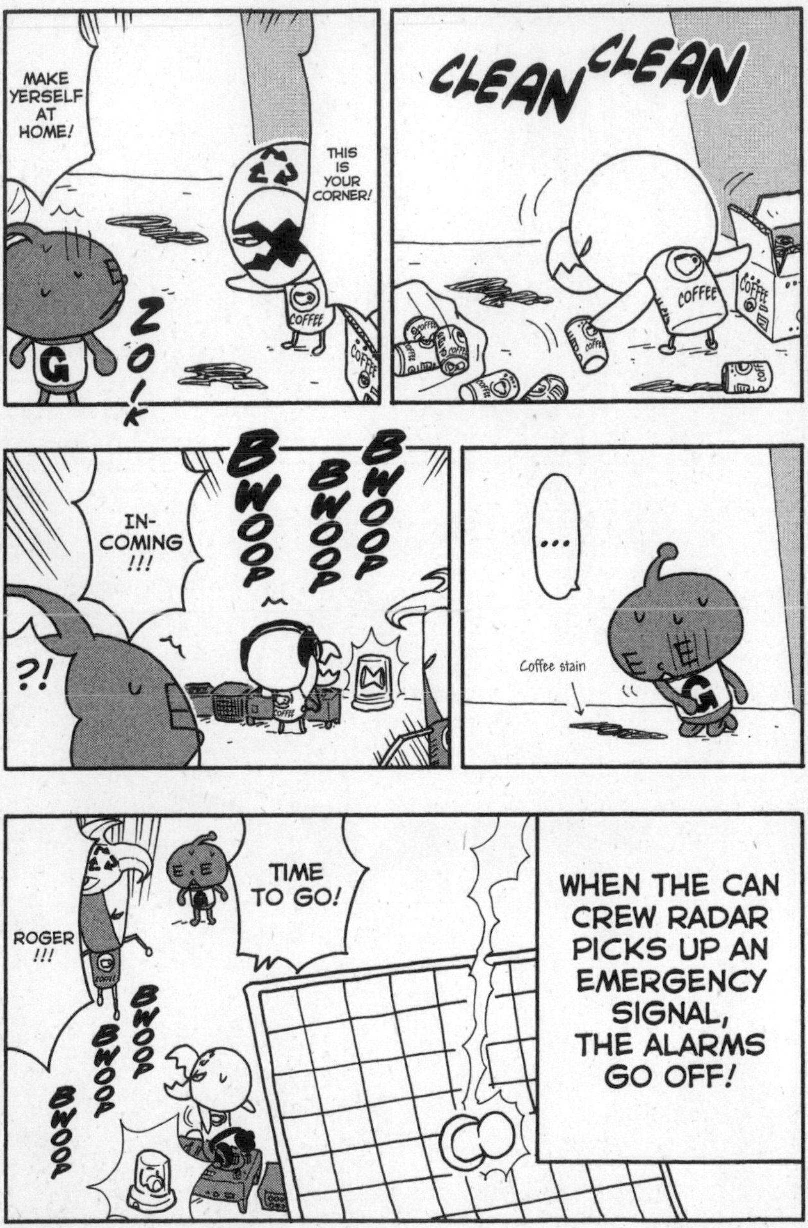

CLEAN CLEAN
MAKE YERSELF AT HOME!
THIS IS YOUR CORNER!
ZOIK
...
Coffee stain
BWOOP BWOOP BWOOP
IN-COMING!!!
?!
WHEN THE CAN CREW RADAR PICKS UP AN EMERGENCY SIGNAL, THE ALARMS GO OFF!
TIME TO GO!
ROGER!!!
BWOOP BWOOP BWOOP

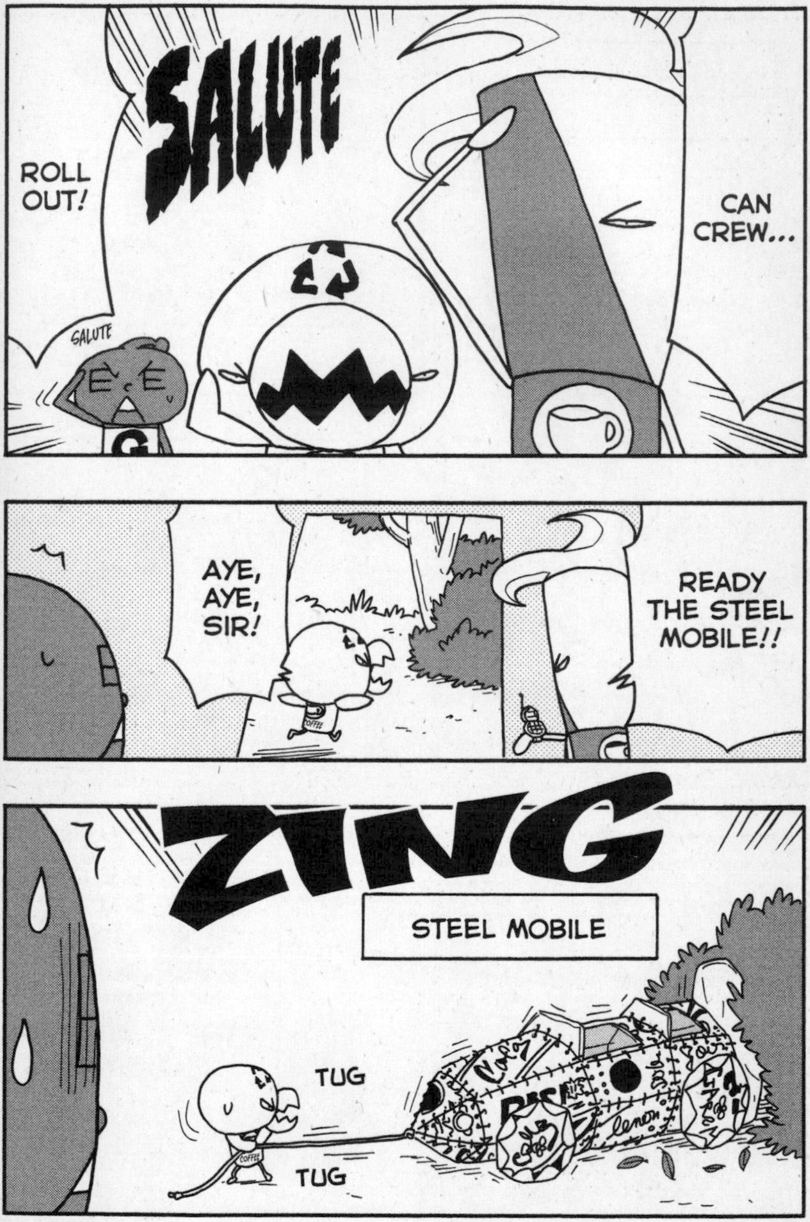
CAN CREW...
SALUTE
ROLL OUT!
SALUTE
READY THE STEEL MOBILE!!
AYE, AYE, SIR!
ZING
STEEL MOBILE
TUG
TUG

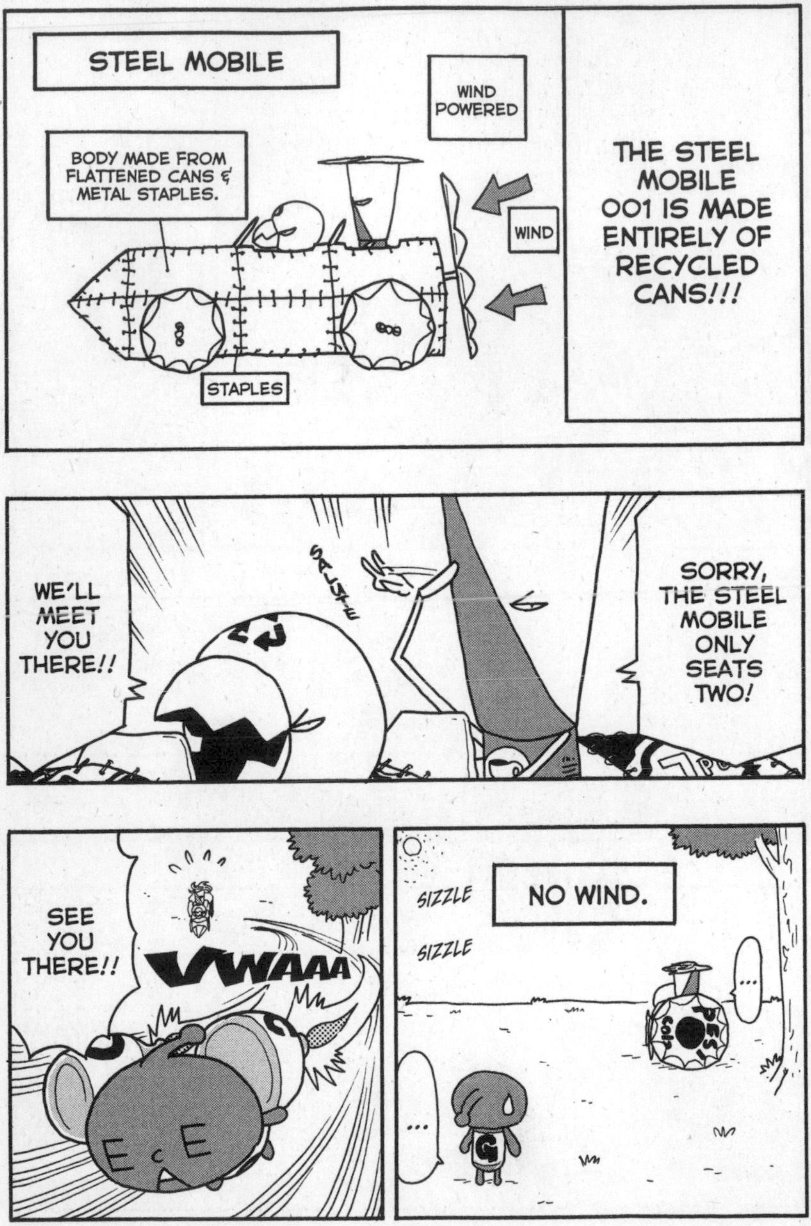
THE STEEL MOBILE 001 IS MADE ENTIRELY OF RECYCLED CANS!!!
STEEL MOBILE
WIND POWERED
WIND
BODY MADE FROM FLATTENED CANS & METAL STAPLES.
STAPLES
SORRY, THE STEEL MOBILE ONLY SEATS TWO!
SALUTE
WE'LL MEET YOU THERE!!
NO WIND.
SIZZLE
SIZZLE
...
...
SEE YOU THERE!!
VWAAA

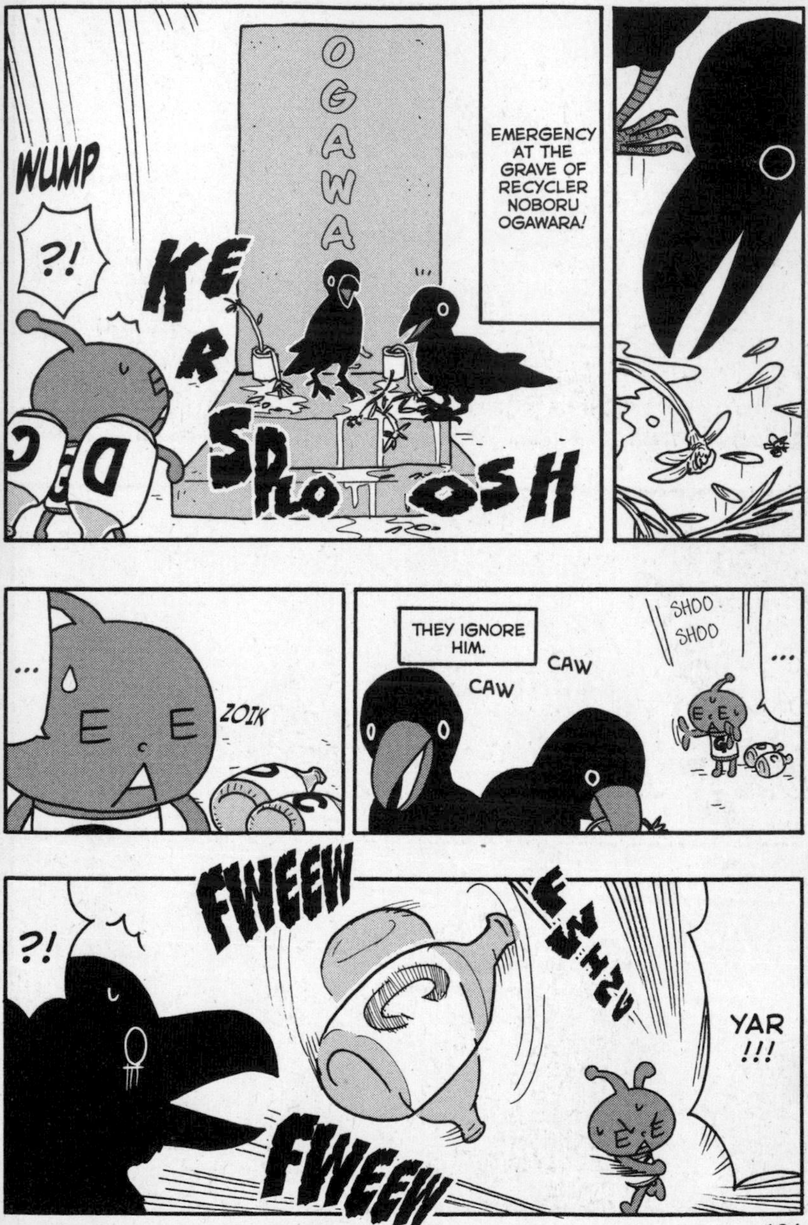
OGAWA
EMERGENCY AT THE GRAVE OF RECYCLER NOBORU OGAWARA!
WUMP
?!
KERSPLOOSH
THEY IGNORE HIM.
SHOO SHOO
...
CAW
CAW
...
ZOIK
FWEEW
?!
YAR !!!
FWEEW

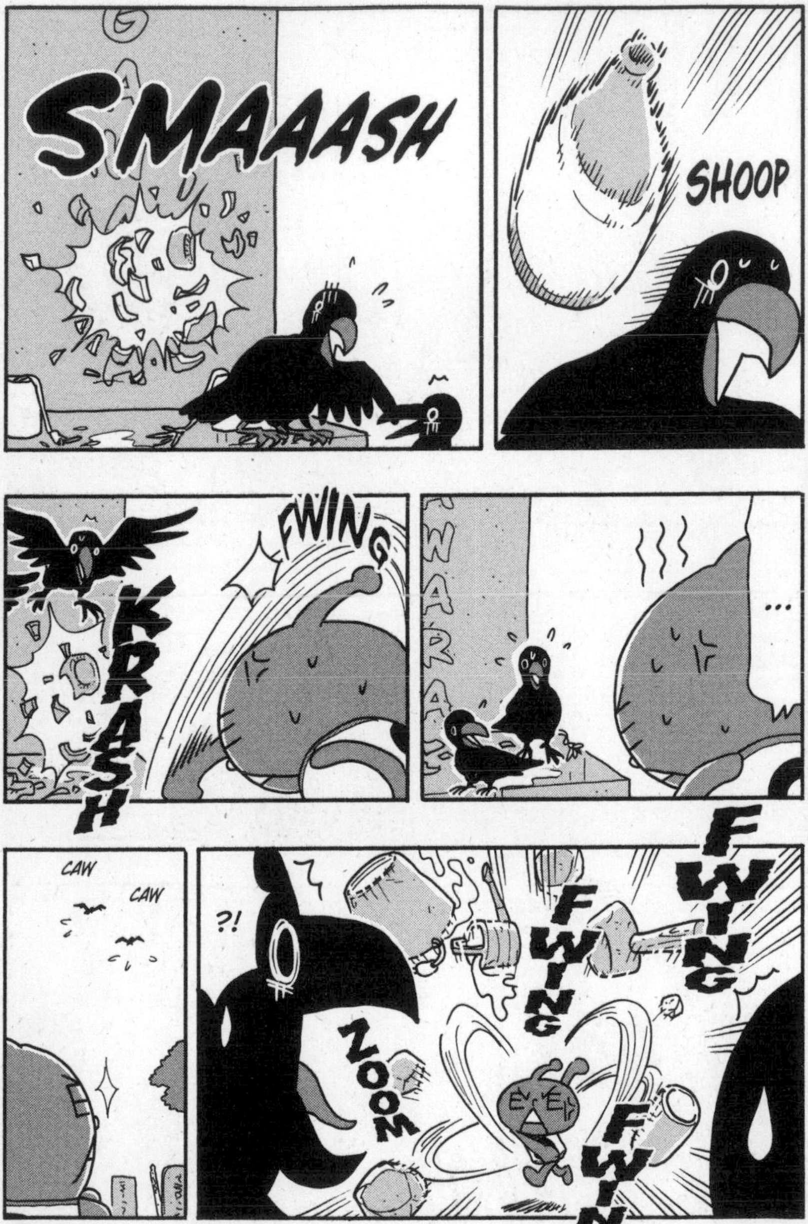
SHOOP
SMAAASH
...
FWING
KRASH
FWING
FWING
?!
ZOOM
FWING
CAW
CAW

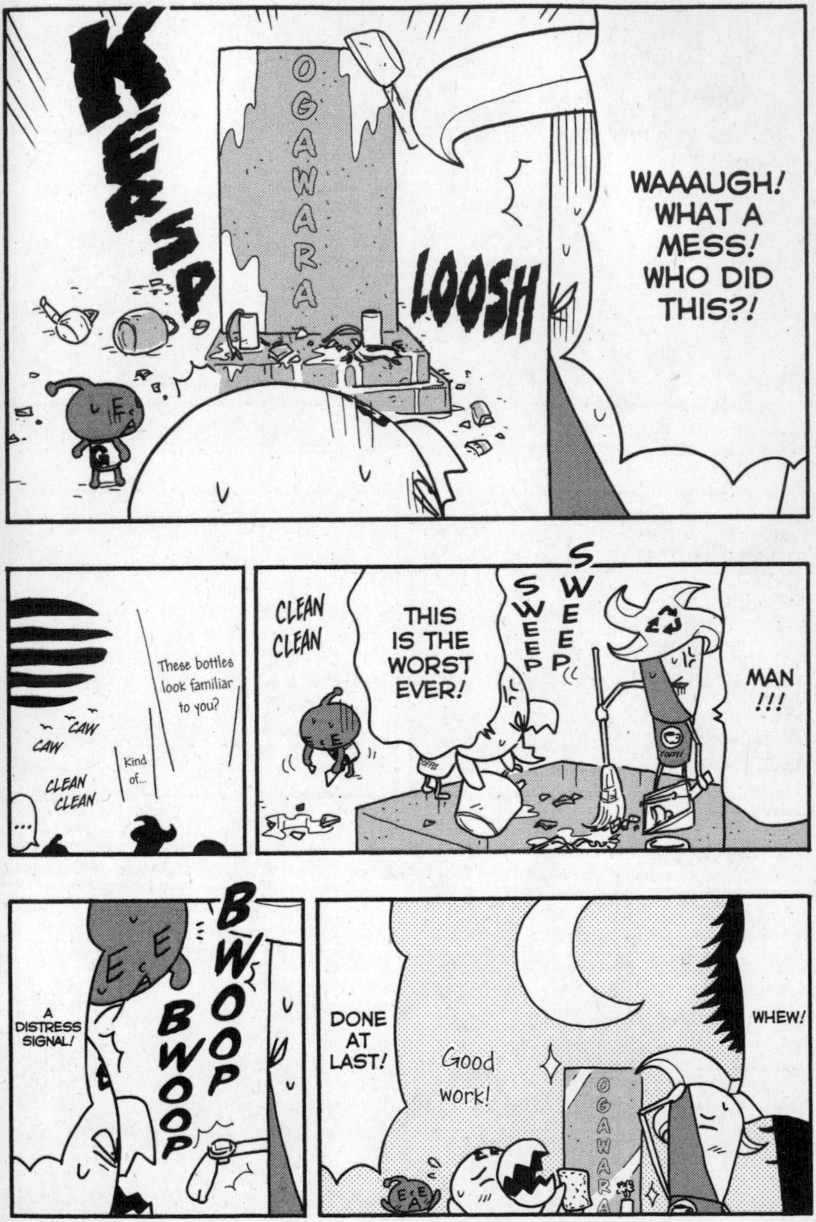

WAAAUGH! WHAT A MESS! WHO DID THIS?!
OGAWARA
KERSP
LOOSH
MAN!!!
SWEEP SWEEP
THIS IS THE WORST EVER!
CLEAN CLEAN
These bottles look familiar to you?
Kind of...
CAW CAW
CLEAN CLEAN
...
WHEW!
OGAWARA
Good work!
DONE AT LAST!
BWOOP BWOOP
BWOOP BWOOP
A DISTRESS SIGNAL!

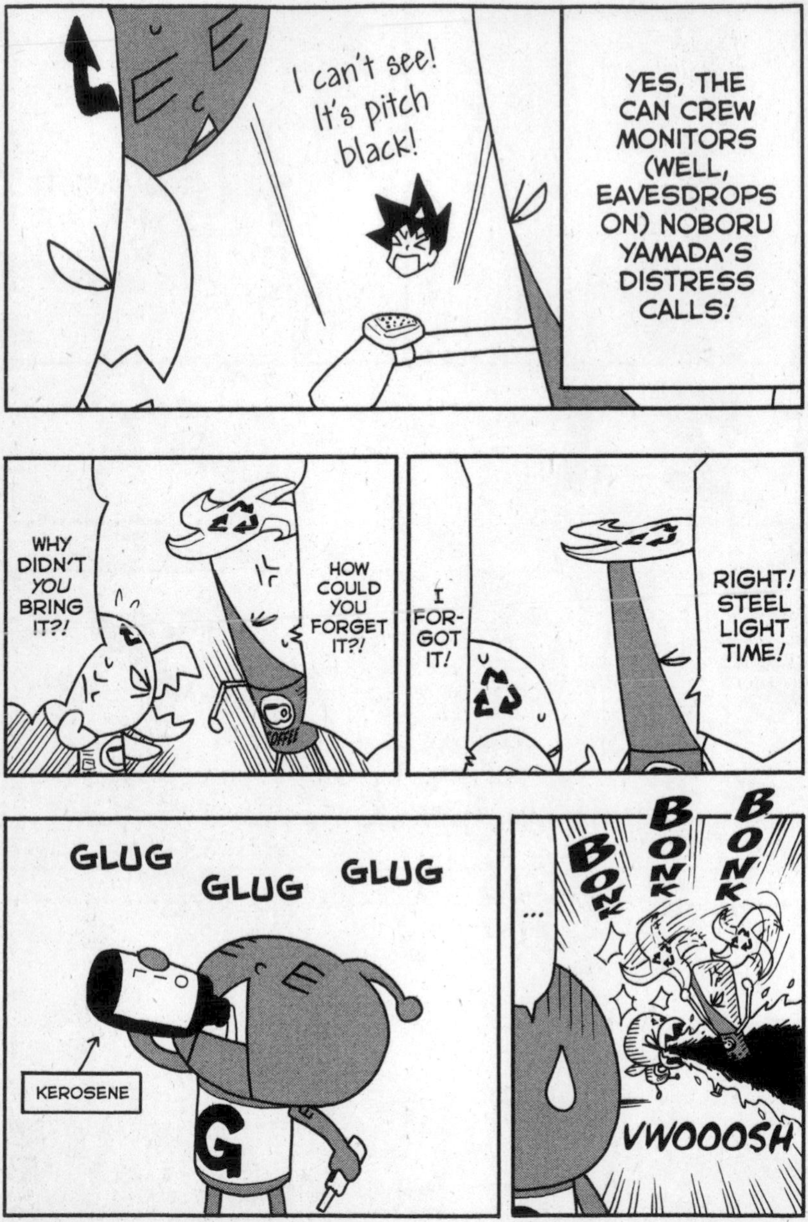
YES, THE CAN CREW MONITORS (WELL, EAVESDROPS ON) NOBORU YAMADA'S DISTRESS CALLS!
I can't see! It's pitch black!
RIGHT! STEEL LIGHT TIME!
I FOR-GOT IT!
HOW COULD YOU FORGET IT?!
WHY DIDN'T *YOU* BRING IT?!
BONK
BONK
BONK
...
VWOOOSH
GLUG
GLUG
GLUG
KEROSENE

 *KIDS, DON'T DRINK KEROSENE! IT'S REALLY POISONOUS!

FWISH

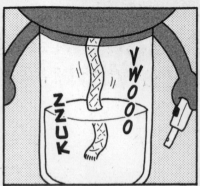

KUNN VWOOO

ZI NG

NICE ONE!

COFFEE

WHOA !!!

COFFEE

So? How'd it go?

SPLASH SPLASH

AUUUGH! A GHOST!!!

•••

?!

TAP TAP

# CHAPTER 16

# Mama and Hikaru Are Worried

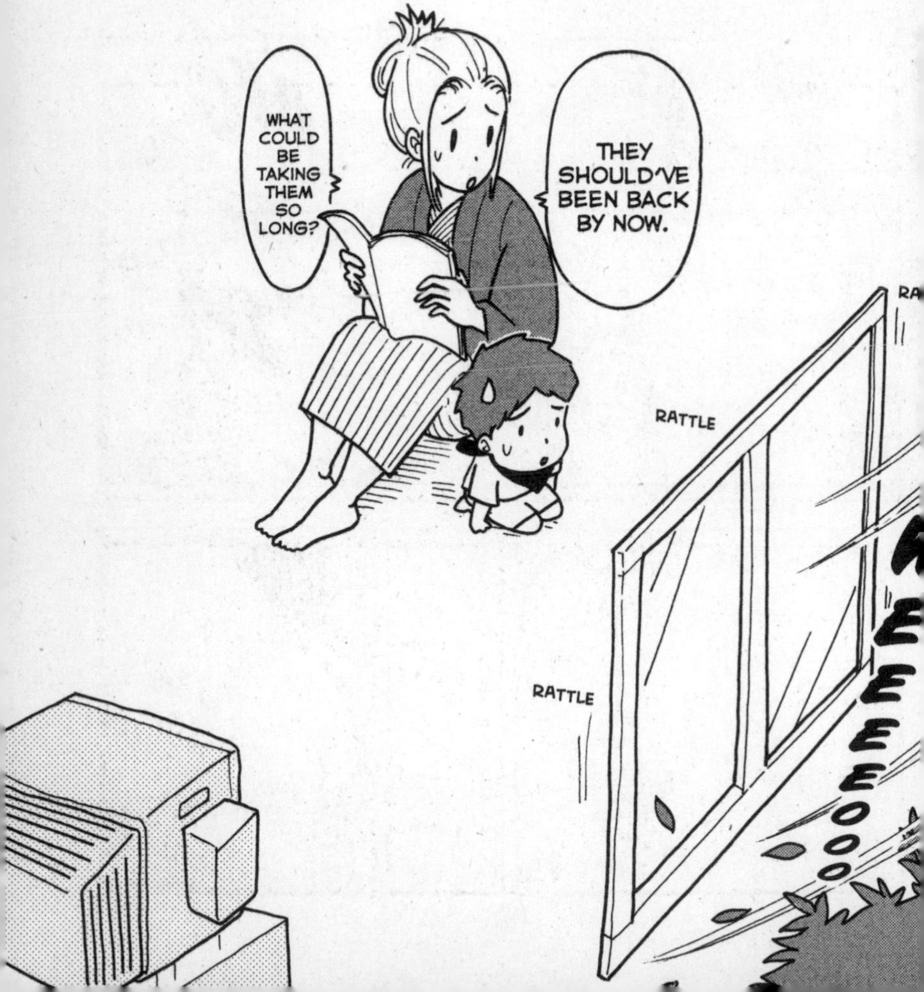
THEY SHOULD'VE BEEN BACK BY NOW.
WHAT COULD BE TAKING THEM SO LONG?
RATTLE
RATTLE

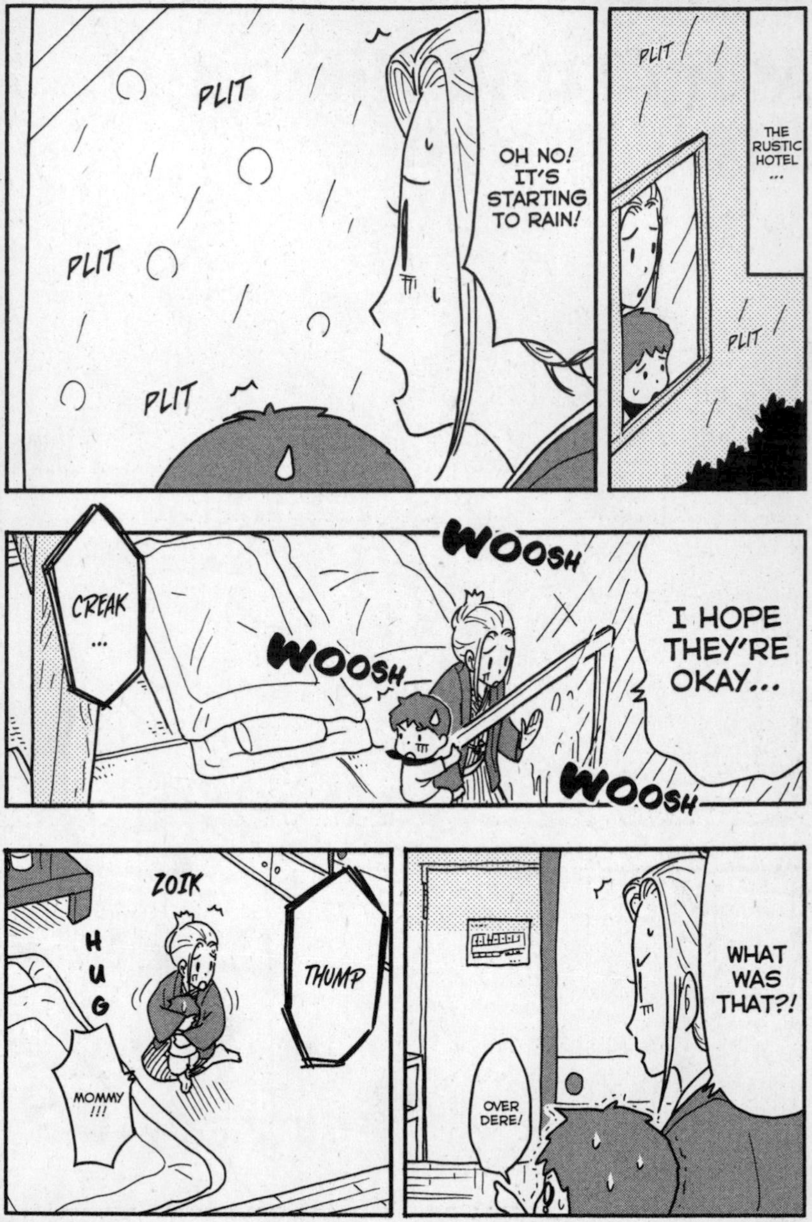
THE RUSTIC HOTEL ...
PLIT
PLIT
PLIT
OH NO! IT'S STARTING TO RAIN!
PLIT
PLIT
WOOSH
I HOPE THEY'RE OKAY...
CREAK ...
WOOSH
WOOSH
WHAT WAS THAT?!
OVER DERE!
THUMP
ZOIK
HUG
MOMMY !!!

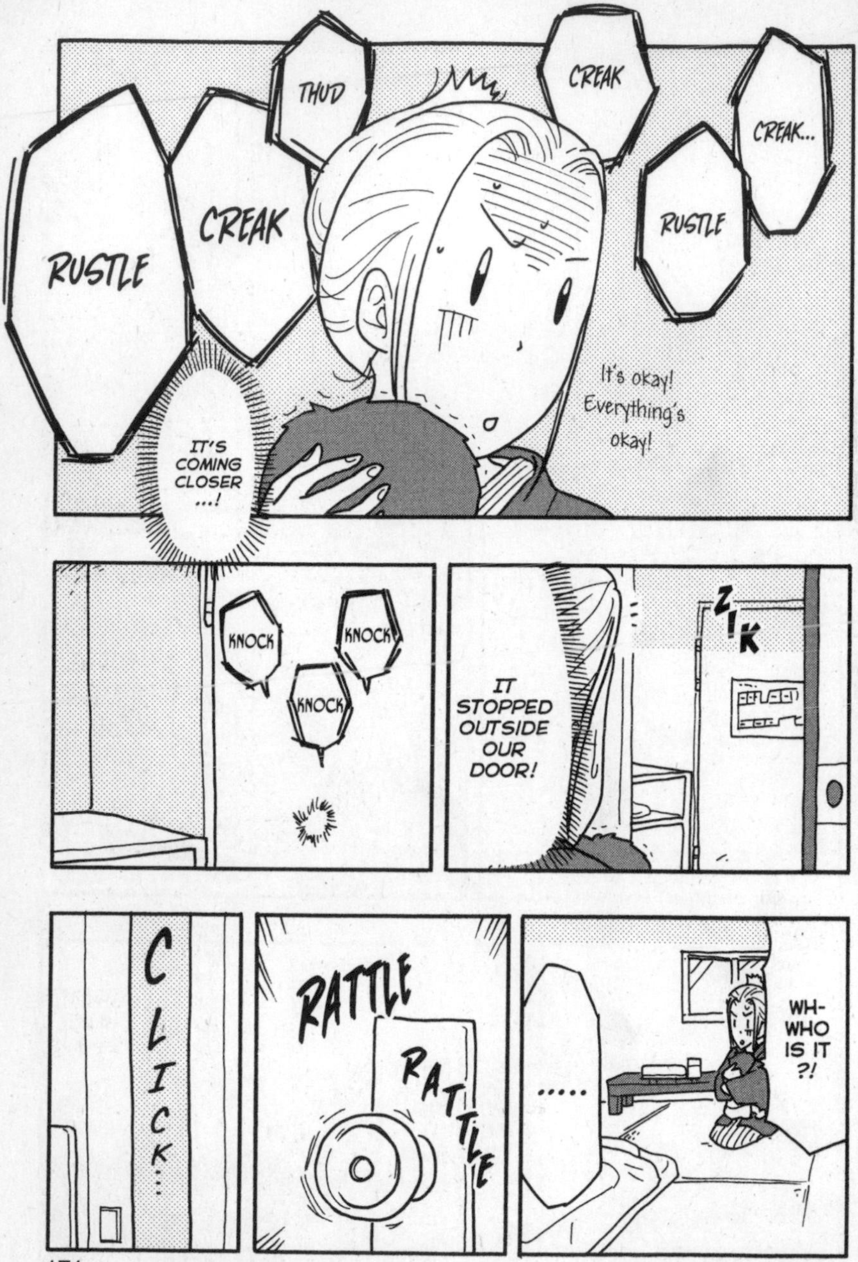
CREAK...
CREAK
RUSTLE
THUD
CREAK
RUSTLE
It's okay! Everything's okay!
IT'S COMING CLOSER ...!
ZIK
IT STOPPED OUTSIDE OUR DOOR!
KNOCK
KNOCK
KNOCK
WH- WHO IS IT ?!
.....
RATTLE
RATTLE
CLICK...

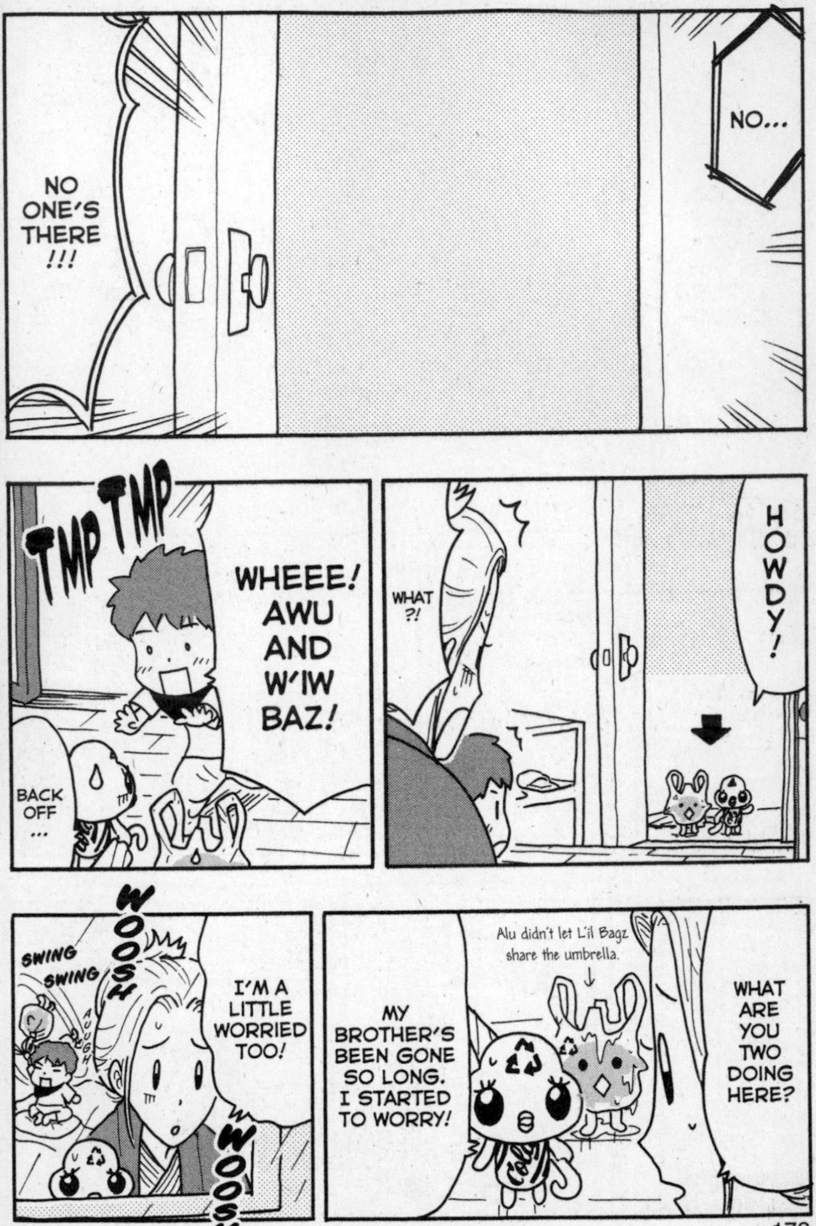
NO...
NO ONE'S THERE !!!
HOWDY!
WHAT ?!
WHEEE! AWU AND W'IW BAZ!
TMP TMP
BACK OFF ...
WHAT ARE YOU TWO DOING HERE?
Alu didn't let L'il Bagz share the umbrella.
MY BROTHER'S BEEN GONE SO LONG. I STARTED TO WORRY!
I'M A LITTLE WORRIED TOO!
WOOSH
WOOSH
SWING
SWING

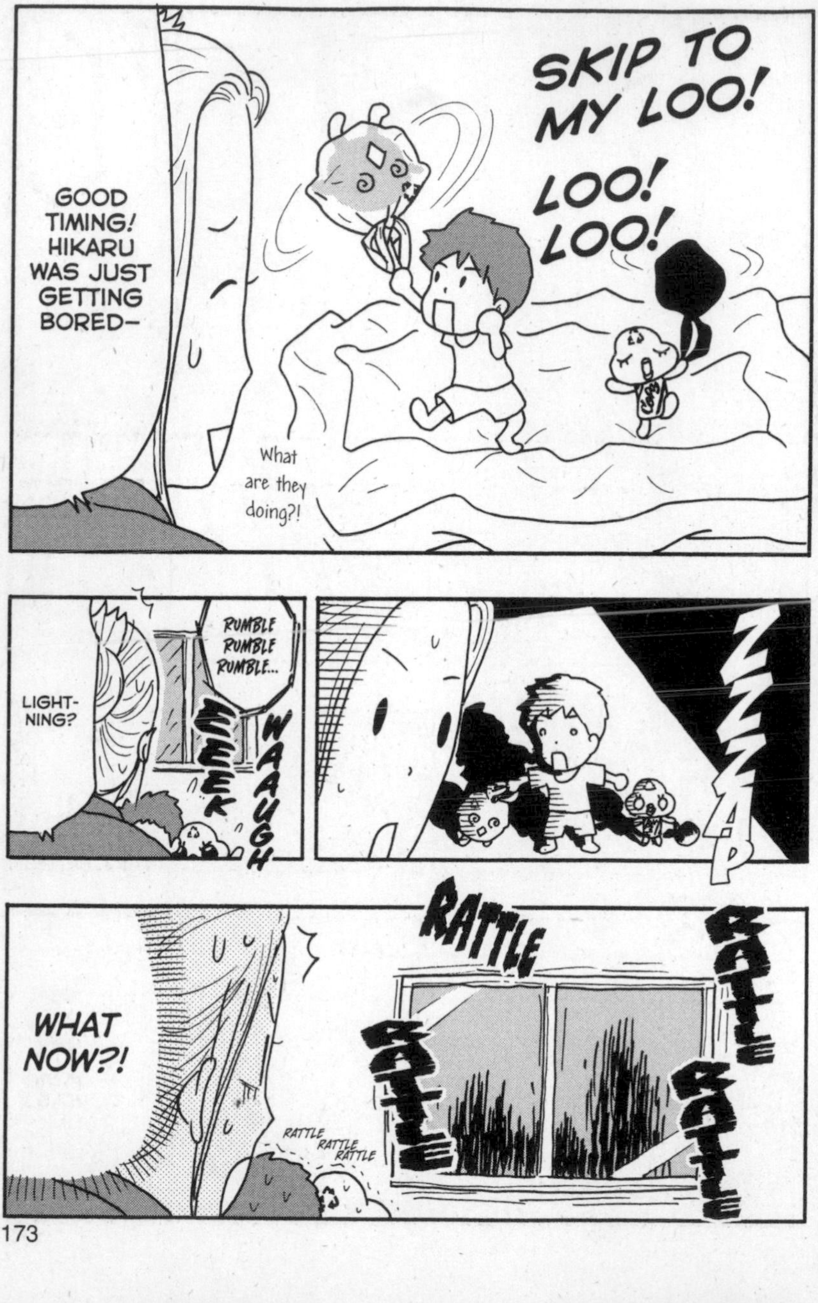
SKIP TO MY LOO!
LOO! LOO!
GOOD TIMING! HIKARU WAS JUST GETTING BORED–
What are they doing?!
ZZZAP
RUMBLE RUMBLE RUMBLE...
WAAAUGH
EEEEK
LIGHTNING?
RATTLE
RATTLE RATTLE
WHAT NOW?!
RATTLE RATTLE
RATTLE RATTLE RATTLE

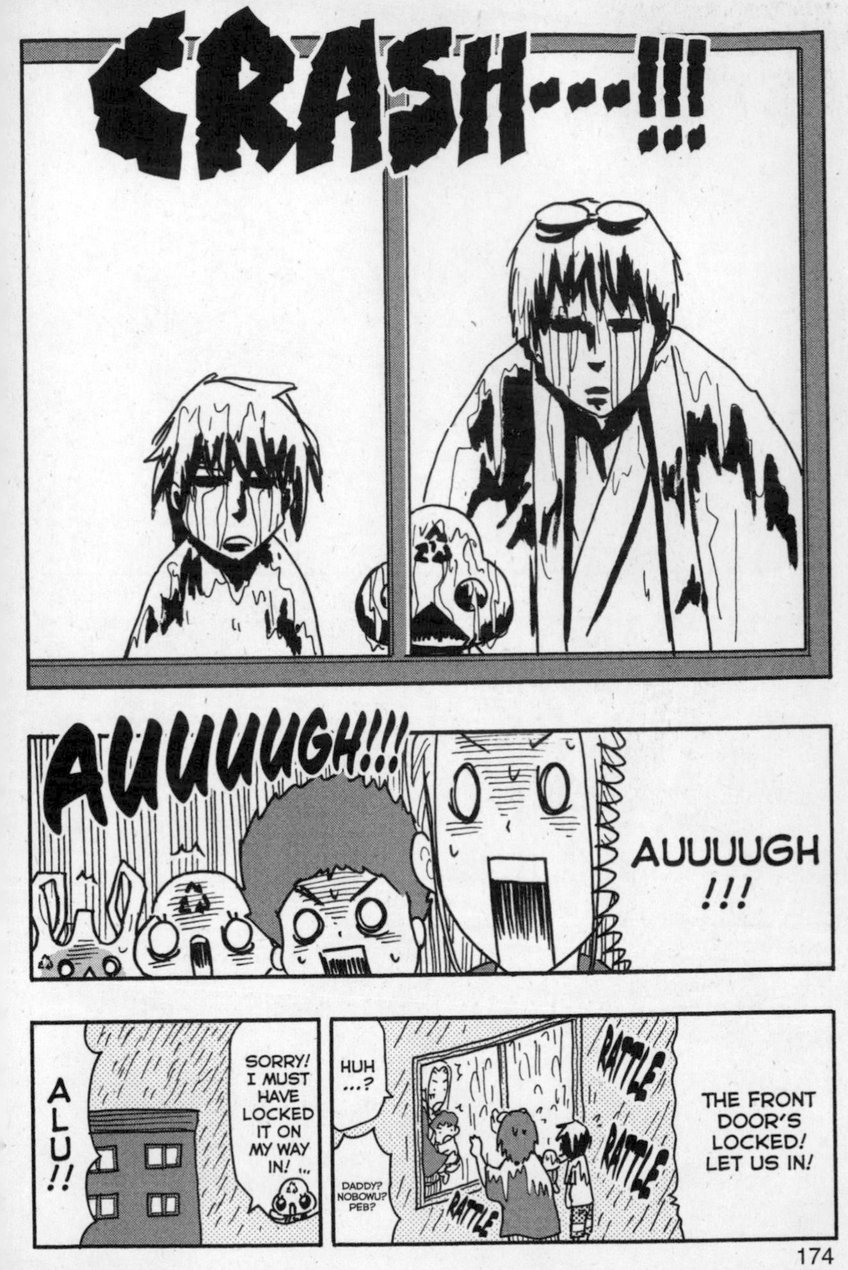
CRASH---!!!
AUUUUGH !!!
AUUUUGH!!!
THE FRONT DOOR'S LOCKED! LET US IN!
RATTLE
RATTLE
RATTLE
HUH ...?
DADDY? NOBOWU? PEB?
SORRY! I MUST HAVE LOCKED IT ON MY WAY IN! ...
ALU!!

# CHAPTER 17
# PET's Carwash

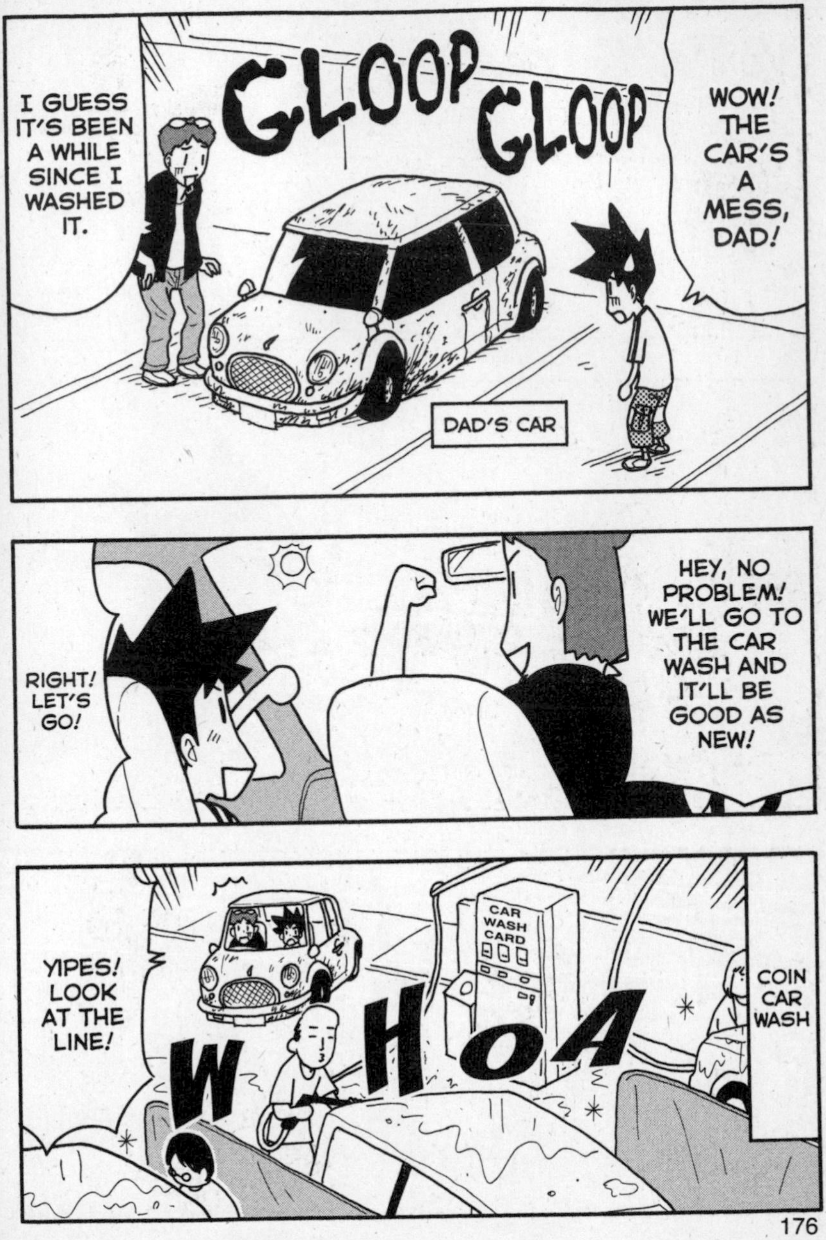
WOW! THE CAR'S A MESS, DAD!
GLOOP GLOOP
I GUESS IT'S BEEN A WHILE SINCE I WASHED IT.
DAD'S CAR
HEY, NO PROBLEM! WE'LL GO TO THE CAR WASH AND IT'LL BE GOOD AS NEW!
RIGHT! LET'S GO!
COIN CAR WASH
CAR WASH CARD
YIPES! LOOK AT THE LINE!
WHOA

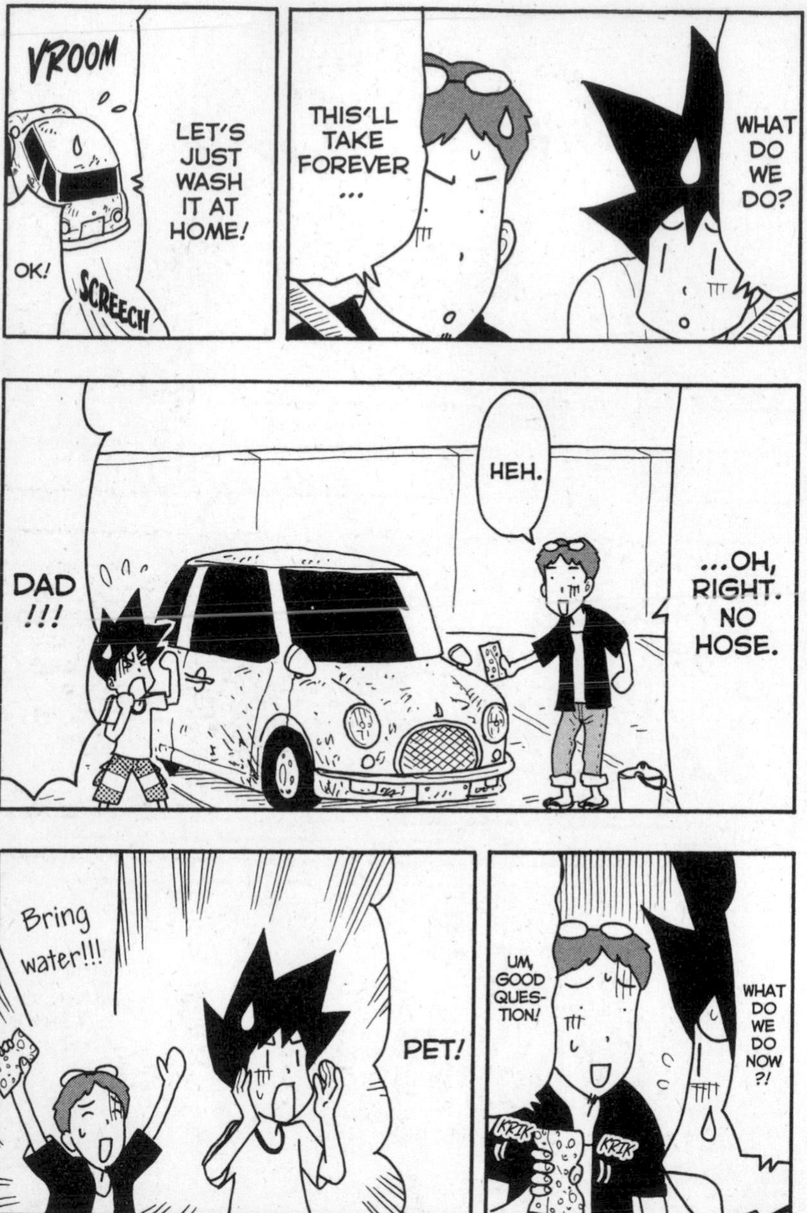
WHAT DO WE DO?
THIS'LL TAKE FOREVER ...
LET'S JUST WASH IT AT HOME!
VROOM
OK!
SCREECH
...OH, RIGHT. NO HOSE.
HEH.
DAD!!!
WHAT DO WE DO NOW?!
UM, GOOD QUES-TION!
KRIK
KRIK
PET!
Bring water!!!

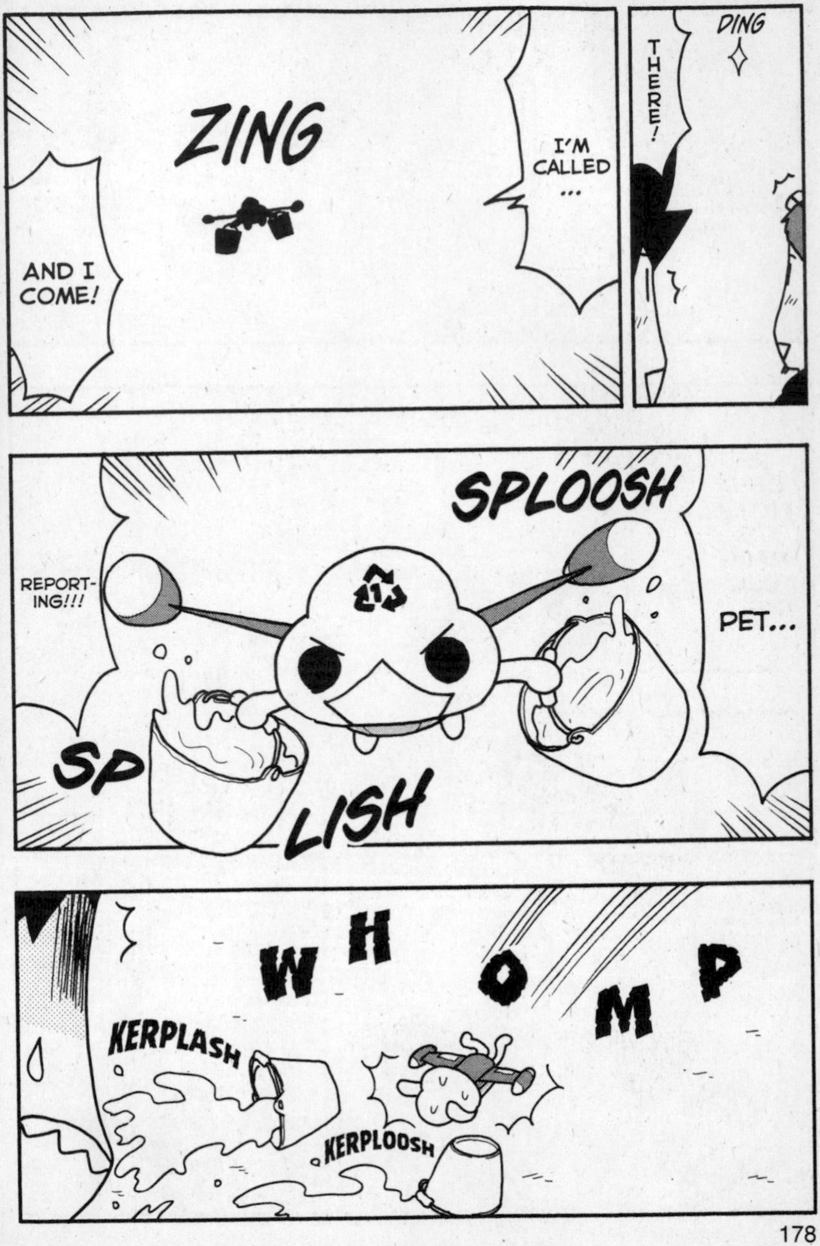
DING
THERE!
I'M CALLED ...
ZING
AND I COME!
PET...
SPLOOSH
REPORTING!!!
SPLISH
WHOMP
KERPLASH
KERPLOOSH

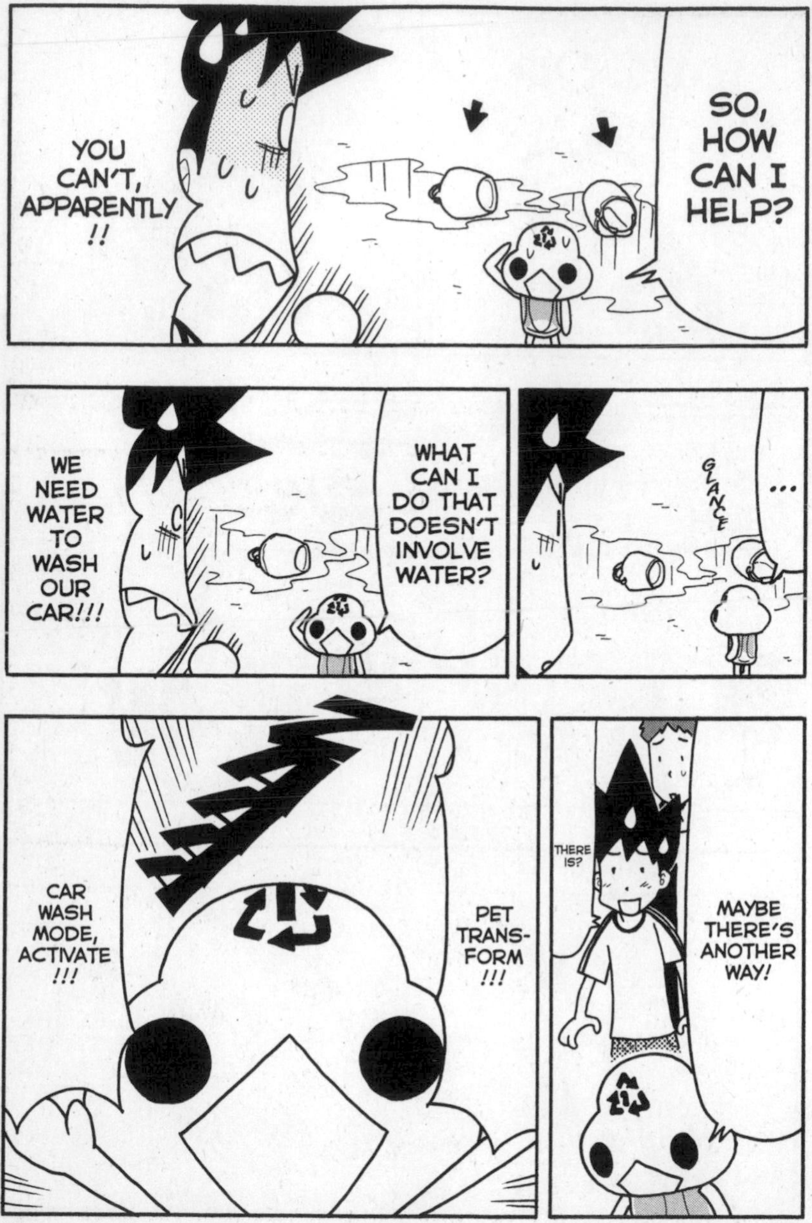
SO, HOW CAN I HELP?
YOU CAN'T, APPARENTLY!!
GLANCE
...
WHAT CAN I DO THAT DOESN'T INVOLVE WATER?
WE NEED WATER TO WASH OUR CAR!!!
MAYBE THERE'S ANOTHER WAY!
THERE IS?
PET TRANS-FORM!!!
CAR WASH MODE, ACTIVATE!!!

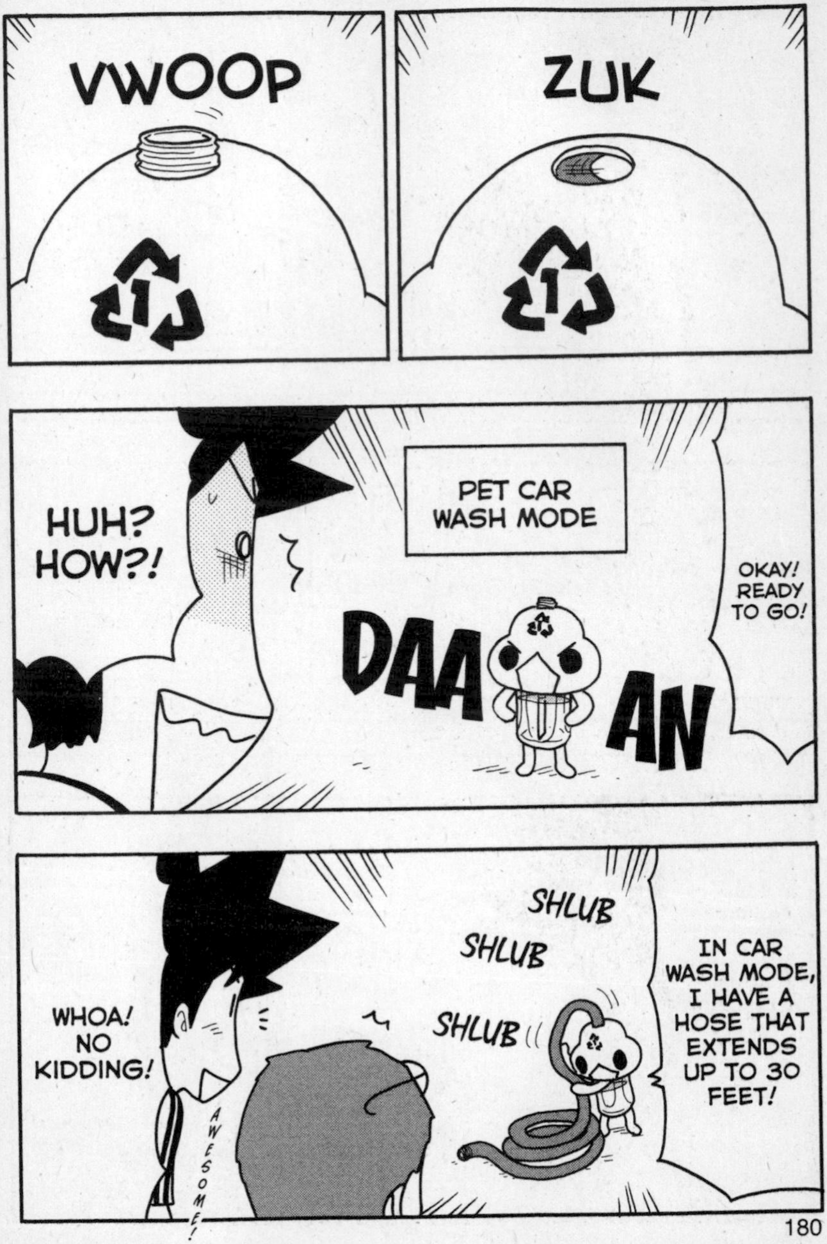
ZUK
VWOOP
OKAY! READY TO GO!
PET CAR WASH MODE
DAA AN
HUH? HOW?!
IN CAR WASH MODE, I HAVE A HOSE THAT EXTENDS UP TO 30 FEET!
SHLUB
SHLUB
SHLUB
WHOA! NO KIDDING!
AWESOME!

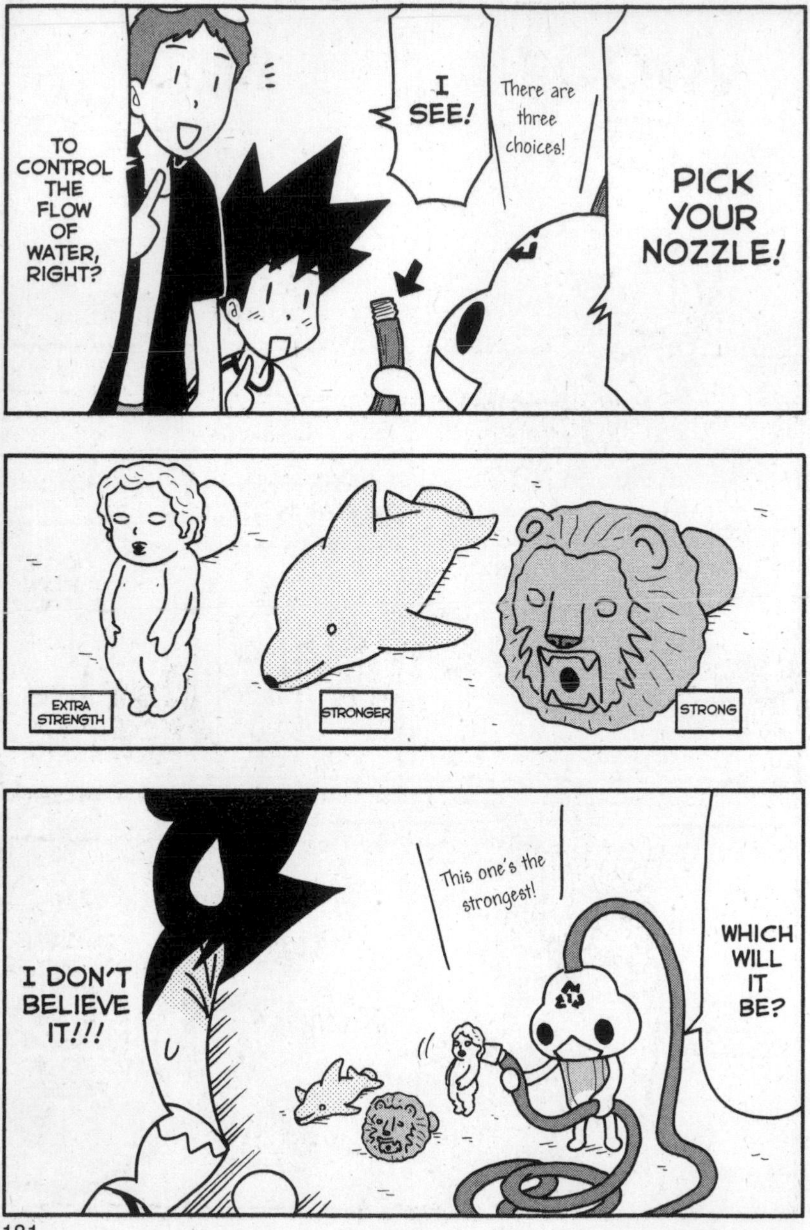
PICK YOUR NOZZLE!
There are three choices!
I SEE!
TO CONTROL THE FLOW OF WATER, RIGHT?
STRONG
STRONGER
EXTRA STRENGTH
WHICH WILL IT BE?
This one's the strongest!
I DON'T BELIEVE IT!!!

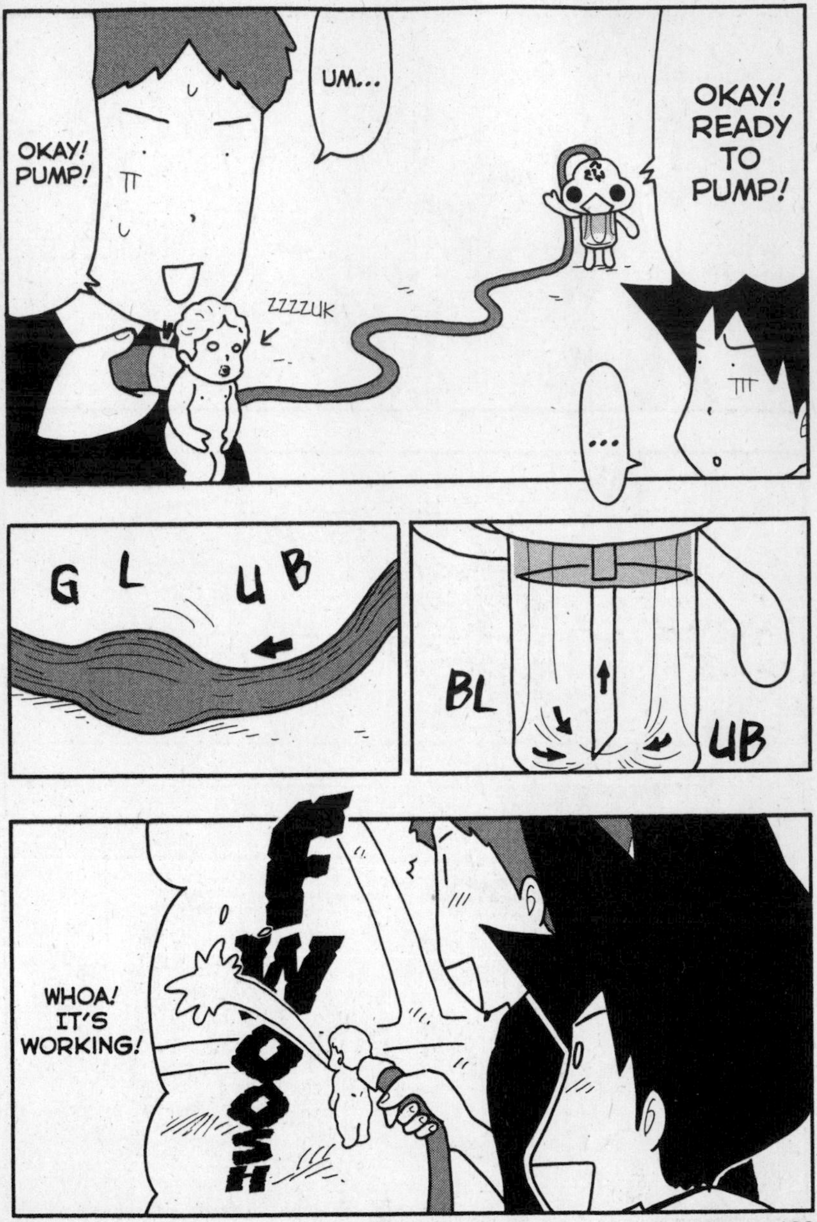

OKAY! READY TO PUMP!
UM...
...
OKAY! PUMP!
ZZZZUK
BL UB
G L U B
FWOOSH
WHOA! IT'S WORKING!

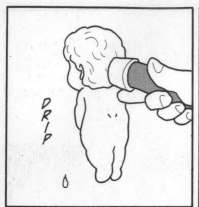

DRIBBLE
DRIBBLE
DRIP
ALL DONE!
Please return the hose to its holder.
ZUB
ZUB
ZUB
THAT'S ALL?!
WHAT WAS THE POINT OF THAT?!
THERE WASN'T ONE!
UM ...
OKAY!
TIME FOR A NEW ATTACHMENT!

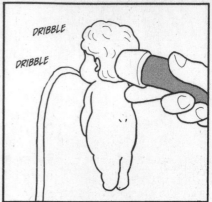

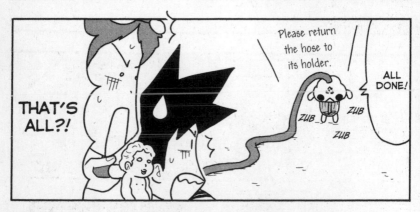

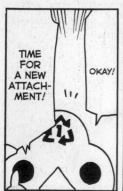

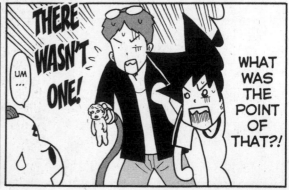

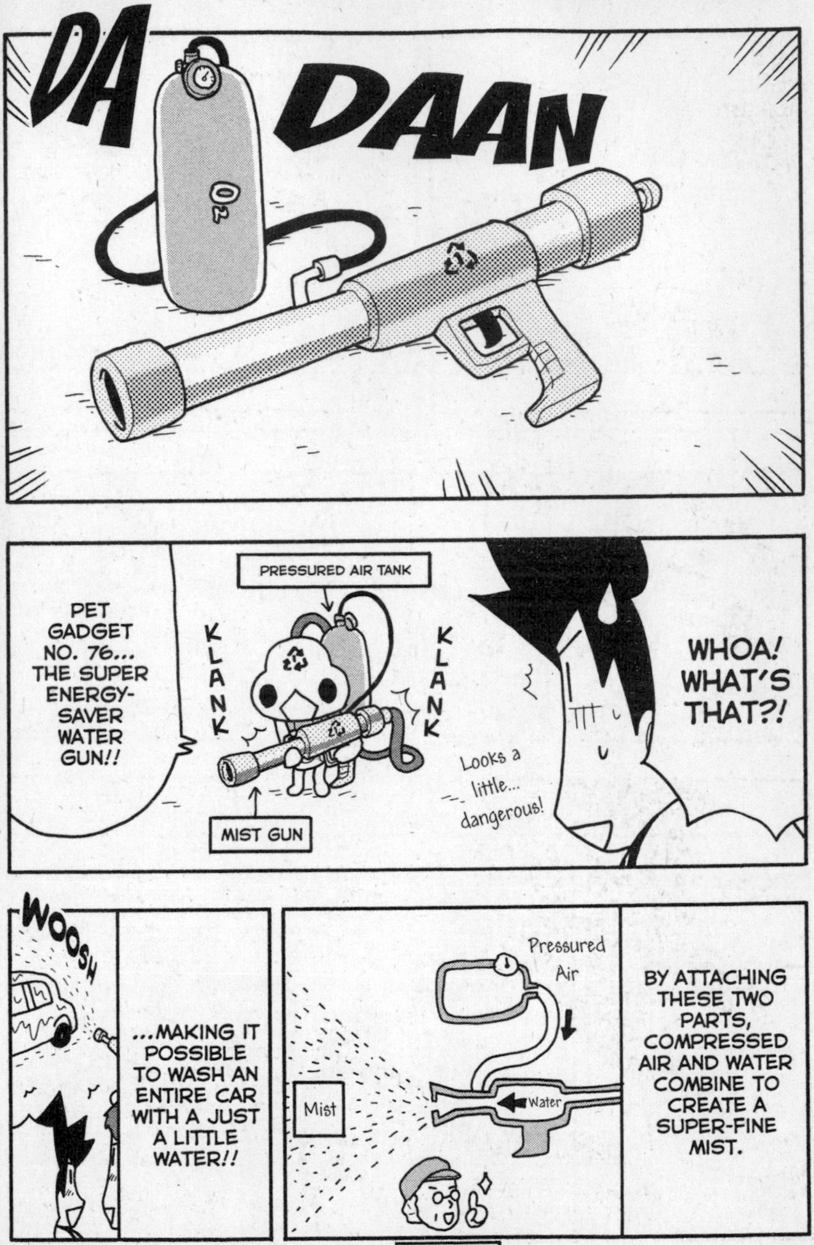
DA DAAN
$O_2$
WHOA! WHAT'S THAT?!
Looks a little... dangerous!
KLANK
PRESSURED AIR TANK
KLANK
PET GADGET NO. 76... THE SUPER ENERGY-SAVER WATER GUN!!
MIST GUN
BY ATTACHING THESE TWO PARTS, COMPRESSED AIR AND WATER COMBINE TO CREATE A SUPER-FINE MIST.
Pressured Air
Water
Mist
...MAKING IT POSSIBLE TO WASH AN ENTIRE CAR WITH A JUST A LITTLE WATER!!
WOOSH

Mr. Morita Gadget Design

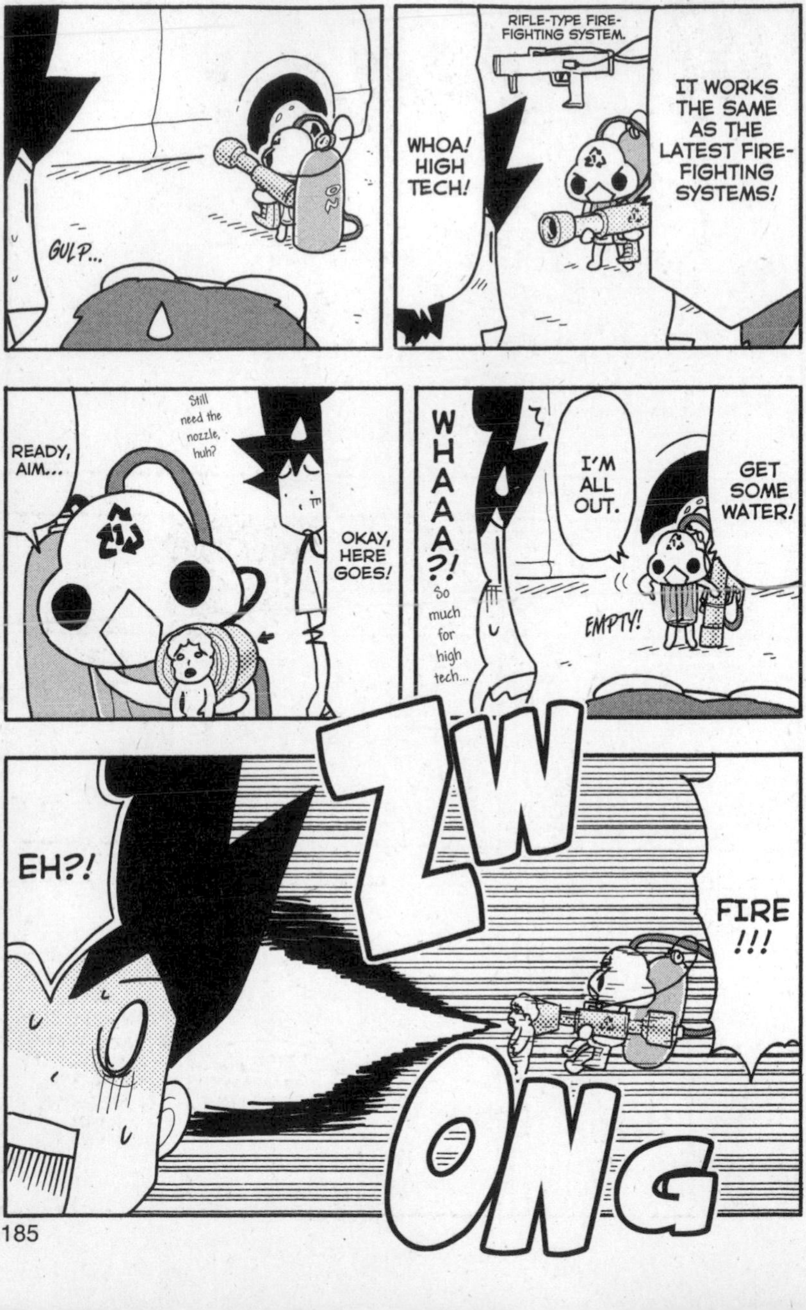
RIFLE-TYPE FIRE-FIGHTING SYSTEM.
IT WORKS THE SAME AS THE LATEST FIRE-FIGHTING SYSTEMS!
WHOA! HIGH TECH!
GULP...
GET SOME WATER!
I'M ALL OUT.
EMPTY!
WHAAAA?!
So much for high tech...
Still need the nozzle, huh?
READY, AIM...
OKAY, HERE GOES!
FIRE!!!
ZWONG
EH?!

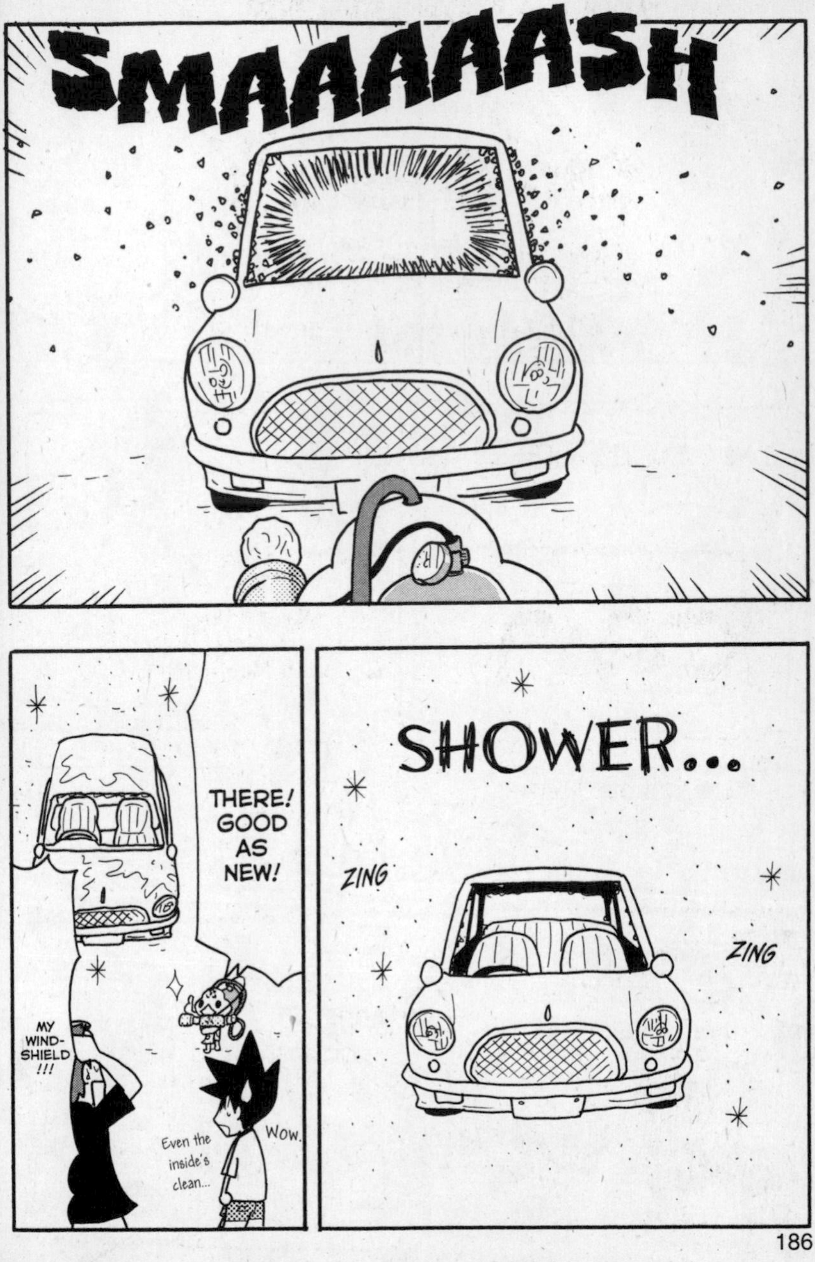
SMAAAAASH
SHOWER...
ZING
ZING
THERE! GOOD AS NEW!
MY WIND-SHIELD !!!
WOW.
Even the inside's clean...

# Can Crew ♺
## Application Test &
## Membership Card

- Please fill in the blank

CAN CREW

Hint: It's our name!

WELCOME TO THE
CAN CREW!

Member No. 003

Member No. 002

Crew
Captain

E E
A
G

COFFEE

COFFEE

**Can Crew**
Membership Card
Member No. 004

Your
Picture
Here

Name

- Listen to the Crew Captain
- Protect Noboru

ANSWER: C

# Special Bonus No. 2

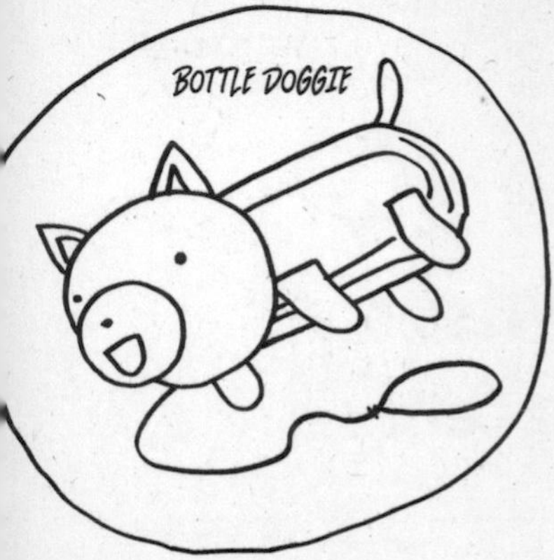
BOTTLE DOGGIE

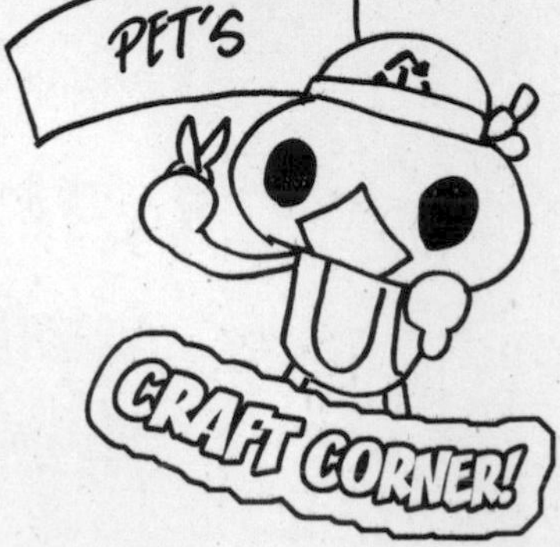
PET'S
CRAFT CORNER!

# MAKE YOUR OWN BOTTLE DOGGIE!

★ CAREFUL NOT TO CUT YOURSELF WHEN USING SCISSORS!

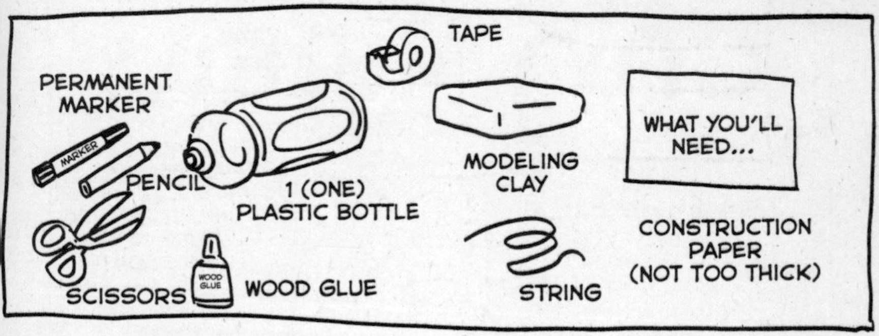
WHAT YOU'LL NEED...
PERMANENT MARKER
MARKER
PENCIL
1 (ONE) PLASTIC BOTTLE
TAPE
MODELING CLAY
SCISSORS
WOOD GLUE
WOOD GLUE
STRING
CONSTRUCTION PAPER (NOT TOO THICK)

① TO MAKE BOTTLE DOGGIE'S HEAD, WRAP THE TOP OF THE BOTTLE IN CLAY

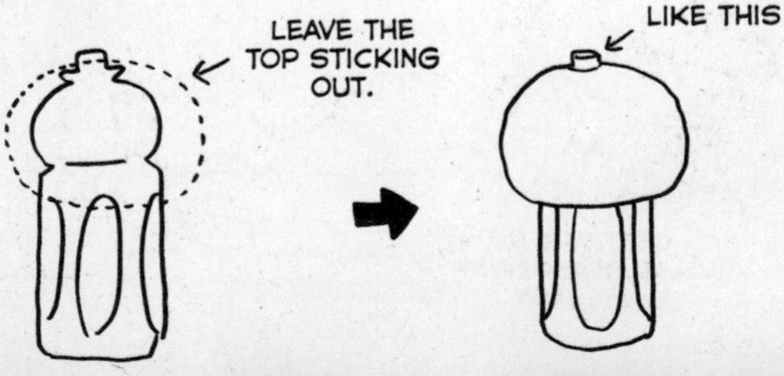
LEAVE THE TOP STICKING OUT.
LIKE THIS

(2) TO MAKE BOTTLE DOGGIE'S NOSE, COVER THE BOTTLE'S TOP WITH ANOTHER BALL OF CLAY.

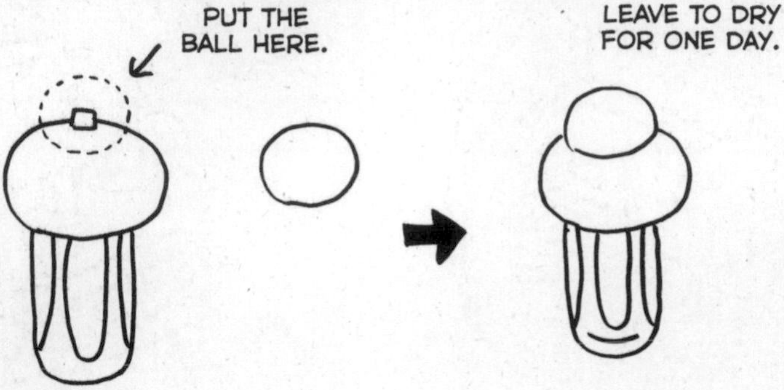
PUT THE BALL HERE.
LEAVE TO DRY FOR ONE DAY.

(3) MAKE BOTTLE DOGGIE'S LEGS AND TAIL.

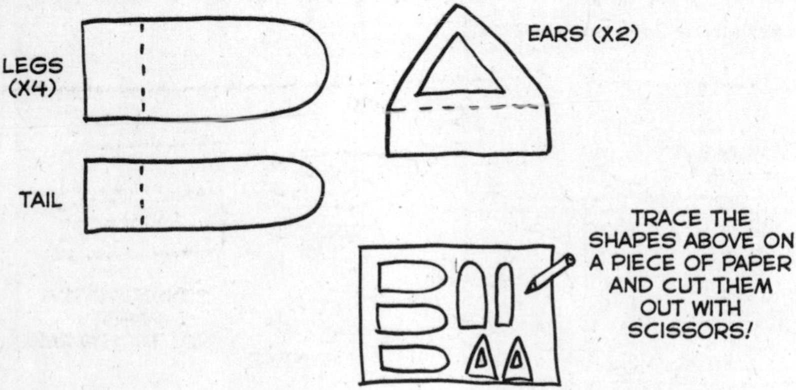
LEGS (X4)
TAIL
EARS (X2)
TRACE THE SHAPES ABOVE ON A PIECE OF PAPER AND CUT THEM OUT WITH SCISSORS!

(4) ATTACH THE EARS, LEGS AND TAIL TO BOTTLE DOGGIE'S BODY LIKE THIS:

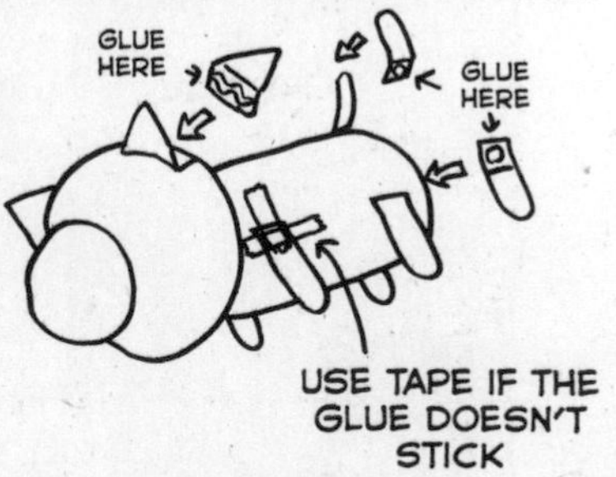
GLUE HERE
GLUE HERE
USE TAPE IF THE GLUE DOESN'T STICK

(5) DRAW EYES, NOSE AND MOUTH, ADD STRING AND YOU'RE DONE!

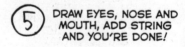

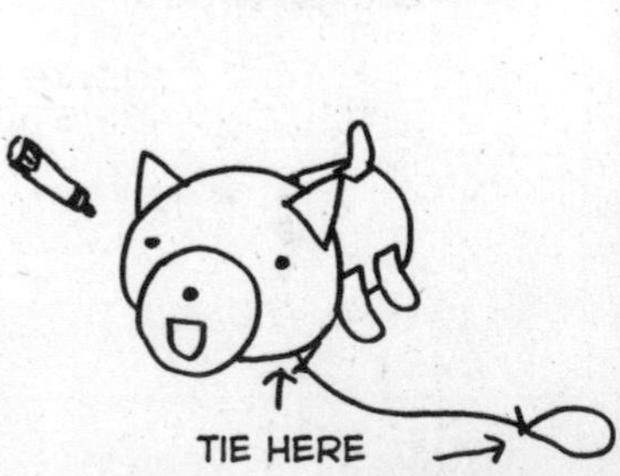
TIE HERE

# from PET's Fans!

SPECIAL BONUS NO. 3

YOSHIMITSU WAHARA - SAITAMA
***RECYCLE TEAM***

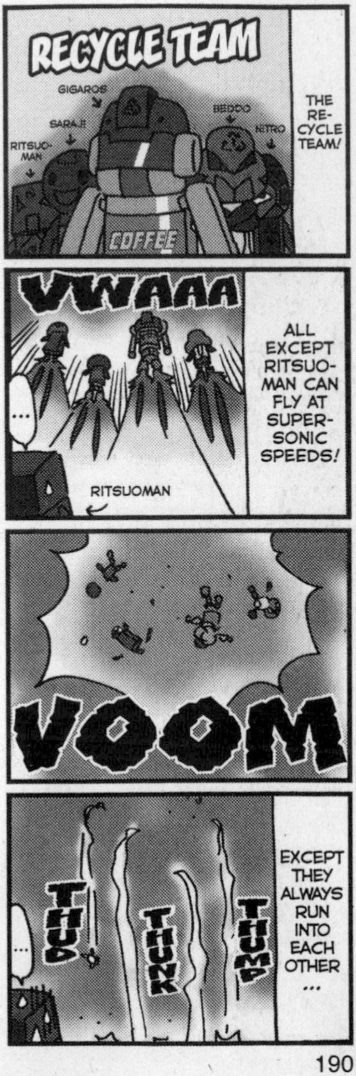

THE RE-CYCLE TEAM!
RECYCLE TEAM
BEDDO
NITRO
GIGAROS
SARAJI
RITSUO-MAN
COFFEE
ALL EXCEPT RITSUO-MAN CAN FLY AT SUPER-SONIC SPEEDS!
VWAAA
...
RITSUOMAN
VOOM
EXCEPT THEY ALWAYS RUN INTO EACH OTHER ...
THUMP
THUNK
THUD
...


MASAKI TAKANO - TOYAMA
***NEWSPAPER MAN***

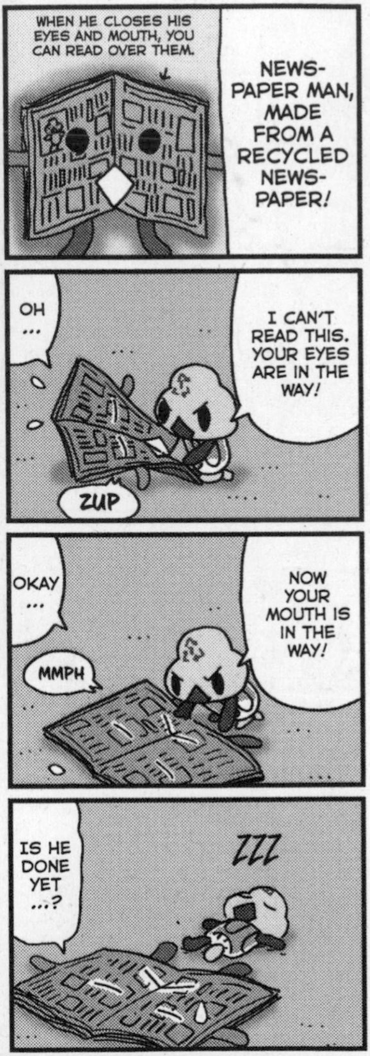

NEWS-PAPER MAN, MADE FROM A RECYCLED NEWS-PAPER!
WHEN HE CLOSES HIS EYES AND MOUTH, YOU CAN READ OVER THEM.
I CAN'T READ THIS. YOUR EYES ARE IN THE WAY!
OH ...
ZUP
NOW YOUR MOUTH IS IN THE WAY!
OKAY ...
MMPH
ZZZ
IS HE DONE YET ...?

# Special Feature
# Recycled Heroes

TATSUYOSHI RYOGOKU - HOKKAIDO
**PET CAP**

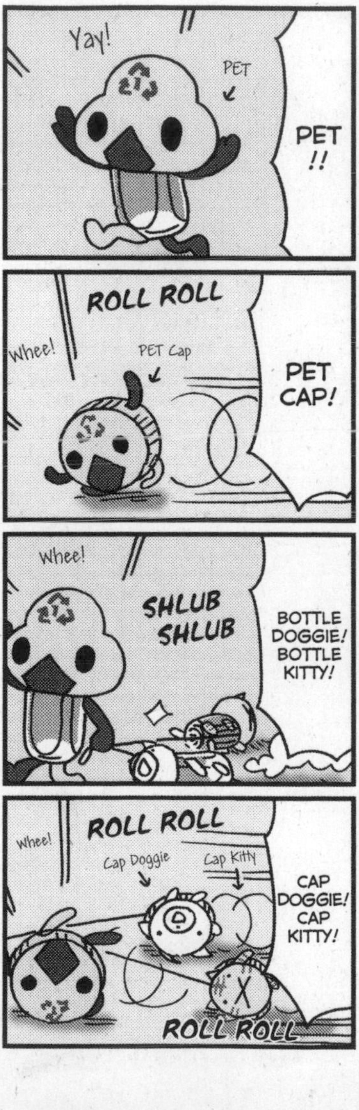
PET !!
PET
Yay!
ROLL ROLL
PET CAP!
Whee!
PET Cap
BOTTLE DOGGIE! BOTTLE KITTY!
SHLUB SHLUB
Whee!
ROLL ROLL
CAP DOGGIE! CAP KITTY!
Cap Kitty
Cap Doggie
Whee!
ROLL ROLL

CHERRY - HIROSHIMA
**GRAPEY!**

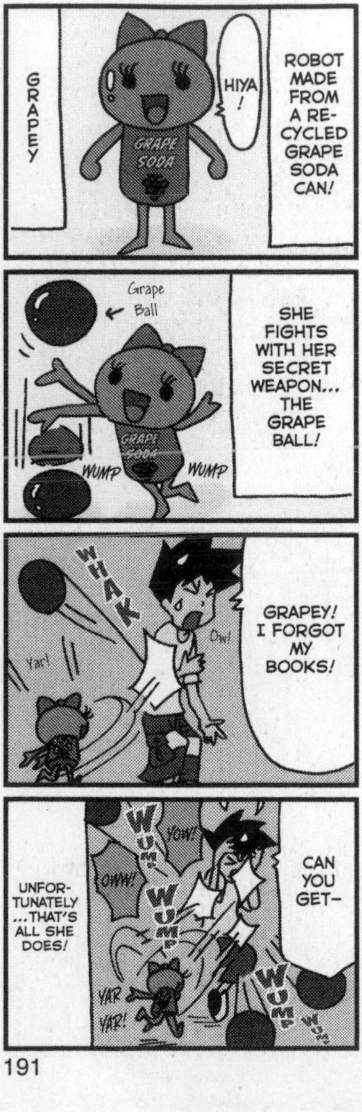
ROBOT MADE FROM A RE-CYCLED GRAPE SODA CAN!
HIYA!
GRAPE SODA
GRAPEY
SHE FIGHTS WITH HER SECRET WEAPON... THE GRAPE BALL!
Grape Ball
WUMP
WUMP
GRAPEY! I FORGOT MY BOOKS!
Ow!
WHAK
Yar!
CAN YOU GET-
YOW!
WUMP
OWW!
WUMP
WUMP
UNFORTUNATELY ...THAT'S ALL SHE DOES!
YAR YAR!

Thanks for reading!
Don't forget to recycle!

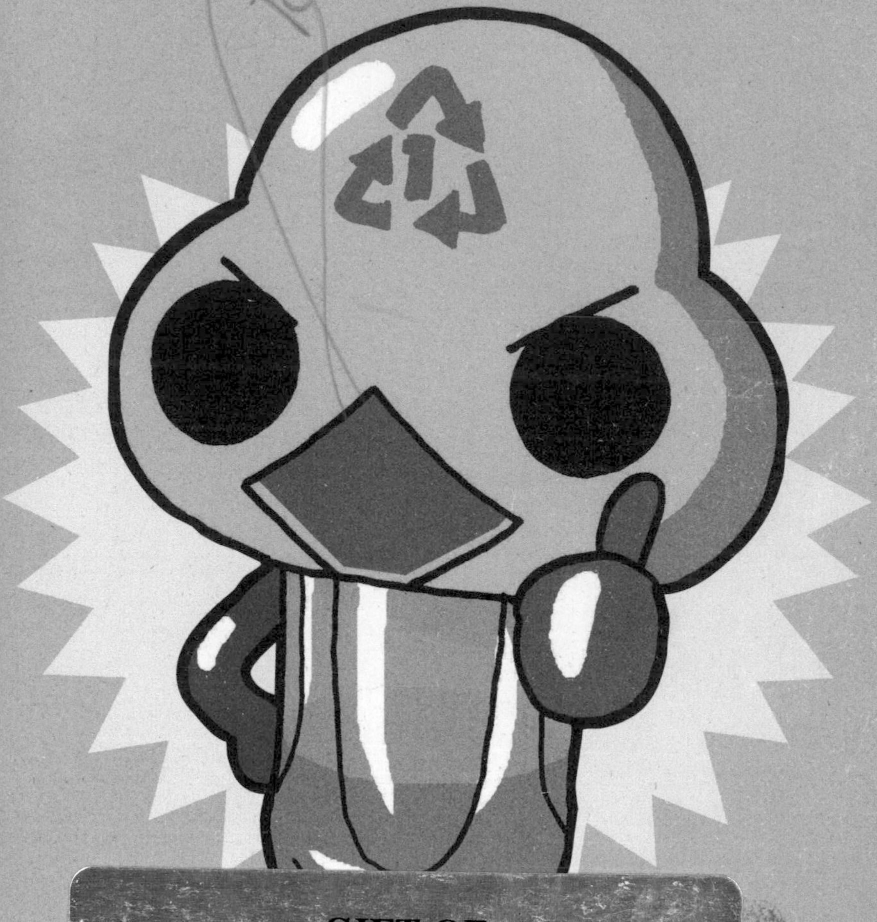